PRAISE FOR DONNA GRANT'S BEST-SELLING ROMANCE NOVELS

"Grant's ability to quickly convey complicated backstory makes this jam-packed love story accessible even to new or periodic readers." - *Publisher's Weekly*

"Donna Grant has given the paranormal genre a burst of fresh air…" — *San Francisco Book Review*

"The premise is dramatic and heartbreaking; the characters are colorful and engaging; the romance is spirited and seductive." — *The Reading Cafe*

"The central romance, fueled by a hostage drama, plays out in glorious detail against a backdrop of multiple ongoing issues in the "Dark Kings" books. This seemingly penultimate installment creates a nice segue to a climactic end." — *Library Journal*

"…intense romance amid the growing war between the Dragons and the Dark Fae is scorching hot." — *Booklist*

Dragon Night ~ Dragonfire ~ Dragon Claimed
Ignite ~ Fever ~ Dragon Lost ~ Flame ~ Inferno
A Dragon's Tale (Whisky and Wishes: *A Holiday Novella*,
Heart of Gold: *A Valentine's Novella*, & Of Fire and Flame)
My Fiery Valentine ~ The Dragon King Coloring Book
Dragon King Special Edition Character Coloring Book: Rhi

DARK WARRIORS SERIES
Midnight's Master ~ Midnight's Lover ~ Midnight's Seduction
Midnight's Warrior ~ Midnight's Kiss ~ Midnight's Captive
Midnight's Temptation ~ Midnight's Promise
Midnight's Surrender ~ A Warrior for Christmas

CHIASSON SERIES
Wild Fever ~ Wild Dream ~ Wild Need
Wild Flame ~ Wild Rapture

LARUE SERIES
Moon Kissed ~ Moon Thrall ~ Moon Struck ~ Moon Bound

WICKED TREASURES
Seized by Passion ~ Enticed by Ecstasy ~ Captured by Desire
Books 1-3: Wicked Treasures Box Set

~

<u>**HISTORICAL PARANORMAL**</u>

THE KINDRED SERIES
Everkin ~ Eversong ~ Everwylde ~ Everbound
Evernight ~ Everspell

KINDRED: THE FATED SERIES
Rage ~ Ruin ~ Reign

DARK SWORD SERIES
Dangerous Highlander ~ Forbidden Highlander
Wicked Highlander ~ Untamed Highlander
Shadow Highlander ~ Darkest Highlander

ROGUES OF SCOTLAND SERIES
The Craving ~ The Hunger ~ The Tempted ~ The Seduced
Books 1-4: Rogues of Scotland Box Set

THE SHIELDS SERIES
A Dark Guardian ~ A Kind of Magic ~ A Dark Seduction
A Forbidden Temptation ~ A Warrior's Heart
Mystic Trinity (a series connecting novel)

DRUIDS GLEN SERIES
Highland Mist ~ Highland Nights ~ Highland Dawn
Highland Fires ~ Highland Magic
Mystic Trinity (a series connecting novel)

SISTERS OF MAGIC TRILOGY

Shadow Magic ~ Echoes of Magic ~ Dangerous Magic
Books 1-3: Sisters of Magic Box Set

THE ROYAL CHRONICLES NOVELLA SERIES

Prince of Desire ~ Prince of Seduction
Prince of Love ~ Prince of Passion
Books 1-4: The Royal Chronicles Box Set
Mystic Trinity (a series connecting novel)

DARK BEGINNINGS: A FIRST IN SERIES BOXSET

Chiasson Series, Book 1: Wild Fever
LaRue Series, Book 1: Moon Kissed
The Royal Chronicles Series, Book 1: Prince of Desire

MILITARY ROMANCE / ROMANTIC SUSPENSE

SONS OF TEXAS SERIES

The Hero ~ The Protector ~ The Legend
The Defender ~ The Guardian

DARK ALPHA'S FURY

REAPERS
BOOK 16

DONNA GRANT®

DARK ALPHA'S FURY
© 2023 by DL Grant, LLC
Cover Design © 2023 by CharityHendryDesigns.com
Formatting © 2023 by CharityHendryDesigns.com
ISBN 13: 978-1-942017-97-4
Available in ebook, print, and audio.
All rights reserved.

Excerpt from: **SHOULDER THE SKYE**
© 2023 by DL Grant, LLC
Cover Design © 2023 by CharityHendryDesigns.com

www.DonnaGrant.com
www.MotherofDragonsBooks.com

DEAREST READER—

Ah, Xaneth. If you've been in any of my Facebook Lives, you've heard me talk about this character for years. He was one of those secondary characters I never intended to continue making appearances. But there he was, book after book after book.

I can't tell you how many emails I got about Xaneth. So many readers were anxious for news of him, to learn what he was doing, and when he would get his own book. I like to keep spoilers to myself because I don't want to ruin the reading experience. However, I didn't have answers to those emails because as a character, Xaneth wouldn't talk to me. He kept to himself. But when he appeared in the books, he was all-in.

Still, he remained elusive. I had a difficult time determining who would have the last book of this series, Xaneth or Balladyn. For a long time, I was sure it was going to be Balladyn, but at the last minute, I knew it had to be Xaneth. And, boy, he and Aisling didn't let me down.

From the moment I put the first Reaper to paper (Baylon in *Dark Alpha's Claim*), I was utterly smitten with them and Death. I wanted to delve more into the Fae after touching on them in the Dark Sword/Dark Warrior series and the Dark Kings. The Reapers gave me that option and then opened an entirely new world to play in.

For those who are lamenting that this is the last Reaper book, let me assure you that while the series is ending, it won't be the last you'll see of any of them. The worlds are interconnected in my Dark Universe, and I never know what characters will show up or where they'll take me.

It's been an absolute pleasure writing the Reapers, their mates, and even the villains. I loved learning about each of the Reapers—their struggles and victories. I adored discovering their love stories and seeing everything they had to go through to find love. And now, I leave you with one of the greatest love stories of them all…Xaneth and Aisling.

xoxox,

DG

CHAPTER ONE

He woke with his arms clutching her. Except, she wasn't there. She was never there. His hands felt empty, as if a piece of him were missing—had always been missing.

Until her.

Xaneth rolled onto his back and fisted his hands, jagged rock digging into him. He still felt Aisling against him, still smelled her jasmine scent. He opened his eyes and stared at the gray sky. Smaller, wispy clouds drifted leisurely against the backdrop of larger, darker clouds. At least his headache was gone.

They used to plague him often after he snuffed out evil, but they had ceased—at least, he'd thought they had. After the battle on the Isle of Skye, they had returned with a vengeance. How he despised them. They caused him to pass out, which left him vulnerable. Like last night—or however long it had been since he'd fallen unconscious.

He took a deep breath and slowly released it. Nothing had

been the same since Skye. He'd had a chance to end the Fae Others' leader but had opted to save Aisling instead of going after Lena.

Xaneth sat and bent his knees to plant his feet on the ground. He wound his arms around his legs and looked at his hands. He'd never felt so helpless, so powerless as he had when holding Aisling's dead body. He should've known that he couldn't do anything to help her. The rage and despair that had welled within him when he realized she had breathed her last had been more than he could handle. He'd been ready to destroy everything.

For her.

Then, inexplicably, she'd taken a breath. He'd been so dumbfounded that he could do nothing but stare at her. He had almost gone back to her. Held her. Touched her. Then he remembered who he was…*what* he was. And he knew he had to leave. His mission was to eradicate evil. Nothing more. Nothing less.

So, he'd teleported away before he did something foolish. At least Aisling was alive. That gave him a measure of comfort. Though he wasn't sure he deserved it.

He fisted his hands once more and hung his head. Skye had been a disaster for him. He could've—and *should've*—ended Lena once and for all. The havoc the Fae had caused was unconscionable. How many more times would he have the opportunity to reset the balance between good and evil? How could he continue walking this realm, knowing he had let his personal feelings get in the way of what he was meant to do?

Xaneth got to his feet and looked at his surroundings. Wind buffeted him on all sides, the air heavy with the scents of salt, driftwood, and seaweed. Water met the horizon in every direction he looked. Beneath his feet, the rocky ground had patches of snow that clung to the last vestiges of winter. He scanned the desolate area, looking for any signs of life. Other than sea lions and birds, he saw nothing.

Where was he? He glanced at the semi-sheltered area of rocks against the rising hill where he had been lying. At least he hadn't been left completely exposed—not that the boulders hid him, but they were better than nothing.

Xaneth leaned his head to one side and then the other, hearing the pops as he stretched his neck. Then he looked up at the tall mound and its steep incline. It wasn't large enough to be a mountain, but it was by no means puny. He could teleport to the peak, but he needed movement after being unconscious. So, he began the arduous trek upward.

By the time he reached the top, his breaths came rapidly. The isle was small, maybe only a quarter mile in any direction. And uninhabited. Perhaps that was why he had chosen it, though he had no memories of it. Other islands were near, and he could even see movement on some. Was he still in Scotland? Xaneth tried to pull up his memories of what'd happened after he left Aisling on Skye, but everything was blank.

How many days had passed? Or was it weeks? How he hated the lost time with no way to account for it.

His thoughts drifted back to Aisling. The moment he'd gone to Skye to join the Reapers and Druids in fighting the Fae Others, he had sought her out—even when he knew he shouldn't have. They had stood shoulder to shoulder in battle.

Not because she couldn't take care of herself, but because he hadn't been able to stay away.

She had followed him for weeks, and he'd demanded that she leave him be. She had finally given up and returned to the Reapers as he wanted. He should've been overjoyed. Except, he had been anything but. He should've kept his distance from her. But that was like asking the moon not to shine.

Xaneth thought of that battle and how he had known that Aisling had his back. That he could count on her. Just as she had known that she could count on him. They had been in sync on a level he hadn't comprehended even existed. He had enjoyed fighting alongside her, as odd and ghastly as it was to admit.

Since he had awoken from his torture at the hands of his aunt, Xaneth had been utterly and completely alone. At first, he'd wanted to change that, but it didn't take him long to realize that he was something different. Something to be feared. That was when he knew he had to stand apart from everyone else for however long he had left.

Even the beautiful Aisling.

Especially her.

Because he craved to be near her.

He fought it every second of every hour. His mistake had been going to her before the battle. Worse, he'd lifted her into his arms when he found her wounded. He swallowed at the memory of holding her. The feeling of her body had been imprinted on his soul, just as her exquisite face. He would never be able to forget her, no matter how hard he tried.

Xaneth glanced down at his damp clothes covered in dirt and blood. Aisling's blood. With a thought, he teleported to one of his safe houses that he'd once used when hiding from his aunt, Usaeil. At one time, he'd believed that was the darkest time of his life. She had been intent on erasing everyone in their family. He had been the last, and he had made it his mission to keep out of her reach until he could end her life.

He'd been damn successful at keeping away from her, too. He'd become known as the Seeker, a Fae who did business with both the Dark and the Light—something that just wasn't done. Yet he'd found a place for himself in that in-between world. He'd even become…if not friends, then friend*ly* with the King of the Dark, Balladyn. They'd agreed to help each other kill Usaeil since she had betrayed them both. Instead, Usaeil had captured Xaneth and murdered Balladyn. At least Balladyn had gotten a second chance when Death made him a Reaper.

Xaneth hadn't had that option. Usaeil had trapped him in his own mind, endlessly torturing him. He had finally gotten free, but it had been an accident. He'd been trying to end his life to stop the horrible cycle of torment and somehow freed himself. When he went looking for Usaeil to exact his revenge, he'd learned that his cousin—Usaeil's own daughter—Rhi had risen against her with the Dragon Kings. Though the Light and Dark army had eventually killed Usaeil. Xaneth would've loved to have been the one to take her life, but it was enough that she no longer lived.

As for him, he knew his time on Earth was measured, and there was nowhere else for him to go. Whether Usaeil had changed him or he'd done it himself when he got free of her torture, he was different. Now, he smelled the unmistakable, vile stench of malevolence. And once he did, he was compelled to hunt it down and end it.

The Fae Others reeked of such vast amounts of evil that it made him gag. The Six—three Dark and three Light Fae— had created the group modeled after the original Others who had attempted to take down the Dragon Kings. Though the Kings had won and stamped out the Others—or so everyone thought. One Fae, Brian, had hidden, while two Druids were allowed to go free because no one believed they could do any harm.

Unfortunately, everyone had been wrong. Brian told certain Fae about the Others, which then led to the Fae Others' creation. Meanwhile, the Druids did the same. As concerning as the Fae Others were, Xaneth knew the one he needed to take out was Lena. She had learned to consume other Fae's magic, making her stronger and more powerful. She didn't need the other five with her to make her power move, so she had killed them and consumed their power, as well.

From the moment Xaneth had laid eyes on Lena, he'd known she was the reason he was still alive. *She* was his objective. Already, she had killed tens of thousands of Fae to obtain their power, and then she brainwashed thousands more to join her faction. With the might she now harnessed, she could enslave everyone to her will if someone didn't stop her.

Lena should never have been allowed to get where she was. No individual, be they human, Fae, dragon, or something else, should ever have that kind of power. It disrupted the balance of the universe in ways that rippled outward for generations.

Xaneth briefly thought about going to Death. He knew

Erith wished to speak with him. Did she know something he didn't? He shook his head. That didn't matter. Death and her Reapers were particularly formidable. The problem was, they were on the defensive and had been from the start. Death was the Fae's judge and jury, and her Reapers were her executioners, reaping their souls. For the most part, Erith kept an eye on the Fae but stayed out of day-to-day issues. Until it was too late—as was the case this time. They'd had the clout to take down Lena when she was still part of the Six before she took her companions' magic and killed them. Doing that had put Lena on par with Erith. Though Erith wouldn't battle her alone. Cael, her lover, was more god than Fae now.

There was a chance Erith and Cael together could defeat Lena.

There was also a real chance they would lose.

Both Erith and Cael were important. Their lives had meaning. Xaneth's didn't. He'd spent most of his life hiding from his aunt instead of confronting her. He was still hiding, though for a different reason. If anyone had to sacrifice themselves, it should be him. He had no one. No family, no friends.

An image of Aisling filled his mind. He shut his eyes and shoved her away.

When he opened them again, he blinked and looked around the cottage hidden deep in the forest. His magic made it appear as if it were in ruins, and if anyone stumbled upon it, they would fear it, the feelings convincing them to run away. The cottage might be small, but everything inside was pristine. He had spent a lot of time here. It was his favorite of his safe houses.

Xaneth snapped his fingers, and his filthy clothes and shoes vanished. He walked naked into the bathroom. He didn't look in the mirror for fear of what he might see. Had his coloring changed? Were his eyes now red since he had taken lives? It was better if he didn't know.

He could use magic to clean himself, but he preferred the shower. He turned on the water and stepped beneath the spray. After scrubbing away the dirt and blood, he washed a second time before getting out and drying off, careful to keep his gaze away from any reflective surfaces. Then he went to the wardrobe. Inside was an assortment of clothing, from rags to royal attire. He grabbed a pair of dark jeans and a charcoal gray, long-sleeve Henley.

Once his boots were on, he ran his hands through his damp hair and felt how long it had gotten. He ran his hands through it again, using his magic to cut it short. As he turned away, his gaze landed on the bed. He paused and, for just a moment, let himself imagine what it would be like to see Aisling waiting there for him.

He could picture her on her side, watching him with her dark, crimson eyes as she held herself up on a forearm, her long, black and silver braids falling to the side. She would run one of her long, blood red nails along her bare thigh and over her hip as she smiled seductively.

Xaneth took a step toward the bed but promptly halted. He shook his head to dislodge the fantasy. It had been a mistake to allow his mind to drift so. It was a slip he couldn't make again. He squared his shoulders and turned from the bed and thoughts of what might have been. Then he took a deep breath and searched for the stink of the Fae Others.

CHAPTER TWO

Dreagan Manor

Aisling's eyes snapped open on the scream that reverberated in the room. She sat up, gulping in huge mouthfuls of air before swiping at the tears that had fallen. She swung her legs over the side of the bed and dropped her head into her hands. Her chest rose and fell rapidly. She listened for footsteps in the corridor, hoping and praying that no one came to check on her.

As each second passed without the sound of anyone approaching or a knock on the door, she let the tension ease from her body. It didn't matter how long she lived, how hard she worked to let go of the past, it would always have a hold over her. That was just the way it was for those who became Reapers. Being betrayed and murdered tended to do that.

Aisling stood and padded barefoot across the plush rug to

the mirror. She stared at her reflection, not liking what she saw staring back at her. She was confused and scared, two things she'd sworn never to feel again. Yet here she was. Right back in the same situation that had caused her betrayal in the first place.

When Erith came to her and offered her a position with the Reapers, Aisling had almost declined. She knew it meant carrying around pain that might never dissipate. The only way to truly be rid of it was death. After everything she had suffered, that was what Aisling thought she wanted: the sweet oblivion of nothingness. The dark abyss.

To this day, she wasn't sure what it was that Erith had said to make her change her mind. The agreement had been out of Aisling's mouth before she even realized it. She could've taken it back, but she didn't. Then, Erith had held out her hand. As soon as Aisling took it, Death had given her just a few tiny drops of her essence. Not only did Aisling return to the land of the living but she also had more power and magic than before.

She had taken her place with the other Reapers and soon came to understand that it was what she had been meant to do. She'd found her place among them despite the endless suffering of the past she still carried with her. She forgot about it some days. But the nightmares always returned when she slept. Always

This time, it wasn't just the past that had filtered through her mind. It was also Xaneth.

Aisling fingered one of her long plaits. She'd started wearing her hair like this after becoming a Reaper. Sometimes, she wore the braids down. Other times, she tied them back. And still others she gathered them atop her head.

Despite the familiarity of her hair, something had changed on Skye. *She* was changed.

She might not be able to put her finger on what it was specifically, but she felt it, nonetheless. She had died on the Isle of Skye. There was no mistaking that feeling. She had already felt it once in that instant before Erith held her soul and made her offer.

What had brought Aisling back? It hadn't been Death. Erith only held their soul that one time. If a Reaper died a second time, they were…gone. So, what had happened? Had it been Xaneth? She had been told that he was the one who'd taken her from the battlefield. But…if it had been him, wouldn't he have waited around? Wouldn't he have spoken to her?

Those were the questions she had asked herself for the past three days without any answers. She was beginning to fear she would never get them. Maybe she wouldn't like what she learned if she did. At least, that was the argument she had with herself. However, she knew it for the lie it was.

Aisling tugged off the band holding the end of one braid and used her fingers to release the plait. Once the hair was free, she looked at it. With a sigh, she began freeing the others. Once they were all unbound, she ran her fingers through her hair. It had gotten so very long. She'd debated cutting it short but then decided to leave it.

Aisling glanced outside at the thick snow. She wanted to walk in the Dragonwood. The forest had called to her since her arrival at Dreagan. After the nightmare, she needed to walk with nature, to feel the hum of magic centered in the woods. With a thought, her sleep clothes vanished, replaced by a thick, black sweater, black corduroy pants, and black snow boots. She added a black coat, scarf, and a fur-lined cap and then teleported to the Dragonwood.

She sucked in a breath as the frigid cold slammed into her. Winter didn't loosen its hold easily in the Scottish Highlands. Aisling started walking, the snow crunching beneath her feet. She and the Reapers from her group had been on Dreagan with Cael and Erith since the battle on Skye, while the other Reapers continued reaping souls. It would be her unit's turn next week. Until then, everyone waited for what was next with the Fae Others. Because there *would* be a next.

Aisling looked at the tall evergreens covered in snow, the precipitation melting in the morning sun. Seeing the land covered in a blanket of white was a beautiful sight. The way the wind whispered silently made it seem like they were on another realm entirely. She stood and drank in the splendor around her. The sixty thousand acres that belonged to the Dragon Kings were some of the prettiest in the country.

She looked through the snow-laden branches to the soft gray sky that matched her mood. Try as she might, she couldn't stop thinking about Xaneth. Where was he? What was he doing? Would he return?

Why had he left her?

He would fight Lena again. Of that, Aisling was certain. Would she be there to see it? To join in? That was the real question. Xaneth had a way of finding the Fae Others like the Reapers couldn't. For all she knew, he could be confronting them right now.

A sound behind Aisling caught her attention. She knew

without looking that it was Eoghan. He was one of the originals from the first group of Reapers, and when Erith added more, Eoghan had taken over her unit as their leader. Eoghan had earned Aisling's respect early, but it was more than that. The Reapers, Death, and Cael were family. It had taken Aisling a long while to fully acknowledge that, but it was true. She loved them. She would die for them. And she knew they would do the same for her.

"You don't have to keep checking on me," she said.

Snow crunched as he shifted his weight. "I disagree. I'm worried about you. We all are."

She didn't want to talk about what'd happened or her feelings. Or, worse, Xaneth. "I didn't think I'd like Scotland this much. There's too much snow, but it's pretty."

"Nothing can beat our Emerald Isle," he said, a smile in his voice. "But I agree. Scotland comes close."

"I don't think Lena will attack in Scotland again. We should stop hiding and seek her out."

Eoghan made a sound in the back of his throat. "You think we're hiding?"

"The Dragon Kings have a protective barrier around their land. We're here. So, yes, I think we're hiding."

"We're waiting."

Aisling jerked her head to the side when he came up beside her. He had moved so quickly and silently that she hadn't heard him. She stared into his quicksilver eyes, the color moving like molten metal. "Waiting for what?"

"Several things." He clasped his hands behind his back and looked into the distance.

"If you have something to say, then say it."

Eoghan sighed as he faced her. "Lena had the opportunity to strike anyone, including Xaneth. Instead, she aimed for you."

"Lucky me. So what?"

"You're too smart to be this obtuse, Aisling."

She bit back her angry retort. "Obviously, I'm not nearly as intelligent as you think I am."

"You're letting your feelings cloud the obvious."

"Let's cut through all this shite, shall we? Just tell me."

"Lena targeted you. *You* are Xaneth's weakness. It was a guess on her part, but she got her confirmation when he left with you instead of attacking her."

Aisling suddenly couldn't draw breath into her lungs. She shook her head. It couldn't be true. She'd know if Xaneth…if he what? Felt something for her? "He wouldn't talk to me. He pushed me away. You're wrong. All of you."

"We're not. And you know it."

She sucked in a breath, her lungs filling with the cold air, making her cough.

Eoghan briefly closed his eyes. When he looked at her, sadness filled his gaze. "Why did you leave to track Xaneth?"

"A feeling." Xaneth had asked the same thing. She hadn't wanted to tell him, and she didn't want to tell anyone else either. It was too much. It would expose too much of herself.

Eoghan quirked a black brow. "What kind of feeling?"

She wanted to walk away, to ignore him. But if she did, she'd have this conversation again. Maybe with him, or perhaps Cael. Possibly Erith. It was better to get it over with now. She looked away. "I felt certain that someone needed to be with him. That he needed someone to watch his back."

"And that someone was you?" Eoghan asked softly.

Aisling shrugged nonchalantly when she felt anything but. "I was wrong."

"You didn't see Xaneth's face on Skye when he saw you wounded." Eoghan paused. "I did."

Her gaze slid back to her leader. She desperately wanted to know what he had seen but couldn't get the words out.

Eoghan took a step, moving closer. "Panic. Helplessness. Determination. Then he gathered you into his arms and vanished. I saw your injury, Aisling. I saw *you*."

She couldn't look away as she said, "I was dead."

"Aye. Yet here you stand before me now."

"I don't know what happened. I've told everyone that. I woke in the cave alone."

Eoghan nodded slowly and let out a long breath. "There's only one conclusion. He brought you back."

"But...how?"

"How does he find the Fae Others? How does he see through our veils when none but the Reapers and Death can? There is much about Xaneth we don't know."

She glanced at her boot in the snow. "He once told me he thought I came to kill him."

"The way Lena reacts to Xaneth tells me she fears him more than us. Even over Erith. He could be the one to kill Lena, but she's going to throw everything at him to prevent that from happening."

"He needs our help." Then Aisling recalled Eoghan's words. If she were Xaneth's weakness, then she couldn't be near him. Lena could and would use her. "He needs all of you."

Eoghan was silent for a moment as he stared at her. "He needs you."

"I don't want to be used against him again."

Eoghan's lips twisted as if her words meant nothing. "You're too smart for that."

She narrowed her eyes at him. "You can't be asking me what I think you are. Not after informing me that I might be his weakness."

"There is no *might*. It wasn't a guess. You're exactly that," Eoghan said, his eyes glittering shrewdly.

She recognized that sly look. Aisling felt the familiar anticipation of a mission. "I'm all ears."

"Xaneth needs to be warned about what's likely waiting when he finds Lena. It would also be nice if he knew we are here to help. You're the only one who has been able to find him. We want you to do it again. After you warn him, convince him to work with us."

Blood drummed in Aisling's ears. Eoghan wanted her to leave Dreagan to look for Xaneth again. She had been successful at first, but then Xaneth had gone out of his way to ensure she couldn't find him. Yet she wanted to know why he had left her. There was a chance she could find him again, deliver the news, and get far from him before the next battle.

And when she next met Lena, Aisling would be prepared for anything the Others' leader did.

"What makes you think I can locate him this time? He made his wishes known."

"He saved you," Eoghan said, a confident smile on his lips.

Aisling wanted to see Xaneth again. If he had brought her back, she wanted to know how he had done it. And why. Besides, she needed to thank him.

"Do I take that look to mean you'll do it?" Eoghan asked.

Aisling lifted her chin. "Aye."

CHAPTER THREE

Don't look.

No matter how many times Xaneth told himself that, he couldn't stop scanning every face in Waterford for the one who haunted his thoughts. *If* Aisling came looking for him again. He didn't expect her to. The safest place for her was far, far from him.

Yet he longed to see her, to look into her crimson eyes. It was such a sharp need. A yearning that grew with every second until he could think of little else.

"Fek," Xaneth grumbled.

What about the Reaper kept her in his thoughts? Her beauty was second to none, but it was more than that. She had battle skills that mesmerized him, fortitude that amazed him, and cunning that continually surprised him. She willingly sought him out, tracking him when she shouldn't have been able to. So much about Aisling captured him, ensnared him, that he could scarcely name them.

Xaneth shook his head to dislodge his thoughts about her. When Usaeil began slaughtering their family, any notions of a future had evaporated. It was about survival, day to day, hour by hour. His days were numbered, and he'd known it. He used each one to keep himself alive.

Until Usaeil caught him.

He was now free of his aunt, but his days were still finite. Each time he sought out and ended evil, he felt more of himself slip away. How much longer would it be until he lost himself entirely? What would he become then? And who would end *his* life?

Xaneth parted his lips, about to call for Erith. He knew the goddess would come. He could ask her to make sure it wasn't Aisling who reaped his soul. If Erith gave her word, she would keep it. Yet if she came, she would want to talk. And Xaneth had nothing to say to her—nothing she would want to hear, anyway. Just as he had nothing to say to Aisling.

Liar.

With Aisling, he *felt*…everything.

Every ache, every longing, every impossible desire. Things that were out of reach for him. They always had been, but now more so than before. And nothing would change that.

Xaneth remained near a building, veiled in the shadows cast by the sun, watching the passersby. Dialects from all over the world could be heard. He saw plenty of Fae, too. Dark and Light mingled freely with the mortals. Humans walked among the Fae without any knowledge of their existence.

If a Fae didn't use magic to tamp down their appeal, humans were inexplicably drawn to them. Mortals couldn't stay away from Fae, and while the Light took advantage of that, no one did it like the Dark. Because the Dark fed off the humans' souls until nothing remained but a shriveled corpse. The mortals had no idea what was happening to them because all they felt was bliss. Being consumed by pleasure wasn't a bad way to go if Xaneth were honest. If he had to choose, that was how it would be. It was better than pain.

He took a deep breath, searching for evil. It was everywhere, just like good, but the kind of malevolence he searched for was more pervasive. He knew Lena's smell and that of the Fae Others, and it wasn't in Waterford.

Xaneth moved farther into the shadows where he felt most at home. He closed his eyes and tried to find the scent. He caught the barest of smells and followed it. When he opened his eyes, he was in another city. Xaneth remained veiled so he could get his bearings. He scanned the area around him. When he saw nothing, he teleported down the street. That was when he saw the welcome sign to Kilbaha. He had only been to the small fishing community on the western tip of the peninsula once before. The quaint village was lush and beautiful—perfect for hiding.

Xaneth glanced at the sky, a bright blue dotted with clouds. He didn't want to walk the streets now, even if he was veiled. He'd wait until night fell where he felt more at home in the darkness. He inwardly snorted. He'd always loved the dark, even as a child. Maybe he had somehow known what would become of him. Because wasn't it only monsters that lurked in the darkest of nights?

He looked at his hands. They appeared normal. They felt normal. And yet he knew they weren't. They had killed, ripped others apart.

And held Aisling.

Xaneth spun on his heel and stalked away to find somewhere better to hide until the sun went down. Soon, he found himself far from the village. When he spotted the Bridges of Ross, he quickened his footsteps, something like excitement stirring in his chest. The last time he had been here was with his family. It was one of the last memories he had of them before they were killed. They'd all had a glorious day.

He paused and took in the natural sea arch of the Loop Head Peninsula, the brisk wind biting into his exposed skin through his shirt. There had been three bridges at one time, but two had fallen into the sea. The Loop Head Lighthouse wasn't far away. There was also the Kilkee Cliff Walk that Xaneth had taken with his younger sister, who had talked nonstop the entire time about everything. He'd ignored her, angry that he'd had to bring her with him. Now, all he wanted was that day back so he could give her the attention she deserved. But that could never be.

Xaneth returned his attention to the bridge. It was a breathtaking spectacle. He walked partway over the natural structure and looked down to see the waves crashing against the rocks sculpted by the ocean, white crests smashing again and again. His gaze moved to the deep blue water beneath him that eventually rolled to shore.

He continued across the bridge until he was on the other side. There, he admired the vast Atlantic Ocean before him. This was a good place to remain until dark, but he would need to stay out of sight since tourists were around, and he wanted to lower his veil.

Xaneth teleported to the beach and found a cave with a

decent entrance and a good-sized cavern beyond it. He settled on a rock outside the cave and considered that in the short time he had been here, he hadn't come across any Fae. That didn't mean they weren't around. The Fae called all of Ireland home. There were more Fae per capita in Ireland than anywhere else on the realm. Honestly, given that, it was surprising there weren't more Halflings—though there were considerably more than anyone realized.

Lena could be in Kilbaha by herself. She had enough power now that she didn't need anyone to guard her, but he suspected that she still had a contingent of soldiers around her, Fae she had shared a tiny bit of her magic with, much like Erith did with the Reapers. Lena was the kind who needed to lord her position over others. And while the stench of the Fae Others had brought Xaneth here, the smell wasn't any stronger than it had been in Waterford. Which gave him pause.

There was no way Lena could know he was tracking her, but on the off chance she did, and this was a trap, he needed to prepare. Xaneth wasn't too worried about Lena tricking him since all he cared about was finding her. It didn't matter where they battled, only that it would happen. And the sooner the better.

Xaneth.

He jerked at the sound of Erith's voice in his head. A part of him wanted to go to her as if he answered to the goddess. But he remained where he was…with some difficulty. At one time, she had called for him often, and it had taken everything he had to squash whatever urged him to go to her. Eventually, she called to him less and less. Then, she stopped altogether.

About the time Aisling came looking for him.

Xaneth squeezed his eyes closed. Why did his thoughts always return to the Reaper? They were on different paths. She had a future. He…did not.

In an effort to stop thinking about her, Xaneth focused on ideas for how to find and kill Lena while watching the various birds on the coastline, the time measured by the crash of each wave on the shore. The hours passed slowly, broken only by a brief rain shower that somehow made the cool wind that much colder. He kept his gaze on the constantly moving sea, following the ebb and flow of the water. Until, finally, twilight came.

That was when Xaneth became anxious to leave the cave. He wanted to explore the village and put it to memory as he located Lena or any Fae Others. By the time he lowered his veil and walked from the cave, the shadows had lengthened, blending into the night. He looked up, the sight instantly capturing him. Xaneth gawked in wonder at the mesmerizing view of the sky and the milky cascade with its billions of stars that created the river of light that stretched across the inky blackness.

For long moments, he simply stood and stared, soaking up the beguiling sight. He'd always loved the stars, tracking the planets' movements, finding the constellations, and even the distant nebulas. It felt like a lifetime since he had indulged his greatest pleasure. He'd looked at the sky so many times, but it hadn't stilled him as it did tonight. If only he could stay and stargaze until dawn.

Xaneth sucked in a long breath and begrudgingly turned

away. Only to come face-to-face with the one person he didn't want to see—Aisling.

She stood, silent as a sentry, her gaze direct and unflinching—and locked on him. Thick, black lashes framed her large eyes, while delicate brows arched gently above them. There was no smile on or softness to her full lips. A gust from the sea swept past them, causing the ends of her hair to dance enticingly. That was when he realized that her long hair was free of its braids. The moonlight highlighted the silver mixed into her midnight tresses. She wore all black—a chunky sweater, pants, boots—the only color her long nails that matched her eyes.

A memory flashed in his head of her lying still, the gaping wound in her chest. He could hardly reconcile that with the woman he saw standing before him now. He wanted to ask how she had come back to life. But he didn't. Because if he spoke with her, he wouldn't want to stop.

Did she have any idea how many times he had wanted to see her face since that day on Skye? Could she know how his hands would forever feel empty after holding her? As if a piece of him had been left with her?

"Nothing to say?" she quipped.

There was a hint of anger in her words, and for the life of him he couldn't understand why. He decided it would be better not to reply. For both of them. So, he shook his head.

"Don't even think about it," Aisling stated in a clipped tone, one daring him not to infuriate her more.

He frowned, wondering how she had known he was about to teleport away.

"If you leave, I'll only find you again." She crossed her arms over her chest and stared at him.

Rather, she *glared*. There was no doubt in his mind she was livid. But why direct it at him? Was it because he hadn't killed Lena when he had the chance? That had to be it. He should have finished Lena. He knew that. But he'd taken one look at Aisling and thought only of her. That couldn't happen again. And if she stayed, it would. He couldn't fulfill his destiny if she stayed.

Xaneth might not have shared a lot of words with Aisling, but he didn't need them to know that she wasn't going anywhere until he replied in some way. So, he came up with the best he could under the circumstances. "I asked you to stay away."

She quirked a brow. "And I asked *you* to talk to me."

"Nothing would come of us conversing." He had to get away. Soon. He couldn't talk to her for all the reasons he had sent her away. Couldn't she see that?

"How would you know since you've not tried it?"

He almost told her they were doing it now. Xaneth opted not to say anything at all.

She shook her head and dropped her arms. "How could you just leave me? Without…anything. Not a word, a touch. *Nothing*."

Xaneth's chest constricted at the anguish in her voice. He couldn't answer her because he didn't have those answers for himself. Worse, it had never entered his mind that she might be angry that he hadn't been there. *This* was why he didn't want to talk to her. It was too complicated, too problematic. He shook his head and took a step back.

Aisling let out a sound that was half laugh, half snort. "You run headlong into danger against the Fae Others and Lena without a second thought, but you can't have a conversation with me? You can't answer simple questions?"

They were far from simple.

"I came to help. That's all I've wanted to do since I started following you," she told him. "To help. I know it's what I have to do. I know it here." She pointed at her chest. "But you won't accept anything I have to offer. Not even my words. So…fine. Leave, Xaneth. Go do whatever it is you think you have to do. But know this. The Reapers will be there. *I* will be there. Fighting. You can't stop that."

He could if he found Lena before they did. Which was exactly what he planned.

She started to turn away but paused. Her crimson gaze locked on him again. "Thank you. For what you did for me on Skye. I owe you."

Xaneth parted his lips to ask what she was talking about when she vanished. He blinked, a frown growing as he tried to think of what he had done other than take her from the battlefield. Maybe that was what she had meant. Perhaps she had needed somewhere quiet to heal.

He looked at his hands and recalled how they had been coated in her blood. How still her body had been. How lifeless.

He scrubbed a hand down his face. Once again, Aisling had found him. Erith must be telling her where to go. But then why hadn't the goddess come herself? He was tired of these questions. Besides, did it really matter? He wasn't a Reaper. He didn't answer to Death.

His gaze slid to where Aisling had stood, looking indignant and beautiful in the moonlight, and wished with every fiber of his being that she was still there.

CHAPTER FOUR

Aisling couldn't remember being so exasperated and incensed. She paced the shoreline of Kilbaha Bay, going over her all too brief and ridiculous chat with Xaneth.

"Why did I even think he'd talk to me? Why did I believe that him saving me meant he, I don't know…maybe *cared*?" She rolled her eyes as anger whipped through her. "He was surprised to see me, but that quickly turned to annoyance."

That was what got her. She'd intended to stay quiet until he spoke, but when she saw his irritation, she'd lost it. Aisling knew she should've waited until he talked. She might think she could help him, but that didn't do any good when he kept refusing.

"If the imbecile wants to die, then let him," she stated.

Aisling stopped pacing and closed her eyes with a sigh. She wouldn't let that happen. No matter how furious she became. Xaneth had endured unspeakable horrors at Usaeil's hands, and whatever drove him now was likely a consequence of that.

He battled the Fae Others better than even the Reapers. Erith had no intention of stopping him. Everyone just wanted to help him defeat their foe.

The difference was, they had been in his shoes and had found their spot in the family. Xaneth not only didn't want his place with a family, but he also didn't want anyone around. And, honestly, she couldn't blame him.

She sank onto a boulder and listened to the waves rolling over the rocks and sand. Her head tilted back until she looked at the stars. He'd seemed awestruck by them. For just a moment, he had lowered his shields. That was all it had taken for her to see him: the lad who'd watched his family be massacred, the Fae who hid everything he was, the rebel who had made a name for himself in both the Light and Dark worlds. The man who had been tortured but had broken free.

In that instant, her broken, battered soul had recognized one of its own.

Aisling leaned back on her hands and regarded the night sky. But it wasn't the stars she saw. It was Xaneth. Tall and broad-shouldered, he carried himself as if ready to unleash Hell on anyone who deserved it. He'd had his large hands clenched, the muscles in his forearms shifting beneath his skin below the shirt sleeves he'd shoved to his elbows.

He had a ruthless air about him. One that only made him more handsome and appealing. From his chiseled jawline to his full lips to his pale silver eyes, he haunted her day and night. His midnight hair was cut short now, the top long enough to show the soft waves. It gave his gorgeous face a lethal look that made her blood quicken.

She knew every inch of his face, having put it to memory

when they first met. She knew the vein in his left temple that throbbed when he was angry. The small scar near his lip. Just as she knew how his body moved during battle. How he made each movement look like a dance.

If only she knew the feel of his body against hers. She had been unconscious when he took her from the battlefield on the Isle of Skye. She had no idea what it felt like to be in his arms. But she had dreamed of it.

She had imagined and fantasized about it.

Every other Reaper had found someone. Even Death had found her soulmate in Cael. Not Aisling. Not that she deserved it. But she could let her fantasies run wild, which was exactly what she had done with Xaneth.

It was wrong. She knew that. It allowed her to believe that something had developed between them when it hadn't. Someone as damaged as she couldn't be put back together to find her person. She had accepted that. She'd been fine with it.

Then she met Xaneth. And *everything* changed. She'd tried to forget him, attempted to ignore him, but it was all in vain. Everything she touched went to shite. The only thing she was good at was being a Reaper, and even that was questionable since she'd left her family to look for a royal Fae who wanted nothing to do with her.

Which meant that Aisling had a choice. She could continue tracking Xaneth to see where he went. If he found Lena, she would be able to call to the Reapers so they could attack. Or…she could find him, give him the message like Eoghan had asked, and return to Dreagan.

Aisling had made a detrimental choice long ago that had defined her life. This was another one. She knew it, even if she tried to tell herself otherwise. Despite the fact that Xaneth had hurt her with his words—or lack thereof—she couldn't leave. At the very least, she had to deliver her message. She should've done it first thing when he turned to find her. Now, she had to find him again. Then, she'd keep far enough away from Xaneth that he wouldn't know she was there.

Lena thought Aisling was Xaneth's weakness. In reality, he was hers. But Lena didn't perceive Aisling as a threat. Regardless, she would make sure Lena couldn't use her against anyone. Aisling wouldn't be the reason the Fae Others claimed victory.

Aisling licked her lips and rubbed her palms on her thighs as she closed her eyes. She thought about Xaneth, focusing all her concentration on him. It wasn't an easy process. It was exhaustive. And painful. Sometimes, it worked. Other times, it didn't. She had looked three places before she found Xaneth in Kilbaha. She hadn't sought him out so many times in one night before, and it was taking a toll. Her head throbbed behind her eyes, but she needed to know if he was still in the village.

She gave up when the pain became too agonizing. Aisling leaned forward and put the heels of her hands against her eyes. The pounding intensified. She had wasted herself on nothing because she couldn't pinpoint Xaneth. That meant she would have to physically look for him instead—if he was even still in Kilbaha.

Aisling dropped her hands and lifted her head. Then, she cracked open her eyes and winced. She needed a few minutes to heal, but time wasn't something she had. Aisling pushed to her feet and turned toward the village. She scanned the distant rooftops until she found one she liked. She veiled herself and teleported there. She had to lean against the chimney as her knees threatened to buckle from the pain that suddenly exploded in her head.

She took in the area, looking for any signs of Xaneth. He liked to hide. That meant she needed to search the shadows. She gripped the side of the chimney tighter, her fingers digging into the brick as she fought a wave of nausea. She had experienced pain before, but nothing like this. She slid down the chimney and leaned her back against it.

"Well, well, well. What do we have here?" asked a deep voice to her left.

Aisling turned her head and looked up at the Dark Fae, who smirked down at her. How had he seen through her veil? That was when she realized she must have dropped it. The Dark had beady, red eyes in a large head. He looked to have more muscle than brains, but at the moment, she wasn't at the top of her game—something she wasn't used to. Maybe she could make him go away. "I want some time alone."

"On a roof?" He laughed, the sound grating. "If you're looking for company, sweetheart, I'm your man."

"No, thanks."

He grabbed her by the hair and yanked her to her feet. "I wasn't asking."

Aisling glared at him as he tightened his fingers in her tresses, pulling tighter. "You're messing with the wrong Fae."

"There's a bounty or your pretty head. I am to collect it."

Aisling couldn't have heard him right. Bounty? By who? Then it dawned on her. Lena, of course. Aisling shoved her hand toward the Dark, her magic hitting him hard enough that the air rushed from his lungs.

He still clung to her hair, so he dragged her with him until he stumbled back and dropped to his knees. His chest had a sizable hole from her hit. Aisling somersaulted over him, landing on his other side. She grabbed his hand that held her hair and twisted at the same time she kneed his elbow. There was a loud crack as the bone broke before he bellowed in pain.

"You bitch!" he screamed as he fell onto his back.

She freed her hair and flipped it away from him. Aisling went to deliver the killing blow when everything went fuzzy. She reached out for something, *anything* to hold onto. What was happening? She blinked and tried to focus on her attacker, but he teleported away before she could finish him.

"Aisling?"

She didn't have to see Xaneth to recognize his voice. He was in front of her, just to her right.

"You're hurt," Xaneth said.

She heard the concern in his voice and wanted to flip him off, but right now, she had to concentrate on staying on her feet. Maybe she shouldn't have tried to look for him this last time. She'd never been able to find anyone like that before. It had only been something she'd developed while searching for Xaneth. But, obviously, she had overdone it.

"What did he do? Tell me," Xaneth insisted. "You don't look well."

Aisling needed to get somewhere quiet and safe.

Instead of answering, she teleported back to Dreagan. At least, she tried to. She found herself on the damp rocks instead. Aisling gripped her head and curled into a ball. She wanted to stay there, but it wasn't safe, especially with the bounty, if the Dark could be believed. She had no idea where she was. Anyone could find her like this. She tried to speak, to call Eoghan's name, but it took too much effort.

The icy waves crashing into her and the bitter wind registered first. Aisling forced open her eyes to see that she was on the beach where she had confronted Xaneth. It took a great deal of effort to lift her head and look around. She spotted the cave before her head fell. Her attempt to teleport failed, causing a kind of terror she had never felt before. She couldn't speak, couldn't teleport, and it felt as if her very skull were breaking apart.

Aisling had been through too much and had overcome so much more to die like this. She gritted her teeth and used her hands and arms to pull herself over the rocks, fighting the incoming tide. It was excruciating and slow, *too* slow for a Fae used to magic coming easily. Each time the water hit her, it was like being blasted with cold. It seeped into her boots, soaking her socks. Her wet hair stuck to the sides of her face, making it difficult to breathe.

She had to pause twice because she nearly passed out, but she pushed against the blackness that dotted her vision. Aisling tried to use her magic to keep herself warm, but it never lasted long. Then, finally, she reached the cave. Tears of joy and pain coursed down her face. The blackness intruded again, and she couldn't push it away this time. Her lips formed Eoghan's name, but she passed out.

CHAPTER FIVE

Xaneth stared in confusion at the spot where Aisling had stood moments ago. He had seen her but had decided to stay away. Then, he'd witnessed her encounter with the Dark. Xaneth hadn't been able to keep himself from watching her deal with the scum. Though it didn't take him long to realize that something was wrong.

His first thought was that the Dark had hurt Aisling. But, like before, he'd said the wrong thing, and she'd left. He wanted that, didn't he? Why did he feel like shite every time it happened then?

Xaneth's concern grew. Aisling had clearly been in pain, her eyes unfocused. The image of her lying so still in his arms on Skye flashed in his mind.

"Fek," he grumbled as he turned in a circle.

He had to look for her and make sure she wasn't injured. The problem was, he didn't know where to start looking. She'd managed to find him, and while he could locate evil, she wasn't that—regardless of her coloring. Or her past. Once a Fae became a Reaper, they retained their coloring from before, but they weren't Light or Dark anymore. They were simply Reapers.

No one knew when the mystery and myth of the Reapers had come into being. One day, they were suddenly a part of Fae culture. Many believed they were made-up stories to get children to mind their parents. Xaneth had assumed the same until he came face-to-face with the Reapers himself—though they hadn't told him what they were at first. He'd figured it out, however.

Yet the terror that ran through all Fae at the mention of the Reapers was very real. Every Dark and Light looked over their shoulders in fear of a Reaper coming for them. The Fae Others had started to change that. They'd begun spreading the truth about the Reapers—as well as the names of each one —to any who would listen. Lena knew the only way to claim control of the Fae was to rid herself of Death and her Reapers. They were the only ones capable of stopping her.

Until him.

Xaneth hadn't been able to do anything to halt the annihilation of his family, but he could—and *would*—put a stop to Lena and the Fae Others. Regardless of the cost to himself—he fully expected his life to be the price. He would gladly give it. Maybe then the weight of failing his family would finally leave him.

Suddenly, the stink of evil enveloped him, so strong it made him gag.

"I had her."

The voice below brought Xaneth out of his thoughts. He

recognized the man as the Dark who had attacked Aisling on the roof. Xaneth moved closer to the edge and peered over. The hulking Dark stood near a streetlight with two other Dark—a woman and a man. Each was dressed in designer clothes, their demeanor that of someone raised with excessive wealth.

"Not for very long," the woman retorted icily.

The big Dark growled as he swung his head to her. "I told you the female was alive. I got her once. I can do it again."

"You failed," the other male replied. He flicked something off his clothes and curled his lip in disgust. "It's our turn now."

The woman's red lips curved into a smile. "The bounty for Aisling is twice that of any other Reaper. She's mine to bring in."

A cold knot formed in Xaneth's gut. Bounty? Holy fek. Xaneth needed to find Lena and end her, now more than ever. But first, he needed to take care of the three below.

Xaneth stood on the roof's edge as he dropped his veil and whistled. All three Fae looked up. "None of you are going anywhere."

The big Dark formed balls of magic in his hands and tossed them. Xaneth easily dodged them and leaped from the roof, landing on the Dark as he shoved an orb of magic into the male's head, releasing all his anger over him attacking Aisling along with it. The male screamed in pain and crumpled. Xaneth landed on his feet as the Dark began turning to ash.

The couple exchanged looks before taking up defensive postures and forming iridescent balls of magic. Xaneth smiled at them. Now that he could see their faces better, he saw the similarities between them—siblings, most likely. Not that it mattered. They were after the Reapers, and whether they were Fae Others or working for them, that put the duo on his to-be-dealt-with list, in the only way he knew how—with death.

The male came at him first. The Dark spun and lunged, his body moving in a mixture of different martial arts maneuvers as he threw orb after orb. Xaneth stalked to the male, ignoring the balls that grazed him and the few that found their marks. He would deal with the pain later. Xaneth waited for the opportunity and grabbed the male by the throat, looking into his red eyes. Fear grew there as the male clawed at Xaneth's hands before lobbing more orbs at him. Xaneth squeezed until he heard the Fae's neck break.

"You monster!" the female shrieked.

Xaneth stepped back and half-turned as she quickly hurled four balls of magic. One landed on his thigh, and another bounced off his shoulder. He gritted his teeth and threw up his hands to block her as she advanced.

She had her lips pulled back, baring her teeth. It seemed she hadn't waited out of fear. She was the more powerful of the two. He felt it in her magic. Saw it in the way she fought. When she reared back her arm to pitch another orb, he dove at her, rolling and coming up on his feet with a ball of magic. He shoved it into her abdomen and heard it as it seared through her clothes and skin.

She froze, shock widening her eyes. She glanced in horror at her wound before looking back up at him. The light began to fade from her eyes. "You can't kill…all…of…us," she choked out before dropping to her knees.

Her body disintegrated into ash before she hit the ground.

Xaneth spun and waited to see if others were waiting to

attack. He winced at the pull of his injuries, but now wasn't the time to deal with them. He needed to warn Aisling. But he had to find her first.

"Bloody hell," he murmured before veiling himself.

Xaneth searched the village, but, as expected, Aisling was nowhere to be found. The sun was breaking the horizon when he returned to his cave to think about his next steps. If he couldn't find Aisling, he needed to contact Death and warn her about the bounties. Just as he had the thought, he drew up short, blinking in disbelief at the sight of Aisling.

He moved toward her and took in the state of her clothes. They were still damp and covered in sand and dirt as if she had been dragged—or had drug herself. He dropped to one knee beside her. Just as he was about to touch her, he paused. She had color in her face again, and he saw no evidence of a wound. Yet he found it troubling that she lay sleeping so near the mouth of the cave. She should've hidden deeper inside.

Xaneth glanced around but saw no one. He returned his gaze to Aisling. Then, he gave in and gently brushed the backs of his fingers across her cheek before moving strands of hair away from her face. Her skin was so smooth. He fought the urge to brush the pad of his thumb over her plump lips, but he knew to do so would make it even more difficult to leave her when the time came.

He dropped his hand reluctantly. He could stand guard over Aisling, but it would be better to alert Death of the bounty. The Reapers would come for Aisling and leave him to continue his pursuit of Lena.

The decision was easy to make. It was harder to carry out, however. It meant that Xaneth had to speak to Erith, when he had been avoiding her. More than that, it meant bidding farewell to Aisling for the last time.

"Maybe in another life, things would have been different," he whispered.

Xaneth forced himself to get to his feet. He took a deep breath and released it, his lips parted to call to Erith when Aisling let out a soul-shattering cry. She thrashed on the ground as if fighting an invisible foe. He was frozen, unsure if he should wake her or not. As he debated, Aisling stilled. Her eyes flew open and landed on him.

She breathed rapidly, and a fine sheen of sweat covered her brow. She swallowed and sat up as her gaze went out to the ocean. Xaneth blinked while struggling to figure out what to do as she composed herself. It would be better if he left. Given the way she put her back to him, she wanted that. Being around Aisling was… It was too much. She made him feel and wish for things that could never be.

Even knowing that, he found himself sitting near her on the rocks, staring out at the ocean. They sat that way for a long time, each lost in thought. It wasn't an awkward silence but one born of trust—the same kind they'd shared on the battlefield.

When he could stand it no more, he looked at her. She had her knees up to her chest, her arms resting atop them. She put her chin on her arms, her long hair blowing in the wind. But the desolation and utter misery he saw made his heart skip a beat. It was gone in an instant, almost too fleeting for him to have seen it at all. Yet he had. There was no mistaking it.

"Lena put a bounty on the Reapers," he told her. "She's paying double for you."

Aisling snorted, a half smile pulling at the corners of her lips. "Damn right."

"She's targeting you. She did it on Skye, and she's doing it now. What did you do to piss her off?"

Her crimson gaze swung to meet his. "I'm a Reaper. Apparently, that's all it takes."

"Aisling," he began.

"I know she's targeting me."

Xaneth blinked at her. "You know?"

"She did it on Skye."

He thought about the look on Lena's face when he glanced her way before taking Aisling. The Dark had been grinning. He'd thought it was because Aisling was hurt but now he wondered if it was more than that.

"Lena thinks I mean something to you. That's why she doubled the bounty on me."

Xaneth's breath locked in his throat. He parted his lips, but no words came. Lena knew. How had she figured out his feelings for Aisling? He'd been so careful.

"At least that's what Erith and the others think," Aisling added.

Xaneth forced his lungs to expand to take in air. If Lena knew about Aisling, then it didn't matter how much distance he put between himself and Aisling. Lena would find her. "You need to let your brethren know about the bounties."

"I will, but we aren't afraid of those she'll send after us."

"You can die," he stated. The shock and disbelief he attempted to hide from this latest news broke through.

Aisling shrugged and tucked her hair behind her ear. "We're more powerful and hold more magic than the Fae.

We've battled her soldiers and have come out on top. I won't be the only one unconcerned with the bounty."

"She's calling each of you out as Reapers. You've kept your identities a secret for a reason."

"Aye. So no one can use us."

He frowned. "Do your families know what you are?"

Something flashed in her eyes before she returned to staring at the waves rolling in. "Nay. No one from our past lives knows."

"That's about to change—if it hasn't already."

Her lips flattened briefly. "We'll deal with it once we dispatch Lena."

"Inform Erith about the bounty immediately."

"Where are you going?" she asked when he stood.

Xaneth hadn't realized how challenging it would be to walk away from her. Or perhaps he had. Maybe that was why he fought to keep her away. Because he knew what being around her would do. "To find Lena."

"You don't have to do everything alone."

Oh, but he did. It was the only way. "I'm not who you think I am."

"I know who you are." She stood and faced him.

Xaneth tried not to look at her, but it was impossible not to be drawn in. She captivated him with her presence, enticed him with a single look. He'd lost the battle before it had even begun, he just hadn't realized it until now. He turned his head and met her resolve. "But you don't."

"Then let me find out."

"You won't like what you find."

"You can't say that. You don't know me."

Yet, he did. He knew her strength, her determination. Her devotion to those dearest to her. Her tenacity when she went after something. What would it feel like to be included in that group? To know that he could turn to her for anything, anytime? It was so tempting, he nearly gave in.

Then he remembered what he was.

"What happened last night?" he asked. The instant he changed the subject, it was like she put up a wall between them.

"Nothing."

He raised a brow. "You didn't look well, and then I found you here, covered in dirt, right at the entrance of the cave."

"I needed rest. Is that what you want to hear?"

"I want to know why you aren't taking care of yourself. You could've been found." *Or worse.* Fek. He couldn't even think about what might have happened if a Fae after the bounty had found her.

She waved away his words as if they meant nothing. "I'm fine, as you can see."

"And the nightmare?" He knew he shouldn't have asked, but he needed her angry. That was how he kept her from him. And prodding and pushing for answers that were none of his business would get him exactly that.

Because he wasn't strong enough to leave her.

If he thought a wall had come down earlier, the temperature between them was downright glacial now. Her eyes turned hard and emotionless. "I don't know what you're talking about."

She did. He knew that. But he also knew she didn't want to discuss it with him, which meant he had to push harder. He steeled himself and said, "Your screaming and thrashing. The sweat that covered you, and your rapid breathing when you woke. Or are you saying I didn't see any of that?"

Aisling took a step toward him, murder in her eyes. And damn if his heart didn't race at having her closer.

"That's none of your damn business."

Then, she was gone.

Xaneth dropped his chin to his chest. It was the right thing to do, but he felt like a complete arse. Aisling had been vulnerable and hurting after the nightmare. That was why he had sat with her. He wanted to know what caused her such pain, but to do that meant befriending her. As it was, their short conversations were too much for him to bear. Everything he did was to save others. Especially her.

He couldn't tell her that, though. Ever.

Xaneth glanced at the place she had been lying when it suddenly dawned on him that he hadn't been felled by a headache after killing the trio of Dark. Why did they hit him sometimes but not every time? When they struck, it left him useless and unable to defend himself—a perfect time for Lena to strike.

That meant he needed to find Lena before she found him in such a state.

CHAPTER SIX

She wouldn't let Xaneth hurt her anymore. Aisling kept telling herself that. Yet she continued putting herself out there for him, letting him wound her. She shook it off. If Xaneth wanted to lash out at someone, then he could do it with someone else. She'd had enough.

Aisling veiled herself and teleported to Limerick, inside an abandoned warehouse near the docks. She made sure she was alone before dropping her veil, replacing her dirty clothes with clean ones, and calling for Eoghan. Within minutes, he stood before her.

"We have a problem," she told him.

His smile vanished. "What?"

"Lena put a bounty on our heads. Every Reaper."

"How do you know?"

She glanced away, wishing she didn't have to speak about Xaneth. "I tracked down Xaneth. In the process, I was attacked. The Fae got the upper hand, but I subdued him. He mentioned a bounty, but I disregarded it, thinking he had me mixed up with someone else."

Eoghan's brow furrowed, and his gaze became intense.

"Xaneth confirmed it and told me that Lena offered double for me."

Eoghan shook his head as he studied the ground, his frown deepening. When he looked at her, his face was lined with worry. "I need to know how Xaneth came by the information and when."

"He told me this morning. Not the previous night when I found him. It must have happened after I handled the Dark."

"*Handled?* You don't handle people, Aisling. You stop them. What aren't you telling me?"

She looked away and crossed her arms over her chest. It was a defensive move. She hated feeling or looking weak, and if she told Eoghan about her episode, it would show just such a flaw.

"Aisling?" he urged, his voice softening.

She couldn't look at him as she said, "In order to find Xaneth, I have to concentrate on him. Sometimes, it works. Other times, it doesn't. But…it takes a lot out of me. Yesterday, I used it multiple times, and it resulted in…pain."

"You said you could find Xaneth, but I didn't ask how. That was my mistake. Have you always been able to do this?"

"No. The first time was when I set out to find him. I thought it was an accident, but the more I focused, the more times I found him."

The tips of Eoghan's brown boots came into her line of sight. He gently took her by the arms and waited until she lifted her head before saying, "How bad was the headache?"

Whatever lie she'd been about to say disappeared as she looked into Eoghan's eyes. He was someone she could trust, and she needed to do that now. "The worst I've ever had."

"Tell me all of it," he ordered.

Aisling tried to look away, but he didn't let her. "It left me debilitated. Weak. I never heard the Dark approach, which was how he got the jump on me. I got away, but my pain kept me from finishing him."

"And?"

Damn. He was relentless. "I tried to teleport to Dreagan."

Eoghan's frown returned. "Tried?"

"I only made it a short distance. Then I dragged myself into a cave. I don't remember anything after that until I woke with Xaneth standing beside me this morning." She left out the nightmare. There was no need to discuss that.

Eoghan released her and stepped back. He was silent as he walked a few paces away before turning back to her. "You made contact with Xaneth?"

"If you can call it that."

"Why do you say that?"

"He still demands to be left alone. As for the news you sent me to give him, let's just say he didn't seem fazed by it. He knows now, however."

Eoghan's quicksilver eyes swirled as they stared at her. "I want to know how Lena discovered you were still alive."

"Maybe she doesn't know. Perhaps she's hedging her bets, just in case."

"She saw Xaneth take you away."

Aisling hated when Eoghan made it sound like Xaneth was worried about her. She had decided that Xaneth would've carried anyone who had fought next to him off that field. "That doesn't mean anything. Besides, he acted like I didn't know what I was talking about when I tried to thank him for saving me."

"Maybe he doesn't know. Remember, we're still figuring out what he can and can't do."

"I think it's better if we let him do whatever he wants. Alone. He's going to reject anyone who attempts to help. He won't even allow a civil conversation."

Eoghan's brow rose again. "Civil? I take that to mean there was an argument?"

"I wouldn't call it that. More like me trying to talk to a stone wall."

She caught Eoghan's grin before he tucked his chin. Aisling almost demanded to know what he found so funny, but she was sure she wouldn't like what he had to say.

"Lena doubled the price on your head because you're Xaneth's weakness," Eoghan said as he looked at her. "If someone brings you in, she's betting it will draw him."

Aisling wrinkled her nose. "So? He wants to find her. What good would that do?"

"It would be on Lena's terms."

"Bloody hell," Aisling murmured.

Eoghan nodded. "Aye. Xaneth is at least speaking to you. You should talk to him again."

"For what? He's made his wishes known. Quite clearly and bluntly, I might add."

"Because he isn't considering the big picture. You need to make him see it."

Aisling knew it would be fruitless, but she could continue

tracking him as she had already decided the night before. Besides, when had Xaneth listened to anything she had to say? "Fine. I'll try one last time. But after that, I'm done."

"You know you can help him. You said so yourself. He needs to know that, too."

Oh, how she hated when Eoghan threw her words back in her face. Despite her hurt and irritation, she knew what she had to do. That didn't mean she had to talk to Xaneth, or even get near him. She could keep her distance while watching him.

"I'm not sure I like that look," Eoghan said.

She shrugged and lifted her chin. "What look?"

"The one that says you'll go, but have no intention of speaking with him."

"You got that from me standing here?"

"I got that from that," he said and pointed at her face.

Aisling flashed a grin. "I'm going back to Xaneth. Isn't that what you want?"

"What I want is for you to find peace."

"I'd like that, too."

"Then talk to him."

She snorted and shot him an incredulous look. "Are you telling me that you think my talking with Xaneth will grant me peace? As if I need a man to do that. I don't need *anyone* to do that."

Instead of being offended by her tone, Eoghan said softly, "I know your past, Aisling. I know your pain."

"No one can fix that."

"You've not let anyone try."

She looked away, hating the tightening in her chest and the

overwhelming anguish that never seemed to go away. It might dim, but that was the only relief she got.

Eoghan sighed. "You went to him because you felt something. Don't push that away now because he said something idiotic."

"Some things can't be fixed, Eoghan." She swung her gaze back to him. "I'm broken. Too broken for anyone."

"Everyone is broken in some way. No one gets put back together exactly as they were before. But that's part of life. The point is to be strong enough to begin healing. Let those broken pieces get picked up and put back into place."

Her eyes burned with unshed tears that she refused to cry. Eoghan was a great leader. This was only one of the reasons she looked up to him. "Some people should suffer for eternity. I'm one of those."

"You're being too hard on yourself."

"Am I?" She was done talking about this. Aisling shook her head to dislodge the past before it took hold. "I'm going back to Kilbaha where I last saw Xaneth."

"Be careful trying to find him. The next time you get such a headache, I expect you to call for me."

He meant every word. It was in his voice and his eyes. Aisling nodded. "I will. Promise."

"Keep me posted. I'm going to Erith now. Good luck," he said.

Aisling sighed once Eoghan was gone. She veiled herself and returned to Kilbaha. Xaneth wasn't in the cave, but she hadn't expected him to be. It didn't take long for her to look through the village. Then, she expanded her search. It soon became apparent that Xaneth wasn't in the area. Aisling was hesitant to use her magic to search for him after the headache the previous night, so she took a little longer and widened her hunt even more. Still, there was no sign of him.

With nothing else to do, she made her way to the cliffs and then down to the shore. No one could see her veiled, but she still wasn't taking any chances. She didn't know why, but she decided to use the cave again. Once inside, she sat against a wall and closed her eyes. Her thoughts went to Xaneth. She found him almost instantly.

She teleported to Roscrea, a market town in central Ireland. It was one of the oldest towns in the country, which meant all the main Fae families had some kind of connection to it. And Lena came from one of the oldest of those lines.

Aisling looked around at the locals and tourists, noting all the Fae. How many of them were looking for her? How many would know Reapers could remain veiled indefinitely? And how many could use magic to force her to show herself?

She knew from experience that she couldn't trust anyone who wasn't a Reaper. That extended to mortals, as well. The Fae weren't above using them for just such a job. That made finding Xaneth more difficult. Aisling smiled. When had she ever turned from a challenge?

She glanced at the rooftops. Xaneth liked to use them, but so had she, recently. It might be better if she remained on the ground for a bit. The sun warmed her as she started down the street. Even though she was veiled, she looked behind her often. She couldn't be too careful.

For the next hour, she scoured the streets of the town without even a single glimpse of Xaneth. She began doubting her magic. She had found him quickly—almost too quickly.

What if he wasn't here? Her magic had failed her before. Yet she didn't seek to use it to look for him again, preferring to remain in Roscrea to continue her pursuit instead.

Just as with Kilbaha, she progressively widened her hunt. She finally spotted Xaneth on the outskirts of town. He stood beneath a huge tree with his back to her, staring down a road. In the distance, she saw the roof of a manor house. When she looked back at Xaneth, he was gone. At least, he was veiled.

Now, all she had to do was keep him within her sights.

CHAPTER SEVEN

Lena smiled triumphantly from the window on the upper floor of the manor. She had come close to losing it all—closer than anyone knew—but everything was falling into place once more. It proved that it was her destiny to lead the Fae. Her people would be great again. They would be feared and respected. And even the arrogant Dragon Kings would kneel before her.

Right before she eradicated them.

Now, her excitement built as she watched Aisling get closer. It had been too easy to lure the Reaper to the manor. Lena had used her new powers to home in on Aisling yesterday, but the Reaper had slipped through her grasp. Today, she had gotten a good hold of her. It was no surprise the Reaper was looking for Xaneth. Lena had expected that and had a plan in place for just such an event.

As soon as Aisling was within her grasp, Lena would find out how the Reaper had survived her strike on Skye. That was a bonus since Lena's main goal was luring Xaneth to her. He would come once she spread the word that she had Aisling.

Lena hoped Death and the Reapers joined in the fun, as well. She was prepared for all of them. They were formidable enemies, and along with Xaneth, they had nearly defeated her. But she'd learned from her failures. Learned and *corrected*. The only outcome this time was victory.

She motioned to one of her soldiers near the door. "Prepare."

It was difficult for Lena to be patient. Death had thought she was clever sharing her magic with the Reapers to give them more power. But they had equals now with Lena's soldiers. The Reapers counted on their veils, but Aisling would soon learn that it didn't matter. Lena's soldiers could see through them, just as Reapers could. Though Lena had to hand it to Aisling. She was being stealthy. It was too bad she had to die. She would've made a good ally. But she would serve Lena better dead.

Lena turned away from the window and rubbed her hands together. Things were about to get fun. She walked from the room onto the landing. She rested her hands on the railing and looked over the side down to the main level. Lena couldn't see through the floor to what awaited Aisling, but she didn't need to since she had designed it herself.

"The female is inside the manor," the soldier stated as he walked up.

Lena met his gaze. "You know what to do."

He nodded and turned on his heel as he barked orders to those near him. They would set up around the manor and even in town to await Xaneth's arrival. Lena might have taken a chance on Skye to see if she'd imagined the looks between Xaneth and Aisling, but when Xaneth had missed his chance to kill her in order to take Aisling away, her suspicions were confirmed.

He'd saved Aisling once. Xaneth would try to do it again.

"Stupid to get your heart involved," Lena whispered. "There is no way to achieve your goals with someone weighing you down. I'll prove that to you, Xaneth. I'll make sure you know exactly what caused your defeat—right before I take your power."

Lena had been wary of the Dragon Kings, Death, and the Reapers, but she had known that with the right attack, she could best all of them. The only one who had given her pause and a reason for concern was Xaneth. He was different than the others. She wished she knew what made him special. All she knew was the way he had zeroed in on her the first time she'd seen him had sent a chill down her spine. She'd known then that she had to take him out first.

That proved more complicated than she liked to acknowledge, though. It was nearly impossible to locate him, but he seemed to be able to find the Fae Others with an ease that unsettled her. It was almost as if he had one goal—her death.

Everyone had a weakness, however. Everyone. No matter what they said. Hers had been her family, but she rid herself of them before anyone else could. Now that Lena knew Xaneth's weakness, bringing the Fae to his knees would be a simple matter. Then she'd kill him.

She would enjoy that. With him out of the way, she could focus on the Reapers. She had Aisling, so she was all but taken care of. Thanks to the bounties on the other Reapers' heads, it would only be a matter of time before she had each of them. Then, only Erith and Cael would remain.

The couple would be challenging—the Reaper-turned-god and his goddess lover. Lena hadn't witnessed Erith's full powers, but with the magic of thousands of Fae flowing through her, Lena wasn't concerned. Goddess or not, Lena would snuff out Erith with a snap of her fingers.

By that time, the Dragon Kings would be focused on her. They had defeated the original Others, but she was much more than they ever were. After she took Xaneth's, the Reapers', Erith's, and Cael's magic, nothing would be able to stop her. She'd toy with the Kings for a bit to make them think they had a chance of winning. They weren't used to defeat. It would be so sweet for a Fae to deliver that blow, especially since the Kings had claimed Earth as their domain and *allowed* the Fae to remain.

Allowed. Every time she thought about it, rage consumed her. Worse, many Fae felt beholden to the Kings for granting them a place to live. As if staying hidden and abiding by ridiculous rules was living. No, it was time for a change. The Fae had talked about it for a long time, but no one had wanted to do anything.

But she did.

And she was.

Lena's lips curled into a smile when she heard the thud of the trap door closing. "Your time has run out, Aisling."

~

Erith stood in Dreagan Manor's library and stared at Eoghan as he delivered the latest news.

"You don't look surprised," Eoghan said.

Erith exchanged a look with Cael. "I'm not. I knew Lena would call us out somehow."

"Ah," Eoghan replied as he crossed his arms over his chest. "That's why we're at Dreagan instead of on your realm."

Cael nodded once. "It's easier to discover what's going on."

"Not to mention react quicker."

Erith looked out a window at the winter wonderland beyond. The Dragon Kings had been more than gracious about offering to share their home with the Reapers.

Cael put a hand on her shoulder and squeezed. "It was the right decision, letting Aisling go to him. She's the only one who can talk to him."

"Yet she told Eoghan that Xaneth doesn't want anything to do with her," Erith argued.

Eoghan snorted. "We all saw his face on Skye when she was injured. He doesn't realize what he feels. Not yet."

"But he will," Cael added.

Would it be too late, though? Erith didn't want to lose anyone, but it was out of her hands. She might be a goddess, but she wasn't all-knowing.

"It was her choice," Eoghan said.

Erith shook her head and moved away from Cael's comforting presence to stand before the roaring fire. "We pushed her."

"She would've gone to him again eventually regardless," Cael said. "That pull brought her to him the first time. It will continue doing that."

Erith looked at the two Fae. "I don't like Aisling being on her own."

Eoghan nodded and dropped his hands to his sides. "Trust in Aisling. She has this."

"Even with the headaches?" Erith hadn't meant to snap, but this was a new development. One of her Reapers was vulnerable, and that frightened her.

Cael made a face. "Aye. I'll admit that one doesn't sit well with me."

"It was the only way we could find Xaneth. The only way to find Lena."

"Aisling isn't alone. She has Xaneth," Cael added. "He won't let anything happen to her."

Erith nodded, praying all the while that Cael's words were true. "Eoghan, please alert the other Reapers about the bounties. Everyone will have to use glamour when they go out. Even when we're veiled and using it, we'll have to be extra cautious."

Once Eoghan left the library, Erith extended her hands toward the fire and rubbed them together, suddenly chilled to her very bones.

"It's going to be fine. Look at every enemy we've faced and conquered. Lena is just another in a long line," Cael told her.

"What if she isn't? She's taking magic from the Fae. If she gets her hands on any of the Reapers, she'll do it to them, too. That means she'd have some of my magic."

"But she couldn't get to you."

Erith looked at Cael and held his gaze. "I won't know that for sure until I face her."

"I've gone through every scenario."

It was what made Cael such a competent, skilled fighter. He was able to methodically go through every movement in battle until he found a way to win. "And?"

"I don't know where the battle will take place. And I don't know who all will be involved."

"Nor do you know how much more magic Lena will have taken by then or what she's capable of."

Cael's lips flattened. "Nay, I won't."

"Which means you can't find the path we need to take until you have all of that information."

"Not unless we set the place and initiate the battle."

Erith knew that wouldn't work. "Lena won't fall for that. She wants this done on her terms."

"Too bloody bad. I want it on ours."

She smiled then, grateful to have him by her side, to be enveloped in his love and care. "We can't force her if we can't locate her. That's why Aisling is following Xaneth."

"And you believe Lena is counting on Xaneth coming to her."

"It's what I would do. She's scared of him and wants to decide when and where she meets him."

Cael blew out a long breath. "It'll give her the advantage. That's what I would do, too."

"For now, we prepare. We've seen what Lena can do, and she's only getting more powerful. I'm sure she's taken more Fae magic since the Isle of Skye."

"Aisling is safe. She'll look out for Xaneth, and he'll look out for her."

Erith heard the hope in Cael's voice. It was the same optimism she clung to with every fiber of her being. It wasn't just that Lena couldn't get a hold of a Reaper's magic—it was so much more than that. Aisling was family. Fierce and loyal. And beloved by everyone in their family.

"The rest of the Reapers know where Aisling is," Cael said, his thoughts running along the same vein as hers. "They're ready and waiting."

"As we all are."

"If Lena harms Aisling…"

Erith held out her hand for him. When Cael walked to her and took it, she pulled him down beside her. "This will be our greatest battle. Lena won't be alone. The others will be fighting alongside her."

"Idiots who drank the Fae Others' Kool-Aid," Cael said with a lip curl. "Some Fae would help us."

"Nay," Erith said. "It's better that it's just us. We don't know who we can trust."

Cael lifted a shoulder. "The Kings are ready to join us."

"Let's hope it doesn't come to that."

"Maybe we should bring them regardless."

Erith lowered her gaze to their linked hands. "We can do this. We *will* do this."

CHAPTER EIGHT

Aisling noted the Fae around the manor—too many for this to be anything but Lena's residence. And the Fae were her soldiers, given their all-black attire. Aisling followed the same trail Xaneth had taken to get to the manor and then went inside. He'd done it all without encountering a single soldier. And, somehow, she had done the same.

She was good, but was she *that* good? At least neither of them had raised any alarms. But something didn't sit well with her. It seemed too easy. Almost as if it were a trap.

The instant the thought went through her mind, Aisling spun around to get out of the manor, but the big, heavy wooden door slammed shut just before she reached it. She lifted her hand to use magic when the floor suddenly fell out from under her feet. Her breath locked in her throat, and a startled shout tumbled from her lips as she plummeted down a narrow passageway. She stretched her hands and feet to grasp the damp stones, but she couldn't stop herself, much less slow her descent.

She landed hard, one knee buckling as she pitched forward. Aisling caught herself with her hands and flipped her hair back as she hastily looked around. The silence of the dark, dank chamber caused an ominous chill to run through her. She tried to slow her rapid breathing, but her heart thudded uncomfortably in her chest.

"Bollocks," she whispered.

It *had* been a trap. But she was a Reaper and could get free. Aisling took a breath to steady herself. She wanted one last look around before she teleported out. Suddenly, a hand clamped over her mouth, and someone hauled her back against a hard body.

"It's me," whispered a deep, velvety voice. "Aisling, it's *me*."

She stilled when she recognized Xaneth's voice. He released her, and she spun to face him. "What have you led me to?"

"*Led* you?"

There were only pinpricks of light, but she didn't need to see his face. She heard the incredulity in his voice.

"I followed *you*," he added.

She shook her head. "That's not possible. You were ahead of me."

He took her hand and pulled her toward a doorway she hadn't known was there. She tried not to think about his warm hand wrapped around hers or how good it felt. His grip was firm but comforting, strong but tender. Her boot splashed in a small puddle. Water dripped incessantly. Xaneth stopped beneath a sliver of light and faced her. "I've been following you since you returned to Kilbaha and came to Roscrea."

A tight knot formed in her chest. She rubbed at it with her free hand, trying to loosen the anxiety that churned faster and faster. "That can't… It can't be."

"I've no reason to lie."

"How did you follow me here?"

"You said the name."

Aisling searched her memory. Had she? She couldn't remember voicing anything.

"Why did you come to Roscrea? How did you know Lena would be here?" As if realizing that he still held her, Xaneth hastily released her hand.

Aisling ignored his quick release and the ache it caused. She fisted her hands, letting her nails dig into her palms to help ground her. "My magic found you in Roscrea. It's why I came. I figured you'd lead me to Lena. None of that matters now. We can leave."

"Nay!" Xaneth shouted as he grabbed her and stepped close. He winced and lowered his voice again. "No magic."

Aisling stilled as their eyes locked. Her heart skipped a beat when their bodies brushed. She wanted to reach up and touch him, to feel him everywhere. He jerked as if comprehending how close they were. He released her and moved back.

He had the ability to cut her to shreds, yet somehow she kept allowing it to happen. If only she didn't crave his touch with such desperation and so much longing it felt as if she might die.

Somehow, she held his gaze and remembered why he had reacted so violently. "Why no magic?"

He glanced furtively to the side. "We're not the only ones in this place. Every time a Fae uses magic, they're killed instantly."

"Well. Fek," she said, utterly deflated.

A quick smile curved his lips. "Aye. I said the same thing."

"Wait," she said with a shake of her head. "If you were following *me*, how did you get inside before I did?"

Xaneth sheepishly said, "The guards were focused on you. I used that to my advantage and came inside. Unfortunately, I did it at the same time they led another Fae here."

"How were the guards focused on me? I was veiled. I still am."

"Apparently, they can see you," he said tightly.

She tilted her head to the side as she lowered her veil. "Are you going to finally admit that you can, too?"

"Aye."

"For how long?"

"Since I escaped Usaeil's."

She wanted to ask so much about that, but Aisling decided that now wasn't the time. "If saw me, then they should've been able to see you."

"As I said, they were fixated on you."

Aisling fisted her hands in anger as the truth slammed into her. "Lena led me here. She knew I would follow you. She wants the Reapers."

"She wants *you*."

"Nay, she wants *you*." Aisling was reminded that *she* was Xaneth's weakness. After swearing not to put herself in such a position, that was exactly where she found herself. "She doesn't know you're here, though, right? That means we have an advantage."

"For now." Xaneth ran his hands through his hair as he looked to the side. "It was pure luck that I found you when I did. I had to get to you before you used magic." His gaze slid back to her.

"Then I owe you even more."

"Why do you think you owe me for getting you off the battlefield?" he asked, his brow puckered.

She shook her head in dismay. "You really don't know, do you?"

"I don't. Please, explain."

"You saved me. I was dead."

His face smoothed as he stared at her in silence. He said nothing, did nothing. Simply stood. Finally, after a long minute, he said, "That's impossible."

"I breathed my last on that battlefield. I remember every second of it. The pain, the…panic." She glanced away at that admission. "I tried to call out to someone, but I couldn't. So, I looked at the stars. Then, everything went black, and the pain left. The next thing I knew, I woke up in a cave alone. Why did you leave?"

He took a step back and ran into the wall behind him. Xaneth kept shaking his head in denial. "I can't. I didn't. I couldn't have…done that," he said with a wave of his hand toward her.

"You did."

Xaneth turned away and scraped a hand over his jaw, the sound of his palm rubbing across his whiskers loud. "How is that possible?"

"I don't really care, but I'm thankful for whatever you did."

He turned his head to her, raking her with his gaze. "Wouldn't I know if I had done that?"

"I don't know," she said with a shrug. "Why did you leave me there alone?"

"If it *was* me, Lena can't know," he said without answering her question.

Aisling realized that he didn't plan to answer her. But she had something else to ask. "Why were you following me?"

"There's a bounty on your head," he said as if that explained everything.

"I'm a Reaper. I can take care of myself."

"I know."

She quirked a brow, wanting more than ever for him to admit why he had trailed her. "Then why follow me?"

"I…" He let out a long sigh. "I didn't want you harmed."

That was probably as much as she would get. But it was more than she had before. Aisling decided it was time to turn the conversation before she pressed her luck, and he cut off his words again. "How do we get out of here?"

"I'm not sure. I've not explored very much."

Because he had been waiting for her so he could be here to prevent her from dying. Again. Aisling might wish that Xaneth had done it because he cared about her, but the truth was, he would've done it for anyone because he was a good guy. It was just who he was.

Aisling shrugged. "Lena set this trap for me. It might be prudent if we split up. I don't want her finding you."

"On the contrary, I want her to know I'm here. It's time this ends."

Aisling saw the determination in his silver eyes. Before she could reply, they both heard something or someone headed toward them. Xaneth grabbed her and pulled her with him into another corridor. She found herself between the damp wall and his hard body. Her breath hitched at the feel of him against her. He felt better than she had dreamed. Warm and solid. If only she could run her hands over him, learning every rise and valley of his firm sinew.

She lifted her gaze to Xaneth's face, but he paid her no heed as he concentrated on the sound—something she should do, too, but she wasn't about to pass up this opportunity. She put the moment to memory, burning it into her brain so she could call it up again and again. She hadn't been conscious when he carried her before, but she was very much awake now, and she absolutely planned to take advantage of every delicious second.

The strength in his body, the warmth that encircled her, the power she felt radiating from him. He wrapped one arm around her, holding her firmly against him, his fingers splayed on her back. His other hand was against the wall next to her head. His breathing was even, and his eyes laser-focused.

She studied the hard line of his jaw covered in a day's growth of beard. His lips were so close she would only have to shift slightly and press hers against his. It was only then that she realized her fingers were splayed across his rock-hard chest. She couldn't remember the last time anyone had protected her—maybe one of her brothers when she was very young.

Yet Xaneth acted as her protector, putting himself between her and whatever headed their way. It made her feel special.

Worse, something inside her blossomed. Even as she basked in the realization, she knew she was treading on dangerous ground.

Suddenly, Xaneth's head swung to her, their gazes clashing. He stared at her for a long moment before his glorious silver gaze dropped to her mouth. Her lips parted instantly as heat and yearning flooded her veins. His fingers flexed on her back. In that instant, she knew he would kiss her. She waited breathlessly.

Someone screamed for help as footsteps pounded against the floor, sounding right next to them. A Fae rushed past, her cries for aid going unanswered. A second later, eerie silence followed a strangled scream.

Whatever had held her and Xaneth vanished in an instant.

He released her and stepped away, looking anywhere but at her as he cleared his throat. "It's better if we keep our distance from others. Just in case."

Aisling nodded since she wasn't sure she could find words. She had never felt as cold as she did in that moment. She'd had his heat, his shelter—even if she didn't need it—and now, it was gone. She motioned for him to go. It took a moment for Xaneth to pick a direction. He continued down the corridor, and Aisling fell into step behind him.

Neither spoke. It wasn't difficult to hear others in the underground maze, but their cries for help always ended in screams that were cut short. Aisling had no idea how many Fae Lena drew to the manor, but there was no way Lena was wasting them. No doubt she gathered their magic to use as her own. Apparently, lining them up and taking it was too easy. She wanted to terrify them first.

Aisling had no idea how long they walked or even where they were from where they had begun. She stared at Xaneth's back and wondered why he didn't want even her friendship. One minute she thought he desired her, and the next, he cut her to the quick. It had never been her intention to feel anything for someone again. The way she was drawn to Xaneth, sought his friendship, needed his touch…it brought up a past that still clung to her like the misshapen fingers of death.

She knew where this road would lead, and yet she couldn't stop herself, couldn't keep from falling for Xaneth. But she was broken. No matter what Eoghan said, Aisling knew there was no way to pick up her shattered pieces, because they were gone —ground to dust and scattered on the wind, long, long ago.

Her fekked-up thoughts and emotions were why she wanted something she couldn't have, something that had never been offered to her in the first place. It wasn't as if Xaneth had flirted. He'd done nothing to make her think that he wanted anything from her. In fact, he had gone out of his way to tell her to leave him alone. She was the one who had sought to find reciprocated feelings when there were none.

She flattened her hand on her stomach as the truth made her stumble and reach for the wall with her other hand. What must he think of her? How sad and wretched was she to continue seeking out someone who didn't share those feelings?

So what if he'd saved her? He would've done it with Torin had he been beside Xaneth in the battle instead of her. There was nothing between her and Xaneth other than what she had crafted in her head. In him she saw…she didn't know what she saw, exactly. A Fae with greatness, a man who struggled to find his way in a world that had done nothing but tear him down. A warrior who battled his demons while tackling evil for others.

She saw a good man that she wanted to help. Whatever fantasies she had needed to stay locked in her head—not bleeding into real life. She could aid Xaneth if and when he required it. She would be the friend he didn't know he needed. That would be enough for her.

It had to be.

CHAPTER NINE

Xaneth had no idea where they were or where to go. The screams and shouts had long since faded as they moved farther from the entry—at least, he thought they had traveled away from it. For all he knew, they were going in circles, and there just weren't any Fae left to die other than him and Aisling.

Aisling.

He turned his head to the side and listened for her footsteps. She remained several paces behind him. They hadn't spoken since he had found himself pressed against her. It had been torture thinking about cradling her against him on Skye, but that was nothing compared to looking down at her and seeing her lips parted and her focus on his mouth.

As soon as he registered that, he'd realized that he held her as if he had a right to touch her that way. As if he knew her body, and she was his to explore. For half a second, he allowed himself to believe that was true—that she wanted him pressing her against a wall. That she looked at him with desire because she craved his kiss.

Even that half a second was wrong. It had given him a glimpse into something he could never have. And *that* was an agony worse than anything Usaeil had put him through.

Xaneth had separated from Aisling as quickly as he could. But even now, his body had an imprint where she had been against him. Her softness, her curves. He'd tried to ignore how she fit against him so perfectly. Attempted to look past the way his blood heated at her nearness and the need—the *hunger*—he had for her. But it was useless. No one could disregard Aisling in any capacity. She commanded attention everywhere she went. It was the way she held herself and took on the world and everyone in it as if she feared nothing.

He was so lost in thought that it took him some time to realize that he walked alone. Xaneth halted and spun around. He searched the dim hallway but found no sign of the Reaper. His heart skipped a beat.

"Aisling?" he called as he retraced his steps, his fear growing rapidly. "Aisling!"

"There's no need to shout. I'm right here."

His eyes scanned the corridor until he found her sitting on the floor, her back leaning against a wall. Xaneth drew in a relieved breath as he made his way to her. Once there, he looked both ways down the corridor. "What are you doing?"

"What are *you* doing?" she replied.

Xaneth's gaze dropped to her in concern. Something in her voice didn't sound right. He went down on his haunches to get a better view of her face. "Are you injured?"

"From walking?" She snorted and shook her head. "Nay.

I'm just tired. We've been walking for what feels like days. We've not seen or heard anything in a long time. There hasn't been a door or a room, just more hallways and dead ends. In case you've not comprehended, we're in a maze. The bitch crafted a maze beneath her manor."

"There's an entry. And if there's an entry, there's an exit."

"Sure. By death. When was the last time you went this long without using your magic?"

Xaneth lowered himself to the ground on the opposite side of the passageway and rested his arms on his bent knees. "I can't remember."

"Exactly. We're Fae. We *are* magic. It's a part of us from the moment we're born. It's natural to turn to magic in any situation, especially ones like this. I can't even call to my friends because the last thing I want is for them to wind up trapped here with us. We can't teleport because that's magic, and we'll get zapped or whatever happens—the end result being death. Lena gets our magic with little to no effort, all the while getting off on terrorizing her kind."

He watched Aisling. Her words had little anger, only acceptance. Submission. And that would never do. He needed her fighting. With him. "The fierce Aisling isn't giving up, surely."

She didn't immediately reply. Instead, she sat there quietly for a long moment. "I'm not surrendering. I'm stating our reality. In case you've not noticed, there's no food or water. I might be a Reaper, but I'm not immortal. As far as I know, neither are you. That means we need sustenance, and in order to get that, we need to use magic. Which we can't."

"There's a way out."

Her head rolled to the side as she looked away. "You don't need to reassure me."

Was he doing that? All he knew was that the words Aisling said worried him—mostly because they were true. They needed to find a way out quickly.

"This isn't the first bad spot I've found myself in," she continued. "I deal in reality. I face the facts. Right now, I just want to rest. I'm tired."

Xaneth extended his legs so one side of his foot touched hers. He didn't know why he needed the contact, but he did. She didn't move away, which surprised him. He'd done everything he could to push her away for so long. He'd ignored Death and the other Reapers. But he hadn't been able to shake Aisling loose. She had relentlessly tracked him, but never abrasively or forcefully. All she had asked of him was to talk, but he hadn't been able to give her even that. In many ways, he still couldn't. But they were stuck together for the foreseeable future.

While she'd said that she wasn't giving up, her words had an undercurrent that vexed him. He had to get her to focus on something—*anything*—else. Xaneth worked his jaw, trying to think of something to say that would draw her into a conversation he had rejected time and again.

"What's it like?" he finally asked.

She rolled her head back to him, no emotion on her face. "What is *what* like?"

"Being a Reaper."

Her red eyes regarded him for a moment, then she shrugged. "It's the best decision I ever made. After so many wrong ones."

He wanted to ask what kind of wrong ones but didn't. Couldn't. He was already delving into dangerous territory by talking to her. "Was it painful? Transitioning into a Reaper?"

"Nay. The betrayal and murder beforehand was, though."

Xaneth stilled. Betrayal? *Murder?* "What?" he croaked, consumed with a mixture of fury and incredulity, each warring with the other for dominance.

Her brows drew together. "Since you knew about the Reapers, I assumed you were aware of how we're chosen."

"Nay." He barely got the word out.

Aisling shrugged one shoulder. "Erith has a few requirements. Each Fae chosen is a highly skilled fighter. And we have to be betrayed…and killed."

"I see." But he didn't. Because each time he thought of someone deceiving Aisling, he wanted to find them and make them pay. Painfully.

She blinked at him before lowering her gaze to her lap. "Erith gives us a second chance as Reapers, and in exchange, we give up our lives, friends, and family from before and dedicate ourselves to her and the team. We're family. We all come in knowing that each of us carries something from our past, that each of us was slain. That binds us."

"So you know what happened to each other?"

"Nay. We only share if we want to. And we never want to."

Xaneth thought about her nightmare from earlier. He wondered if it had anything to do with her betrayal and murder. He instinctively knew that it did. Deep-rooted rage coalesced within him. He wanted—nay, he *needed*—to avenge her. But surely she had already done that. "Did you take revenge on those responsible for you becoming a Reaper?"

There was a brief pause before she shook her head.

Xaneth seethed. Had it been a man? If so, what had he been to Aisling? Xaneth wanted to traverse whatever hell or underbelly the bastard had gone to and kill him again. And again.

"Right at the point of death, Erith contains our soul," Aisling continued, unaware of his thoughts. "She told me who she was and offered me a place with the Reapers. She told me the rules and what I would have to do if I accepted her terms. It was a good offer, but I hesitated."

That made him frown, especially after her statement that it had been the best decision she'd ever made. "Why?"

"If I agreed, I knew I would carry the past with me." Her eyes met his. "If I refused, death would erase it all."

"In the end, you accepted Death's offer."

Aisling nodded slowly. "I wanted to do something good with my life. Until that point, I wasn't exactly someone who contributed to society—human or Fae."

Xaneth twisted his lips as he shook his head. "I've seen you with the Reapers. That can't be true."

"You didn't know me before. This," she said as she waved her arms around herself, "is the product of a second chance. What I am now is nothing like I was before."

"Who were you before?"

She didn't look away as she said, "A killer."

Xaneth could've told her that was obvious by her coloring, but he had interacted with many Dark and knew that not all of them were murdering psychopaths who needed to be put down. "Everyone has a past."

"We don't only get a second chance when becoming

Reapers. There must be something in the few drops of magic Erith gives us that changes us. We look the same, but we have added magic and powers, and the trappings that once conformed us are no longer there."

"Is that why she takes Dark and Light Fae?"

A small smile played on Aisling's lips. "She doesn't wipe away our pasts, but it's something like that. We all get to start anew with the knowledge from before. It allows us to make better choices. To *do* better. We don't see each other as Light or Dark. We're simply Reapers."

"It's too bad all Fae can't be like that."

"Or any species."

He dropped his head back against the wall. "The bond between the Reapers is something special."

"Erith usually kills any Fae who discover who we are. She didn't do that with you. Why?"

Xaneth drew in a breath and released it as he shrugged. "I honestly expected her to take my life. I never learned why she didn't."

"We never stopped looking for you."

At the mention of his capture by Usaeil, he stilled.

"Never," Aisling added.

He swallowed, uncomfortable with that knowledge. He had been on his own for so long, only counting on himself, that it was an odd feeling to know that others had been trying to help. They had continued reaching out to him, even as he slapped their hands away.

"I'm sorry Usaeil captured you."

Xaneth lifted his gaze to the ceiling high above them. "She was after me for so long. I watched her wipe out my family, one by one—my little sister being the last. I hid instead of helping her."

"There's nothing shameful in that. You couldn't help your sister. You had to think of yourself."

"Everything about that is inexcusable and reprehensible. I promised I'd protect her. I failed."

"It was Usaeil," Aisling said. "She was older and had others at her disposal to track you. The blame lies with her. Not you. Don't carry that."

He found himself staring into Aisling's crimson eyes. "I told myself that, but it never dulled the pain. I knew it was only a matter of time before she found me. I learned to sneak around. I even ventured into the Light Castle when she still sat on the throne. I came within feet of her, and she never knew."

"Ballsy," Aisling replied with a grin.

Xaneth chuckled. "More like insane. She always made it seem as if she could find me anywhere. I wanted to see if that was true."

"What did you do when she didn't recognize you?"

"I expanded my business."

"Ah. The Seeker."

He linked his fingers together. "I knew if she ever came after me that I'd need friends all over. That was why I started working with both the Light and the Dark. Everyone wants something, and I made sure I could get it for them."

"People trusted you."

"When I gave my word, I kept it." He lifted a shoulder. "Until Usaeil hired me to find Thea."

CHAPTER TEN

Aisling couldn't stop looking at Xaneth. From the moment he had escaped Usaeil, he'd been reserved and aloof. Now, he was relaxed. Even his body had softened from its usual state of tenseness. She didn't know why he was talking, but she would enjoy it while it lasted.

She had met Xaneth after he'd kidnapped Thea for Usaeil. The Reapers had gotten involved because Thea had pulled Eoghan from the Hell realm. Aisling had known about Xaneth but had never come face-to-face with him until that time. It didn't take her long to discover that he wasn't just any Fae. He was a royal. When Usaeil went back on her word about lifting Xaneth's banishment, Xaneth allowed the Reapers to rescue Thea—putting Xaneth in Usaeil's crosshairs once more.

"Your aunt didn't take your betrayal well," Aisling said.

Xaneth grunted. "She deserved it and so much more."

"Do you think she knew who you were when she hired you?"

"I didn't think so at first, but maybe she did. She would've killed me if all of you had not been there."

Aisling shifted to get more comfortable. "After eluding her for so long, why did you take the job?"

"It was good money—and another way to be next to her to see if she realized who I was."

"That was risky."

His silver gaze darted away. "I got tired of hiding."

"But then she knew who you were. She knew you as the Seeker."

"Aye." His lips flattened. "Things went to shite after that."

The Reapers hadn't known that Usaeil had captured Xaneth until they couldn't find him. "We eventually found the house she had you in. The room." Aisling tried not to think about the empty bed she had discovered or the thoughts that had gone through her head regarding what might have happened to Xaneth. "But you freed yourself."

"You wouldn't have wanted to be there to see that."

He wouldn't meet her gaze. Aisling's heart went out to him. "Was it bad? What she did to you?"

"She trapped me in my own mind."

His tone was flat, the words hollow, but she still heard the pain in them, the agony of what he had endured. She wanted to reach out to him and give him comfort. But she kept her hands to herself. Instead, she pressed the side of her foot more solidly against his.

Xaneth's shoulders lifted as he inhaled. "I was running for my life the entire time."

Aisling froze. She had wanted to ask about his torture but hadn't dared. Things like that weren't shared—at least, not willingly. She certainly wouldn't be the one to ask him to delve into those memories just so she could satisfy her curiosity.

"There was a monster after me," he continued, looking across at the wall somewhere over her head. "It got near me once and slashed. Those wounds were very real. The pain worse than anything I'd ever experienced. I couldn't sleep, couldn't rest. It was always there. Always able to find me. I don't think I've ever been so exhausted or drained. Or scared. I was utterly alone without a clue where I was. And all without my magic."

Aisling's lips parted as shock went through her. He was once more in a place he didn't know without his magic. At least he wasn't alone this time. She wasn't so sure she would be as calm as he was if their positions were reversed.

"I jumped from a waterfall." He shook his head as if reliving the experience. "I was desperate to get some space from the beast so I could eat and maybe shut my eyes for a second. Something about the place I swam to looked familiar, but I didn't dwell on it. Not until I was catching some food and remembered that my father had taken me to the spot to teach me how to fish." His eyes met hers, the look in them solemn and intense. "I went to other places and found other memories. That was how I realized I was in my mind."

She stretched out her leg near him to offer what comfort she could, hoping he would take it. After a moment, his leg lengthened against hers. "It's impressive you figured it out. Usaeil wanted you frightened and running to keep that from happening."

"Aye," he replied softly.

"How did you get away?"

"I faced the creature coming for me."

Aisling's brows shot up, though she shouldn't have been surprised. It sounded exactly like something Xaneth would do. "And?"

"I thought it was the monster I had been running from, so I fought it. In doing so, I realized that *I* was the beast."

Her breath came faster with every reveal. She swallowed hard. "Yourself?"

"Everyone has two sides. Each decision we make gives one side a win."

"Aye. Good and bad. Feed the good…you're good. Feed the bad, you're evil."

He grew still. "The monster was both sides of me, working together. The battle went on for hours, days, I know not how long. I was only aware that I had to defeat it to get free. I don't know how I knew that, but I did."

"You won. You're free."

"Did I? Am I?"

She frowned in confusion. "I don't understand. You're sitting here with me. You're no longer being tortured."

"I didn't win, Aisling. Not in the way you think. I didn't kill that thing. I *became* it—a living, breathing monster."

"You call yourself a monster, but I call you a hero. You're fighting the same fight we are. You seek out evil and destroy it."

His smile was sad as he said, "You've not seen what's really inside me."

"I know you. The Fae who stood alone against Usaeil, who defied her in keeping Thea hidden so the queen couldn't kill her. The Fae who found a way to live with both Dark and

Light alike—and befriend those of each. A Fae who broke free of torture meant to kill him. A Fae who took me from a battlefield and brought me back to life." She leaned forward. "A Fae who followed me here because there is a bounty on my head. And one who made sure I didn't use magic and die in this horrible place. Monster? No, Xaneth, you aren't some brute. You're the opposite in every way. You're good, decent. Noble. And that has nothing to do with your royal blood and everything to do with *you*."

"How I wish your words were true."

"They are," she insisted.

He looked down and shook his head. "You've not seen me when I go after evil."

"You forget that I fought beside you on Skye, as well as the encounters with Lena. I've seen you."

"Of course."

But she knew he was giving in instead of agreeing. What was he hiding? What didn't he want her to know? "Don't do that," she said.

He lifted a thick brow as he met her gaze. "Do what?"

"Retreat. Tell me."

"I'd rather not. I like this picture you paint of me. It's how I want you to see me."

Did it matter to him how she saw him? "It *is* how I see you."

"After. It's how I want you to see me *after*."

She searched his face, trying to determine what he meant. But she knew. He didn't expect to live after his battle with Lena. She swallowed past the lump in her throat, emotion choking her. "It's how I'll always see you."

There was a real smile on his lips this time. She knew pain, every Reaper did, but she suspected that Xaneth's went much, much deeper. He might have told her about the torture, but he had no doubt glossed over things. Yet she couldn't deny the happiness she felt that he had shared that part of himself. With her. Almost as if they were friends.

Aisling wanted to wash away his pain with her kisses, to hold him until she mended every scar on his soul. It was wishful thinking, of course. But if given the opportunity, she would gladly do it.

"How are you able to see through my veil?"

He shrugged. "I don't know. It only happened after the torture."

"Have you always felt like…?" She couldn't even say *monster*.

"Nay," he said with a shake of his head. "Again, after."

She slowly leaned back. "What about smelling evil? Was that after, too?"

"Aye."

"Your need to end evil?"

"After," he answered.

She bit her bottom lip. "Your speed and power match that of a Reaper. I would even suggest that it exceeds ours."

"I had more magic than the average Fae because of my royal blood, but nothing like what I have now."

"There can only be two reasons for that."

His brows snapped together as his silver eyes filled with doubt. "You can't seriously think it has to do with the torture."

"Maybe. Or the fight for your freedom. You said you battled yourself, yet you claim you're a monster now."

He blinked, his face going slack as he contemplated her words. "What you're suggesting isn't even possible."

"How is magic possible? How is Erith here but no other gods or goddesses? I don't know. It just is."

Xaneth released a long breath. "What I do know is that I have one purpose: to end Lena and the Fae Others."

"That's good to hear because that's what I'm trying to do," she said with a grin.

He didn't return the expression. "You can't be near when I clash with Lena. None of the Reapers can."

"You're going to need our help. Lena will have others with her."

"I know."

She glared at him, crossing her arms over her chest. "Do you have a death wish?"

"Do you really want me walking around? What happens after I kill Lena? What happens when I stop looking for evil and just look for someone to slaughter?"

"You don't know that will happen."

"You don't know it won't," he replied softly. "I'd rather die in battle than force a friend to put me down."

All her anger vanished in an instant. "You consider me a friend?"

"Aye. Though I think you'll come to regret it one day very soon."

"You make it sound like we're going to get out of here. I doubt we will."

His silver eyes blazed with determination. "We will get out."

She wanted to believe him. It was easier to cling to that

thin thread of hope than let reality take hold. Eventually, reality would intrude again. Until then, she would allow hope to blossom within her. Xaneth had called her a friend and opened up about himself. Maybe he'd done it to ease her mind, or perhaps he really did think of her as a friend. Either way, she was glad he was here with her.

He climbed to his feet and held out his hand. "Shall we?"

She slipped her fingers across his palm and allowed him to pull her up. "We shall."

This time when they began walking, she stayed at his side. She didn't hide the smile either. She'd had nothing to grin about for too long. Now, she had a friend and a connection she hadn't had before. That was more than enough to smile about.

CHAPTER ELEVEN

"Something is wrong," Lena stated as she paced the front room on the main floor of the manor. "Very wrong."

She should've felt Aisling's magic by now. There's no way the Reaper could've gotten out of her maze. It was inherent in every Fae to use their magic to get out of a situation. It was why she had set up the labyrinth as she had. No one lasted more than a few hours in there. No one. So, why didn't she have Aisling's magic?

Lena halted and spun to face the soldier behind her, standing with his feet apart and hands clasped behind him. His hair, more silver than black, was trimmed short, and his red eyes held hers. Berach had risen through the ranks to become her captain. Not because he was a skilled warrior but because the others before him had died. Still, he was proving to be more than adequate at his job. If not, she'd kill him—every soldier knew that.

"You said the Reaper was in the maze," she stated.

Berach bowed his head. "I saw her enter the manor myself. She's locked away."

"Then why haven't I felt her magic?"

Calmly, Berach said, "Perhaps you have gained so much power and magic from other Fae that you no longer feel when you take."

"I still feel it," she told him and began pacing again. "If Aisling is in the labyrinth then she somehow knows not to use her magic." Lena jerked to a stop as she whipped her head around to Berach. "She is still in the maze, correct?"

"No one can get out. You've made sure of that."

That didn't answer her question. Lena had devised the trap to ensure that no one could get out unless they knew exactly where to go—and she was the only one who had that information. Fae wouldn't spend the time looking for a door or some other way out. They would try to teleport, and if those in the labyrinth didn't have the power to teleport, they would still use magic to escape. Either way, everyone ended up dead, and she with their magic.

"Aisling isn't that intelligent. She's a warrior," Lena said, more to herself than to Berach. "She only knows how to fight. I expected her death within minutes, an hour at the very most. It's been over fourteen hours and…nothing."

"She's in there. Your decoy led her straight to the manor, just as you predicted," Berach said.

Lena turned her gaze to him. "Are you suggesting I should wait?"

"I'm *suggesting* the Reaper is already dead. Perhaps she didn't have the power you think she did."

Lena quirked a brow. "Is your magic more potent since becoming one of my soldiers?"

"Aye."

"You match the Reapers in nearly every way. Are you now telling me that if I killed you and took back what I gave that I wouldn't feel it?"

A muscle in Berach's jaw jumped as he realized he had backed himself into a corner.

Lena waved away whatever words he might try to say. "She's in there. Find her. I want to know where she is." Just in case the Reaper had decided to walk the maze to get out.

"There's another reason you've not thought of," Berach said.

Anger bubbled within Lena. She could take this Dark's life with a snap of her fingers. And she was seriously contemplating it. The only thing that made her hesitate was realizing it would behoove her to listen. *Then*, if she didn't like what he said, she could kill him. "What's that?"

"She saw someone use magic and perish, which is why she hasn't. That has given her time to look around the labyrinth."

As much as Lena hated to admit it, he had a point. "You think she's trying to get out?"

"I think she realized it's a trap. And that she wants to find you."

That was something Lena hadn't considered. No Fae had survived the maze yet. However, if Lena wanted to be victorious, then she shouldn't underestimate anyone—especially not a Reaper.

"You may be correct." She smiled at the soldier. "Send in the *cú* hound."

Berach's smile was slow as he turned on his heel and strode from the room to carry out her orders. Now that she had worked the problem plaguing her since Aisling's arrival, Lena could relax and wait for the influx of magic from the Reaper.

Lena walked to the pale-yellow brocade settee that had been in her family for generations. Everything about the manor sickened her. She had hidden the truth of who she really was for so long—from her husband, her son, her brother, and his family. Even the Six who had ruled the Fae Others with her.

Until she hadn't needed any of them anymore.

The manor had been her escape, the place she could go to be herself. Every other room in the home had been redecorated to match her dark side, but not this one. This sitting room had been left for the occasions when someone visited. But now, there wasn't anyone to call on her. At least not anyone she was hiding her true nature from anymore.

She ran her fingers over the cloth of the lounger. With a thought, red and silver replaced the bright, happy colors around the room. First the settee turned to a deep red silk. The two tufted chairs faded from turquoise to a dark gray velvet. The Oriental-style rugs vanished, replaced by fringed, hand-knotted, red Turkish rugs.

"Much better," Lena said with a smile as she sank onto the settee.

She reclined against the cushion and crossed one leg over the other. Her wide-legged black wool trousers, and a matching double-breasted blazer that contoured to her curves looked amazing against the red. She sucked in a breath as magic poured into her from the maze below. It wasn't much, but every little bit counted.

And Fae were so easily led. It took next to nothing to get them to travel to the manor. Then, it was only a matter of getting them through the right door—again, entirely too easy—before they were in the labyrinth.

The more magic Lena took, the more powerful she became. She couldn't believe that none of the other Six had thought to do as she had. Even the original Others hadn't gone this route. It was ironic. Had they, she probably wouldn't be here today—none of them would. Including the Dragon Kings. Not that she was worried. The Kings time on this realm was dwindling rapidly. And they didn't even know it.

For the moment, however, her focus was on Death and the Reapers. Not to mention Xaneth. They had joined forces three times against her. The first hadn't been planned. It was a good thing, too, because she hadn't been prepared—not for them or Xaneth.

The second time, she had expected it, but it had only been days after the first skirmish, right after she had consumed her family's magic. The rush of that had been unlike anything she could even try to describe. She had been so overcome by the sheer force of everything inside her without any time to try to wield it when Xaneth suddenly showed up. The second time she'd faced the royal Fae, she'd gotten in a good strike that had knocked him out.

She wished she could've killed him then and there, but Chevonne, her niece and the last member of her family, had attacked. Lena fingered her wounded ear, the top part missing. Magic hid that, but she knew what Chevonne had done.

Then came the Isle of Skye. That had been meant to be

her crowning glory. Not just because she'd killed the other five who governed the Fae Others with her, but because she meant to wipe out Xaneth and the Reapers. That attempt, too, had been foiled. That time by Balladyn, the previous King of the Dark, who was now a Reaper with a Druid by his side. That defeat had come close to ending all her dreams.

Which was why she had taken the time to come up with a plan that would ensure her success in every way. And why Aisling not dying yet made her anxious. Lena didn't care if she had to sacrifice every last soldier with her, she *would* end Aisling's life. She could always make more soldiers, but she needed a Reaper's power to get a taste of Death's capabilities and understand her potency.

Lena was so close to being unstoppable. All she needed was one Reaper to fall to her. She suspected she could take on the goddess already, but she wanted to be sure. Needed to know positively that she could win against Death.

Another burst of magic entered her. Lena briefly closed her eyes and felt the tension melting from her body. How had no one thought to take magic from others to enrich theirs? If even one King of the Dark had tried it, the Light could've been wiped away long ago. No one would've had to listen to their sanctimonious shite, telling the Dark they were evil and wrong.

But Lena would show them all.

Including those working so hard to form a Fae council. In all the ages of the Fae, no one had attempted such a thing. That was because the Fae didn't want it. Not then, and not now. They only thought they did. Once she removed all the obstacles in her path, she would show the Light and Dark that they only needed to bow to one person—her.

Lena stopped herself from thinking too far ahead. That was what had happened to her ancestors, the Muldowneys. They had allowed themselves to get too greedy, which had brought about their downfall. The family had changed their surname to Quinlan and walked the straight and narrow of the Light Fae for so many generations the past had almost been buried forever. Then, Lena uncovered the truth.

As soon as she learned who she was descended from and how the Muldowney family had been feared and respected as they wreaked havoc within all the Fae, she suddenly knew she wasn't the different one in her family. It was everyone else. From that day on, Lena had silently plotted her way to power.

Her answer to it all? The Others.

If they had never come to Earth, if they had never set out to destroy the Dragon Kings, then she wouldn't have found out about them. She wouldn't have sought out the five like-minded Fae. Once they formed the Six, it was incredibly easy to lure other disillusioned Fae into their larger group.

It was Lena's idea to take a small portion of those Fae. The others, the Six, split their magic after killing them. At first, Lena had feared the Six would realize that she'd stopped being a Light somewhere along the way and had turned Dark. Oddly enough, none of them had. Then, she'd killed *them*. Making her the one in charge. The only one.

And being on top felt wonderful. Right, even. As if she had been destined for this since before she was born. This was only the beginning. She had so much more planned for the Fae once she stood without enemies coming for her.

There were too many Fae. Her soldiers rooted out the weak ones and brought them to the manor, where they died in the maze, giving Lena their magic. The population was dwindling considerably, but there was still so much more to go.

It would come, though. She had no doubt. Then, she would let the Fae loose on the humans. The silly mortals thought they could do whatever they wanted. The Dragon Kings had given up the realm to them, but she wouldn't. The humans needed to know their place. They were food for the Dark. And with their overpopulated cities, the Dark could feast as they'd never feasted before.

This magnificent realm the mortals had decimated would bounce back with her care—and the removal of those who thought only of themselves.

Lena leaned her head back against the settee. "Soon," she whispered.

CHAPTER TWELVE

Xaneth had made a promise to Aisling that he intended to keep. Not just for her but also for himself. He probably shouldn't have said it, but he'd looked into her eyes, and the words had just fallen from his lips.

But that was how things were with Aisling.

Anytime he was around her, he said and did things he wouldn't normally do. Like talking to her. He hadn't meant to share so much of himself. Yet, at the same time, it had felt right. She hadn't looked down her nose at him, hadn't pitied him. She'd listened and accepted. Perhaps he should've realized she would do that, but it had still come as a surprise— a good one, but a surprise, nonetheless.

Now, they were walking again. He shortened his strides so they could walk together. He didn't want to like her beside him, but he did. Too much, actually. There was no going back now, however. He'd crossed the line he'd tried so hard not to cross. He'd known speaking with Aisling would be easy. He'd known he would enjoy it.

It was one of the reasons he had pushed her away so determinedly. Not that it had gotten him anywhere but exactly where he'd attempted *not* to be. Yet, even then, he wasn't angry about it. It was Aisling, after all. The way she looked at him with her crimson eyes, the way her lips curved into a smile. Her throaty voice that made him want to drag her into his arms and kiss her until they were both breathless and needy.

He wouldn't. Of that, he was sure. He might not be able to send her away now, and he had caved with the conversing, but that was where things ended. He was sure he wouldn't cross that line. Nothing and no one could make him do that.

Xaneth didn't know how long they walked this time. He saw Aisling's fatigue, felt his. The Fae were a hearty species but they still needed sustenance. It had been some time since he had eaten anything or even had water. He could only hope that after Aisling had woken in Kilbaha after the headache that she had gotten food. Otherwise…

He focused on putting one foot in front of the other. The tunnels were eerily quiet. The only sound that of their footsteps and the endless dripping water. He didn't think anything was down here with them, but neither he nor Aisling wanted to test that theory.

When he next pulled himself out of his musings, he noticed that neither of them was walking with quite as much gusto as before. He touched Aisling's arm to get her attention. Her head whipped to him, and surprise shone on her face, showing she had been lost in her thoughts.

"Let's rest," he said.

The fact that she didn't object told him how weary she was. They sat across from each other once more. He planted his feet on the ground as he rested his arms over his knees. Aisling sighed when she leaned her head back.

"I think we might be lost," she said.

He chuckled. "It's a real possibility."

"I confess, I've not been paying attention to which tunnels we've taken. And we don't have breadcrumbs to leave to backtrack."

Xaneth frowned. "I've not paid attention either."

The only time they had turned around was when they'd come to a dead end. There had been a lot of those. It became frustrating.

"How much longer do you think we have?" she asked.

He held her gaze and shrugged. "I can't say."

"I won't hold you to your promise to get us out. I never intended on it."

"I don't give vows lightly. I made it. I will keep it."

Her smile was soft as she tucked her hair behind her ears. "Some things are out of our control."

Not this. This was a maze. Something he could figure out —if only he could keep his mind on the task. "We just need to concentrate more on where we're going."

"Sure."

"You're not giving up, are you?"

She lifted a brow. "I don't know the meaning of the word."

But something flashed in her eyes. Something that looked suspiciously like capitulation. "I'll carry you if I have to."

"I'm fine."

"Your eyes say differently."

She released a long breath and looked at the floor. "I was thinking about the past. I gave up once."

"There's nothing wrong in acknowledging that."

"There is."

That's it. Two words. Nothing else to explain what she meant. The tightness he saw on her face told him that whatever memories she had delved into were dark and perilous. He needed to pull her out of them quickly. "You might need to carry me."

Her gaze lifted to his, and he saw in her red depths that she knew exactly what he was doing. "Are you afraid I can't?"

"Oh, I've no doubt you could lug my arse anywhere you wanted."

Her lips pulled into a hint of a smile. "I absolutely could."

"I know."

Her soft laugh made him grin. He loved the sound and wanted to hear more.

She tilted her head to the side as she regarded him. "Talking to me isn't so bad, is it?"

"Nay."

"You don't have to worry about me," she said, suddenly serious. "My life before I was a Reaper might have been questionable, but not now. Eoghan and the rest of the lads… we've accomplished things that have made me feel as if I've made up for some of my past actions. I'm not afraid of dying. I just don't want Lena to take my magic."

Xaneth's chest tightened at her words of death. The image of her so still in his arms on Skye flashed in his mind, making his hands clench. "It isn't your time to die."

"I'm not saying it is. I'm merely stating things that you need to know if you have to decide to leave me behind."

"Nay." He said it more harshly than intended.

She gave him a flat look. "I'm a realist, remember? I'm pragmatic. I see the facts before me. It's easy to identify the outcomes."

"Stop." He didn't want to hear this. Not now. Not ever.

"Xaneth, I—"

Their heads snapped to the side at the fearsome howl of an animal that rang ominously through the tunnels. Aisling was on her feet first. Xaneth joined her and stared down the darkened tunnel in the direction they had come.

"You heard that, right?" Aisling whispered.

He nodded. "Aye."

"Any ideas what it might be?"

"Nothing good."

The next howl was long, the sound unnatural in the maze's silence.

"Lena might have gotten tired of waiting on me to die."

Xaneth turned his head to her. "We have two options. We fight or we run."

"Three options," she said, looking at him.

He quirked a brow in question.

"We know it's coming. We set a little trap of our own."

Xaneth couldn't stop the smile. "It's no wonder you're a Reaper."

She shrugged, but he saw by her smile that she was pleased with his words. "Thought you might like that."

"What are you thinking?"

Aisling turned and pointed to two openings on either side

of the tunnel. "We each take a side. That thing will have to choose which one of us it wants. Once it decides, the other joins in, and the two of us kill it."

"You're forgetting one thing."

"That we can't use magic? I've not forgotten," she replied with a mischievous smile. "Have I told you how much I love hand-to-hand fighting? We Fae don't do it too much because of our magic and all, but it does come in handy."

When another bay filled the tunnel, Xaneth looked in that direction. "Whatever Lena is sending will be lethal. We don't know the size or even what it is, but I doubt we can outrun it."

"Exactly. Whatever it is, our best chance is making it choose. It'll turn its back on one of us, giving us a slight advantage."

"That's assuming there is only one of them."

"I only heard one howl."

So had he, but he didn't want to bet his—or Aisling's—life on that. If there were two, well, they were fekked.

"We can do this. We have to," Aisling said.

Xaneth nodded and turned to her. "Let's get into position."

They walked the short distance to where the tunnel branched off in two directions. He was about to turn to his side when she stopped him. He glanced behind him before facing her.

She held his gaze and gave him a firm nod. "We can do this."

"Aye."

"Be safe."

No sooner were the words out of her mouth than her lips

pressed to his. It was the briefest of touches, but it went through him like wildfire. Before he knew what had happened, Aisling was gone to her corridor.

He blinked, struggling to come to terms with what had just occurred. She had kissed him. On the lips. Bloody hell. What had she done? Did she have any idea what a tailspin this sent him into? Especially when he had promised himself that he wouldn't cross that line—a line she had walked over as if it didn't matter.

As if she hadn't known it was there.

Xaneth had been afraid to move, afraid he wouldn't feel her mouth on his. He parted his lips and curled his bottom one now, his upper teeth holding it as his tongue swept across it. The taste of her filled him, exploded through him with enough force that he rocked back on his heels.

It was too much. *She* was too much. He'd had control of himself. He'd known the line he couldn't—wouldn't—cross, and he'd kept his focus on it. In one instant, she had obliterated his intention and thrashed his objective. With one kiss, she had ignited something within him that wouldn't be denied. A fire that now raged out of control.

He wanted to go after her and demand she never do that again. But he knew if he did, if he got close to her, the blaze within him would take over. He barely held his monster in check. He feared he would let his guard down with Aisling, and the thing he desperately hid from everyone, including himself, would be freed.

Xaneth fisted his hands and backed into his opening. She shouldn't have kissed him. Her touch had been agony enough. Now, he knew how soft her lips were. He knew her taste.

The howl sounded again. It was much closer. Xaneth looked through the darkness to where Aisling waited across the hall. The creature Lena had sent was after Aisling, but he wouldn't let it get anywhere near her.

She kissed me.

Xaneth heard a growl and realized it came from him. The beast that he kept caged strained to get free. Because Aisling was in danger. Xaneth struggled to hold the monster back, because if it got loose, he wasn't sure who or what he'd become. And he wasn't ready for that. Not now. Not after Aisling just kissed him.

She kissed me.

The sound of something running toward them reached Xaneth. When he breathed in, he was overcome by the stink of evil. He fought to keep the monster within him leashed. He and Aisling had a plan, one that would work. Then he thought about the lengths Lena was going to in order to kill Aisling, and his control snapped. He couldn't hold back the beast within him any longer. Nor did he want to.

There was another howl, one that loosened something dark and lethal within him. Xaneth stepped into the corridor and turned. His gaze locked on the enormous hound that barreled toward him, its teeth bared. The animal sniffed the air, sniffed *him*, and tried to alter its direction to go around him. But Xaneth wasn't about to allow that. The hound was evil, which meant he had no choice but to kill it. The fact that he would be keeping it away from Aisling was a bonus.

Killing evil was what he did.

It was who he was. For better or worse.

The dog was quick and tried to slip past Xaneth. But he

was quicker and grabbed the hound's tail, flinging the animal back in the direction it'd come. The animal rolled a few times before coming to its feet and shaking itself. It slowly faced Xaneth and lowered its huge head. It peeled its lips back to show large teeth as it growled, drool dripping from its mouth.

Xaneth widened his stance and released his own growl. The two were locked onto each other. The hound's muscles bunched as it readied to pounce. Xaneth steadied himself, but it didn't prepare him for the force of the animal as it launched itself at him.

CHAPTER THIRTEEN

Aisling listened to the growls, snarls, and teeth gnashing with growing alarm. Surely…that couldn't be Xaneth in the hall with whatever was after them. But she knew it was. She ran to the doorway and looked one way. As she swung her head in the other direction, she caught a blur of fur and teeth that came right at her face. She leaned back, but she wasn't quick enough. A large paw swiped at her, striking her, and cutting her shirt. She flew backward and landed jarringly on her back.

Immediately, she got to her feet and approached the door more hesitantly. This time when she looked out, she spotted Xaneth as he fought what appeared to be the biggest dog she had ever seen. Whatever the animal was, it wasn't natural. Its jaws clamped down on Xaneth's left forearm. Xaneth yelled, the sound a mixture of anger and pain.

Aisling stepped out into the corridor to help. The instant she did, the dog locked on her with its yellow eyes. The animal released Xaneth and tried to get to her. Xaneth wound his arms around the animal's chest and jerked back, causing Xaneth to land heavily on his back with the dog on top of him.

"Keep back!" Xaneth yelled at her.

Aisling immediately ducked out of sight. She wasn't used to sitting out a battle, but the dangerous look in the animal's eyes left her chilled to the bone. It wanted her dead. And she knew it wouldn't stop until she was. How could she leave it up to Xaneth to fight it on his own, though? She couldn't. They had a better chance of defeating it together.

With her decision made, Aisling crept to the doorway a third time. She had to be stealthy and join Xaneth when the dog couldn't see her. Every time Xaneth grunted, she imagined what kind of wound the animal had inflicted. The dog yipped in pain a few times, but it never lasted long enough to suit her.

She peered around the corner to see Xaneth on his feet. The dog was on its hind legs, towering over him. Xaneth had one hand around the animal's lower jaw, shoving the great head away. His other hand had a hold of one of the dog's front paws. It was then she saw that the animal didn't have the regular paws of a dog. These nails could retract like a cat's, and like a feline, the talons were razor-sharp. Her gaze raked over Xaneth to see that his shirt was in tatters, and the cuts beneath looked as if the dog had both clawed and bitten him.

Even with Xaneth holding the animal, its gaze was locked in her direction. It would be so easy to subdue the creature if she could do magic. But if she did, it would mean her death. Still, she couldn't just sit here. Not while Xaneth battled the animal—a creature that was after her.

Aisling took a breath and stepped out into the hall. The

animal renewed its efforts to get to her. Xaneth bellowed as he struggled to keep his hold on the dog. She started walking toward the two of them.

"Let it go," she told Xaneth.

He didn't acknowledge her. She didn't know if he couldn't hear her over the dog's growls and his shouts, or if he chose to ignore her. It didn't change her mind. She kept walking, closing the distance. When only a few feet separated them, the dog managed to knock Xaneth away.

Aisling's heart clutched when she saw how far Xaneth went flying. Then the animal's glowing yellow eyes were on her. She lifted her chin. "You came for me, didn't you? Well, here I am."

The dog looked behind it at Xaneth, but he wasn't moving. Aisling wanted to look at Xaneth herself, but she didn't dare take her eyes off the animal. She had no intention of dying in the maze, either by Lena's hand or via the dog's. She was a Reaper, chosen by Erith because of her skills. Aisling could keep up with any Reaper. She didn't need Xaneth to protect her.

"Hey," she called to the animal. "Turn your attention back to me. I'm the one you want."

The large head turned her way. She couldn't make out the dog's coloring in the dim light, but the fur looked dark. Spots on its body appeared wet. She hid her smile because she knew that Xaneth had done some damage to the creature.

The dog lowered its head. A long, rumbling growl filled the corridor as it slowly took a menacing step toward her. Her heart thudded in her chest, and blood rushed in her ears. She was more than accustomed to battle and the tension that filled the air before a clash. It was no different now.

Don't use magic.

She repeated the mantra over and over in her head. It was second nature to her, but if she fell back on it, it would mean her death. She hadn't survived Hell to be given a second chance with the Reapers only to blow it now.

"I'm not going to be an easy kill," she told the animal. "Lena should've come herself. It proves what a coward she is."

That caused the dog's growl to grow louder, longer. One side of its lips peeled back. Aisling saw something behind the animal and realized it was Xaneth silently climbing to his feet. She was overjoyed that he wasn't harmed, but she wanted to keep the dog's attention on her. She felt Xaneth's gaze on her, sensed the lethal danger that radiated from him.

The instant the animal launched itself at her, Aisling ran toward it. She dropped to her knees and slid when it leaped, raking her long nails across the dog's stomach. Xaneth rushed the animal from behind, jumping over her and tackling it when it landed.

Aisling put a foot out to stop herself and turned on one knee to see Xaneth and the dog rolling around on the ground. She rose and started toward them when she noticed that Xaneth had his hands on the animal's snout and lower jaw, pulling its mouth open. She halted in her tracks, transfixed, utterly gripped by the ferocious, savage sight before her.

Xaneth's teeth were bared, the ropey sinew in his arms straining as the dog clawed at his chest and legs, growling and yelping to get away. Xaneth threw back his head and released a loud bellow. A moment later, there was a loud crack of bone. The animal went quiet and then limp. Xaneth released the dog to crumple to the ground and took a step back. His chest heaved as he stared down at it.

Then his gaze swung to her. Aisling had witnessed Xaneth fight the Six and their soldiers, but she had been fighting alongside everyone else and had missed exactly what Xaneth could do—the barely leashed violence, the narrowly restrained fury. The sight was beautiful and brutal. And it called to her like nothing ever had before.

His expression shuttered, and he turned away. He got two steps before grabbing his head and going down on one knee. Aisling rushed to him. She went to touch him but then thought better of it as pain contorted his face. She had never felt so helpless and unsure of what to do. His words from earlier suddenly came to her.

"Stop fighting it," she told him. "Be who you are. Just as you were when you fought the beast during your torture and the dog just now. Don't hide from it. Accept who you are. Accept all of yourself."

The more she spoke, the more he relaxed. She had been grasping at straws, trying to think of something that could help him, but she hadn't realized how true her words were. So, she kept going.

"You're Xaneth. A royal Light who survived cruelty no one else could. You can find evil. Find the enemies we're searching for. That's nothing to hide from. It's something to embrace and use to your advantage."

His hands fell away from his head. His chest still heaved, but the pain disappeared from his features. She swallowed heavily and reached out to put her hand on his back. At the last moment, she let it drop to her side.

"Accept who you are," she said. "Everything about you. It's the only way to live. The only way you *can* live."

Xaneth's dark head lifted. His hair was wet with sweat and blood. A lock dropped over his forehead, and she fought the urge to smooth it away. His silver eyes met hers. He said nothing as he climbed to his feet. He had to steady himself against the wall, and then he took a deep breath.

"You're going to regret all of that," he said.

She stepped over the dead animal and faced him. The dim light kept most of his face in shadows. She wished she could see all of him. "Why? Because you think you're a monster?"

"You saw what I did." He motioned to the dog at his feet.

Aisling lifted her chin. "I saw a man who did what he had to do to survive without using magic. That isn't a monster. You aren't a villain. You're a hero."

"I'm far from that."

"Not the way I see it."

His jaw hardened. "Do you have any idea how hard I've worked to keep that…other side of me locked away?"

"And that's where you went wrong. Use it. Use the strength it gives you. It isn't a beast or a monster. It's you. You're two sides of a coin."

"Usaeil released something within me that no one could've foreseen."

Aisling shrugged. "You say she released it. I say she set it free. Maybe instead of thinking that what happened is some atrocious mistake, look at it as a gift."

"A gift?" he asked with a snort of skepticism.

Her eyes narrowed as she fought against the anger that threatened. "Look what you can do. Something not even a Reaper can. Stop hiding from who you are. Embrace it. You might find that your life becomes easier."

"You act like you know what I'm going through."

"In a way, I do. If you think coming back from the dead and becoming a Reaper was easy, you're mistaken."

He swallowed and stared at her for a long moment. Then he ripped off what was left of his tattered shirt and wiped the blood from his face and chest with it. "Next time I tell you to stay away, stay away."

"Need I remind you of who I am? Because I'm not some damsel in need of saving." She turned on her heel and started walking.

Behind her, she heard, "Obviously."

They walked in silence with her leading the way. She had no idea where she was going, but she wanted to get as far from the carnage as she could. Earlier, they had stumbled into a small room where they had to retrace their steps. She was looking for something similar so they could rest. Despite Xaneth's bold words, she could tell the fight had taken a lot out of him. Truth be told, she was finding it more and more difficult to put one foot in front of the other. She was hungry, but more than that, she was thirsty.

Finally, after several attempts, she found the nook she was searching for. She walked in and went to a far corner, sliding down the wall to sit on the ground. She no longer cared that everything was damp and it seeped into her clothes. It felt good to be off her feet.

Xaneth stood in the doorway. "We should keep going."

"We need to rest."

"I don't think that's a good idea."

"Anywhere else, I'd say it wasn't. But this room allows only one way for something to come at us."

Xaneth glanced behind him. "It only leaves us one way out, as well."

"I need to shut my eyes, and my feet are throbbing. If you want to stay awake, be my guest, but I'm going to take a break." She closed her eyes.

A few moments later, she heard the scrape of his boots as he walked into the room and sat. She peeked to find him in the corner to her left. Aisling hid her smile and let herself relax as she hadn't in hours—or days. It was hard to determine how much time had passed while they had been in the maze.

"Thank you."

His softly spoken words jarred her. She blinked open her eyes and looked at him, but he had his head leaned back, and his eyes were closed. She studied him. "You're welcome."

"I didn't know that fighting the…thing within me caused the headaches. They would always make me pass out afterward."

Leaving him vulnerable.

He cleared his throat. "I still think you're going to regret it."

"I don't," she replied and closed her eyes again.

CHAPTER FOURTEEN

Xaneth closed his eyes, but he couldn't rest. His mind was going nonstop. All because of Aisling.

He'd been ashamed and mortified that she had seen him at his worst while killing the hound. He had given into his beast, the absolute fury within him, and had torn the animal apart. A Fae would never have done that. That begged the question: Was he Fae?

When Xaneth had looked into Aisling's eyes, he had wanted to hide. He'd turned away, and in that instant, the pain in his head had exploded with more force than ever. Just like all the times before, he knew that he was about to fall unconscious, and that was the last thing he could allow to happen.

While he fought against it, her voice had reached him through the panic and fog of pain. He latched on to the sound of her voice as if she were a lifeline. Her words had been soft but firm. Almost immediately, the agony in his skull slowly started to ebb. At first, he didn't hear what she said, but once he did, he reacted without thinking. Did exactly as she bade— even as he realized it was what he had been struggling against from the very beginning.

Yet she had been right. By accepting that other side of him, the monster within, the pain had not only retreated but disappeared entirely. How many times had he staggered to some place to hide as the pain washed over him before he became unconscious? Too damn many. And all he'd had to do to stop it was embrace the other part of himself.

The monster.

He'd thought he would feel differently, but he didn't. Not now, at least. He turned his head to the side and opened his eyes to look at Aisling. In his time as the Seeker, he'd had many acquaintances. None he'd ever considered a friend, though. To trust was to put himself in someone else's hands. Someone who could betray him to his aunt.

He'd spent so many decades among others but ultimately alone, separate. He had accepted his fate while plotting to kill Usaeil to take back the life he had been denied. Then, he'd come across the Reapers. He wouldn't call them friends, exactly, but he trusted them. Possibly because of Aisling.

He trusted her completely.

He suspected that he always had but was only now admitting it. He wouldn't allow himself to hurt Aisling or harm any of the Reapers. If he turned into what he feared, he wasn't sure how he could hold to that promise, but he would do his best.

Xaneth took a deep breath and released it as he rolled his head back. As Aisling slept, he took stock of his body. After the battle with the hound, he'd wanted to do nothing but sleep. Now, however, he felt fine. Better than fine, actually. He'd wanted to keep walking, but one look at Aisling had told him that she needed to rest.

His gaze was drawn to her again as if some invisible line connected them. She was constantly in his thoughts, even his dreams. He thought about the kiss she had given him. Should he mention it? She hadn't touched him after the battle. Did that mean she regretted it? Despite her being a Reaper, he couldn't imagine how he had looked. Maybe he had repulsed her.

Xaneth glanced down at his bare chest. The cuts from the hound's claws and the punctures from its teeth had healed, but dirt and blood covered him, and his jeans were still damp from the wetness that seemed to coat everything in the labyrinth. As he sat, his mind went over and over the brief touch of their lips. He imagined kissing her…deeply, thoroughly. It was the first time. He had yearned to taste her since she'd sassed him when they first met.

The memory of that encounter brought a smile to his lips. Nothing seemed to bring her down. She didn't care what stood before her, she met it with a straight back and a lifted chin, daring it to stop her. She was more than capable of handling herself. Otherwise, she wouldn't be a Reaper. Yet he couldn't seem to halt the protectiveness he felt for her.

He looked at the wadded remains of the shirt in his hands. Xaneth silently climbed to his feet and tied it around his waist by the sleeves. He wouldn't leave anything behind to alert Lena that he had been there. It disturbed him how intent the Dark was on getting Aisling—to get to him.

Xaneth's head turned as he looked at the Reaper. He recalled the dread and horror when he'd seen her injured on Skye. Had Lena seen him leave with Aisling? Did she know that he… Xaneth paused. That he what? That he respected Aisling?

Aye. He did. But he respected all the Reapers.

Admit how you feel about her.

He couldn't. To do so would require opening himself to something he didn't dare. That didn't mean someone else hadn't seen what he couldn't name—someone like Lena.

Xaneth closed his eyes and shook his head. That would explain why Lena had doubled the bounty on Aisling's head. Lena wanted Aisling because she knew that he'd come for her. Apparently, it didn't matter what he might or might not admit to himself. Lena had connected the dots.

He blew out a breath and walked to the entrance. Xaneth leaned a shoulder against the cool, damp stones as his gaze slowly moved around the dim corridors and the many doorways. Only the sound of water dripping broke the quiet. At least there weren't any more screams from dying Fae as there had been near the entrance.

If just anyone could take a Fae's magic, then it would happen all the time. It took an immense amount of power. Xaneth had heard rumors that Usaeil had begun to take magic from Druids before her death, but not even his aunt had turned to the Fae. Things would be vastly different if she'd been able to do that.

Lena hadn't just stolen others' magic to grow hers, she'd learned how. Where had Lena learned such magic? While the Fae were made of magic, some things took knowledge and study. Unfortunately, he wouldn't know to what extent her command had grown until he faced her. That would happen soon. He felt it in his gut. Everything was leading him to that point.

He pushed away from the door to explore. It was easy to get turned around and backtrack in a maze without knowing it'd happened. He didn't go far before he retraced his steps to return to Aisling.

As he walked to the alcove, something on the wall snagged his attention. He halted and searched the area where he thought he'd seen it. He narrowed his eyes and moved his head from side to side before lifting and then lowering it. Still nothing. He must have imagined it. Then he took a step and saw it again. This time, he walked to the wall and stared at the area. Finally, he pressed his cheek against the stone and spotted the red arrow.

Xaneth whirled around and raced to Aisling. He touched her shoulder, and she came instantly awake. When she looked up at him, he said, "I found something."

"What?" she asked as she got to her feet.

He should've held out his hand to her as before. Would she have taken it? Perhaps it was better if he didn't know. After the kiss, he'd be crushed if she didn't want anything to do with him. She hadn't touched him since his fight with the hound. And for some reason, that really bothered him.

The irony wasn't lost on him. After all the times he'd pushed her away, making sure he *didn't* touch her, now it was all he thought about.

He motioned for her to follow him. "Come."

Xaneth walked to the red arrow. Now that he'd found it,

he couldn't believe he hadn't seen it earlier. He grinned at Aisling, waiting for her to acknowledge it.

After a moment, she shrugged. "What am I supposed to look at?"

"You don't see it?"

She shook her head, a small frown marring her forehead. "I see lots of the same things we've seen since entering this bloody maze."

"You don't see this?" he asked and pointed at the arrow.

Aisling looked at the stone and then him. "I see a stone. Like all the others."

"There's a red arrow. Put your face against the wall. That's how I saw it."

She did as he requested, then stepped back and threw up her hands in defeat. "Still nothing."

He returned his finger to the arrow. "Right here."

"I don't see it," she said with a sigh.

Xaneth dropped his arm to his side. "There's an arrow. And it's pointing this way."

"I wish I could see it. Maybe it's because of something Lena did."

"Maybe." But Xaneth couldn't help but wonder if it had something to do with that other half of him that he had fought for so long. "I think we should follow it."

Aisling nodded in agreement. "Let's go."

"It could be another trap."

"It could be a way out," she argued.

Still, he hesitated.

Aisling took his hand and tugged him to follow her. "Keep

an eye out for more of the arrows. If there's a chance we can get out, I say we take it."

The joy that burst within him at her touch was heady. But as soon as she had him walking, she released him. Xaneth missed her hold. He almost reached for her again but held himself in check. He was a half step behind her, his eyes searching for more of the arrows. They didn't walk long before he spotted one telling them to go left. He didn't have to hunt hard for the indicators now. He could see them as if they glowed, but Aisling still couldn't make them out.

Their steps quickened as they followed arrow after arrow, taking them this way and that. Not once did they hit a dead end. The longer that went on, the surer Xaneth was that this could be the way out. The maker of the labyrinth would need to have an exit, something that only they could find.

Once more, they traversed a long distance, but the hope within them kept them going when they otherwise would've stopped. He was conscious of how Aisling's feet had begun to drag, though she didn't complain or ask for a break. Just as he was about to say they should rest, he saw it. Xaneth grabbed her shoulder to get her attention.

"What is it?" she asked.

He looked up into nothing but darkness. "The arrow points up."

"Then up we go."

He glanced over to see her grinning. Her exhaustion was evident, but neither of them would quit now. "I'll lift you."

"Look at the stones here. They aren't as smooth as the other walls. I can climb them," she said.

Xaneth nodded. It would be better if he remained behind

in case she lost her grip. That way, he could catch her. "The arrow is right here. Climb up."

Their eyes briefly met before she popped her knuckles and set her foot on a slightly protruding rock, then straightened her leg to reach her hand for another. Her hold was solid as she began to climb. Xaneth didn't take his eyes off her.

When she got far enough above him, he followed. It seemed the wall went on forever, but suddenly, Aisling grunted.

"I hit something," she said.

He heard hinges squeal in protest. Then sunlight spilled in and over them.

CHAPTER FIFTEEN

Aisling closed her eyes and relished the fresh, clean air for a moment before hurrying out into it. Her fingers sank into the cool blades of grass, and it brought tears to her eyes. She had begun to believe that she would die in the maze. She took in great lungsful of air and lifted her face to the sun.

The warmth that fell on her made all the dampness she had endured during her confinement in the labyrinth fade away. Her hunger, however, did not dissipate.

Aisling opened her eyes to see Xaneth standing on the other side of the opening. Her gaze ran over his bare chest, seeing him in all his glory now. She marveled at his hard body, the defined sinew creating ridges and valleys she longed to explore. She didn't see the dirt or blood, she only saw his chiseled abs, muscular arms, thick chest, and broad shoulders. His narrow hips where jeans hung just low enough for her to spot the sexy V of muscles that made her swallow suddenly.

How had she missed all of this? But she knew. The hunger and dread of the maze had her focusing her attention on other things, which was probably a good thing. Perhaps she should stop ogling something she could never have. Her gaze lifted to his face to see it set in hard lines, his lips flattened in concern. She climbed to her feet and turned her head to see what had agitated him. That was when she saw that they were on a tiny island, no more than ten square feet, surrounded by nothing but water from horizon to horizon. Yet they weren't the only things here. Four Fae doorways surrounded them, forming a square.

"I don't like this," Xaneth said.

Aisling glanced down into the hole they had emerged from. She tugged it shut, liking the firm thud she heard. Once closed, she couldn't make out that there was an opening there at all. After dusting off her hands, she asked, "Do you recognize this place?"

"Nay. You?"

She shook her head. "We have to be in Ireland, right? There's no way the maze could've extended anywhere else."

Xaneth's silver eyes met hers. "We did walk quite a ways."

"Scotland, maybe?"

"That's assuming we're still on Earth."

She scoffed at his words. Then, she immediately sobered. "Should we teleport or use one of the doorways?"

"My concern is the doorways. Why are they here? If the exit is for Lena, then she could teleport anywhere she wanted to go. Why have these?" he asked and motioned to the four doorways.

After the labyrinth, Aisling was scared to use her magic. Though they were free of the maze's confines, they were still very much in the world Lena had fashioned. "We have to do something. I need water."

Xaneth walked between two doorways to the water's edge. He knelt and put his finger in it before tasting it. He frowned and faced her. "Saltwater."

Which meant she still had nothing to drink. Or eat. Whenever Aisling got free, she would happily find Lena and make her suffer her own maze. Only Aisling would block the exit so Lena didn't have a way out.

"So." Aisling faced one of the doorways. "Looks like we're trying one of these."

"We don't know where they lead," Xaneth cautioned.

She jerked her gaze to him. "We can't stay here."

"We teleport, then."

It was an easy solution. Why, then, couldn't she do it? Because she was terrified now. Lena had done that to her. Just one more reason to hate her.

Xaneth's brows briefly drew together as he faced her. "We're out of the maze."

"Then why the doorways? You asked that very question. It makes no sense. It's either another trap, or we're on another realm."

He looked at each of the doorways. "Or it's just another game. If anyone happened to make it out, Lena would want them confused and frozen in fear."

"I'm not frozen," Aisling snapped.

Silver eyes watched her carefully. "I didn't say you were."

"You implied it." It had been a lifetime since she had felt such trepidation, but still, she recognized it. Loathed it. It churned like a swirling ball of black goo in her gut, moving faster and faster as it grew. She had sworn she would never feel anything like it again—being a Reaper meant that she never would.

And yet, here she was.

"I'll teleport first," Xaneth began.

"Nay!" she all but shouted. At his confused look, she turned to the side and crossed her arms around her middle. In a calmer voice she said, "I don't want to be left alone."

A beat of silence passed, then, "We have to do something. We can't remain undecided. That's what she wants. If we try a doorway, we might end up right back in the maze."

"Or free."

"Aye. Maybe. It could also lead us to her."

Aisling's head swung to the side to spear him with a look. "That's exactly what we want."

"Not now, it isn't."

"Because you think I'm weak."

"Because you're angry."

She barked in laughter. "Oh, that's rich. Need I remind you about that dog thing? I saw your rage."

"That's different."

Her brows rose. "Really?" She snorted and put her hands on her hips. "How, exactly?"

"It's how I fight. It isn't how you go into battle. You're calm. Tranquil, even."

That brought her up short. "How would you know?"

"I've seen you."

Three words. But they hit her square in the chest.

Xaneth took two steps toward her. "When you go into battle, you size everything up in one glance. You know where you need to be in a split second. You move with grace and speed that leaves others unable to keep up. Your body and mind calculate not only your positions, magic, and moves, but also your opponents. Within seconds. It's riveting to watch. Even better to be fighting beside you."

She swallowed, unsure what to say or if she should reply. What did one say to such beautiful words? *Thanks?*

"You don't let emotion get in the way," Xaneth continued. "I don't want to test that theory. Not with Lena."

Aisling could only nod.

Xaneth lowered his gaze and looked away as if he regretted everything he'd said. He raked a hand through his hair. "If you aren't ready to teleport, and I don't want to go through one of the doorways, let's try something different."

"Like what?"

The words were barely out of her mouth before a water bottle appeared in his hand. She gaped at him. Had she known what he intended, she would've stopped him. He must have known that, which was why he hadn't told her.

Aisling didn't hesitate to call her own water. Except she created an entire gallon of it. She lifted it to her lips and drank deeply, pausing often to let it settle. When she drank it all down, she lay on the ground and looked up at the sky. She felt better with every second that passed. How long had they been in the labyrinth?

She glanced at Xaneth. He was still shirtless, and she considered asking him to remain that way. She doubted he would even understand why she wanted to look. After all, he hadn't mentioned the kiss. That wasn't to say she wanted to have a long discussion about it, but he acted as if it hadn't happened. Like it didn't affect him.

When she had to force herself not to linger.

It had been a split-second decision—something she regretted now. Though it wasn't as if she could take it back. It had felt as if death hovered next to them, and she had given in to her desire to know what his mouth felt like against hers. Maybe it was beneficial that he hadn't mentioned it. What would she say if he did?

"I didn't want to die without kissing you."

Or… *"Since I know you don't want me, I took advantage of the moment."*

Not exactly things she wanted to say aloud. And the more she tried to come up with decent replies, the more she realized how impulsive her actions had been. A kiss! With someone who had no interest in her. Men did that to women all the time and didn't think they did anything wrong. She shouldn't get a pass simply because she'd thought she was going to die. She owed him an apology. However, that meant bringing up the kiss. And, honestly, she'd be happy if he completely forgot about it.

For her, it was imprinted on her mind—the softness of his lips, the way he had stilled at the contact.

She hadn't given him time to push her away, but she wondered what it might be like for him to drag her against him, to slant his mouth over hers and really kiss her. And not just a brush of the lips. A true kiss. Passionate, hot, and deep.

Aisling sat up and bent her knees so her legs lay against the ground. She glanced down at her clothes and grimaced.

"Aye. I know," Xaneth said.

She looked over to find him clean and clothed once more.

"I couldn't stand my smell," he said.

His crooked smile nearly did her in. She flicked her hair over her shoulder. "Is that your way of telling me I stink?"

His face went slack. "Nay. I…I–"

"I'm teasing," she told him with a laugh. "But you're right. It's time to get out of these clothes."

She hesitated for only a fraction of a second before she called to her magic to clean herself and replace her clothes. She instantly felt better. She touched her hair, happy to have it dry and clean once more.

It was hard not to notice the way Xaneth's eyes followed her hand as she ran it through her tresses. She liked the way his face softened as he watched her. What she wouldn't give to discover what thoughts ran through his mind. Suddenly, his eyes met hers before he hastily looked away, the moment broken.

"Ready to leave?" he asked.

She looked at the Fae doorways. "Nay."

"You're not seriously considering going through one of them, are you?"

"I think it's time I called in my team to investigate."

A muscle twitched in Xaneth's jaw. "One of them could be a trap. All of them could be. Would you send your fellow Reapers into what we just came from?"

He had a point. Fek! Something about the doorways kept drawing her attention. Maybe Lena had designed it that way. They were possibly all some kind of trap like the maze. And she wouldn't wish that on her brethren.

"We'll return," Xaneth said.

We. Did he really intend to stay with her? Aisling expected him to get away from her as soon as he could and return to pursuing Lena. Well, maybe not pursuit. They knew exactly where she was. They just had to confront her now.

Yet Xaneth hadn't left. He'd remained. She hoped it was because he wanted to and not because he thought she might do something reckless. Whatever the reason, she wasn't ready for them to part ways.

"All right," she agreed.

Lena drummed her fingers on the arm of the chair, her impatience getting the best of her. It had been hours, and she still didn't have Aisling's magic. She speared Berach with a look. "The *cú* should have had her by now. Call the hound back."

She tried to stay seated as he walked out of the room to do as she bid, but in the end, she got to her feet and paced. It should've been a simple exercise to get Aisling's magic. How did the Reaper continue staying just out of her reach? It didn't matter. Lena would win in the end. She always did.

Long minutes passed before she barked for Berach. He returned without the confident expression he usually wore.

"What is it?" she demanded.

"The hound isn't returning."

Lena's eyes narrowed. "That can't be possible."

"We're still calling for it."

But she knew if it were alive, it would've already found Aisling and returned. The fact that it hadn't brought in a tide of fury. "She killed my hound. She'll pay for that."

CHAPTER SIXTEEN

Xaneth didn't relax when Aisling agreed to go with him. That meant she wanted off the island, but that didn't mean she would stay with him. And did he even want that? After making sure he was alone for so long? He absolutely did—though he shouldn't.

All because of a kiss.

He didn't want to think about her not touching him as often. It left him…raw. It would've been better if he had never learned her soft lips or gentle touch. But he had, dammit. There was no going back from that.

As he stared at her, he almost asked why she had kissed him. Then, he realized it might come out wrong, especially since he was so wound up. He contemplated asking why she hadn't done it again, but he knew the answer. He didn't need her to say it, to give the words form. They were enough in his head.

"Where do you want to go?"

Her voice jarred him out of his musings. Xaneth shrugged and tore his gaze from her. Within seconds, he was staring at her again, noticing how the sun made her red eyes brighter, how the wind caught her long locks, the black and silver strands tangling with each other in a wild dance. He wanted to touch her hair, to slide his fingers through the length.

To hold her firmly against him.

"We know where Lena is," he replied. "There's no telling how long she'll be here. I'd like to regroup before going back for her."

"Going back with me, of course."

He almost smiled at her feisty assertiveness. Aisling didn't like to be left out of anything. "I'd rather go alone, but I've learned that you'll find your way no matter what obstacles are in your path."

Her answering grin was both sexy and enigmatic. "It's good you recognize that now. It took you long enough."

How was it that she could make him forget the horrors he'd endured? That she could wring a smile from him in the darkest of times? Pull him from the depths of pain and agony? She made him forget all the ghastly misdeeds he'd suffered. She quieted his riotous mind and soothed the savagery within him. If only he could…

Xaneth didn't allow himself to finish the wish. He thought of the line he'd promised himself he wouldn't cross. He had to remember that. So, she had kissed him. It had been so quick, could it even be called a kiss? And she didn't know about the line. Which meant he couldn't claim that she'd crossed it.

It didn't matter what his heart and soul craved above anything else. He knew the monster he was, that other half of him he struggled against. Aisling had helped him accept what he had been fighting. He might not like that he had become this thing, but if he could use it to his advantage and remove the evil that sought to harm her and the Reapers, then Xaneth would gladly do it.

Her smile slipped. "What is it?"

If only he could tell her. If only he dared. But he wouldn't burden her with such things. Aisling was a fixer. He should've seen that earlier, but he'd been too intent on getting her away. Now that he comprehended her ability to home in on a problem and find a solution, he knew to keep his mouth shut. "Just thinking."

"About?" she asked with a pointed look.

"Where to go."

"Bloody hell," she said with a laugh. "Getting answers from you is like pulling teeth. Where are we going?"

Xaneth knew one place they could go. "Somewhere to rest and regroup."

"Where is that?"

"Do you trust me?"

"Aye," she answered without hesitation.

That shouldn't have made him rejoice, but it did. "It's—"

"Show me," Aisling said as she walked to him and took his hand.

Xaneth stared at their joined hands and knew he was treading very close to that line. He tightened his fingers around hers before teleporting them to the house where Usaeil had kept him prisoner.

"Veil yourself," he whispered when they arrived.

She did as he requested, and her veil included him because their hands were still clasped.

"You've *got* to be kidding me," she said softly. "This place?"

He shot her a quick grin and leaned close to her ear—a veil could hide them, but others could still hear them. "No one wants any part of this place. Let's make sure we're alone."

Though he was loath to release her, he put up his own veil and let go of her hand. She took the main floor while he checked upstairs. Then they cleared the dungeons below. Once they knew the house was empty, they lowered their veils.

"So," she said, "I see you can keep your veil up for as long as you like."

He glanced at her before ascending the stairs to the main floor. "There is a lot I can do since waking from the torture."

"Only Reapers can do that."

"And Erith."

Aisling paused for a moment. "Aye, she can, too."

"I'm not a Reaper."

"Are you telling me you're a god?"

He chuckled at the comment, shaking his head as he waited for her to reach the landing. "Truthfully, I don't know what I am."

"Which means you could be a god."

"I'm fairly certain Erith would've recognized that and told me."

Aisling quirked a brow as she cut him a dark look. "Really? So, you've spoken with her?"

Ouch. When Aisling struck, she went for the jugular. Not that he blamed her. "You know I haven't."

"Why not?"

Xaneth walked to a room where the doors stood half-open. He pushed the double doors wide and entered the library. When he awoke from the torture, he'd combed through every inch of the mansion, searching for Usaeil, but he hadn't really *seen* any of it. He sank onto a plush sofa. "I knew she would try to talk me into joining her."

"Would that be so bad?" Aisling paused beside a chair and leaned against it.

He shrugged, trying to find the words to articulate what had been going through his head. "When I woke, I only wanted to find Usaeil. Once I learned of her death, I found myself seeking out the worst evil. I couldn't stop myself, couldn't control it. I wasn't sure what I had become or even who I was anymore. I thought it better to keep away from anyone, but especially those I knew."

"But we're not evil. You wouldn't have harmed us."

"I didn't want to take the chance."

Aisling sighed, the sound long and forlorn. "All we wanted was to know that you were alive and okay."

"I'm far from all right."

"I disagree. From what I see, you're more than fine."

The fixer at it again. Xaneth fought the smile he wanted to give her. He wasn't sure what kind of Dark Fae she had been with such a good, soft heart. "I will admit that I don't think I could've carried on this kind of conversation when I first woke."

"You spent a lot of time avoiding us. Me."

He'd hurt her. He hated that, but he'd had no choice. "I did it to protect the Reapers. You."

"I know."

"But you kept coming. Why?"

She half-sat on the arm of the chair and tucked one leg under her. "I suspected that you might need a friend."

Until he'd made sure she couldn't locate him. That didn't last long, though, as he soon found himself on the Isle of Skye, fighting alongside the Reapers, Druids, and even the Dragon Kings against the Fae Others.

"We should've won," Aisling said.

He wasn't surprised to find that her thoughts were the same as his. He nodded. "I had a chance. I could've killed Lena."

"Why didn't you take it?"

He looked deep into her crimson eyes. Something in the depths held him. He thought of different things he could tell her, but he didn't want that. He wanted her to know. "You were injured. Dying."

"That's something we all leave to chance when we go into battle."

True, but he hadn't been able to let her die.

Her finger moved over the fabric of the chair, following the design. Neither of them said anything. He prayed she wouldn't press him or ask why he had chosen her over Lena. He hadn't thought about the answer himself, and he definitely didn't want to give it to her.

"I died," she said softly. "And you brought me back."

Xaneth remembered the despair, the anguish. The deep, profound sting of grief that had consumed him when he realized there was no life in her body. He'd been able to think of nothing but Aisling. Not seeing her again, hearing her voice. Looking into her beautiful eyes. He knew what loss was.

He'd seen every member of his family be slaughtered, yet it was the stunning Reaper who had brought him to his knees. Utterly wrecked his heart that he thought long empty.

He'd raged at the world, at everything. He'd been so distraught that the magic within him had felt as if it were tearing his skin apart. He'd released it before he knew what he'd done. Had that been what'd saved her? Had it been an accident? Could he do it again if he had to?

His thoughts drifted to the night he'd found a Dark teenager and his friend tormenting his Light half sister and her puppy. The Dark had killed the puppy. At least, that was what Xaneth had thought. But before he left, the puppy was very much alive, and the young Light was smiling. Had the puppy only been injured? Or had he…had he brought it back, too?

"If it was me who—" Xaneth motioned, having a hard time with the words.

She lifted her brows. "Brought me back to life?"

"Aye. If it was me, I didn't do it on purpose."

"You're not denying it anymore?"

He rubbed a hand over his jaw and rested his other arm along the back of the sofa. "I just remembered a puppy." He told her the story, all of it. "I didn't mean to kill the kid."

"He was Dark. You and I both know if you're Dark, you're evil."

Xaneth eyed her. He couldn't imagine Aisling being evil. And he'd known Balladyn when he was King of the Dark, and Xaneth hadn't sensed anything evil about him, either. "He was an adolescent," Xaneth repeated.

"Who tortured an innocent animal and harassed his half

sister. He deserved what he got. Don't feel guilty. He knew what he was doing. Trust me on that. He made his choice."

Xaneth wished her words could absolve him of that sin, but it didn't wash away quite so easily.

"I do think you brought the puppy back to life," she said, her lips curved into a smile at the corners. "You did it without even knowing it. Same with me. I wonder what you could do if you put your mind to it."

The only thing he'd really put his mind to was ending the Fae Others. Yet now, he wondered if there was something positive he could do besides ridding the realm of evil. He lowered his gaze, letting that thought sink into him.

When he looked back at Aisling, her head rested against the side of the chair, and her eyes were closed. He decided to let her sleep. Except when he rose to leave, he stopped and faced her. He gently lifted her into his arms and laid her on the sofa. Xaneth called a blanket to him and covered her before walking away.

CHAPTER SEVENTEEN

Xaneth roamed the house while Aisling slept. He ended up standing in the doorway of the room Usaeil had kept him in. The mattress was still rumpled and stripped of blankets. He hadn't been tied to the bed, but there hadn't been a need. Usaeil had crafted the worst sort of prison.

If anyone had asked him a year ago if he would survive such confinement, his answer would've been nay. He'd never thought of himself as being that strong, mentally or physically. He still didn't know how he'd gotten free or even how the idea had come to him.

Yet, here he stood.

Liberated.

At least, he thought he was. What if he was still stuck in his head? What if this was nothing more than another of Usaeil's tricks? It would make sense. Because Xaneth couldn't see Aisling tracking him as she had. Nor would she leave the

Reapers to do it. Then there was Erith. The goddess should be able to find him anywhere he went.

And would he really be the one to take out Lena? Him? Who just happened to be born with royal blood but had done nothing to save his family? Who hadn't stopped Usaeil? Why would he be the one to break free of a mental prison that should've kept him locked inside for eternity, slowly driving him mad?

Xaneth shook his head. It shouldn't be him. In any reality, it *wouldn't* be him. Did that mean everything he'd done since supposedly waking up from the torture had been more of a mind fek?

The thought left him nauseous. It made sense. Usaeil was too powerful for him to overcome. If Erith and the Reapers had had a hard time with Lena, then it made no sense that someone like him would have anything to contribute.

He looked down at his hands. He recalled holding the hound's mouth open, the feel of the bone snapping, and the animal going limp in his arms. Then again, the beast that had chased him in his mind had been all too real. Xaneth had felt every slash of its talons tearing through his flesh. His stomach had twisted with hunger. His body struggled with exhaustion. He'd felt the wind against him, the water he'd swum in, the fish he'd caught. It had all been as real as everything around him now.

"Did you really think I'd let you go so easily?"

Xaneth winced at his aunt's voice in his head, her laughter causing him to squeeze his eyes closed.

Maybe this was the real torment. Manipulating him so he

believed he was free and doing something meaningful. Working with someone he cared about.

Xaneth turned away from the room and walked to the stairs. He set his hands on the wood and looked over the railing. The Reapers hadn't tried to reach Aisling, nor she them. That wasn't normal. He might not know the intricacies of the group, but he didn't think they would send Aisling out on her own after Lena—with him.

He looked around. The world wasn't cast in the gray it had been in his torture, but he didn't trust it. It could be another trick.

Again, he heard his aunt's laughter in his mind.

Xaneth gripped the balustrade so tightly he heard the wood crack. How could he determine if any of this was real? He couldn't trust himself or anyone else. And if he couldn't trust anyone, then he couldn't remain with Aisling. That thought brought him up short, turning him cold because he liked having her near. But he wasn't special. Never had been. He couldn't bring her or the puppy back from the dead.

And that meant nothing—including her kiss—was real.

That was a blow that made his knees buckle. He caught the railing to keep himself upright, but the anguish and agony left a gaping wound in his soul. He'd thought he'd known true suffering before. He hadn't known anything. Not until this moment.

He closed his eyes, his heart racing. He'd assumed he had gotten free. Believed he had outwitted Usaeil. He'd imagined he had reconciled with the monster within. Thought Aisling…

What did he do now? How could he get free? If he did, how would he even know? Would he die locked in his mind?

Right now, that sounded preferrable to what he was going through.

Soft hands touched him.

Xaneth batted them away and stumbled backward. He found himself staring into Aisling's crimson eyes, worry making her brow wrinkle.

"Hey," she said in a soft voice. "It's just me. Let me help."

"Why?"

She blinked, her frown deepening. "Because I'm your friend."

"Are you?" He took a few steps away from her. If only he could believe her.

Aisling lowered her hands and observed him for several seconds. "What happened? I knew being here wasn't a good idea. Why did you want to come back?"

Why had he chosen this place? At the time, it had seemed like a good idea since few knew about it, and no one would look for them here. Now, it seemed like a colossal mistake.

"Talk to me, Xaneth. Please," Aisling begged.

He shook his head. He'd known it was wrong to get close to her. He'd let his guard down. He'd trusted her. He'd...

"Why me?"

"Excuse me?" she asked, clearly taken aback.

"Why me?" he asked again. "Why follow me? Why track me? Why befriend *me*?"

Her gaze searched his. "We've been over this."

"Tell me again."

"Because I..." She paused and licked her lips.

Xaneth laughed sardonically. "Can't find the words, aye?"

"What the bloody hell happened?" she snapped.

"*Why me!?*"

She blew out a frustrated breath, her lips pinched, and eyes slightly narrowed. "I'm a friend. I tracked you because I felt in my gut that you needed help. *My* help."

"And Erith was fine with you walking away from the Reapers to do that?"

Aisling blinked, and he saw the slightest hesitation in it.

"That's what I thought."

"You know nothing," she spat.

Xaneth crossed his arms over his chest. "Enlighten me."

Her nostrils flared, anger rolling off her in waves as her red eyes glittered with fury. "I left the Reapers because I knew it was imperative that you had someone to watch your back. I risked Erith's wrath to find you. And for what? This? To be grilled every time I turn around? I've done nothing but help you. And to think I believed you might care for me since you brought me back from the dead. Guess I know the truth now."

"No one can bring someone back from the dead," he retorted.

She snorted loudly. "Did you forget Ulrik? The Dragon King can do exactly that."

Damn. He had forgotten about the dragon. "Fae do not."

"Do you want me here?" she demanded.

It was Xaneth's turn to pause. He definitely wanted her with him, but he didn't trust her—or himself.

"Fine."

Before Xaneth knew what he was doing, he grabbed her wrist. It happened so fast that he was surprised he had caught her before she teleported.

"What the fek?" Her gaze leaped from him to his hand. "What did you do?"

His chest heaved, and blood rushed through his ears like a drum, making it difficult for him to hear her.

"You stopped me from teleporting," Aisling murmured, shock in her voice as her eyes went wide.

Xaneth immediately released her. Sound came rushing back to him. "I-I…" He didn't know what he'd done or why.

"Tell me what's going on right now." She poked him in the chest with each word. "I said, *now*," she stated in a low voice filled with righteous anger.

Xaneth ran a hand down his face. "I'm sorry for stopping you. It's best if you leave. Forget you know me. Forget…me."

"I'm not going anywhere until you tell me what brought all of this on."

He stared at her, thinking she'd leave if he were silent for long enough. Instead, she crossed her arms over her chest and stuck out her hip, her expression expectant as she tapped a toe angrily.

What would it hurt to tell her? He knew she'd convince him it was all real. As long as he steeled himself, he could speak about anything he wanted. Xaneth swallowed. "What if I didn't get free of my mind?"

Her expression softened as the words hit her. "You think you're still being tortured?"

"I heard Usaeil's voice. I heard her laughter."

"When? Since you woke? Or only when we returned here?"

Unable to help himself, he looked through the doorway into the room Usaeil had held him in. "When we came back."

"Well, then," she said and dropped her arms to her sides. "There's your answer. Being here reminds you of that bitch. You're probably hearing the things she said to you while she was torturing you. I assure you, this is real. You aren't locked in your head."

"I knew you'd say that."

"Because it's true."

He slid his gaze back to her. "I'm nothing, Aisling. I happened to be part of the royal family but was so far down the line that I was nobody. These…powers I have now? Where were they when I needed to defend my family? Myself? Where were they when I had to defeat Usaeil?"

"Waiting," she said softly. "For the time they were needed. That time is now. As powerful as we Reapers are, as formidable as Erith is, we can't defeat Lena without you. *You're* the one she fears."

"I'm no one."

"So was I. Less than that, actually. Yet Erith found me. Look at me now. Do I deserve to be here? I don't know. Sometimes, I think I do, but I often question why I was given a second chance. I struggle with a past that still haunts me. I worry that I'll let my friends down. That I won't be there when they need me someday."

He frowned. "Like when you followed me."

She nodded, exhaling through her mouth. "Exactly like that."

"I don't deserve to be here. I certainly don't deserve the things I'm able to do now."

A whisper of a smile crossed Aisling's lips. "Let's agree to disagree on that one. You see, I think you're special. Very much so. I hate what Usaeil did to you, but at the same time, I know you can do the things you can now because of what she did."

Xaneth couldn't hold her gaze and looked away. Everything Aisling said made sense. He wanted to believe her, but he couldn't.

"Nothing I said helped, did it?" she asked, hurt coloring her tone.

He shook his head.

"Is there anything I can do? Say?"

Xaneth faced the railing and gripped it once more. "Nay."

"I think you should leave this place. It isn't good for you."

He tried not to react to her telling him to leave, but it was like an uppercut to the jaw. He clenched the wood so tightly that his knuckles turned white, and the wood cracked again. It became difficult to breathe. He struggled to pull air into his lungs. With each mouthful, he needed more. Urgently.

"I'd stay if I thought it would do any good," Aisling continued. "I thought we'd become friends. Now, I see that was my mistake. I won't subject you to being around me anymore. You've told me enough times to leave you alone. I should've respected your wishes from the start. I...I'm sorry I didn't."

She was leaving. This time for good. Xaneth didn't know how he knew it, but he did. And it left him shaken to his very core.

He turned to her. The sadness on her face pushed him over the line he swore he wouldn't cross. He took a step toward her. She didn't retreat, didn't run. Xaneth closed the distance between them and wrapped his arm around her waist. Slowly, he pulled her close.

She never looked away from his gaze. One of her hands came to rest on his chest and caressed upward to his neck. And then her fingers were in his hair, her long nails gently scraping his scalp. Her other hand rested on the waist of his jeans.

With his free hand, he cupped the back of her neck and held her against him. If he kissed her, he wouldn't be able to let her go. Ever. If he gave in to the desire thrumming through him, hot and sizzling, he would be hers.

Body and soul.

Xaneth looked into her dark red eyes before dropping his gaze to her parted lips. The silky strands of her hair slid through his fingers as he brought her closer and lowered his head. Their noses brushed, and then their lips.

The shock that went through him at the contact left him stunned, dazed. Astonished. And hungry for more. He moved his lips over hers, gently, softly. She sighed and melted against him. Xaneth slid his tongue into her mouth when she parted her lips. He moaned at the sweet, exotic taste that was Aisling's alone.

She clutched at the waist of his jeans when he deepened the kiss, letting the hunger and yearning he'd locked away loose. Everything he had denied himself—the need, the desire, the longing—rushed through him like a whirlwind.

And she answered with passion, matching him in every way.

CHAPTER EIGHTEEN

Aisling was in Heaven. It could only be Heaven, it felt so good. So *right*. Xaneth kissed as he did everything—with everything he was. He coaxed, he teased, and then he swept her off her feet with a kiss that curled her toes.

It became so heated and passionate they both needed more, craved more. He moved his hand to her lower back and pressed her against his arousal, allowing her to feel the hardness between them. He held her firmly, securely. His rigid cock against her was like a drug, and she hungered for more. Suddenly, she found her back against a wall as he continued kissing her as if he were starved for her.

Aisling tore her mouth from his, her breaths coming in great gasps. He sought her again, but she put her fingers over his lips. "Not here. Anywhere but this place."

Before the words were out of her mouth, Xaneth had teleported them. She didn't even register where they'd ended up because he took her lips once more. Only the sound of waves crashing told her they were somewhere near the coast.

"I need you," he ground out.

She knew how much those words had cost him. For all of Xaneth's power and magic, for all the evil he'd wiped away, he still held himself apart from others as if he didn't think he belonged. In response, she kissed him as if there were no tomorrow.

Abruptly, Xaneth released her and stepped back. Aisling had to grab hold of him to keep from falling on her face. She thought he might have changed his mind, then she looked into his eyes. The blatant, palpable desire that stared back at her made her heart catch. His chest heaved, showing he was as breathless as she.

He held out his hand to her. She took it, and then saw they were in the cave on Kilbaha. A large fire roared at the back of the cavern, and a pile of thick blankets and plush pillows lay behind the flames. Xaneth made no move to bring her to the bedding, but she didn't plan to wait for him. She removed their shoes with a thought and then pulled him after her.

Once on the pile of blankets, she faced him. "You have no idea how long I've wanted this."

"I have an idea," he murmured before taking her mouth again.

This kiss was slow and sensual, carnal, and altogether hedonistic, awakening parts of her that only he could touch. He kissed her thoroughly, completely. Until she could barely stand. Only his strong arm wrapped around her kept her upright.

She used magic to remove his clothes so she could touch

him at her leisure. Her hands smoothed over his thick shoulders, coasting over the bulges of his arm muscles before moving back up again. She caressed his impressive chest and then moved down to his stomach. Her palms inched around to the back of his waist and then to his firm ass.

He groaned and rocked against her. Aisling was on fire for him. She slipped a hand between them and wound her fingers around his cock. It was hard as steel, smooth as velvet. She pumped her hand slowly up and down his length before smoothing her thumb over the head of him.

Xaneth's breath caught. The next thing she knew, she was on her back with him over her, one of his legs between hers, and she was naked.

"Two can play that game," he murmured with a soft laugh.

She smiled, but it quickly vanished when he bent his head and wrapped his lips around a turgid nipple. He drew the pebbled flesh deep into his mouth and pulled. She arched her back as pleasure shot through her, searing her body and landing at her center. Aisling cried out as his tongue flicked back and forth over the stiff nub.

With the soft blankets at her back, the warmth of the fire mixing with the cool sea breeze blowing into the cave, and the heat of Xaneth's hard body against hers, her senses were overloaded.

His large hand smoothed down her side, his touch tender yet firm. The way he embraced her, caressed her, showed his desire. His hunger. She lifted her hips to move against him. How many times had she dreamed of exactly this? How many times had she wondered if she would ever know the feel of him against her?

And now, here he was.

His mouth kissed from her breast, gliding over her collarbone and up her neck before he licked across her jaw and seized her lips once more. She groaned with contentment when she finally felt his full weight atop her. He felt so *good*. Better than any fantasy she could've come up with.

As Xaneth drank deeply from Aisling's kiss-swollen lips, he wondered why he had ever warned himself about giving in to his desires for her. The line he'd sworn not to cross was a distant memory. The woman who had tempted him beyond reason was in his arms, warm and willing. She was as passionate a lover as she was a fearsome warrior. It was like he was a jigsaw puzzle. She fit perfectly. A missing piece that opened an entire world he hadn't dared to think existed.

He couldn't stop touching her amazing body. Her skin was soft, her curves enticing and seductive, and her soft cries of pleasure? They only pushed him to touch, kiss, and lick more of her.

Xaneth turned his lips to the other side of her jaw and down her throat. He licked her collarbone and kissed downward until he feasted upon her other breast. Her nipple was hard and puckered when he drew it into his mouth and softly tugged. His cock jumped at her moan. He could play with her breasts for days, but he wanted to explore more of her.

He shifted his body down more. She widened her legs, allowing him to settle between them. He glanced up to find her watching him. Xaneth grinned before parting her women's lips and lowering his head to lick the delicate area before circling her clit. She sucked in a breath, and her head fell back onto the blankets.

Hiding a smile, he focused all his attention on her.

Aisling gripped the bedcovers tightly, her body straining against Xaneth's magical tongue. How did he know exactly where to touch her? He applied just the right pressure and kept at it until she soon spiraled toward pleasure.

She was so absorbed in what he did with his tongue and the tightening of her body that she gasped when he gently inserted a thick finger inside her. He moved it subtly, but that was all it took for the waves of climax to crash over her. Aisling's back arched as her body jerked. The beautiful, undulating currents of ecstasy swept her away.

Her body went boneless as the last vestiges of the orgasm rolled through her. She felt his finger inside her still and cracked open an eye to look at him. The way he watched her sex continue to clench around his finger made her stomach tighten with desire once more.

"By the stars, the feel of you," he murmured. Then he added a second finger and slowly turned them from one side to the other.

Aisling groaned at how amazing it felt.

"I want to make you come again like this," he said, his voice thick with need.

She lifted her hips as he moved his fingers inside her. "I'd rather feel you."

His eyes burned with a hunger that left her breathless. She started to sit up and take him in hand again, but he was over her before she could. He braced his hands on either side of her head and looked at her.

"If this is a dream, I don't want to wake up."

She touched his face. "It isn't a dream."

He bent his arms and lowered himself just enough to press his lips against hers. Aisling found his cock and stroked it. He moaned, the sound rumbling in his chest. If she didn't want to feel him moving inside her right then, she would have turned him onto his back and had her way with him. But that would come later.

Aisling guided him to her entrance. She bit her lip when he brushed her sensitive clit. Then he slipped inside. She opened her eyes to find him watching her. Their gazes locked, held as he thrust once, twice, and filled her fully. She sighed as her body stretched to accommodate him.

Nothing would ever feel as wonderful as Aisling. Xaneth accepted the realization as fact because that was what it was. Feeling her warm wetness, he marveled that he hadn't caved sooner. There would be no one else for him. Not in this lifetime. Or in the next. His heart would forever belong to the remarkable, exquisite woman in his arms. Even if she was nothing but a figment of his imagination, someone sent by

Usaeil to torture him, he would gladly endure anything—just to hold her, kiss her.

Love her.

He began moving his hips, his length sliding in and out of her. She felt divine. Perfect in every way. Seeing the pleasure move across her face and how her breathing hitched made him desire her all the more.

Words he dared not say threatened to fall from his lips. To stop them, he kissed her heavenly mouth.

She clung to Xaneth. With every drive of his hips, every movement of his thick cock inside her, she felt as if she were coming alive for the first time. As if everything had suddenly fallen into place. Aisling lifted her knees so he could go deeper. His tempo gradually increased as his hips thrust, pushing him deeper, faster. Harder.

"Yes," she whispered. "Don't stop."

His silver eyes had darkened to a stormy gray of pleasure. He gave her another lingering kiss. There was something there, something she wondered about but would never ask. It was the same thing she held within herself. Something that didn't need to be voiced now, not when they had this.

Her thoughts halted as her body took over once more. She met him thrust for thrust, searching for the pleasure that awaited them both. Her body tightened a heartbeat before the second climax struck.

"Aisling," he called as she felt his seed spill inside her.

The walls of her body clamped around him, milking him

as he continued moving, her orgasm prolonged with each thrust. She clung to him and cried out as a third climax swept her away.

When she came to, Xaneth was still on top of her, still inside her. He gently touched the side of her face and smiled down at her. She returned his grin, happier than she ever remembered being.

"Wow," he said.

She chuckled. "You can say that again."

He gently pulled out of her before rolling onto his back. He turned his head toward her and quirked a brow. "Are you a cuddler?"

"I am."

"Thank goodness," he said with a smile.

She moved to curl against him, her head on his chest as his arm went around her. She listened to his heartbeat, the crackle of the fire, and the crash of the waves. "I don't ever want to leave this place."

CHAPTER NINETEEN

The blood. There was so much blood. Too much. Aisling stared in horror at the sight, certain the victim was dead. She told herself not to look. The sight would be frozen in her brain. She knew what she would find, but her eyes landed on the motionless figure, barely discernable given the sheer amount of blood.

Her heart sank, and a keening cry rose from somewhere deep inside her. She reached out, desperate to take hold of the outstretched hand, to make contact one last time. Her fingers were breaths away when the hand turned to ash.

"Nay!" Aisling screamed.

Someone spun her around, and she saw a face contorted with utter contempt. "Did you actually think all of this would be yours?"

She didn't have a chance to respond as the blade entered her side, slipping through her ribs as easily as a hot knife through butter before piercing her heart.

. . .

Aisling jerked awake, struggling against who held her.

"It's me. Aisling, it's me," said a calm voice.

The richness penetrated the fog of her brain, and she focused on the face above her. Xaneth. She stared into his silver eyes as she took a deep breath and blinked away the remnants of the nightmare.

He gently smoothed hair away from her face, worry clouding his expression. "You're safe now."

She didn't push away when he lay back and pulled her against him. His hold wasn't tight. It was comforting, reassuring. Aisling concentrated on the beat of his heart and stared at the shadows from the fire moving across the cave wall. She waited for Xaneth to ask about the nightmare, but he said nothing. He allowed the unanswered questions to lay silently between them. Whereas she had hounded him in the maze for answers to all her queries, he patiently waited for her to decide if she wished to talk or not.

After everything he'd shared, she should do the same. But how did she begin? She hadn't spoken about it with anyone. Ever. Erith knew because she had seen it. Eoghan knew because the Reaper leaders needed to know everyone's history to adequately deal with any issues that may arise. Neither had said anything to Aisling about it.

Maybe it would be good to talk about it. To face it. Going over it in her head had done nothing. The nightmares never stopped. It was the same thing every night. Sometimes, it went longer. Other times, they were cut short like tonight. But it always featured the same people.

Aisling sat up and crossed her legs as she faced the fire. She rubbed her hands over her arms to warm them, suddenly colder than she had ever been. Something soft touched her hand. She glanced down to see that one of the blankets had been draped over her. She turned to look at Xaneth over her shoulder. His met her gaze but remained silent.

She sighed and returned her attention to the dancing flames. "I come from a large family. There were eight of us—three girls and five boys. My brothers—three older and two younger—took it upon themselves to protect their sisters at all costs." She smiled, recalling how she had strained against what she felt were the confines of her family. If only she had known then what she did now.

"We were respected in our community. Firmly middle class. But it was a good life. I knew nothing but happiness, even if my family shielded me more than they should have. But then again, that's what parents do, isn't it?" She tugged a strand of hair from her eyelashes. "I often trained with my brothers, who were in the Light Army. One day, one of their commanders saw me and asked if I was interested in joining. It was a way out, so I took it. I loved every moment of it. Each new weapon, the battle magic they threw at me. I learned and mastered. I moved through the ranks rapidly and saw a bright future ahead of me that was so close I could practically reach out and touch it.

"I had new friends and traveled to different places. One week, we were in Cork. Some friends and I went to a human pub where lots of Fae gathered. We were curious to see if any mortals drew our attention. That's when I saw him across the room, through the throng of people. The way his red eyes watched me was both unnerving and exciting. My friends and I left soon after, but I couldn't stop thinking about the Dark.

So, I went back by myself the next night, looking for him. I don't know why. Maybe I thought I could handle anything a Dark might throw at me. It was rather cocky of me considering the closest I'd been to a Dark was passing one on the street. But I wanted to explore the feelings that seeing him had produced. I hadn't been able to stop thinking about him or the grin he'd shot me, as if he knew that I found him attractive but was too hesitant to do anything about it."

Aisling brought her knees to her chest and rested her chin on them as her arms locked around her legs. "He wasn't there. I was relieved but also disappointed. No one had caught my eye the way he had. My friends said it was his dangerous air. I soon accepted that explanation because I couldn't think of any other reason. I went back to my training and tried to forget him, but he kept popping up in my thoughts randomly. Nearly a year later, I saw him again—this time in Dublin. I felt someone watching me in the pub, and just like before, he stood there as still as a statue, simply observing me. I wasn't the same naïve girl I had been, though I wasn't as mature as I thought I was either.

"Other Dark surrounded him as his entourage. He motioned for me to come to him. I shook my head and gave him a look that told him he had to come to me if he wanted to talk. And he did." She paused, back at the pub with the loud music and conversation, the crush of bodies. "At the time, I was thrilled. The connection I'd felt across the room was undeniable up close. There were no words between us as he took my hand and led me outside into the shadows. The attraction and danger swept me off my feet. I didn't tell anyone about him. Not my friends, not my family. We kept our relationship secret from his friends, too. The passion between us was all-consuming. More powerful than I knew how to handle. The way he talked to me, how he treated me, it was like I was his queen. He showered me with the attention I'd been longing for, and all the while, I fell deeper and deeper under his spell."

Aisling paused, the words harder than she'd thought to get out. She licked her lips and wondered what Xaneth's expression was. She could look at him, but she knew if she were to continue, she couldn't. So, she kept her gaze on the flames. "I believed I could make him see that being Dark was wrong. I'd always believed that if we could turn Dark, then a Dark could turn Light. I intended to make that a reality for him so we could be together in front of the world instead of hiding. But he had other plans. I fell in love with him so hard and fast that I never saw his manipulations. I was deliriously happy and only saw what I wanted to see in him.

"I told everyone around me that it was my idea to leave the army, but I know now that it was all him. He knew just what to say so I'd do what he wanted. Once I left the Light Army, he became even more controlling. Again, I didn't see it. I had what I thought I wanted—him. I was happy that we were together day and night. Eventually, I cut off contact with my family altogether. They had discovered who I was with and made their displeasure known. He was livid and hurt, and through that, convinced me that my family didn't care about me. Said they were trying to control me. The irony was lost on me at the time."

Aisling briefly closed her eyes when she felt Xaneth's fingers splay across her back. It was a simple gesture, one that told her he was there and listening, offering her comfort if she needed it. She drew in a shaky breath. "I was completely under his thumb by then. More and more of his friends began coming around. It was disconcerting to have so many Dark near, especially since I was the only Light. He assured me that no one would ever harm me. I had no reason to doubt him. With the new Fae in my life, I saw another side of him. If he asked someone to do something, they did it. Without question. Without fail. And that included me. If someone didn't do as he asked, they saw his true wrath. It terrified me. Before I even knew what had happened, I was Dark."

Her voice hitched at the word as she recalled the first time she'd looked in the mirror and saw that her silver eyes had been replaced by red. She had cried for hours. "All that time, I thought I was converting him, but he had been steering me to *his* purpose. He became my world—everything I wanted. Everything I did was for him and him alone. I lost myself. I lost the person I had been, the one with dreams and aspirations. I turned my back on the love of my family and friends. I embraced all that was evil. Because that's what he wanted me to do.

"Over time, I saw less and less of him. I wasn't allowed to leave the house unless he was with me. No one came to visit unless they came with him. He chose what I wore, who I spoke to, what I ate, how I acted. I wasn't allowed to look any male Fae in the eye unless he gave me permission. I catered to him in every way. In all things. No chains bound me, but I stayed anyway. Because I thought I loved him. Because I thought he loved me. Because I thought that was how relationships worked.

"I was so desperate to please him that I never stopped to ask myself what I wanted. I couldn't have even if I'd wanted to. He had a dark side—even for a Dark Fae. I learned very quickly never to anger him. No one had ever laid a hand on me in anger before him. I thought my training in the army would've prepared me for such abuse, but it didn't. Nothing could have. It wasn't just the physical abuse, it was also the psychological and verbal abuse that came along with it. I became a shell of the person I had once been."

Aisling swallowed and released a long breath. Those words had been tough to get out, but the next part would be even more difficult. "Things changed some when I became pregnant. He was overjoyed and once more showered me with all the love and attention our relationship had started with. I had one acquaintance who was the wife of another Dark he knew, and he allowed me more access to her. I still couldn't go out, but she could come to me. We spent every hour we could together, getting ready for the arrival of my baby. All the gloom and darkness of my life faded as I anxiously awaited my child's arrival. I told myself I had to endure all the horrible things to know what true happiness felt like. My entire pregnancy was amazing. I couldn't stop smiling, even when he was in one of his moods. Every day was something new and joyful. I eagerly counted down the days until I could hold my baby. And when it came, I hardly felt any pain. I was so elated to finally hold her. She was tiny and perfect, and I knew my heart would burst with joy."

Aisling didn't stop the tears that fell down her cheeks. She never did when she thought about her beautiful baby girl. Aisling sniffed as her view of the fire blurred from her tears.

Xaneth's thumb gently moved back and forth, reminding her she wasn't alone. He was here. She wanted to bury her head against his chest and forget the rest. But it needed to be said. She had come this far.

"I didn't care that he left me at home because I could spend all my time with her. She surprised me every day. And the unconditional love I saw in her eyes melted my heart. He adored her, but it was nothing like my love for her. He began spending time away from us. There was always an excuse, and I accepted them all because I honestly didn't want him there. I feared he would dim her light as he had with mine, but I still loved him. Then my friend told me that he was having an affair. It was a blow I didn't anticipate. I had given him everything, and that was how he treated me? So, I confronted him about it. He admitted it. Said I gave our daughter the attention that should have gone to him, and my punishment was him seeking out someone else's bed."

Even after all this time, thinking about that still caused a rush of cold fury to rise within Aisling. She felt herself tense and forced herself to relax. She drew in a breath, taking solace in Xaneth's presence. "I don't think I've ever been so hurt and angry as I was then. After hours and hours of tears, my daughter made me smile. That was when I realized that I was only truly happy with her. In that moment, it was as if a light bulb had turned on. I saw how miserably wretched my life had been, to the point where I couldn't remember the last time I had been happy. I'd always done what he wanted, meekly accepting his words as he'd taught me to do. That night, I began to plan my escape with my daughter. She was still so small, but I knew I could make it happen. I had to. Because I saw what the future held for us, and I didn't want any part of it.

"I didn't say anything to anyone. Not even my friend. She talked about his cheating, but I didn't react. I began to suspect that she might be sharing things with him. No matter how I looked at things, I couldn't understand why he had allowed her to become my friend. My blinders were off, and I finally saw everyone for who they were. My job was to protect my child at all costs, and I planned to do that. Over the next few weeks, I noticed how my friend tried to get information out of me. I finally had enough and told her I would no longer give her anything to bring back to him."

Aisling shook her head and snorted. "I was so full of myself. I should've kept my mouth shut. But after being restricted and hampered, I was finding my feet again. I didn't originally see her for the threat she was. She laughed in my face and told me she was the one he had taken to his bed. She then told me she wanted my life and would get it." A knot of pain filled Aisling's stomach. "I would've stepped aside for her, but I knew he wouldn't give me up. He'd told me countless times that I was his and would always be his. That if I tried to leave him, he would stop me. Which meant I had to be careful. I'd only have one chance to escape, and I had to do everything myself. I managed to get word to my eldest brother to see if my family would help, but they had cut me out of their lives. They wanted nothing to do with me or my child because I was Dark, and I couldn't blame them. Still, it hurt. So very much."

Xaneth silently sat so his shoulder rubbed against hers. He took one of her hands in his, gently holding it.

Aisling glanced at him, unable to maintain eye contact.

"All I had to do was teleport out—once I was free of the house anyway. He had spelled it so no one could jump in or out of the home or garden. I only needed to get one foot over the line, and my daughter and I could be free. I planned to go somewhere he'd never find us. It was a good plan. I was readying everything to leave that night when I walked into my daughter's room and saw the…the blood."

She choked on the word as images flashed in her mind of that fateful day. Xaneth tightened his fingers over hers. Her heart beat rapidly as if she were back in that room and experiencing the horror again. "My darling girl was gone. Her blood co…covered everything. Her eyes were open and staring at me. I got there in time to see the light fade from her. I could barely make out her face with the savagery. I saw her little hand hanging over the side of the crib, and I reached for her. I needed to touch her once more. But I wasn't in time. She turned to ash before I could get to her. I didn't protect her. I hadn't been able to stop her murder. All of that was going through my head when someone jerked me around. I found myself looking into my friend's eyes. She reminded me that she wanted my life, and said she was there to take it. She was pregnant and said she would give him a child to replace mine. That she was replacing me. Then, she stuck a knife between my ribs."

CHAPTER TWENTY

Xaneth couldn't speak for a full minute. He was appalled, stunned, and outraged at what Aisling had endured at the hands of someone who had claimed to love her. Then there was the so-called friend. It was far worse than what he had borne. If it weren't for the nightmares, he wouldn't know about the horrors of her past.

She leaned against him slightly. He wanted to gather her in his arms and hold her tightly so nothing would dare harm her again. Yet Aisling's strength kept him from doing just that. She had overcome the past to stand on her own among those who could squash others with merely a thought. The fact that none of the Reapers did that spoke to each of them individually.

Xaneth looked down at their joined hands and saw that he held her too tight. He loosened his hold, forcing himself to acknowledge how much her story had touched him. That she had trusted him enough to share it. He'd wanted to know, but he had realized pressing her about it would get him nowhere. Then, she had told him on her own. He was overcome with emotions.

Aisling laid her head on his shoulder, her long hair brushing his arm and side. "Erith lets us decide if we want to take revenge on those who killed us. A few have."

"Did you?" Because if she didn't, he would be happy to do it on her behalf. He was already planning just how he would do it.

"Nay."

He rested his cheek against her head, wishing there was something—anything—he could do or say to take away her pain. He wanted to heal her hurt and undo the damage heaped upon her.

"That isn't true," she said. "For a long time, I wanted revenge. I planned all of it out to the second. The way I'd find them, what I'd say. What I'd do. That kept me going. It was little consolation, but I eventually discovered that he'd known nothing about her plan. He'd been so furious with her that he tried to kill her. She managed to get away, and he sent others after her. She kept hidden until she had her child. A son. She went back to him and presented the lad, hoping it would make up for things. He took the child from her. She repeatedly tried to get the boy back, but he secreted the baby away. She was inconsolable after that. Ultimately, she took her life."

"Good." Xaneth didn't hide his satisfaction. In his opinion, the female deserved worse.

Aisling nodded absently. "As for him, he controlled the child for years. I feared the lad would grow up to be as corrupt as his father, but he had more strength than I ever had. He escaped before he turned Dark. He changed his name and carved out a place for himself with the Light. As for my ex, he found another woman he could control and repeated everything he did with me. Though her family stepped in and made sure he left her alone for good."

"I hope that means they took his life."

"They did," she answered softly.

Xaneth fought not to pull her into his arms. She wasn't some frail, vulnerable female in need of his protection, but that didn't mean he didn't want to do just that. She deserved only happiness and joy for the rest of her days.

He hated the man who had hurt her and tried to extinguish what made her unique. More than that, he hated the Dark for having experienced her love. That she had given all of herself to him, only to be abused and demeaned in such a way. The man had taken the spirited Fae and turned Aisling into nothing more than the husk she had been. Yet Aisling had clawed her way back after that and the tragic death of her daughter, as well as the betrayal of a so-called friend. That took an inner strength he wasn't sure many had.

"Thank you for telling me," he said.

She turned her head slightly and kissed his shoulder before replacing her head. They sat like that for a time. Since everything he thought to say sounded hollow, he figured the best thing would be to just sit with her. Then he lay back, and she curled up next to him. Something in his heart eased at how she sought him out. He stared at the ceiling of the cave and memorized the feel of her body against his and the way it fit perfectly. She fell asleep quickly. She had released a ton of pent-up emotions, so he wasn't surprised.

It was some hours later before his eyes grew heavy. He slept lightly, waking each time Aisling moved. The sky was just beginning to lighten when he woke and gently extracted himself from her. He didn't know how much time they had at the cave, and he expected it was shorter than either of them hoped. His first instinct was to keep them hidden so they could spend as much time as they wanted together. But that wasn't feasible. Not when Lena and the Fae Others were still out there.

Xaneth sat beside her and watched the sky gradually lighten through the cave entrance. He would go to Lena today. He wanted to go alone, but Aisling would fight him on it. He knew it. He'd always thought to take on the Fae Others himself. Not because he thought he could do it alone, but because he didn't want anyone getting hurt. If he died, then so be it. He was a monster.

Yet Aisling had told him he wasn't. He believed her because he desperately wanted it to be true. She looked at him as if he were extraordinary and irreplaceable. She made him feel both. Right or wrong, there was no going back for him.

"That sigh sounds as if it carries the weight of the world."

At her voice, Xaneth turned his head toward Aisling. She wore a sleepy smile, but her gaze held a measure of concern. Xaneth leaned on his elbow alongside her. "Just thinking."

"About?"

"Lena."

"Ah." Her gaze searched his. "I'll follow you, you know."

He grinned and tugged on a long strand of her hair. "I know. I've accepted that."

"You have?"

"You don't have to sound so surprised. You're…persuasive."

She rolled to face him, the corners of her mouth turning up. "That, I am."

"You didn't wake with a nightmare."

Her fingers skimmed his bare shoulder, moving to his chest. "It's the first time I've slept soundly in ages."

It didn't matter if it was because she'd talked about the past or because she was with him. It was enough that she had rested well. "Talking about it must have helped."

"Or it could've been the company I kept."

He would like to claim he was the reason, but he wouldn't. "Hungry?"

"Starving, but Eoghan's shouting my name."

"Ah. Our interlude is over." The sadness that swept through him was as thick and dragging as quicksand.

She leaned toward him and pressed her lips to his. "For the moment."

They got to their feet and called their clothes. Xaneth removed the blankets and replaced them with an array of food. Aisling mumbled her thanks around bites. She got in three mouthfuls before she said Eoghan's name.

The Reaper appeared almost immediately. The widening of his eyes told Xaneth that he hadn't expected him. Eoghan's gaze slid to Aisling, where she was eating.

"It's been a rough few days," Xaneth said.

Eoghan returned his attention to him. "Since Aisling is otherwise occupied, why don't you fill me in?"

Xaneth told him about Lena, the maze, the hound, and the escape. By the time he finished, Aisling had taken her last bite. Xaneth grabbed a scone and halved it before slathering it with butter and sinking his teeth into it.

"It's amazing you two got out," Eoghan stated.

Aisling nodded as she glanced at Xaneth. "Had he not seen the arrows, we'd likely still be there."

Eoghan's sharp eyes studied Xaneth. "Seems there's a lot you can do."

Xaneth decided it was better to take another bite than answer.

Eoghan crossed his arms over his chest as a frown marred his forehead. "At least we know where Lena is."

"If she's still there," Aisling replied. "It won't have taken her long to find out the hound is dead. She might continue looking for me, but she also may leave."

Eoghan nodded slowly. "It's good that she didn't know Xaneth was there."

"Very," Aisling agreed.

Xaneth grew uncomfortable when both of them turned their gazes on him. He swallowed the last of the scone and asked, "What?"

"I wish we knew everything you could do," Eoghan said.

Aisling smiled as she said, "What he can do is quite impressive."

For the first time in ages, Xaneth felt his cheeks warm. He liked that she thought so highly of him. Would that she always did. "If I go after Lena, Aisling will follow."

"Aye," she replied.

"I think it's better if the Reapers join us," Xaneth finished.

Eoghan's smile was wide. "I'm glad you said that. Do you have a plan?"

"I do."

CHAPTER TWENTY-ONE

Lena stared down at what was left of the *cú*. Her ire grew, churning violently. How dare Aisling kill her prized pet? Lena fisted her hands. It had taken her decades to craft the *cú* as she wanted it. The hound had been her most faithful and devoted servant. It had never questioned her, never sought to take her power. The *cú* had simply wanted to follow orders. Now, he lay dead, ripped apart as if he had been nothing.

"She wasn't alone," Lena said as she studied the brutality of her pet's death.

"You can't mean Aisling," Berach said from her left. He hadn't stopped looking nervous since they walked into the labyrinth.

Lena turned to spear him with a look that made most drop to their knees. "Of course, I'm referring to Aisling." Lena pointed at the hound. "She couldn't have done that."

"I know the power you've given me. I think I could've taken on the hound."

His confidence astounded her, and not in a good way. Lena faced him. "Is that so?"

"Aye."

"When I create another one, let's put it to a test."

Berach frowned briefly. "You make it sound as if I couldn't."

"Because you couldn't. None of my soldiers could. And that means none of the Reapers could have either."

"I don't understand," Berach said with a shake of his head.

She turned her back on him. "You aren't meant to."

Berach hurried to catch up to her. "If you don't think Aisling was in here alone, then who was with her?"

Lena couldn't figure that out. No one had been with Aisling when she came to the manor. Yet Lena knew for certain that Aisling couldn't have taken down the hound without magic, and Lena would have the Reaper's power if Aisling had used any.

Lena halted suddenly. "Aisling understood that in order to stay alive, she couldn't use her magic."

"She must have seen another Fae die by doing just that."

"Maybe," Lena murmured. She tapped her finger on her leg as her mind sorted through things. "That doesn't explain the *cú*. No magic was used to kill my hound."

Berach glanced behind him. "Then someone used their hands."

Had she underestimated Aisling? Could the Reaper be that strong? Lena's magic had taken her down easily enough during the battle on the Isle of Skye. Lena had been sure she was dead, yet the Reaper was very much alive.

"Maybe there's more to the Reapers than you first thought," Berach said.

Lena slid her gaze to him and simply stared until he glanced away. Unfortunately, he might have a point, and she didn't like that at all. She and the rest of the Six had found out about the Reapers from Brian, a cowardly Light Fae who had been part of the original Others. He had been the first she'd killed and taken magic from. Once Lena discovered the Reapers were very real and not some legend, she had set out to learn all she could.

It hadn't been easy. Death made sure to keep the Reapers a secret, but not secret enough because Lena had been able to uncover things. Once she dug deeper, things eventually fell into place. She had been wrong about how many Reapers there were. Everything hinged on how strong the Reapers were —even Death, herself.

Lena knew she could take on the goddess. Or she *had* believed that. Now, she wondered if Death and the Reapers were toying with her. No. That couldn't be right. They fought too hard to let innocents die. Which meant she wasn't wrong about their strength—or the fact that Aisling wasn't alone in the maze. But who was with her?

Fury rushed through Lena with such force that she swayed. "Xaneth."

"He's here?" Berach asked, glancing around.

"Nay, you idiot. He was with Aisling."

Berach's brow furrowed deeply. "How? We only saw the Reaper."

"That's right. We were too focused on her following my

trap. Xaneth must have been following *her*. Or was ahead of her. It's the only way she isn't dead."

"So they're still down here?"

That was the question, wasn't it? Lena had every intention of facing Xaneth, but on her terms. Not down in her labyrinth where she couldn't use magic. She didn't answer Berach as she began walking again, following the arrows only she could see to lead her out of the maze. It took time to reach the exit, time that caused her apprehension and alarm to build.

She and Berach had talked openly, loudly. Were Aisling and Xaneth waiting to attack them somewhere up ahead? Or, worse, had they found the way out? That couldn't be possible. Only she could see the arrows leading to the exit. Yet with every step, she began to consider the possibility that the couple *had* escaped.

"Could they have known you set a trap for Aisling?" Berach asked.

Lena clenched her jaw. "Possibly."

"I'm not too eager to face them when I can't do it properly."

Neither was she. Lena quickened her pace. She expected Aisling or Xaneth to jump out at her from every corner. Her nerves were stretched tight by the time she reached the wall and began the climb upward.

For once, Berach didn't ask questions. He kept his head on a swivel until she was high enough that he could climb up after her. Lena opened the lid and exited. She dusted off her hands and waited for Berach before shutting the opening once more.

"Where are we?" Berach asked.

She ignored him and searched for any signs that the couple

had found the exit. They had been in the maze for three days. They had two more days, tops, before they succumbed without water. When Lena didn't find anything to alert her that Xaneth and Aisling had escaped, she smiled.

All this time, she had prepared herself to meet Xaneth in battle. Without even meaning to, she had captured him in the maze where he would die slowly and painfully alongside the Reaper. Lena had been excited to get a Reaper's magic, which would've helped her against Xaneth. Acquiring Xaneth's along with Aisling's would make fighting Death and the other Reapers as easy as killing humans.

"Which doorway do we take?" Berach asked as he looked between the four.

Lena's good mood had returned. She faced him and shrugged. "There are three wrong options and one correct."

"Where do the three wrong one's lead?"

"I'd suggest not finding out."

"And the correct one?"

Her smile widened. "Dublin."

He paused as he looked about the tiny isle. "You created this in case anyone ever figured out the maze."

"I needed a way out, but, aye. It was in case someone managed to find the way."

Berach laughed as he shook his head. "There's no way Aisling and Xaneth came here."

"That's right."

"They'll die in the labyrinth."

Lena was delighted at the thought. "They certainly will."

"So, which doorway leads to Dublin?"

"Why would you use a doorway when we can teleport back to the manor?"

He blinked at her in confusion. "Then…why have the doorways?"

"To make someone doubt, just as you are. You assumed that you had to take a doorway, especially after coming out of the maze, where you can't use magic."

"Oh, that's clever," he said in awe.

"I know."

Berach's gaze was approving as he looked at her. "You're going to do great things for the Fae. I can't wait for the removal of the Reapers and Death."

"Don't forget the Dragon Kings," she cautioned.

He lifted one shoulder nonchalantly. "They won't matter by that time. Their deaths will be an afterthought."

Maybe she had been wrong about Berach. Perhaps he was a better second in command than his predecessor. "It won't be long before I right things to how they should've always been. The Dragon Kings have lorded over all for far too long. They relegated us to second-class citizens. Us. The Fae! Had the audacity to put humans above us. That was the Kings' mistake."

"What was the Reapers'?"

"That falls to Death. The goddess claimed the right to decide the fate of the Fae. She alone stands as our judge and jury. And we're supposed to accept that? I may not know when she took that role, but she hasn't always been around. We were fine before her, and we'll be better without her. If power gave her the ability to decide our fates, then I'll take it from her once I crush her into nothingness."

Berach's smile slipped. "What if there are other gods or goddesses?"

Lena snorted. "If there were, they would've already shown themselves. Death is on her own. Oh, her lover, Cael, might have some of her magic, but I'm not worried about him." The only one she had really been concerned about was Xaneth, and he was about to be taken care of.

Everything she had been dreaming of and planning for was finally coming to fruition. The Fae had been hindered and told to hide their true selves for too long. They wouldn't repeat the catastrophe of the Fae Realm here. She would see to it. Once she took charge of all the Fae, Earth would be their playground.

There would no longer be talk of a Fae council. There would no longer be those vying for the Dark or Light thrones. There would only be her. When she thought about all the Fae bowing to her, Lena got a rush. They would soon sing her praises.

The Fae had been divided for far too long. No longer would the Dark be looked down on. They would be equal to the Light in all ways. No more would the Light be told to sleep with humans for only one night. Let them enjoy the mortals for as long as they wanted. After all, they would only exist to satisfy the Fae's appetites.

Lena imagined her ancestors, the ones who had been killed because they'd followed their baser instincts, looking down at her with pride. They might have failed, their hope lost, but she had discovered her roots. And she would succeed where they hadn't. Everyone would once more shout the Muldowney surname. It would be respected by all.

"Come," she told her captain. "Let's go back to the manor. I've got all the time in the world to wait for Xaneth and Aisling to die in my maze."

Berach bowed his head before teleporting away. Lena hesitated for a moment and looked around the island. She had erected a shield around it. From the outside looking in, only a tree grew in the middle. From the inside looking out, there were miles and miles of water, when, in reality, the shore was only a quick swim away.

Illusions. It was something the Fae didn't use often enough. It was too bad Aisling and Xaneth hadn't made it up here. She would've liked to know how long they would stand here debating which doorway to take. There was a slim chance they would decide to chance teleportation, but she doubted it.

The minds of the weak were so easy to bend—and break.

"It's too bad you're going to die in the maze, Xaneth," she said into the wind. "I would've enjoyed meeting you in battle."

CHAPTER TWENTY-TWO

"You can't be serious." Aisling could only look at him in
disbelief. Eoghan departed to fill Erith and the others in on the
news some time ago and returned to let them know the
planning would happen on Death's Realm. And yet, Xaneth
didn't want to go. Not after everything they had been through.

He briefly looked away. "I can't leave Earth, even if it is to
go over my plan with Erith and the Reapers. I have to be here.
I hunt evil, Aisling."

"It isn't as if we'll be gone for months or even weeks. We're
talking days."

"I can't."

She was trying to understand, but she couldn't. "Explain it
to me, please." She knew her words were clipped with anger,
but she couldn't help it.

Xaneth ran his hands through his black locks. "You're tied
to the Reapers, to Erith, correct?"

"You know I am."

"That's how it is with my situation. I wish it were otherwise, but it isn't. I have to be here."

Aisling closed her eyes for a moment and nodded. She might not comprehend his ties, but she accepted it. When she looked at Xaneth, she shot him an apologetic smile. "I get it. I just…" She floundered for words, trying to find the right ones so she didn't sound irrational. "It would be better if you were there with us, is all. Also," she said with a shrug, "I don't like you here by yourself. You should have someone watching your back."

"You'll return soon."

She didn't want to leave him. Not now. Not ever. The same feeling that had caused her to leave the Reapers to look for Xaneth made her stomach clench now at the thought of departing.

"I'll be fine," he assured her. "Like you said, it's just a few days."

Aisling shook her head, waving away his words. "It isn't that. I mean, it is, but it's…I've got a bad feeling."

"About?" he asked, his brows drawing together.

She squeezed the bridge of her nose with her thumb and forefinger. "I don't know. It's the same feeling that made me search for you to begin with."

"Try to explain."

Aisling quirked a brow at him as she dropped her arm to her side. "Did you not just hear me?"

"Aye."

She could've sworn his lips twitched. She glared at him, daring him to laugh.

Instead, he calmly said, "What I mean is for you to look

deeper into those feelings."

Aisling immediately shook her head. "No."

"All right."

Once more, Xaneth surprised her. She expected him to push to know her rationale, but he gave her space. Time to consider the scenario, contemplate her reaction, and reflect on the motives behind it. "Damn you."

It was his turn to raise a brow. "What did I do?"

"You didn't push."

He eyed her dubiously. "I don't understand."

"Most people would've asked me why I refused so quickly. Just like others would've prodded to know about my nightmares. You didn't do either."

"I figure if you want to talk about it, you will."

She sighed loudly. "I bury my emotions. I've done it for so long that it's second nature. Losing my daughter sank me into a deep depression. It was a long time before I could properly take my place among the Reapers. Erith never pushed me. She was there when I needed her and not when I wanted time alone. I knew I had a duty, so I did what I did best."

"You pushed aside your anguish and grief."

Aisling nodded. "I became what Erith needed—what I had promised. I know she would've given me as much time as I needed, but I also required something that I could hold onto just to keep going. Being a Reaper helped, but it also hindered me because I never let myself sit with those emotions, I never looked at their root cause. And I never let myself heal."

"I understand. I did the same for many years."

"How did you stop?"

His crooked grin was so boyish it made her heart skip a

beat. "I'm not sure I have. But someone recently told me to accept all of myself. I'm trying to do that."

She didn't think, she just reacted. Aisling grabbed his face and brought it down so she could kiss him. His arms went around her. What she'd meant to be a brief kiss soon turned into a raging inferno as the flames of desire licked greedily around them.

Aisling was the one who ended the kiss. She fought to calm her breathing. When she finally opened her eyes, Xaneth watched her with such yearning in his silver depths that she sagged against him.

"I don't want you to go," he whispered.

Her stomach fluttered, his words making her feel as light as air. The feelings were so perfect, so pure, they would be imprinted on her mind and soul for an eternity.

"I pushed you away because you were a temptation I knew I wouldn't be able to resist—or want to." Xaneth gaze swept over her face softly, tenderly. "I knew it would only take one kiss. I was determined to keep that from happening. Then you kissed me in the maze."

She smiled, thinking about it. "I did."

"You have no idea how long I've wanted you, how much I've craved to know the feeling of your body against mine."

Her smile slipped, but she was careful not to let him know. As wonderful and exciting as his words were, she also understood what they meant—she was indeed his weakness. If she'd ever had any doubt, she didn't anymore.

Lena had killed her. It had happened so quickly that Aisling hadn't been able to react. She wouldn't be here now without Xaneth. Who could say if he would be able to do that again? And even if he could, *should* he if it meant choosing her over ending someone as evil as Lena?

"Stop," he told her. "Whatever thoughts are going through your head, don't listen."

Aisling smoothed her hands down the sides of his face. "Can you read minds now?"

"I know you. I know every line of your face and the subtle expressions others miss because they're not paying attention. The way you hold your body when you're confident, happy, sad, angry. Or determined. I know how you press your lips together just a fraction when someone irritates you. I know the way your body tenses when you realize something you don't like."

She fought the sting of tears that burned her eyes. She loved him. Loved him with all of her being. That was what had brought her to him. That was what had made her follow him for weeks and allowed her magic to track him when she'd never been able to do such a thing before. It wasn't the power Erith had given her. It was her love for Xaneth.

And that was why she didn't want to be apart from him. She feared losing him and not being there to fight alongside him.

"Don't," he pleaded, his hold tightening.

"I'm not doing anything."

"You're pulling away. Putting up a wall between us."

Aisling smoothed back a lock of hair that had fallen onto his forehead. "You would've killed Lena had I not been injured on Skye."

"I made my choice. I'd make it again."

"As I would for you. You're my weakness, just as I'm yours. Lena will use me against you."

Xaneth said nothing, simply stared at her.

"You can't allow that to happen. No matter what."

"Don't ask that of me."

"I am. Because if I don't, and Lena gets away again, killing more, you'll carry that around with you. It might take a while, but you'll eventually come to resent me for it."

"I wouldn't."

She nodded, smiling softly. "You would. I know because I would, too." Aisling moved out of his embrace, instantly missing his warmth. "Perhaps it would have been better if we'd never experienced what's between us. What I know is that what's happening outside this cave is about more than the Fae Others. It's about more than the Fae. It's about this world and everyone in it."

"I *will* kill her," he stated flatly.

Aisling's heart clutched painfully. "I know. I'm going to be right beside you when you do. But only if you give me the promise I've asked for."

"I'm the happiest I've ever been, and you're asking me not to come to your aid if you're injured? To stand by and watch you die?"

"Aye."

His nostrils flared as he stared at her for a long, silent moment. "Fine. I ask the same."

"Agreed." Though she wasn't sure she could hold up her end of such a vow. But she would try.

Xaneth shrugged as he relaxed. "It won't matter because you won't be wounded again."

She didn't say anything since she knew Lena would come straight for her. It was no matter. Aisling would be prepared for the bitch.

"I know Erith wants the Reapers safe from Lena, but as far as the plan, I th—" Xaneth halted mid-word. A look of fury came over his face as he whirled around with a growl. Then, he was gone.

Aisling knew that sound. He'd smelled evil. The problem was, she didn't know where he had gone. She had no idea how far away he could sense such malevolence, but she counted on him being close. Aisling veiled herself and jumped to the top of the cliff above them to look around. She saw nothing until a scream of fury had her jerking her head to the side.

"The lighthouse," she murmured and jumped to the location.

A Dark female seduced a mortal male at the base of the structure. He was so enthralled with her that all he cared about was the pleasure she promised. He had no idea that he was slowly dying in her arms.

The scream had come from one of the two other Dark who fought with Xaneth. Aisling lowered her veil and went after the Fae with the mortal. She grabbed the female's short hair and literally threw the Dark over her shoulder. The man bellowed in rage. He jumped to his feet, uncaring that his pants and underwear were lowered to his ankles and his shoes still on. When he tried to take a step toward Aisling, he fell flat on his face. She ignored him and faced the Dark she had just interrupted from enjoying her meal.

The female bared her teeth and then blinked, surprise coming over her face. "I know you," she said.

Aisling motioned at the Dark with her fingers. "Then come and get me."

Twin orbs careened straight for Aisling's head. She dodged both, but as she straightened, another hit her in the abdomen. The pain of it took her breath. This wasn't the first time she'd been struck in battle, and it wouldn't be the last. She shoved aside the pain and kept her focus on her opponent as her body began healing.

Every time Aisling tried to close the distance between them, the Fae backed away. Aisling blocked a sphere coming at her chest and flipped forward to avoid the one aimed at her legs. When she landed, she shot six orbs at the Dark rapid-fire. Three found their marks. The Fae howled in pain, her red eyes blazing with hatred.

Aisling reared back her arm, getting ready to end the fight when the Fae vanished. She remained in position in case it was a ploy, but the female didn't reappear. Aisling turned to Xaneth in time to see him finishing off the last of the trio. They shared a look before the mortal's howl caught their attention.

He'd had sex with a Dark. There was no relief for him now. No matter how many times he sought out his own kind, he'd never find the release he had with the Fae. Aisling wasn't sure how old the man had been when the three had found him, but he appeared to be close to sixty now.

"It would be a kindness to end his suffering," Xaneth said as he came to stand beside her.

Aisling had seen dozens of people locked away in mental hospitals after encounters with the Fae. It *would* be a kindness to end the human's life, but she wouldn't do it. She looked at

Xaneth. Out of the corner of her eye, she caught a blur of movement. They watched in astonishment as the mortal rushed to the edge of the cliff and threw himself off.

"Bloody hell," Xaneth murmured.

Aisling was silent, her mind on the Dark who had gotten away. "The one I fought left. She recognized me."

Xaneth nodded once. "Then we'd best prepare. They'll descend shortly. We need to leave."

A part of Aisling didn't want to run, but now wasn't the time to implement Xaneth's plan. Or was it?

Xaneth frowned at her when she didn't budge. "What?"

"Why not let them bring me to Lena?"

"Have you lost your mind?"

Aisling grinned. "Erith can track me. She can tell you where they're holding me."

"That's assuming Lena doesn't kill you the moment they present you to her."

"She won't," Aisling stated. "She wants to make sure you come for me."

"I don't like it."

Aisling shrugged one shoulder. "But it's a good plan."

"It's a dangerous one."

"Isn't everything? It can work. You know it."

Xaneth glanced at the water before nodding reluctantly. "We need to talk to Erith and the others. But here on this realm."

"I know just the place," she replied with a grin.

CHAPTER TWENTY-THREE

Xaneth breathed in deeply, contentment coursing through him as he stood atop a mountain deep in the Scottish Highlands. Dreagan, home of the Dragon Kings, was sixty thousand acres of pristine countryside with such rugged beauty that he was awestruck. There wasn't a hint of evil for miles. The last time he had felt like this was before Usaeil captured him. He knew he couldn't remain here forever, but it was tempting.

He turned his head to find Aisling watching him. Her crimson gaze gave nothing away. She had two plaits on either side of her head, running from her temple to her nape, where the rest of her hair was gathered and then braided together, leaving the length to fall over her right shoulder.

The sun managed to peek through the thick, gray clouds threatening rain, its rays falling on her. He wanted to take her and run as far as they could from Lena, the Others, and anything that could tear them apart. It was a dream, a fantasy, but he wanted it more than anything.

Yet the need to seek out and end evil was too much a part of him now to turn his back on it. Not to mention, Aisling was a Reaper, first and foremost. They could never run. They *would* never. But he let himself dream about the life they *could* have. The love, the happiness. Possibly children.

"I knew you'd like it here," she said as she came closer.

Xaneth turned his gaze back to the view of the mountains. He'd seen a herd of red deer galloping over a nearby slope. The cry of a golden eagle pierced the silence. He could envision how Earth had been long before the humans and Fae came to disrupt the dragons' world. "Makes me wonder why the Kings ever leave Dreagan." He looked at Aisling. "Or allow the Fae here."

"Well, let's not forget that two of the Kings are mated to Fae. Shara is with Kiril."

"Ah. The Dark Fae who turned Light." Oddly enough, his aunt had helped Shara make that change—something Xaneth didn't understand at all.

Aisling slid her hands into the back pockets of her black jeans. "Then there's Rhi."

"Rhiannon. Legendary Queen's Guard, briefly Queen of the Fae, lover of Constantine, King of Dragon Kings, and my cousin." Something no one had known until right before Usaeil died.

Usaeil had killed nearly all her children, but Death had stepped in and saved Rhi. Xaneth wondered if Erith had known what that simple act would do in the years following. Every Fae—Dark or Light—knew of Rhi. She was one of the most infamous Fae of all time. Not only because of her love affair with Con but also because of her skills and power.

Rhi could've taken over the throne. The Light had begged her to do just that, but Rhi realized the best thing for the Fae was a Council. She had helped to begin that process, but it hadn't taken off as most had envisioned once Rhi stepped back and focused on her life with Con.

"The Kings friendship with the Reapers is what grants us access," Aisling said.

Xaneth grunted. "But I'm not a Reaper."

"I don't think you're a simple Fae either."

He glanced at her. "I think we're going to find out soon enough what exactly I am."

"You still aren't thrilled with me and the others being here, are you?"

It wasn't the Reapers he minded. It was Aisling. The thought of her intentionally offering herself as bait made his chest feel too tight, as if the world rested there, trying to crush him. He thought of the promise he'd given her. He wasn't sure he could keep it. Even when he'd given it, it had left a sour taste in his mouth.

"They're here," Aisling said.

Xaneth turned around to find Erith, Cael, and Eoghan. Death's petite frame strode toward Xaneth, her long, blue-black waves pulled into a high ponytail. She wore a solid black ensemble that fit her like a second skin and impossibly high stilettos. Her lavender eyes gave nothing away. Beautiful couldn't begin to describe Erith. Cael, her lover and mate, was on her right. The tall Fae had once been a general in the Light Army before he'd been betrayed and killed. His once-silver eyes were now purple, though that was the only outward sign that he had become a god.

Eoghan stood to Death's left. The Light Fae had been to Hell and back, literally. And he'd survived. His eyes were the color of molten silver from the experience, and moved like it, as well. He and Cael were the last two members of the first Reaper unit, and now each led their own team. Xaneth had learned about the Reapers when he met Eoghan, who had been searching for his mate, Thea.

The trio stopped before him and Aisling. Xaneth had never expected to work with the Reapers after waking up from his torture. He certainly hadn't imagined that he would find himself wishing for a life with Aisling. He couldn't help but wonder if he really was awake. The doubts he'd had about that returned. What if Usaeil still lived? What if this was just more torture? What if she instigated all of this? What if…?

He shook himself to hear Eoghan speaking.

"…know about your plan," Eoghan told him.

Xaneth nodded, hoping he hadn't missed anything crucial.

"I want to amend it," Aisling said.

Cael lifted a hand. "We've told your team everything. They should be arriving shortly."

As if on cue, they arrived. There were nine total. Xaneth recognized the original group that consisted of the Dark Fae: Dubhan, Cathal, and Balladyn, and the Light Fae: Bradach, Rordan, Torin, and the newest member, Ruarc. Some of them weren't alone. Balladyn had brought his Druid mate, Rhona, with him. They had been the two who'd ultimately stopped Lena and the Fae Others on the Isle of Skye.

Next to Rordan stood Fianna. The Light's brother had betrayed and murdered her while working with the Fae Others. She was now a Reaper. The Dark Fae, Breda, stood alongside Torin. Xaneth's gaze landed on Chevonne next, who he had fought with against Lena, her aunt.

He and Chevonne had a lot in common. Their aunts had killed their families, tried to kill them, and sought the kind of power no single person should ever have. He bowed his head to Chevonne, and she smiled at him.

Xaneth met each Reaper's gaze. He had pushed them away, along with the aid they'd offered. He wasn't sure why, other than he had feared the violence within him. And believed he needed to be alone.

Because of the brutality and savagery that consumed him. The thing keeping him going instead of dwelling on his imprisonment and the suffering he'd endured at his aunt's hands. Even now, it felt like there was a wall—a thin one, but a boundary, nonetheless—keeping all of that away so he could focus on his task.

He wasn't sure how long it would hold if he survived the battle with Lena. *If* he was even awake at all right now. That could be the real torment. It would be too easy to fall into that once more. On the off chance this was real, he had to focus. At least he wasn't running for his life from some beast intent on killing him. At least he could rest.

At least there was Aisling.

Xaneth heard her speaking and pulled himself from his thoughts once more.

"…Dark got away. She recognized me." Aisling motioned between them. "Xaneth and I knew she would be back with others."

Eoghan's lips flattened as he replied in a tone laced with anger, "Because of the bounty Lena placed on our heads."

"Yours more than the rest of ours," Bradach pointed out.

Aisling nodded in agreement. "I think we can use that. I think Lena targeted me because she knows if she can get her hands on me, it'll bring Xaneth."

"How does she know about the two of you?" Cathal asked.

Cael shrugged as he crossed his arms over his chest. "It could be because Xaneth took Aisling off the battlefield. It could be something else. That doesn't matter now."

"No, it doesn't," Aisling said. "What matters is that she wants to use me."

Torin's brow furrowed deeply. "You're going to her willingly?"

"I am. Think about it. I *let* her capture me, then Erith can find me and bring the rest of you. All the while, Lena will think only Xaneth will come."

"That's a lot of *ifs* in there," Balladyn pointed out.

Too many for Xaneth's comfort. Yet he couldn't find a good reason to convince Aisling that it wasn't a decent plan. And he'd been trying since she'd brought it up.

Chevonne blew out a breath. "I don't know, Aisling. I know my aunt. She'll have thought of everything. There's a chance she'll kill you as soon as she has you."

"Ah, Lena will," Breda replied. "If for nothing else but your magic."

Chevonne continued. "You probably won't even see it coming. There won't be time for you to do anything. You saw how quickly she killed my family. Even the rest of the Six."

"In a fekking blink," Rordan grumbled.

Aisling sighed loudly. "It's a chance, I know. I've thought

about all of this. I'm willing to take the risk to give us a possible advantage. One, I might add, we need."

"Xaneth?"

He looked at Erith, who hadn't said anything until now, and met her lavender eyes. He knew what her question was, but he still wanted her to say it. "Aye?"

"What do you think of Aisling's suggestion?"

Xaneth felt Aisling's eyes on him. He didn't look her way. He couldn't. If he had his way, Aisling would be locked somewhere Lena could never get to her. Xaneth knew that wouldn't happen, but for Aisling to use herself as bait? He could barely breathe thinking about it. With every fiber of his being, he wanted to say that he hated the idea. Instead, he said, "I can see why it might work."

It wasn't an agreement. But it wasn't a rejection either.

Still, it wasn't what Aisling wanted to hear. He felt her disappointment like a punch to the gut.

"Don't do it," Chevonne told Aisling. "Lena has shown us who she is. We have to attack as one unit or not at all. If we aren't together, she'll pick us off one by one. The Reapers, along with Erith and Cael, are strong enough to stop her. Then there's Xaneth. She's terrified of him. We need to use all of that."

Xaneth glanced away and found himself meeting Balladyn's gaze. There had been a time they had struck up a friendship of sorts. In Balladyn's red eyes, Xaneth saw sympathy and understanding. Xaneth had attempted to hide his turmoil about Aisling's proposition, but apparently, he hadn't done it well enough if Balladyn had seen through his words. And if the Fae had seen it, then so had Aisling.

The peace Xaneth had found on Dreagan was rapidly slipping away. The tighter he held onto it, the faster it fled. Just as the firmer he held onto Aisling, the quicker he lost her.

Xaneth ran a hand down his face and closed his eyes, his gut knotted in turmoil over what his heart wanted and what he knew was a sound idea. He needed to be honest with Aisling. About the promise he'd made her, about his thoughts on her plan—about how he felt about her. Other than clearing his conscience, what would the words do?

Ever since he'd found out about the Fae Others and Lena, he'd solely focused on taking them down. He'd known with absolute certainty that he could defeat Lena. He still felt that. After her, though? After the Fae Others were disbanded? That same conviction told him that he would die. He didn't know by whose hand, but it didn't matter. He knew he didn't have long to live. So, why should he get his heart involved? Except he already had.

The Reapers needed Aisling as much as she needed them. She couldn't die, and if she used herself as bait for Lena, that was exactly what would happen.

Something touched his arm. He looked down to see Erith. When he blinked, the others had moved farther away, leaving the two of them alone.

"I told them I needed a moment," she said.

Xaneth turned to face her. "With me?"

"You don't want Aisling to do this."

It wasn't a question. "There's a chance she could be killed."

"It's her right to choose this."

"And it's *your* right to refuse her."

"Are you asking me to tell her no?"

Xaneth struggled to find some kind of equilibrium in a world that was quickly spinning out of control. Instead of answering, he asked, "Do you like her suggestion?"

"I think she sees a good opportunity. And, no," Erith said firmly. "I don't want to lose her. I don't want any of my Reapers to die, but it's a chance each of us takes every time we go into battle. But that's who we are, Xaneth. It's what we do."

He knew what it felt like to lose Aisling. She had died in his arms on Skye. He couldn't go through that again. Not when he knew what it felt like to hold her against him. Not now that he had fallen in love with her.

"She got you here. She's the one who helped you stabilize whatever was going on after you woke. Aisling is stronger than even she realizes. Don't underestimate her. She's a fighter, and she always finds a way. You know that best of all."

It was all true, but did he have the strength to let her carry out the plan? Could he willingly put her in Lena's hands, knowing the Dark could kill Aisling? Of course, he couldn't. But if the situations were reversed, he'd be damned if he let anyone prohibit him. What right did he have to stop her?

"I don't know if I can let her go," he whispered.

Erith smiled sadly up at him. "Think about how she feels about you wanting to meet Lena on your own."

"It's what I'm meant to do."

"And who's to say this isn't what Aisling is meant to do?"

Xaneth shook his head. "She's destined for something more. She can't die with Lena."

"Then we make sure that doesn't happen."

He dragged in a ragged breath. "If I lose her, I can't guarantee what will happen to me. What I'll become."

Erith placed a hand on his arm and nodded. "Let's focus on Lena for now."

CHAPTER TWENTY-FOUR

Aisling tried not to stare at Xaneth and Erith, but it was impossible. She didn't know why Death wanted a private word with him. Normally, Aisling didn't give much thought to what Erith did, but now, she wished she stood right there with them to hear every word.

"You did what none of us could," Eoghan said.

She turned her head to him, not realizing he had come up beside her. She blinked, registering his words. "You mean by becoming such a pest that Xaneth had to talk to me?"

"You make light of it, but that had something to do with it. You're also leaving out the most important part."

"What's that?"

"If he hadn't wanted to talk to you, he wouldn't have. That same gut reaction you had to go searching for him is the one that let you know he needed you."

Aisling snorted. "Xaneth doesn't need anyone."

"I disagree. The last time we saw him, he was wild. Angry. Brutish, even. Look at him now."

Her gaze swung back to Xaneth. All she saw was a formidable Fae who had suffered unimaginable pain and then broke through it to become something else. Something stronger. Something even more formidable than who he already was—and that excited her.

Aisling drew in a deep breath. "He thinks himself a monster."

"Monster? Nay. Though I would say that you helped tame him."

She chuckled at the thought of *taming* Xaneth. "No one can subdue him. Besides, he's far from that. All I did was tell him to accept himself. He did the hard work."

"But you were there when he needed to hear that."

Aisling glanced at the ground before looking at Eoghan. "Perhaps. Or maybe he would've done it on his own eventually. He's the one who broke free of Usaeil's torture. He didn't need anyone for that."

"Aye." Eoghan was silent for a moment. "I believe Xaneth could take on Lena by himself—and win. But she'll have others with her. It's better if we're in this together."

Ah. So that was what Eoghan wanted to discuss. Aisling shouldn't have been surprised. "You don't like my idea to use me as bait?"

"I didn't say that."

"You implied it."

One side of his mouth lifted in a grin. "I think Xaneth is worried about Lena hurting you. Again. Don't forget he's the one who took you off that field. He's the one who held you as…"

"I died," she whispered. She kept forgetting that. All she'd thought about today was coming back and finding herself alone.

"It's obvious something has developed between the two of you. I think it's always been there. However, that also puts you both in precarious situations."

Aisling kicked at a small rock near her foot. "Meaning he doesn't want to see me hurt. Nor I him."

"Meaning, all he's thinking about is holding your lifeless body in his arms. My guess is it keeps running through his head, which would explain his hesitation to your idea."

"I made him promise not to choose me over Lena again."

A deep frown lined Eoghan's face. "Will you do the same?"

"Of course." When he studied her solemnly, she said, "At least, I plan to try."

"We all have parts to play in the road of life. Sometimes, those parts are easy. Other times they're demanding. Occasionally, they're uncomplicated, but generally they're complex, tricky avenues crammed with thorns and more obstacles and hurdles than we know how to navigate. There are periods we don't think we can go on, and moments we can't imagine how we got through it. Both you and Xaneth are survivors. You're fighters. He won't stop you, just as you won't prevent him from doing whatever he has to do in order to put an end to Lena. Because both of you know that is the necessary outcome."

His words touched her deeply. Eoghan put it into a perspective she hadn't thought about before, proving once again why he was such a great leader. "Would you let Thea be the bait?"

Eoghan paused as he considered her words. "I'd caution her on all the reasons—and there would be many—why putting herself in danger terrified me. Then I would show her all the ways she could protect herself until I could get to her." His smile was tender with understanding. "When you love someone, it's easy to hold tight and think you're protecting them. But if you love them, then you have to let go."

"I'm not holding tight."

"Are you not?"

Aisling's gaze was drawn back to Xaneth to find his eyes on her. She thought about how she had tracked him from one place to the next, how she had prodded him to speak about his past. She had interjected herself into his life, and now she was thinking about a possible future. With him. Which meant she sought anything and everything to keep him from facing Lena alone.

Yes, she was holding on tight. Clutching him as if he were the only way she could face the next decade, the next year... the next day. As she stared at Xaneth, she saw him for who he was: a warrior. A fighter for the vulnerable and helpless. Someone who saw his role and accepted it, no matter what the ending might be. He was, to put it simply, a hero. The kind of Fae she had always secretly searched for but never thought existed. And yet, here he was. Standing before her.

"Thank you," she told Eoghan. She looked at him and smiled through the threatening tears.

He nodded. "Anytime. That's what family is for."

The Reapers were her family. Not the ones who had

disowned her for turning Dark. Not the supposed friend who had killed her daughter and then her. The hodge-podge group around her now, who came from different walks of life and had found a unit of love and acceptance among themselves. They weren't blood, but they were more of a family than Aisling had ever had. They were the ones who accepted her for everything she was, who were there for her to lean on, but also gave her the freedom to be the Reaper she needed to be.

It was only right that she do the same for Xaneth. Because he was also family.

A few moments later, Xaneth and Erith walked over. Xaneth came to stand beside her and brushed his hand against hers. Aisling linked her pinkie with his. His gaze was warm when it met hers. The pit that had opened in her stomach slowly began to recede. She might have to call on Eoghan's words later, but for now, she had found solid footing again.

Erith caught her attention. "Aisling, are you sure you want to do this?"

"Nay," she admitted. "But I think it's the only way."

Cael asked, "What if Erith can't find you?"

"I will," Xaneth declared.

Aisling's knees went weak at his statement. She knew without a doubt that he would come for her.

He looked at her and nodded once. "I will."

"I know." The words came out as a whisper. The vow she saw in his eyes and heard in his words made her lightheaded.

No one had ever looked at her that way before.

Erith nodded. "Then it's settled."

"Let's move onto Xaneth's plan," Cael said. "I've looked at it from all angles. It's sound. It's our best option."

Balladyn added, "But we should be prepared to change tactics."

"Absolutely. Lena is the coldest bitch there is. She'll come after us in ways we'll never expect," Ruarc replied.

Xaneth was the one who broke eye contact first as he looked at the others. Aisling dragged air into her starved lungs and listened as they went through each detail of the plan. The second group of Reapers would come in from another angle after the battle had been raging for a short time. This would be the final battle between them and Lena. Someone would come out on top.

Halfway through talking everything out, two dragons, one silver and the other red, flew their way. Aisling tugged on Xaneth's finger to alert him. His eyes lit up when he saw the two enormous dragons headed toward them.

Ulrik, the King of Silvers, and Guy, the King of Reds, tucked their wings and dove from the sky. They shifted before hitting the ground, each landing on one knee with their hands on the earth, fully clothed. The two got to their feet and greeted Erith and Cael first. The smiles shared were genuine.

Guy's pale brown eyes ringed with black turned to her and Xaneth. He walked to them and smiled in greeting. Wind swept through his shoulder-length, honey brown hair. "Welcome to Dreagan," he said to Xaneth in a thick Scottish brogue.

"It's stunning," Xaneth replied.

Ulrik walked over. His gold eyes crinkled at the corners from his smile as he nodded to Aisling and then faced Xaneth. "Rhi and Con will be sorry they missed you. You'll have to return when they get back from Zora."

"I'd like that."

"So," Ulrik said as he faced the group, "we didna get Lena on Skye. I take it with all of you gathered now that you're planning another attack?"

Eoghan nodded once. "We are."

"Then we'll prepare," Guy answered.

Erith held up a hand. "We're not asking that of you."

Ulrik and Guy shared a look before Ulrik addressed her. "We've been friends for a long time. The Reapers have been there for us when we needed it. We've returned the favor. That doesna end now. Lena is a threat no' just to the Fae but also to the humans and us."

"We want in on this," Guy added.

Ulrik nodded in agreement. "I'm no' alone in this. Every King wants to join you. However, since half of us are on Zora with Con, you'll have to deal with those who are here."

"You mean the best of the Kings?" Guy said with a wink.

Ulrik chuckled. "Exactly."

Aisling watched unease fall over Xaneth's face. He didn't say anything, but she knew he was thinking of the additional people in danger. She leaned close and said, "Regardless of who fights, everyone is in jeopardy."

"I know. I don't have to be happy about it. This isn't the Kings' fight."

Ulrik looked at him and said, "The Dragon Kings protect this realm. Always have. Always will. The Fae Others might no' be after us yet, but we all know they're coming. We wiped out the original Others. We'll be there to lend aid against Lena."

"Then I suppose we'd best fill you in on what we have so far," Erith said.

As Cael began outlining everything, Xaneth tugged Aisling away from the group. When they were alone, he turned her to face him. She watched his Adam's apple bob as he swallowed.

"I don't want you to go to Lena, but I know it isn't my decision," he said. "It's yours. I meant what I said earlier. I *will* find you."

She nodded slowly. "Why do you think I suggested the plan in the first place?"

The concern on his face smoothed away as his lips slowly curved at the corners.

CHAPTER TWENTY-FIVE

Lena drummed her fingers on the windowsill as she looked out across the land that had been in her family for generations. Her closest neighbor was a mortal who, thankfully, was a recluse and never ventured anywhere near the manor.

It had been hours, and she still didn't have Aisling's or Xaneth's magic. Had she miscalculated? Had the pair gotten out?

"Nay. That's impossible," she murmured to herself.

She might not know what Xaneth was, but she had sensed immediately that he was the one she needed to be the most concerned about. No matter how many times she tried to pinpoint exactly what made him a threat, she couldn't come up with an answer. She just *knew*.

Was it the look in his eyes when he saw her that first time? Was it the way he came straight for her as if he had been sent to kill her? Perhaps he had. Maybe that was the reason he made her skin crawl with apprehension. He fought like a Fae possessed. And with more strength than even her soldiers or the Reapers. Xaneth's gaze was wild, his attacks violent. No matter who stepped in his way, he had remained locked on her.

Xaneth was everywhere she saw Death and the Reapers. He was one of them, without a doubt. Yet he didn't seem like a Reaper. It was almost as if he stood slightly apart. Xaneth's strength and power frightened her. She didn't know where he got it. If it was from Death, then why hadn't the goddess given the rest of the Reapers the same? Perhaps she couldn't. Xaneth might have been an accident. Or he could be something else entirely. Neither option pleased Lena.

Because she didn't know the extent of Xaneth's magic, she couldn't say for sure if he could get out of the maze. She didn't have definitive proof that he had been in the labyrinth with Aisling either, but it seemed a logical deduction. While her soldiers were powerful, they couldn't have ripped the hound's head apart. That meant that neither could the Reapers. Xaneth, however, was another story.

She could've caused such destruction, as could Death. The only other person was Xaneth. Lena had noticed there was something between Aisling and Xaneth during one of their first battles when the Reaper hadn't been able to take her eyes off the Light. Lena's proof that they were a couple came during the battle on Skye.

That was why Lena had tricked Aisling so the Reaper believed she followed Xaneth to the manor. It appeared, however, that she had been the one deceived. Aisling must have known what'd happened and called for Xaneth. Lena fisted her hand at the idea that she'd had both of them in the maze. As the minutes ticked by without confirmation of their deaths—and subsequent transference of their magic—she could no longer deny that the couple had managed to escape.

Had they stumbled upon the exit? That was doubtful. It was hidden for just that reason. Unless someone knew the arrows were there, showing the way, there was no way to find it. Did that mean one of them had been able to see the arrows? Fear skated through Lena. The only one who might be able to was Xaneth.

More proof that she needed to be concerned. And careful.

Xaneth being in the maze made sense. Either he or Aisling must have seen one of the Fae die from using their magic. That was how they had gotten past the first part. Their only recourse had been to walk the winding corridors. As for the *cú*, that, too, had to be Xaneth. Then him again to get them out. If he hadn't been there, Aisling would surely be dead, and Lena would have the Reaper's magic.

She drew in a steadying breath. There had been no word from her other three traps. If Xaneth or Aisling had fallen into one of them, she would've been alerted immediately. That meant they had either happened to choose the correct doorway or they had teleported away. Her bet was on jumping. The couple could be anywhere now.

A firm knock sounded on her door before it opened. Berach said, "I've just gotten word. Aisling was spotted in Kilbaha."

Lena closed her eyes as anger rose swiftly and surged through her. She had been right. About all of it. It was a difficult blow, especially with all the planning she had done.

She had thought of everything. Well, everything except for Xaneth.

"What happened?" she asked.

"A trio of female Dark were having a bit of fun with a mortal. She said a Light male attacked two of her friends. She didn't get a good look at him, but it was Aisling who fought her. The female said her companions died. She got away to gather others to go after the Reaper."

Lena turned to face Berach. "Let me guess. Aisling was gone."

"Aye."

But that gave her an idea. "Captain, put the word out to everyone in the organization to look for Aisling and Xaneth specifically. If they're spotted, I want them to alert my soldiers. No one is to take action except for the soldiers."

"I'll see it done," he said with a bow of his head before walking out.

Lena smiled in anticipation. "You think you're clever, Xaneth, but you're not nearly clever enough to beat me. You and Aisling want to fight us? I'll give you both a battle you weren't expecting."

Erith flexed her hands. In all her endless years, from the time she had floated in space searching for something, anything, to becoming the Mistress of War, to stumbling upon the Fae and transforming herself into Death, and finally to forming the Reapers, she had never expected the course of her life to head in this direction.

She had longed for a tribe and others to connect to. At the time she'd formed the Reapers, she hadn't realized that she was trying to create a family for herself. It had taken centuries of mistakes before she saw that in order for her to be a part of a family, she had to open herself to them.

She looked around at the men and women who were that and so much more. Some Fae, some Halflings, but all remarkable people who loved and fought with everything they had. She had loved Cael from afar, but watching her Reapers find love had made her take a hard look at herself and what she had been missing—and take a leap of faith.

Because of that, she didn't just have a family, she had Cael.

The love and community she desperately sought had been right in front of her the entire time. She'd lowered the walls around her heart and had found more joy and happiness than she thought possible. She had then opened her realm to the Reapers and their mates, giving everyone a haven to live in and escape to when needed.

Though she often told the Reapers she wasn't all-knowing, she did know some things. That was what troubled her the most about Lena and the Fae Others' rise. How had she missed it? If it had come to her attention sooner, she could've… Her thoughts trailed off because she knew she wouldn't have done anything.

She didn't rule the Fae. She never wanted that. She hadn't stopped Usaeil or those who ruled the Dark. She wouldn't have stepped in with Lena either. The role Erith claimed was that of judge and jury at the end of a Fae's life. She had judged Usaeil many, many years before, but Erith had known that she couldn't disrupt Usaeil's journey because it was connected to so many others—Rhi, Con, Balladyn, Xaneth, and countless more. Unfortunately, the same was true for Lena.

Cael came up and put a comforting arm around her. She leaned against him for a brief moment. He was always there when she needed him to talk to, to allow her to unload her burdens for a short time, or just to hold her. He was her sounding board, her friend, a shoulder to lean on, and her lover. With him, she had found happiness that had always been just out of reach.

"Don't think about what you could've done," he said softly. "Lena's soul wasn't reaped for the same reasons you don't take any Fae's lives for simply being evil. How many times have you told me there's a balance?"

"That balance has shifted considerably," she argued.

Cael put a finger under her chin and tilted her face to his. "Take a look at our group. Consider those who have stood against us and are now vanquished. Look at our friends and allies. You put all of it together. You saw each of us during some of the best times of our lives. And our worst. You didn't care who was Light or Dark. You looked deep into our souls and saw who we truly were, the Fae we could be."

"You were already that Fae," she said with a smile.

He winked at her. "I was just waiting for you to notice."

She faced him and placed her hands on his chest. "This might be the time we lose."

"We might. We might not. I didn't think about that when I battled Bran for my life. I fought him for you, for us, for our family. Is that what went through your mind when you faced him?"

Erith gazed into Cael's purple eyes and felt some of the tension fall away. "I only thought of you."

"The Reapers are strong because of our bonds with each other. It doesn't matter what Lena throws at us, we'll be ready."

"As will we," Ulrik said as he walked up. Beside him was his Druid mate, Eilish.

Erith looked from the couple to the group of Reapers who stared back at her. Some of their mates stood with them, while others remained on her realm, guarding it. She was scared to lose any of them. Without a doubt, it would destroy her. Yet it would be that same love that gave her the strength to face this next evil. Together, all of them would defeat Lena and put an end to the threat hanging over Earth.

"The plan we have is a good one," she told them. "Lena is cagey, however. It won't take her long to realize what we're about, and she'll try to swing things to her advantage. She might even achieve it. But we can't give up. We've faced Lena before, but this will be our final battle. Aisling is putting her life in our hands. It's time for us to disband the Fae Others for good. It's time to reap Lena."

Eoghan rubbed his hands together as he looked at his team. "We're ready."

Erith's eyes shifted from one set of Reapers to the other. "You know what to do. The moment we hear from Xaneth or Aisling, we'll know Lena took the bait."

The Reapers teleported out in twos, leaving Erith and Cael with the Dragon Kings.

She nodded and reached for Cael's hand. Once their fingers were linked, she said, "Now, we wait."

CHAPTER TWENTY-SIX

Xaneth strolled along the one-lane wooden bridge next to
Aisling, catching the various scents of evil that had assaulted
him since leaving Dreagan. This was where he belonged,
though. Out in the mix of wickedness and malevolence.
Xaneth focused on the area around him. Clontarf. The pretty,
affluent community was a Dublin suburb situated on Dublin
Bay that brought in scores of tourists. It was dotted with
beautiful parks but was known for the eleventh-century battle
that happened here, and Clontarf Castle, built in the 1830s,
that had since been converted into a hotel.

They continued along the bridge that connected the
mainland to Bull Island, where they were headed. Scores of
sightseers made the trek across the picturesque bridge to visit
the nature preserve, golf club, and Dollymount Beach. Xaneth
couldn't help but notice how everyone around them was
oblivious to what was about to happen, unaware of the danger
Aisling willingly walked into.

"It isn't too late to change your mind," he said.

Aisling smiled but kept her gaze on the water. "I know."

Xaneth tried to soak up the quaint beauty around him, but he couldn't stop himself from searching every face he saw—both Fae and human. Putting himself and Aisling out in the open made him uneasy, even if it was the plan.

"I can do this."

He jerked his head to her. "I don't doubt that."

"I just thought you might need to hear it."

Xaneth drew in a long breath and then slowly released it as he looked ahead. The wood creaked as a car drove past, the pedestrians safe in their walkways on either side. He glanced behind him and spotted a young family gaining on them. Xaneth guided Aisling to the railing and paused. They faced the water and quietly waited for the group to pass.

He watched the water moving steadily with the current. "I want to stop you from doing this."

"I know." She gently placed her hand atop his on the fence. "When all this is done, we can laugh about it."

He frowned at her words.

"You don't think you'll survive?"

Xaneth felt her eyes on him. He swiveled his head to hers. "Nay."

"But…" She paused, her crimson eyes troubled as her brow furrowed, and her lips pinched. "We're here. Together. You're not doing this alone anymore."

"I've known from the beginning," he reluctantly explained. "From the time I woke from the torture, I was driven to find evil. Not just any malevolence, mind you, but the foulest, nastiest sort. The kind that threatens everything. Even as I hunted it, I knew I'd find it—and that it would cost me my life."

Aisling lifted her chin, defiance in her steady gaze. "You were wrong about the monster within you. You're wrong about this."

He wasn't, but arguing the point would do no good. He wished she was right. He wished it with every fiber of his being. But Lena was too strong for even Erith to face on her own.

"This thing between us is far from over." Aisling faced the water once more. "It isn't."

Xaneth regretted being so frank, but he wanted to prepare her. The problem was, he couldn't prepare *himself* for the inevitable. Not after having Aisling in his life. She was... everything. A companion to fill the emptiness, a friend he thought he didn't need.

A lover he had ached for.

Her inner strength and the steel in her that kept her going when others would've crumbled staggered him. Her battle skills were breathtaking. The sheer expanse of her power astonished him. Her determination was a force on its own. Her loyalty to those she cared about was second to none. Her beauty was enthralling.

It would be excruciating to watch what was building between them end. Then again, he wouldn't be here to see it. But he knew it, and that was almost worse. It would be far crueler than anything he'd suffered at Usaeil's hands.

Xaneth looked at the clouds rolling above them, listening to the squawk of gulls and the soft rolling of the waves onto the shore. He inhaled the scent of sea and salt that hung heavy in the air. Then he looked at Aisling's profile. He put everything to memory, not wanting to forget a single second. If he were lucky, he might be able to remember this in the nothingness of death.

He winced when the smell of something foul reached him, angry that his contemplation had been disturbed. Aisling's fingers tightened around his hand, alerting him that she was aware of his every movement.

"Where?" she asked.

"On the island."

She faced him and nodded, her chin lifted in determination. "I want Lena stopped. Today. She's done enough damage and has taken enough lives. Besides, I have a future with you that I want to get to."

Xaneth turned his hand and slipped his fingers between hers. He hadn't thought his admiration for Aisling could grow, but it did. She was utterly incredible. He parted his lips and almost said the words in his heart, but he hesitated a heartbeat too long and then decided against it.

His finger rubbed against the black-stringed bracelet Eilish had given Aisling. It had been his idea—a safeguard for Aisling to be found in case Lena blocked Erith's ability to locate Aisling and he was dead. Lena wouldn't expect the Reapers to fall back on Druid magic, but Xaneth wasn't taking any chances with Aisling's life.

She smiled, but it didn't quite reach her eyes. Outwardly, it appeared as if Aisling were ready for Lena to take her, but Xaneth could feel the small tremble in her. He thought about teleporting them away to begin the life they both longed for, but it was just a dream—though one he held close. It was the only way he could get through the plan that had been put into motion the moment they'd started across the bridge.

Xaneth gave her a nod. She returned it. Then they started toward Bull Island. Every step was like a blade twisting in his heart. He wanted to stop this nightmare. It was unfathomable that he was about to willingly let the woman he loved go into the hands of his enemy, one who was known to kill Fae to steal their magic. Yet if he wanted to have the advantage over Lena, he had to proceed. Despair and misery heaped upon his shoulders, joined by rage and resentment until he could barely stand upright. How was he ever going to be able to go through with this plan?

"There's a lot I want to say," Aisling said, breaking into his thoughts.

Xaneth glanced at her. "I'm listening."

"I mean after. It's important. You're going to want to hear it. That means you have to be around when this shite is finished."

He felt his lips curve into a smile. That's what Aisling did. She was the light penetrating the deepest of nights, showing him a way out. "A long conversation, then?"

"Very," she stated firmly. "Too long to be conducted now while in the middle of a mission."

Only Aisling would do something so clever and ingenious to get someone to do what she wanted. It was one of the millions of reasons he loved her. "There are things I'd like to say to you, too."

"After."

"Of course." He smiled. In the direst of situations where everyone's life hung in the balance, she could wring a moment of pleasure out of him. It was the most precious thing he'd ever experienced. He wondered how different his life would've been had he met her centuries ago. Yet she wouldn't be the Fae she was now, and neither would he.

She was a balm to his battered soul and splintered mind.

His wrecked heart.

Mere hours were all he'd had with her. And a million lifetimes wouldn't be enough. It didn't seem fair that they'd had such paltry time together. He wanted to rail at the universe and denounce the destiny that seemed set before him. All for her. For more time with a Dark, who had beguiled him, utterly and instantly with a single look.

He had fought against it, against *her*, but he had lost the battle the moment they met. His heart and soul belonged to her. They always had.

Always would.

Xaneth grimaced at the putrid smell of evil that assaulted him, yanking him from his thoughts. He and Aisling were nearly to the island. With Ireland's mild winter climate, there were tourists all year. They walked and drove the streets of Bull Island, mixed among the Fae.

"Xaneth," Aisling whispered.

He glanced to the right and saw the five Dark who didn't hide their coloring among the humans. "I see them."

"We need to get somewhere secluded."

Xaneth looked at the group of Dark, who watched them raptly. They were the stench he smelled. Fae Others. Exactly what he and Aisling had wanted to find. As soon as Xaneth's feet were on the isle, he paused and returned the Darks' stares. "Care for some fun?" he inquired.

The one in front smirked. "Always."

"Then follow us."

The Dark snorted. "What's wrong with right here? Afraid of hurting a few mortals?"

Humans passing near them looked over in shock before hurrying away. Xaneth ignored the mortals and kept his focus on the group. "If you want to finish this, then come find us."

He and Aisling turned in the other direction and began walking. Just in case the Fae Others thought to ambush them, they cut between buildings and avoided the main thoroughfares where tourists and locals gathered. The problem was, Bull Island wasn't that large.

The isle had been Aisling's choice. She knew of a location where locals kept to themselves. They didn't hurry there, though Xaneth wanted to. Instead, they kept an even pace. Neither of them looked behind them to see if the Fae Others followed. Xaneth could smell their nearness. When they finally reached the windswept beach, he was pleased to see that no one was there, likely thanks to the cloudy winter day.

"Ready?" he whispered to Aisling.

She squeezed his hand in response. They turned in unison to face the five Dark who had already begun to spread out and encircle them. Xaneth wasn't sure how he would be able to let anyone take Aisling, despite it being their plan.

Two of the Dark attacked her first. It was all Xaneth could do to keep his attention on the three nearest him. He fought not to turn and see if Aisling needed help. He told himself repeatedly that she was a Reaper and could handle herself. But it didn't work.

"We were told not to attack you," the Dark leader said as

he held out his hand and let an orb of magic form. "The two of you looked so adorable, though. And I thought…why not?"

"You don't know who we are, do you?"

"Why should I?"

Xaneth jerked his head toward Aisling. "She's a Reaper."

The leader snorted and glanced at his two friends. "Right. If she were, she wouldn't be with the likes of you."

"Oh, I'm something much worse," Xaneth replied before flinging balls of magic toward each of his three opponents.

They weren't expecting it. The Dark to his right didn't move in time, and the orb landed on his shoulder, eating through the skin, muscle, and bone until the limb fell off. He howled in pain as he dropped to his knees and began turning to ash.

The other two were quicker. They didn't come to their friend's aid. Instead, they launched simultaneous attacks on Xaneth. He dove to the side, putting some distance between him and Aisling so she wasn't struck by a sphere meant for him. He came up on one knee and flung his arm wide, releasing an orb as he did. The leader ducked to avoid it, but the second Fae wasn't so lucky. The ball grazed the hand about to release an orb. He grabbed his wrist and squealed in pain as the magic fell and rolled uselessly in the sand before melting the area around it.

Xaneth rushed the wounded Dark and grabbed his neck, twisting until he heard a crack. The leader let out a bellow of rage as the wind caught the ash from the Fae in Xaneth's hands. Xaneth seized the orb the leader tossed at him. It burned his hand, but Xaneth didn't release it as he stalked to the Fae, whose eyes widened in shock and terror.

"I did warn you," Xaneth said as he shoved the ball into the Dark's chest, pushing it deep.

Xaneth didn't let up until the leader's cries of pain cut off, and his ashes swirled in the wind. Xaneth searched for Aisling. He found her standing a short distance away, watching him. He swept his gaze over her, looking for injuries but seeing none.

The evil was vanquished, but his blood still ran hot. She started toward him. Xaneth strode to her and yanked her against him, their lips meeting in a fervent clash as they each sought to get closer. He wasn't thinking about Lena, the Others, or battle as his body ached for the one woman who matched him in every way.

Xaneth removed their clothes with a thought as she wrapped her legs around his waist. He grabbed her hips and lifted her before pushing inside her with one thrust. She broke the kiss as her head fell back with a cry of pleasure.

He moved in and out of her, hard and fast, his only thoughts the pleasure that consumed them and the release they both sought. He'd never taken anyone so roughly or passionately before. There was only need.

An unquenchable, undeniable craving for Aisling.

She gasped, her body stiffening a heartbeat before he felt her sex clench around him. Xaneth didn't fight the climax as it swept through him so quickly he had to fight to stay on his feet. In the end, he dropped to his knees, still holding Aisling, lost in the ecstasy he only found in her arms.

He had no idea how long they stayed like that until he opened his eyes. Aisling's head rested on his shoulder, both of them still breathing heavily. The cool wind felt good on his heated flesh. The strands of her hair tangled around his face. It was Heaven.

She lifted her head and smiled as she said, "I like this side of you."

He grinned, his heart bursting with love. He would tell her now. He wanted her to know what she meant to him. How important she was. Her gaze moved past his shoulder as her smile slipped. Xaneth saw movement behind her and spotted Lena's soldiers.

CHAPTER TWENTY-SEVEN

A cold knot of dread filled Aisling. While she battled the Dark, she hadn't thought about Lena or the plan. Obviously, neither she nor Xaneth had it on their minds when they surrendered to passion. But there was no ignoring it now—not when the soldiers began to appear. She wanted to halt time, freeze everyone and steal another second of utter bliss.

Xaneth's arms tightened around her for a heartbeat, letting her know more were behind her. Had she made the wrong decision? Had she been hasty in offering herself up to Lena? Because now she wanted to take it all back, return to Dreagan, and forget all of this and what awaited her.

But that wasn't who she was. Nor was it Xaneth. She met his gaze and lost herself in the silver depths. One second. That was all they gave themselves before disengaging and clothing themselves at the same time. Aisling called her sword to her. The pommel filled her right palm, its comfort that of an old, trusted friend. The weapon had been with her since her time in the Light Army. It never failed her. She spared Xaneth a glance and saw that his face was set in hard, determined lines. Yet she saw in his eyes that they could halt the plan with a single word from her.

But she wasn't going anywhere. The future she wanted could only exist if Lena weren't a part of it. And to get that, the plan had to move forward.

"Be safe," Aisling told Xaneth.

A muscle ticked in his jaw. "Stay alive. No matter what. I will find you."

She parted her lips, ready to tell him that she loved him when the attack began. Aisling released a battle cry as she used the sword to block and knock away orbs as she threw her own with her left hand. She kept her feet moving, spun, pivoted, and lunged. She shifted left, then right before feinting a step back, only to roll and come up on her feet to thrust her blade into a soldier who got too close.

Like every Reaper's, her sword had been forged in the Fires of Erwar. One knick by such a blade was enough to kill a Fae. She smiled in triumph at the dead soldier. The feeling didn't last long as a pulse of magic threw her back. They'd planned for her to be taken, but she wouldn't go without a fight. Aisling jumped to her feet and fired off a volley of orbs as she rushed the soldiers. When she neared, she somersaulted over them, swinging her blade as she did.

By the time she landed, two more soldiers were crumbling to ash. Aisling swung her sword around her as she eyed the group circling her. They had separated her from Xaneth. She wanted to look his way, but she knew he could take care of himself. Everything they planned was going exactly as it should.

That didn't mean she wasn't scared or second-guessing herself. She'd had the Reapers around her for so long. After them, it had been Xaneth. Now, she had purposefully allowed herself to be isolated. She felt the bracelet on her wrist. It wasn't the only item Eilish had spelled, but it was a visible reminder that she wasn't on her own.

"What are you waiting for?" Aisling taunted the soldiers, who continued eyeing her.

She felt the movement of air behind her. Aisling whirled, but it was too late. They struck her from all sides, and it felt like the ocean was pulling her under its depths. She tightened her hold on her blade even as her vision dotted, and blackness crept in at the corners. She felt herself falling, and thought she heard Xaneth shout her name as if from a great distance.

Xaneth seethed with rage so intense it threatened to tear him apart. He glared at Lena as she stood smiling while one of her soldiers unceremoniously hefted Aisling over his shoulder. Xaneth had to let Lena take Aisling, but at that moment, he didn't care about the plan. He just wanted to save Aisling.

And kill Lena.

"I know the feeling," Lena said. "I want to end your life, too."

Xaneth glanced at the remaining soldiers around him. They stood between him and Lena. He could get through them, but would it be in time to stop Lena from taking Aisling?

As if reading his mind, Lena chuckled. "If you want me, come and find me. And in case you need an incentive, I'll keep a hold of your lover to make sure you do."

"Fight me now," Xaneth dared her, even knowing she wouldn't.

Lena's red eyes narrowed. "Our time is coming. Be ready. It'll be your last day."

Then she and Aisling were gone.

Xaneth bellowed his fury. The monster inside him demanded release. And he gave it.

"Come on. This is tiresome. I didn't strike you that hard with my magic."

Aisling winced at the voice as she fought against the fog in her brain. Whoever it was, she didn't like them. But they kept talking. The voice was grating and annoying. Aisling struggled to wake up and open her eyes, if for nothing more than to make the woman shut up permanently.

It took a great deal of effort for Aisling to open her eyes. The sight of a bright blue sky without a cloud met her gaze. She blinked when she looked at the sun and raised her arm to shield her eyes. A soft cushion of grass greeted her when she sat. She sank her fingers into the blades. Her head felt muddled, and her body was sluggish. She struggled to remember what'd happened.

She cupped her hand over her eyes, which allowed her to see past the sun's glare. The moment she spotted a doorway at her feet, her stomach clenched as her entire body thrummed with unease. She looked to the right to find another doorway. To her left, another. She didn't need to look behind her to know there was a fourth there.

"It's about time. I have a schedule, and you're going to cause me to be late."

Aisling stilled, her heart thudding against her ribs. Lena. Of course. How could she have forgotten? She'd been on the beach with Xaneth, setting their plan in motion. Xaneth. She missed him already. How long had it been since they'd taken her? How had he faired? Those were answers she wouldn't have for some time. Aisling drew in a breath and stood, then looked down at her feet in confusion when she felt the grass tickle her toes.

"Ah, yes." Lena laughed. "Did you honestly think I wouldn't take your clothes and shoes? As if I'd leave anything easy."

Aisling glanced at the white pants and boxy shirt resembling scrubs worn by medical professionals. She scrunched her toes in the grass and faced Lena, trying to determine if the bracelet was still on her wrist. She brushed her arm against her leg but felt nothing. Three more tries gave her the same information.

The leader of the Fae Others wore a thin, red sweater, high-waisted, wide-legged, red pants, and matching heels. Her short hair was mostly silver with only a little black showing at her hairline over her left eye. Lena grinned as she crossed her arms over her chest. She stood near the shore, the water brushing the backs of her heels. "There you are. Now, as I'm sure you've noticed, you're back on the island. Just to be sure your friends didn't used any tricks to find you, I've had everything removed from your body. Your clothes, your shoes. Jewelry. I'm sure there was a plot to get the upper hand, but I have plans of my own."

Aisling really wanted to slap that smirk from her face. The only reason she didn't was because she knew Xaneth and her friends would succeed. She only had to stay alive and bide her time.

Lena's smile grew. "Xaneth had that same look on his face when I took you. The two of you made it too easy. It would've been prudent for you two to keep your feelings hidden, especially from me. I expected more from you."

"I don't care."

Lena's expression hardened, her eyes shooting daggers. "You will soon."

Aisling lifted her chin in defiance. The sound of a howl, one she'd never thought to hear again, reached her.

"Did you think I only had one *cú*?" Lena dropped her arms and motioned to the doorways. "I'll give you a hint. One returns you to the maze. Another will deliver you to Dublin where you can reach your friends. The other two?" She shrugged, delight curving her lips. "You'll have to find out for yourself. And just to make things interesting, I added four more doorways. There could be ones that free you. Or…not," she said with a shrug of indifference.

Aisling forced herself to show no outward emotion. Lena thrived on that.

"Just so we're clear on your current predicament," Lena said and snapped her fingers.

Aisling sensed movement to her left, where a soldier

emerged from between two doorways. She was shocked to see him since she hadn't realized he was there.

"Come to me," Lena ordered him.

The soldier tried to teleport. Instantly, he was struck down, his magic moving to Lena as a white light. Pleasure filled Lena's face before she grinned. "I couldn't make it too easy for you. I'm sure you understand."

"Enjoy all of this, because your time is drawing near."

Lena chuckled as she shook her head, pity on her face. "I give you less than an hour to live. Then, I'll have your magic, and your friends will follow. As will your lover. None of them, not even Xaneth, stands a chance against me once I have your power. Have fun, though don't take too much time. The *cú* will be here soon. I think we both know you'd fare better going through a doorway than facing my hound. Farewell."

Aisling didn't move until Lena was gone. Then she looked at the eight doorways around her—four standing in a square, and four others behind the originals, set in the spaces between. One of the inner four should take her to Dublin. Though she didn't trust anything Lena said. Then again, Lena knew that and could very well have spoken the truth.

"But which one is to Dublin?" Aisling whispered to herself.

She didn't want to end up back in the labyrinth. No doubt other similar places waited beyond the other doorways. Yet she couldn't stand here undecided. She had to *do* something.

The hound howled again.

Aisling didn't know where the sound came from, but it didn't matter. The animal was coming for her. She couldn't use magic against it, and she no longer had her sword. Aisling had seen the hound's size and witnessed how it moved. The only way for her to survive against it was by using magic.

"Fek," she said between clenched teeth.

Fight or flight. She couldn't freeze, not now. That meant certain death. She had to take a chance using one of the doorways. Aisling walked to each of them and stood at their entrance. Though she knew it was impossible to see anything through them, she tried. She inhaled, seeing if she could smell anything.

After facing each of the eight, she stood back in the middle once more. "I have a one in eight chance of getting to Dublin. Not exactly great odds."

Whatever awaited her on the other side of whichever doorway she chose, Aisling would have to be ready to fight—without falling back on her magic. Lena loved to toy with people and make them suffer mentally and physically. Aisling had to keep that at the forefront of her mind.

She walked to each of the doorways, stopping before a purple one. She looked it over carefully. It didn't look any different than the others. Her intuition wasn't helping her pick. Aisling jumped when she heard the hound's cry. It was closer now. Much closer.

Before she took a step, she checked her hair. Her braid was still intact. Aisling grinned. Lena had thought she'd taken everything that could be tracked. Eilish had spelled the bracelet, a buckle on her boots, and the hair tie that bound the end of Aisling's plait. If there was a way for her friends to find her, they would. It was all she could ask for.

"I trust in you, Xaneth," she said before crossing the doorway's threshold.

CHAPTER TWENTY-EIGHT

Xaneth didn't stop until every last soldier was dead. He stood on the beach, breathing heavily as ash drifted around him. He needed to kill more. The monster inside him demanded it, commanded it. The stench of evil was pervasive now.

His gaze sought out the spot where Aisling had fallen. He knew she wasn't there, but he walked to the location anyway. He fell to his knees and touched the sand as if he could somehow touch her again. His fingers brushed something hard. He moved aside the grains and spotted her sword. Xaneth grasped the pommel as he thought about her, the way she had looked at him with such love that it made his breath catch.

Through the haze of his anger and the need to find Aisling, he remembered their plan. *His* plan. He dropped his chin to his chest. He didn't know how long it had been since Lena had taken Aisling. It could've been minutes or hours. All he knew was that she was in his enemy's hands.

"Erith," Xaneth bit out. Within seconds, the goddess and Cael stood before him. Xaneth lifted his gaze to her. "It's done."

Death's gaze dropped to the sword in his hands. "She's strong."

Aisling's strength didn't matter. Xaneth knew Lena's depravity. She would batter Aisling until the fierce, beautiful Reaper was a shell of herself. Xaneth had to get to her before then. "Find Aisling's location," he demanded.

Erith hesitated. "I…I can't."

"Then I will."

"That isn't the plan," Cael said.

Xaneth snapped his head to Cael. "The plan has changed."

"We all want her back," Erith said. "We will find her. But first, we have to stop Lena. You know this. We put the plan together."

He shook his head. "It doesn't matter. None of this matters without Aisling."

"Usaeil's spells lost their hold when she died. The same could happen with Lena," Erith said.

Xaneth's gaze narrowed. It was a valid point. "Lena is waiting for me." He swung his eyes to Cael. "Eilish needs to find Aisling. That's the only way I'll do this."

"I'll make sure of it," Cael replied and teleported away.

The beast within Xaneth was untethered now. He'd kept it under control before, but now he didn't care. Lena's words came back to him. She wanted him to suffer, and he was. But it was nothing compared to what he would do to her.

"Xaneth."

He looked down at Erith's hand on his arm. Xaneth tightened his grip on Aisling's weapon and met the goddess's gaze.

"Remember what we talked about on Dreagan. Trust in Aisling. Trust that she knows what she's doing."

Each time he thought about Aisling suffering, he felt nothing but wrath. "That was easier to do before Lena took her."

"I know." Erith's gaze lowered to the sand. "I had to watch my enemy torture Cael. I've never felt such..."

"Madness? Ire?"

She nodded. "Aye. Madness. Indignation. But the need to destroy those who had hurt him and avenge his pain consumed me—along with the guilt."

Xaneth studied her silently, waiting for her to continue.

Lavender eyes held his. "Because I was the reason Cael suffered. *I* was the reason they attempted to take his life."

He looked away, each word like the dull edge of a blade scraping over his tattered heart. Each word a truth he didn't want to hear but needed to.

"The only way Aisling survives is with you," Erith said.

Xaneth swallowed and nodded. He would do whatever he had to do. For her. For the love he held for her.

For the future he'd gotten the tiniest glimmer of, the glimpse of what could be.

Because Xaneth knew what he had to become to defeat Lena and find Aisling—he had known all along. It was why he had pushed everyone away and had wanted to do this alone. His heart broke at seeing the future that had been within his grasp fading before his eyes, but it was worth it to stop Lena and rescue Aisling.

Anything would be worth Aisling. Even death.

Xaneth inhaled a deep breath and climbed to his feet. "Lena expects me."

"Do you know where?"

"My guess is the manor."

Erith nodded once. "We'll be there. Just like we talked about. Hidden and waiting."

"There won't be anything left of Lena by the time I'm finished with her."

"I don't care who ends her. She disrupted the balance, and she must be stopped."

Xaneth turned his back on Erith. "She will be. You'd better take hold of me if you want to know where I'm going."

He didn't wait to see if she grabbed him before he jumped to the manor. Xaneth didn't go to the back door as he had when following Aisling. This time, he stood on the front lawn. The gray stone manor had flowering vines growing up the front. It looked charming and idyllic from the outside, but there was no denying the reek of wickedness pouring from inside it.

"Good hunting," Erith whispered from behind him.

Xaneth didn't look at her. Instead, he ran his eyes over the numerous windows of the three-story structure. Where was Lena? Was she inside waiting, or would she come outside? He thought about the maze and briefly pondered if Aisling was inside again. He shut those thoughts off because he'd forget Lena and go in search of the woman who held his heart if he didn't.

It was only because he knew that Aisling would want him to focus on their enemy that he was able to keep his mind locked on Lena. He remembered Lena's smile, the confidence she had that she would get all she wanted. Xaneth might not know what he was, but he knew he had been created to best her.

He'd believed the Fae Others were his targets, but he now realized that it was Lena. Without her, none of this would have happened. She had executed Fae—both innocent and guilty. That had been her goal all along. She had duped the other members of the Six from the very beginning while biding her time until she could strike. And what an attack it had been.

Xaneth would never regret taking Aisling from the battle on Skye, but he wished he had also rid the world of Lena then, too. Instead, he stood here now with no idea if Aisling were alive or not.

The manor's door opened. Xaneth stared at it, waiting to see if anyone would walk out. There were no soldiers, but he wasn't fooled. They were around. Lena, for all her bold talk, would never face him alone. Even with all the power she had amassed, she would let others do the dirty work and come in at the last minute to take the prize for herself.

Minutes ticked by. No one came out to meet him. So, Lena wanted the battle inside. Was it because she didn't want anyone to see? Probably not. Most likely, it was because she'd set a trap. And she could determine who entered and who didn't. Which meant the Reapers and Kings might not be able to help as they wanted.

Xaneth grinned. As if anything could keep his friends out. Lena wanted this battle? She would get every ugly, horrendous moment of it. Then Xaneth would shove it down her throat and snuff out her life once and for all.

He almost remained on the lawn to see how long it took Lena to come to him, but he was tired of waiting for the encounter. He'd met her thrice on the battlefield. He looked back on parts of each encounter and realized he could've beaten her—he *should've* beaten her.

There would be no more *should'ves* and *could'ves* after today. One of them would die.

Xaneth tightened his grip on Aisling's sword. She wasn't with him, but her blade was. That would have to be enough. He started toward the open door. He saw only darkness within at first, but as he neared, he made out the black-and-white-tiled floor and the large, round entry table that stood empty.

He paused at the threshold. The beast within him rumbled, ready for the showdown that had been building for far too long. Xaneth welcomed that side of himself, greeted the monster with a willing smile—and entered the manor.

If Xaneth expected to be attacked immediately, he was wrong. Nothing but silence and stillness greeted him. As if the house had been deserted.

"It's not nice to keep a lady waiting, Xaneth." Lena's voice drifted around him, coming at him from all angles.

He walked farther in, rounding the entry table in the foyer. The room was good-sized with stairs to his right. Rooms with shut doors were on his left, and beyond, a hallway. "You're no lady."

"Oh, *touché*," she said with a laugh. "It's too bad I have to kill you. I like your spirit."

"I can't say the same."

She chuckled. "Here's your one and only chance. Instead of me killing you, we could work together."

"I'd rather eat glass."

"That's too bad. Though I expected that response."

His gaze lifted to the second floor. Xaneth slowly scanned the area and turned in a circle, looking behind him as he looked on the landing that encircled him. "Why are you hiding?"

"I have a plan. As I'm sure you did. Not that it matters. I wouldn't have allowed anything you tried anyway."

Xaneth almost laughed at that since she had done exactly as they wanted. But he needed her to think otherwise. "Where's Aisling?"

"You know, I was just telling her it would've been better if the two of you had kept your little affair a secret. By being so open, I was able to use it against you both."

The beast inside Xaneth demanded a reckoning, but he kept a tight leash on it. For now. The time for the retribution they both craved would come. "Where is she?"

"I'd say she was having fun, but we both know that's not true. Let's just say that the seconds of her life are ticking down. Rapidly."

Xaneth clenched his fist as he fought not to start busting through walls to try and find Lena so he could kill her.

Lena tsked. "A Fae with your kind of power should never be at another's mercy, and that's exactly where you are. All because you have *feelings* for someone. I've used that against you. That makes you weak."

He thought about how strong being with Aisling had made him. How she had urged him to accept himself, making him more powerful than ever before. Weak? Aisling made him many things, but weak wasn't one of them. "Do you plan to talk me to death?"

"Oh," she said with a tsk. "I've struck a nerve."

She certainly had. He was going to kill her as painfully as possible. "I came here for Aisling. And to kill you."

"How adorable. You think you can take me on."

"You're the one who's scared. I can smell it on you."

"I'm not scared," she bit out tersely.

Xaneth smiled. "Who's hiding from who?"

Just as he'd hoped, his words found their mark. Lena appeared at the top of the stairs, looking down at him. Her lips were pinched, and her hands were fisted at her sides—a clear sign he had scored another hit. But he didn't want to trade verbal barbs. He was ready for another kind of battle. Because each second wasted in conversation was another gone not finding Aisling. All Xaneth could hope for was that Eilish's magic worked, and the Druid found Aisling.

"You want a battle?" Lena asked. "Then a battle you shall have."

Soldiers poured out of the rooms, filling the area around him. Xaneth bellowed and swung Aisling's sword as he unleashed Hell.

CHAPTER TWENTY-NINE

Aisling pitched forward, lurching awkwardly. The platform on the other side of the doorway was barely wide enough for her feet. She flailed her arms as she struggled to find her balance while screaming at herself internally not to use magic. The sun blinded her, the heat oppressive as she squinted, her eyes frantically searching for something to grab hold of to steady herself. Then, she fell.

Panic cut through her, its icy fingers gripping her throat in a choke hold. Aisling turned her body and instinctively reached out for something, anything. Her fingers found purchase, and she held on for dear life. Her body slammed against a hard surface, nearly making her lose her grip, but she managed to hold on and kept still as she waited to catch her breath.

The burning of her fingers was the first thing that drew her attention. The rock and pebbles of the ledge she clung to dug into her fingertips, and it felt as if it had come directly from the center of the sun. She tried to adjust her grip, but she slipped, nearly plummeting in the process. Her heart leaped into her throat as she grabbed hold once more.

Aisling pressed her forehead to the stone and briefly closed her eyes. Her breaths came in hard gasps, and blood roared in her ears. She had no idea how far down it was. She was hesitant to look in case she lost her grip for good. Her anxiety was sky-high, and dread was becoming a close, personal companion—both of which she hated. Was this how humans lived? She had no idea how they did it. If only she could use her magic, this wouldn't be an issue. But she wasn't about to test that just yet. Maybe never.

Swallowing hard, Aisling slowly turned her head to get a better view. She saw her bare feet dangling next to a column. She moved her head gradually to peer over the side of her arm. Pain radiated from her fingers, and her arms shook with the effort it took to hold herself. Finally, she saw the ground. It was difficult to determine the distance, but from her current position, it looked too far for her to drop without seriously harming herself. Yet she couldn't stay here. Whether she fell or jumped, she had to do something.

"Same thing I said about going through the fekking doorway," she grumbled.

Aisling tried to pull herself up to the skinny platform to go back through the doorway and try another. She managed to get her chin up, but it was a struggle after hanging for so long. When she attempted to throw her leg over, it caused one of her hands to slip completely until she dangled by only one.

"Fek!" she shouted, her heart pounding erratically until she grabbed hold with both hands again.

Never, in all her long years, had she ever feared falling. She'd always had magic to turn to. But thanks to Lena, Aisling was terrified now. She had to stay alive to keep Lena from stealing her power. Yet if she didn't use magic, she could die. And if she did, it would play right into Lena's hands.

"I really loathe her."

Aisling pushed all thoughts of Lena aside as she concentrated on finding a way up or down. With the height of the doorway, this might be her only chance to get where she needed. That meant she had to try one more time to pull herself onto the ledge. After hanging for so long, her upper body hurt and trembled, and she knew her time was running out.

She made sure she had as good a grip as she could get, then kicked out a leg. She might have made it if she had been wearing shoes, but her heel slid off too easily. Still, it was better than her first attempt. So, she tried again.

Aisling knew it was a mistake as soon as she did it. Her fingers were too tired to hold on for that long. She lost her grip with one hand again. Then, her other hand slipped as she reached to find a better grasp of the ledge. Her gaze quickly searched for something to grab. In her panic, Aisling stretched for the first thing she could find as she felt herself falling.

She squeezed her eyes closed when her head bashed sharply against the stone, and agony bloomed at the impact. But she managed to find purchase once more. She opened her eyes to discover that she gripped a flourish from the top of the column. A glance up showed she had dropped several feet— too far to climb up and return through the doorway.

Tears stung her eyes, but she refused to give in to the

emotion. Aisling looked down again, and her gaze locked on a heap of what appeared to be a fallen pillar. Maybe if she slid down the column, she could reach the bottom without harming herself. Then she remembered that she was a Reaper. She healed.

"But can I here?"

Fury once again shot through her. It was because of Lena that Aisling questioned everything now. Her arms hurt from holding her weight. If she were going to fall, she wanted to do it by choice, not because she couldn't hold herself any longer.

Aisling gauged the distance and focused on what appeared to be a clear spot. She took a deep breath and then let go. She stayed near the column as she fell, watching the ground rise rapidly as the air rushed by her loudly. When she neared the bottom, she used her hands and feet to push away from the column to miss the jumble of stone.

She landed hard on the cobblestones with bent knees. Her hands caught her when she tumbled forward, her hair braid falling over her shoulder. Aisling flung her plait out of the way and took stock of her body. She felt some minor pain in her knees and ankles, but she was already healing, the pain diminishing with each heartbeat. She scanned the area and saw no signs of people or animals.

Slowly, she straightened and turned in a circle, wincing at the heat of the cobblestones beneath her feet. She stood in a city, long since abandoned if the crumbling ruins and eerie silence were any indications. Aisling tilted her head to look up at the doorway. It was a considerable distance away. A Fae wouldn't hesitate to teleport to it, but that was using magic.

The four columns that held the narrow platform were

mindbogglingly tall. There were buildings next to it, but nothing tall enough that would allow her to climb back to the doorway. Just as she'd feared.

The longer she stood there, the more her feet burned. She hurried to a building that cast a shadow and sighed in relief. Aisling regretted not taking a look at the city while she was hanging from the ledge. She had no idea how big the place was, if people were about, or if the entire thing had been abandoned. And if it had, why? Whatever the reason, Lena had used this place because of it. The maze had appeared safe at first, but Aisling had quickly discovered that it was far from that.

She looked at her feet. Being barefoot was inconvenient, but at least she knew she could heal. She would have to wait until nightfall to explore the city or risk the soles of her feet blistering. In the end, she chose to chance the injury. The sooner she learned what this place was, the better.

Aisling explored the building nearest her, finding nothing but dust and debris among the collapsing and cracked rock. Still, she went to the next and the next and the next. She found a set of stairs outside on the fifth building that led to a roof. The stone burned her soles, but she didn't stop—and was she glad she didn't.

When she reached the top, she finally got a view of the city. It was huge. Bigger than she had imagined. A myriad of rooftops met her gaze. Some had detailed spires, others pitched roofs, and some were plain. She must be on the side of a tall mound as the structures lowered with each level. There was plenty for her to explore, however. She sought to see the edge of the city and found a wall far in the distance. Aisling turned to look behind her, but she saw nothing but the columns that held the platform with the doorway.

Aisling vaulted over the side of the roof and landed at the bottom before hurrying into the shade. She leaned against a wall and rolled to the outer edges of her feet to give her soles time to heal as she planned her next move. Every sound she made seemed amplified in the stillness. If anyone or anything were about, they would've been alerted to her presence by now.

If anything was there. That didn't mean she would let down her guard. Something could be waiting for her to make a wrong move. The cry of the hound still echoed in Aisling's head. For all she knew, Lena could send it here. Or there could be something even worse lying in wait. That sounded exactly like something Lena would do.

Aisling was more of a face-it-head-on type of person. Lena preferred psychological warfare. Aisling wished she was here now. She would love to land a few strikes on Lena, but she knew Xaneth and her friends were taking care of the Dark.

"I just have to stay alive," she reminded herself.

Xaneth had promised to find her. Aisling touched the end of her braid. Eilish would help him. Aisling planted her feet on the ground and straightened. She was a Reaper. She knew about survival. She would do whatever it took until her family found her.

Dreagan

"What the bloody hell do you mean?" Cael said in a low, menacing voice.

Eilish blinked helplessly at the Reaper-turned-god. "I-I..."

"Careful," Ulrik told Cael in a threatening tone.

Eilish swallowed and looked at her mate. "Cael has every right to be upset."

"He doesna have a right to talk to you like that," Ulrik stated without looking away from the god.

Cael's purple eyes narrowed.

Eilish stepped between the two men. She looked from Ulrik to Cael. "I'm going to keep trying. I did warn everyone that this wasn't a guarantee."

Cael bowed his head and took a step back. "Keep trying. I'm needed at the battle."

"We're coming," Ulrik replied.

Eilish turned to give Ulrik a quick kiss. "Be careful."

"You, too."

Then, they were gone. Eilish put a hand to her forehead. She had spelled three items to help find Aisling. She should at least have *some* idea where the Reaper was. Instead, there was nothing. It was as if Aisling no longer existed.

Eilish dropped her hand to her side and hurried from the room as she called to the other Druids at Dreagan. The other six quickly met her at the base of the stairs. She looked into their faces—Darcy, Esther, and Gemma. She hadn't intended to ask for their help, but she knew they wouldn't hesitate to give it.

"There's a problem," she told them. "Lena took Aisling as intended, but now I can't find her."

Darcy's brow furrowed. "Nothing from the three items?"

Eilish shook her head.

"Then we'll find her together," Gemma declared.

"Just what I was hoping for." Eilish motioned for the ladies to follow her to the conservatory.

The four of them gathered in a circle and linked hands to let their magic flow between them, their power growing incrementally. Eilish began the chant that would give her the location of the items she had spelled. It took great effort, but she finally found one.

"The bracelet," Eilish said as she strained to see it clearly. The piece of jewelry kept going in and out of focus.

Esther said, "Is that…water?"

"Yes!" Eilish said in relief. They had one item, and she now knew its location. She stopped the chant and dropped her hands. "I'm going to find her."

"Not alone, you aren't," Gemma replied.

Eilish didn't argue. She held out her arm, waiting for them to grab hold. Then she clicked her silver finger rings together and teleported them to the bracelet.

CHAPTER THIRTY

Ireland

Erith saw a bright light shooting through the roof of the manor and straight into the sky before billowing outward like a mushroom. She had seen that before. It was the same kind of shield Lena had used on the Isle of Skye. The one impenetrable even by the Dragon Kings. There wasn't time to tell the others what was happening. All she could do was dive out of the way, coming to her feet just as the barrier slammed into the ground.

She searched the grounds to see if everyone had gotten inside in time. She spotted Eoghan, Fintan, Rordan, and Fianna near her. Dubhan and Kyra were on the right side of the house. Cathal, Bradach, and Maeve were on the left, but she didn't know about the back side.

She glanced behind her to find the other members of the

first wave of Reapers. Including Cael. She met her lover's eyes through the blockade. It was déjà vu all over again. The same thing had happened to them on Skye, but they had been victorious then. They would triumph again.

"*I love you,*" she mouthed.

His solemn expression softened as he mouthed it back to her.

Erith faced the manor. Nothing would separate her from Cael. Nothing. She glanced at the Reapers within the shield and nodded. Everyone knew what they had to do, regardless of which side of the barricade they were on.

The coppery scent of blood pervaded the room, and ash floated on the air like snow. Xaneth didn't notice any of it as he cut his way through the soldiers.

There was a never-ending line of them. He spun in a circle, slicing and cutting with the sword and tossing magic. He didn't care how many got in his way. He would get through each and every one of them. Because nothing would stand between him and Lena. Not this time.

Xaneth felt a sting and the slight pull on his skin when an orb found its mark. But he didn't slow, didn't stop. Too much was at stake. Too many lives hung in the balance.

Aisling.

He pushed her from his thoughts as he focused on the battle. Lena had put him in a position that kept him hemmed in on all sides. One wrong move and the soldiers would be on top of him. They were strong, but they didn't have a monster inside them as he did. They weren't fighting to save the person they loved.

That made him unstoppable.

Xaneth lifted his gaze to Lena to find the Dark grinning from her vantage point on the second-floor terrace. He stopped his attack. Her smile slipped as the soldiers hurled magic at him. Xaneth clenched his teeth at the pain and closed his eyes. He called to the beast, urged it forward. It answered willingly, gleefully as he gathered his magic.

The agony of his wounds made his knees buckle, dropping him to one knee. Xaneth focused on his magic, the wild rush of it, the raging, tempestuous force that he hadn't dared to call forth until now. There was no denying the violence he felt, the utter savagery that swarmed him.

He welcomed it, sought it as it gained strength. When he could hold back the ferocity no longer, he released it. He threw back his head, flung his arms wide. He saw the blast of his magic erupt outward, throwing the soldiers backward and into each other and the walls.

Xaneth locked his gaze on Lena as he got to his feet. Her face was ashen, alarm clouding her eyes. He jumped to the landing near her as Erith and the Reapers rushed into the manor and engaged the soldiers.

"There's no running from me," Xaneth told Lena.

The leader of the Fae Others stiffened her spine. "I'm not running. You think I'm afraid of a display of power? If you want to see strength, then I'll show you strength."

A burst of air surged from his mouth as Lena's magic

slammed into his midsection and threw him backward. Xaneth grunted as he crashed into the railing before hurtling through three walls and finally landing on his back. He shook his head, dazed by the impact. He felt a pull and winced at the discomfort that shot through him. When he looked down, he saw a sliver of wood the size of his forearm embedded in his right side.

He grabbed the end of it and held his breath before pulling the shard out. Xaneth gasped at the agony. That kind of wound shouldn't have caused that much damage. He lifted the wood to his nose and sniffed, gagging at the scent of evil.

Xaneth tossed the wood aside and gingerly touched his wound. He drew back his hand to see it coated in blood. His body began to repair itself, but the process was slower than usual. Xaneth couldn't wait for the injury to heal. He climbed to his feet and stepped over the rubble as he made his way to Lena. Her sly smile at the sight of his wound made him even more determined to finish this game they'd been playing.

"Score one for me. I hope that injury doesn't slow you down," she stated.

Xaneth felt like his body was nearly healed. He glanced at the ground floor to see Erith spinning in a circle, her black sword slicing through soldiers with ease. He waited until he stood a few feet from Lena before saying, "For all the magic you've taken from the Fae, I would've expected you to do more than that."

Just as he'd hoped, her eyes narrowed in anger. "I could take your life and your magic with a snap of my fingers."

"Really?" He twisted his lips. "Then why haven't you done

it to me? Or the Reapers?" He held her gaze. "It's because you can't."

"Are you so eager for your friends to die?"

Xaneth thought about Aisling being held somewhere, most likely enduring some sort of misery so they could put this plan into action. He thought about Erith and the Reapers fighting below. He thought about the Druids who'd stepped forward to lend their aid. He thought about the Dragon Kings, who refused to back down from the fight. There wasn't a person involved who didn't know what was on the line and didn't understand that they might not come out of this with their lives.

"The only life I want is yours," Xaneth said as he lunged for Lena with his weapon.

She stepped away just as the sword came at her, but not fast enough to prevent the blade from slicing her sweater. Xaneth couldn't tell if he'd drawn blood or not because she wore red. But he *had* gotten close.

"That was a mistake," she said and lifted a hand to snap her fingers.

Cael had been here before. He knew the terror and uncertainty of wondering if he could get to Erith and the others in time. He had lost control of his emotions on Skye when he and Erith had been separated. He wouldn't do it now.

"I'm really beginning to hate this bitch," Ulrik said from beside him.

Cael fought to remain calm. "We missed getting inside by seconds."

Balladyn put his hand on the barricade. While invisible to the naked eye, it flashed around Balladyn's palm when he touched it. He tried to push his hand through, but it didn't budge. Balladyn looked at Cael and shook his head.

Cael had already known he wouldn't be able to get through, but Balladyn had been on the other side of the shield during the battle on Skye. He didn't know what Cael and the Dragon Kings had gone through to break down the barricade. In the end, nothing they had done had worked. Balladyn and Rhona confronting Lena had destroyed the barrier. Now, both of them were on the outside with him this time.

"Well," Rhona said tightly. "I don't like this. What do we do?"

Cael wished he could see Erith, but she was inside the manor now. Though she was a goddess perfectly capable of taking care of herself, he preferred to be by her side to watch her back. After so many centuries of fighting together, it was difficult to be apart from her. Especially in situations like these.

"Nothing we did last time worked," Ulrik said into the silence.

Cael sighed. "So, we try something different." He looked at the others. "Xaneth and Aisling spoke about the maze. I think it's beneath the manor."

"You want us to go into a maze where we can't use magic?" Balladyn asked, confusion lining his face.

"Nay. I want us to go belowground. The barrier only goes so high, so I think it only extends so deep."

Ulrik chuckled. "I like it."

They all stepped back. Cael was the first to open a large hole in the ground. He went deep before testing to see if the blockade still stood. Then, he went deeper. One way or another, he was getting into the manor to fight alongside Erith.

A jolt of shock went through Eilish as she retrieved the bracelet she had given Aisling from the water. She stood on the banks of the loch, speechless at her find. Houses dotted the shoreline. A few boats floated along the tranquil water. The only other thing there, was a tiny island with a dead tree. Nothing that would give any indication of where Aisling was.

"I found Aisling's boots," Esther called.

Regret filled Gemma's face. "I see clothes farther out in the water."

Eilish fisted her hand over the bracelet. "They were here. Aisling wouldn't have taken these things off herself. Lena or her goons must have done it."

"Did they get the hair tie? That is the question," Darcy said as she walked up.

Gemma and Esther joined them and held out their hands. "We search again. Our magic found the bracelet."

"But not the boots," Esther pointed out.

Eilish pocketed the bracelet and grabbed their hands. She began the chant, focusing all her energy on Aisling and the hair tie. No matter how much magic she used, no matter how many times she sourced her fellow Druids' magic, all she saw was the loch. Every time.

She sagged forward, her hands on her knees as she hung her head. "Nothing but this damn loch."

"We'll try again. As many times as needed."

Gemma said, "I agree with Esther. We can do this."

"Absolutely," Darcy replied.

Eilish hoped so because she didn't want to face Xaneth if she couldn't find Aisling.

Erith lifted her sword to block an orb meant for Bradach and took a moment to look up where she saw Xaneth and Lena. Erith didn't like the sight of so much blood pouring from the wound on Xaneth's side.

The sight of more soldiers appearing snagged her attention. Every time she thought they had killed the last of them, there were more. It was as if they multiplied with every death. She'd felt each time she gave a few drops of her magic to the Fae to become Reapers. She couldn't imagine how much Lena had given to create her soldiers. Then again, Lena had known she needed the soldiers to fight this battle. Without them, Lena couldn't have fought against the Reapers herself. Not yet.

Out of the corner of her eye, Erith saw Cathal go down after being hit with magic. Dubhan stood over him until he got back to his feet. Erith waved her hand, ending the lives of five soldiers running toward her. She glanced up in time to see Lena lifting her hand as if she were about to snap. She knew exactly what that meant.

Erith let out a war cry as she thrust the blade of her sword into the ground. The floor cracked with the force of her magic. It began to splinter, cracking slowly at first and then rapidly in two directions as she covered herself and the Reapers in a shield to keep out Lena's magic.

Erith looked at Xaneth, knowing she hadn't been able to include him. She held her breath as Lena snapped.

CHAPTER THIRTY-ONE

Exhaustion wore Aisling down. The heat of the ground continually blistered her feet within seconds of stepping onto the sizzling earth. Her body continued healing, but it was happening slower and slower as she depleted her energy.

Aisling ventured into one building after another, finding nothing new, even after hours and hours of searching. The sun was finally beginning to set. She hadn't paid much attention to it since she was intent on discovering if the city had people or animals that might attack. Her throat was irritated from the sand everywhere, her eyes burned from the intensity of the sunlight, and her stomach clawed at itself with hunger.

She hadn't fully recovered from her stay in Lena's maze. Now, she was here. And alone this time. She tried not to think about what Xaneth or her friends were doing. She did her best not to wonder where the battle was or who might be injured. But she failed on both accounts.

Aisling leaned a shoulder against a wall and briefly closed her eyes. She couldn't remember ever being this tired. She fought to keep her scratchy eyes open and focused when all she wanted to do was lay down and sleep. She pushed away from the wall and took a deep breath. She had a few more hours of searching left. She forced her feet to move, putting one foot in front of the other.

She exited the room and stepped over a broken chair near the doorway. She turned to the left and headed down a wide hallway with peeling paint. The house was enormous, and the rooms numerous, hinting at the past opulence. She wondered who had lived here. Where had they gone? What had driven them away?

Her thoughts halted when she saw a light flicker in one of the rooms up ahead. Aisling was instantly on alert. She crept forward. When she neared where she'd seen the glimmer, she flattened against the wall and slowly moved to peer around the corner. She blinked, thinking that her mind had to be playing tricks. She could only stand and stare at the many candles situated around the dining room, setting the room ablaze with light. Gone was the rubble and trash. In its place was an immaculate room with polished marble floors, soaring ceilings, elaborate stone carvings on the tall columns, and lavish paintings depicting mountains, fields of wildflowers, bright blue skies, and a stunning waterfall.

A table that could easily seat thirty sat in the center of the room. And spread from one end to the other was enough food to feed an army. The aromas made her stomach grumble with hunger. Yet Aisling saw no one about.

She hesitated to go inside. Why did this room look different than the others? Obviously, it was meant to lure her. But… why? Who was responsible? As far as she knew, no one was in the city.

Despite her reluctance, the food drew her. She cautiously crossed the threshold and made her way to the table. She was so ravenous, the smells made her dizzy. It would be so easy to grab something. Just one bite. That was all she needed. But just as her hand hovered over some sliced meat, she paused.

What if the food was a trick of some kind? What if this was how Lena intended to kill her? Aisling snatched her hand back and hurried out of the room and the house. She ignored the burning cobblestones with their dusting of sand as she raced to the next structure. She took her time exploring it. The sun was nearly below the horizon by the time she reached the top floor. Aisling looked out and tried not to despair.

She gazed into the distance at the gate, which seemed farther away than ever. She knew she had covered significant ground. She looked behind her but only saw rows of buildings rising with the columns holding up the doorway in the distance.

Her throat clogged with unshed tears as she leaned against a wall and slowly slid to the floor. She let her legs fall open to rest and heal her feet. The scent of food followed her, causing her stomach to loudly remind her that it needed sustenance. She ignored it and her dry mouth.

The meal was a trick. Why would she eat anything in this place? There was no telling what Lena had done to it. The only food Aisling would eat would be what she got for herself. Though she would need something soon. She was weary, and while sleep would likely help some, she needed nourishment more.

Maybe that was Lena's real deception: that everything in this place was fine, but Aisling was too scared to use magic to find out, thus making her starve to death. When all she had to do was have the guts to use what she had been born with —magic.

Aisling held out her hand, ready to call water and food to her. But she couldn't do it. She'd promised Xaneth that she would stay alive. One wrong move would give Lena what she wanted most of all. And Aisling couldn't do that. She wouldn't. All she had to do was give her friends some time to win the battle and find her.

She dropped her hand and closed her eyes as a tear crested her lid and rolled down her cheek. Within seconds, she was asleep.

Xaneth saw Lena raise her hand. Seemingly in slow motion, he watched her snap her fingers. And all he thought was, *nay*.

He didn't know how, but he knew he wouldn't die. He felt a tug on his magic, a pull on his body—then nothing. When he remained, Lena's eyes widened, and trepidation drained her face of color.

They both looked at Erith and the Reapers at the same time. Xaneth briefly met Death's gaze to find her shielding herself and her people. He swung his head back to Lena as anger contorted her face.

"Not today," he said and jumped the short distance separating them.

He wrapped his hand around her neck and squeezed, but Lena wasn't going down without a fight. Her nails lengthened into talons as she clawed at his arms, face, and chest. Between raking her nails over him, she shoved her repugnant, revolting magic into him. The unrelenting assault was too much. He felt himself weakening, even as he squeezed his fingers tighter, trying to crush her neck.

Lena's red eyes were wild with fear and determination. The sheer amount of hate rolling off her was suffocating, the reek of her evil nauseating. But Xaneth didn't let go. He knew he couldn't. This was why he was here, why he had the monster within him—the one slowly taking over.

Xaneth watched Lena glance at his friends. The instant Erith lowered the shield, Lena would attempt to take their magic. That simply couldn't happen. Xaneth fought against the rising tide of Dark magic, grappled with his waning strength.

And he did the only thing he could think of, he teleported them both away.

~

"Stop!"

Cael lowered his hands and looked askance at Ulrik. "What?"

The Dragon King pointed at the ground. "Did you no' feel it?"

"Feel what?" He didn't have time for this. They needed to get inside the barrier.

Ulrik merely smiled. "Magic, brother. The realm's magic is helping."

Cael jerked his head back to the hole he had opened in the ground to see it expanding as if on its own. The earth parted, and steps appeared, leading down. He could only stare in shock at the sight before him.

"Erith always talks about the balance," Balladyn said from Cael's other side. "I never expected the realm to take a side."

Ulrik chuckled. "Never underestimate the planet."

"Well? What are we waiting for?" Balladyn asked.

Cael glanced at the manor where Erith fought. "Hold on, my love. I'm coming."

He was the first one down the stairs.

"Nothing," Eilish stated in frustration.

They had been using their magic to find Aisling for hours with no results. She blew out a frustrated breath. They had each poured every ounce of magic they had into the locator spell, but nothing they did showed them anything more than the exact area they were in.

Eilish glanced at the silver finger rings on her hand. She could teleport anywhere she wanted, but that did little good when she couldn't find Aisling. She had spelled three items, and even that hadn't worked. Eilish might have miscalculated. Lena was used to dealing with Fae magic, and Eilish had believed a Druid enchantment wouldn't even register for her. But it seemed Eilish might have been wrong.

She sighed and straightened to find Gemma staring across the loch at the island. Eilish frowned at her friend's penetrating gaze. "What is it?"

Esther rubbed her hand over her face and looked from Eilish to Darcy to Gemma. Then she, too, looked at the island. "What do you see, Gem?"

"Each time we search for Aisling, we see this area," Gemma said.

Eilish nodded, biting back words of annoyance at the reminder.

Gemma's head swiveled, and her light blue eyes pinned Eilish. "What if it isn't the area we're meant to see? What if it's the island?"

Eilish blinked and then jerked her head to the tiny isle. "Shit."

"How did we miss that?" Darcy asked.

"They're Fae," Esther said. "There could be Fae doorways we can't see."

"Shara!" Eilish shouted.

Within moments, the Fae stood before them, her expression anxious as she looked between the four of them. "What is it? What's wrong?"

"Do you see anything there?" Gemma asked as she pointed at the island.

Shara turned to follow Gemma's finger. An audible gasp came from the Fae as her silver eyes widened. She shook her head of black hair, the thick, silver stripe near her face the only proof that she had once been Dark. "Aye. There are Fae doorways."

"Bloody hell," Esther murmured.

"Mummy."

Sleep had Aisling firmly in its grasp, holding tightly with a grip that refused to let go. All she wanted to do was slumber for days—weeks, even.

"Mummy!"

"Coming, sweetheart," Aisling murmured as she rubbed her eyes and yawned.

She pushed to her feet and started out of the room, bleary-eyed. Still half-asleep, she stumbled a few times and had to use the wall to right herself. Aisling made her way down the hall and turned into a bedroom.

"What's wrong, my sweet?" she asked, yawning again with her eyes closed.

Silence met her words. Aisling was instantly awake. She spun in a circle, gazing in surprise at the remains of what had once been a bedroom. A broken child's bed sat against a wall, a forgotten doll lying in the middle of the room, stuffing hanging from its midsection. Aisling's heart pounded, and a roar filled her ears. Stark, brutal fear brought her to her knees. But there was also hope.

That emotion choked her and caused her to bend over, giving in to the wail of sadness that erupted. Because she had heard her daughter's voice. It hadn't been a dream. For all of her nightmares, Aisling had heard her daughter's laugh but never her voice. Not once.

Aisling gripped her head and lowered her forehead to the floor as she screamed. The grief she hadn't confronted, the anger she had buried, and the guilt she had never admitted flooded her. It took hold and dragged her under until she had no choice but to feel every one of those emotions that she had locked away to become the Reaper her team needed.

Aisling sobbed uncontrollably as images of her sweet, beautiful daughter played in her mind.

CHAPTER THIRTY-TWO

Xaneth threw Lena away from him and grinned when she hit the wall with such force that it cracked. She fell to the floor, getting her clothes wet and dirty. Her gasp of indignation was music to his ears.

"I wouldn't if I were you," he cautioned when she lifted her hand to form an orb of magic. "Take a look at your surroundings."

The outrage melted from her face, turning to one of disbelief and then alarm. She slid her red gaze back to him in apprehension. "What have you done?"

"I had such fun in your maze that I thought you'd want to experience it firsthand."

Her nostrils flared as she got to her feet. Her neck moved as she swallowed and dusted off her hands on her pants. "It's no matter."

Xaneth laughed at her indifferent words because the

tension in her body and her tight lips said something else entirely.

"You shouldn't find this funny," Lena snapped.

"Oh, I don't," he replied. "Nothing about what you've done to your people is even remotely humorous."

"I can get out of the labyrinth easily."

"You'll have to get past me first."

Lena searched the walls until she found the red arrow near Xaneth, pointing the way past him. Her gaze met his. "Do you honestly think I'd fashion something like this and not create an instance where I could use my magic?"

"Aye. Because you never imagined a scenario where you'd be down here not of your own free will."

Her eyes narrowed, telling him that he was right.

Xaneth spread his arms wide. "Go on. Take your best shot at me." When she did nothing, he dropped his arms to his sides. "This is between you and me. Not your soldiers. Not my friends. You want freedom, you'll have to kill me."

"So, this is what you resort to so I can't use my magic? You know I'm more powerful."

"What I know is that I was created for just this moment. This…*thing* inside me wants your death, and nothing will stop me from achieving that."

Lena came at him before he finished speaking. She moved with whirlwind speed, striking with her nails, and kicking. Xaneth lifted his arms and blocked a swipe of her long claws over his face as he turned to the side and used his leg to prevent her stiletto heel from connecting with his knee.

He spun and elbowed her in the face so hard her head

snapped back, but she struck, equally as fierce, with a jab to his kidneys.

"Where the fek is Xaneth?" Eoghan bellowed as they fought.

Erith sliced off a soldier's head and then turned to knock away another's ball of magic. "They teleported out."

"Where?" Maeve asked.

Erith wished she knew. She hoped Xaneth had been the one to take Lena and not the other way around. She turned to face two soldiers coming at her. Erith dispatched them quickly enough.

Her chest heaved with exertion as she looked at the Reapers. They were the only ones left standing. The air was heavy with ash from the dead, making her cough.

"Well," Bradach said with a grin, "that was easier than expected."

Erith's smile faltered when more soldiers rushed out of the rooms until they were surrounded. There was no time to do anything but fight back. The soldiers pushed into them, crowding their group to limit their movements, but the Fae soon learned that was a mistake. Maeve and Fi teleported to the second floor, where Lena and Xaneth had been. Dubhan and Fintan jumped to the stairs.

Every time a Fae fell, regardless of whether they were Light or Dark, Erith's ire at Lena grew. The thirst for power and control had brought the Fae to this madness. Lena had started the Six, but it was that group of Fae who'd begun the Fae Others and used manipulation and promises to sway the

Fae to their side, killing half to consume their magic and swelling their ranks with the other half.

So many had died—innocent and guilty alike. Erith's heart hurt for what had become of the Fae without the leaders they were accustomed to. The Fae council hadn't taken off as everyone had thought, leaving room for someone like Lena.

Erith wished she were the one fighting Lena. If it were her choice, she would be. But it was Xaneth's path. All Erith could do now was make sure that she gave him the opportunity he needed to end Lena.

Ash exploded in Erith's face as she impaled a soldier on her blade. She turned and dropped to one knee, dodging an orb before using one hand to flip over. She used her legs to swipe the feet out from under the female soldier and sent a blast of magic that killed her instantly.

"Fek me," Cael murmured as he came to the end of the stairs. Before him was a section of earth about five feet wide, holding Lena's barrier in place. Below it, a tunnel opened, encircling the manor where the barricade was.

"Con is going to be so pissed that he missed this," Ulrik said as he came up behind him.

Cael exchanged a look with the Dragon King before they took off in opposite directions. He soon discovered their tunnel wasn't the only one the magic had opened. He heard the other Reapers' voices as he ran. He found them as he came to another opening that led to the manor.

"Cael!" Torin shouted.

Baylon flexed his hands. "Did you do this?"

"The magic of the realm did," Cael explained as he turned down the tunnel and headed toward the manor.

There was no more talk as they ran. Cael didn't know what awaited them, but he had to trust that the magic would get him and the Reapers into the manor to help Erith and the others. The ground shook around them, but Cael never slowed.

"Don't let us down," he whispered to the magic.

He might not be of this realm, but it had been his home for some time. The fact that it had never occurred to him to ask it for help was sobering. But that didn't matter now. Defeating the Fae Others was what mattered.

Just ahead of him, Cael saw a small explosion and light from above. He didn't hesitate to jump up and through the hole. He found himself inside the manor on the first floor. So many soldiers were gathered, there was barely room to move. Cael didn't see Erith or the Reapers, but he knew they were around. Otherwise, the soldiers would be gone.

Cael stalked to the nearest soldier, who had yet to see him. "Hey!" Cael yelled.

The soldier turned, and the battle began.

"We need to get onto the island," Eilish said.

Shara shook her head. "The tree is an illusion. With so many doorways on that tiny piece of land, you could walk through a doorway without even knowing it."

"That's why you're here," Gemma said with a grin.

Eilish caught the Fae's eyes. "We need to find Aisling. Our magic has led us back to that isle again and again."

Shara bit her lip and returned her gaze to the isle. "That's probably because she went through one of those doorways."

"Any way we can tell which one?" Esther asked.

Shara shook her head. "No."

Eilish wanted to scream. She didn't need to ask to know that Lena had put Aisling on that island and forced her to pick a doorway. "Why didn't Aisling swim to shore?" she asked, just realizing that.

"Maybe she couldn't." Gemma crossed her arms over her chest. "That sounds like something Lena would do to ensure Aisling's choices were narrowed to what was directly around her."

Darcy wrinkled her nose. "It would also explain why she didn't teleport out and find the Reapers."

"Fuck," Eilish bit out. She squeezed the bridge of her nose with her thumb and forefinger, then dropped her arm to her side and looked at the women around her. "My gut tells me that Aisling is in danger."

Esther walked closer to the water's edge. "I figure we have two choices. We leave and hope Lena is removed from this earth so Xaneth can return here and look for Aisling. Or,"—she paused and looked at the others—"we try to find her ourselves."

"She's alone." Gemma compressed her lips. "I wouldn't want to be alone."

Darcy shrugged as she raised her brows. "Do we go after her then?"

"You have no idea what's through those doorways," Shara said, her voice pitched high in disbelief.

Gemma turned her head to Shara. "She's alone."

"What if you can't use magic? Remember, that was how Lena confined Xaneth and Aisling in the maze," Shara pointed out.

Eilish ground her teeth together. She had forgotten that part. "Then we don't use magic."

"Aisling wouldn't waver if she were here and trying to find one of us. I say we go," Esther said.

Gemma grinned. "I'm ready."

"Fek," Shara said into the silence. "All of you are right. I'm coming."

Eilish shook her head. "We need you to make a note of which doorway we take. You know, in case we don't come back. Then Ulrik will know what happened."

"And tear the fekking universe apart," Shara muttered. She eyed Esther, Darcy, and Gemma. "Same with Nikolai, Warrick, and Cináed."

Esther rubbed her hands together as she stared at the island. "We're Dragon Kings' mates. We live as long as they do."

"That doesn't mean we can't suffer," Darcy added.

Eilish exchanged a look with Shara.

"Stay on the shore," the Fae warned before she and Eilish teleported the others to the tiny piece of land in the middle of the water.

~

It was still dark out when Aisling opened her eyes. She was lying on her side, looking out one of the broken windows. She had never cried herself to sleep before. It was an exhausting, draining experience. She might have felt rested except for that. As it was, her head was stuffy, and her heart heavy with the onslaught of all the emotions.

She pushed up to a sitting position, then got to her feet. Instead of searching the rest of the structure, she made her way outside and onto the street. In the silence, she still heard her daughter's sweet little voice in her mind, which kept the pain constant and achingly horrific.

It was all she could do to keep going. Her explorations of the buildings hadn't given her any clues as to who the people were or where they had gone—or even if anyone was still in the city. The scope of the metropolis hinted that it had been a thriving community at one time. There had to be a reason everyone had abandoned it.

She took advantage of the night and the street's cooler stones to walk. Her target was the wall to leave. She didn't want to spend any more time here than necessary. Something about the city felt *wrong*. It was odd that she hadn't sensed anything amiss upon first entering. It was only after she had fallen asleep and heard her daughter's voice that she began to sense that something wasn't quite right.

Maybe it wasn't the city. Perhaps she was the one who was *wrong*. Everything Aisling touched went awry eventually. Things started off well enough, but with plenty of time, things usually went sideways. All she had to do was look at her life for justification.

She'd had a supportive, loving family. She'd had a place in

the Light Army. She'd had friends. She had given all of that up for what she'd thought was love. Aisling snorted. That hadn't been love. It had been about control. *Him* controlling *her*. And she had been too weak to notice the small changes, turning her into someone she didn't recognize.

But even that relationship had begun to deteriorate. She'd become everything he professed to want, yet he hadn't been satisfied. Then, she'd gotten pregnant. Her daughter was the brightest light of her life. That wee bairn's birth had shown Aisling just how far she had sunk and how miserable she had been. Instead of dealing with it, Aisling had turned her attention to her daughter, giving her all the love Aisling had to offer and more.

As the child grew, Aisling realized she wanted a better life for herself and her child. But she hadn't even been able to do that correctly. A mother should be able to protect her child from danger. Aisling wiped away tears and kept walking. She came to a sudden halt, her head jerking up. Had that been a…voice?

She turned to look back the way she had come and strained to hear. She held her breath listening intently. Then she heard it again. Her name.

"I'm here!" she shouted and started running. "I'm here!"

She ran so fast she tripped and fell, slamming her shoulder into the corner of a building. Aisling righted herself and kept running. She didn't stop until she ran out of breath. She listened for her name again, but she didn't hear anything.

Where were they? Where had they gone? It was so far to the doorway, but if that was where they were, she would go back. Aisling started jogging. She was so focused on putting one foot in front of the other while listening for her name that it took her a while to see the lights flickering from one building to the other, keeping up with her.

She slid to a stop, her breathing loud to her ears. Who was controlling the lights? And what did they want? Aisling forgot about the voices she'd heard and studied the outside of the house. Then she slipped through the narrow space between the door hanging by one hinge and the frame.

CHAPTER THIRTY-THREE

Lena stumbled backward and wiped the blood from the corner of her mouth. Something within Xaneth delighted at the sight of it. He would spill much more before he was finished with her.

"You think you have me at a disadvantage," Lena stated.

Xaneth shrugged as he considered his next move. "I've planned this moment between us for a long time."

"You'd leave your friends to fend for themselves?"

"They came to keep yours entertained while I dealt with you."

Lena's brows rose as she walked to the other side of the corridor. "You talk as if I have a reason to fear you."

"It's a fact I've noted."

She rolled and squared her shoulders, positioning herself in the middle of the hall. "I'm sorry to disappoint you, Xaneth, but I can fight with more than magic. I've been at this a lot longer than you."

But she didn't have his beast inside her, the one gnawing at him to be free so it could unleash its fury upon her. He raked a scathing gaze over her. "I know exactly what you've been doing skulking in the shadows, lying to your family and friends."

"It's taken me a long time to get here, and I'm not going to give up so easily."

"I don't plan on stopping until there's nothing left of you."

"Then there's no more to be said."

Xaneth flexed his fingers. "There never has been."

Lena struck quickly, her fists punching his face and abdomen. He dropped down onto one knee and jabbed his balled fist into her stomach. She grunted, but she didn't go down. Her blows turned to his head.

Xaneth lifted her as he got to his feet. He grabbed her legs and swung her. She shielded her head with her arms as she collided with the wall.

Erith pivoted and flung out her left arm, releasing an orb of magic. The soldiers shifted slightly, giving her a glimpse of a familiar face. "Cael," she whispered at the sight of him.

After that, she spotted the rest of the Reapers and even the Dragon Kings.

Erith redoubled her efforts. Eventually, they would run out of soldiers to fight, but she wasn't sure when that would happen. Lena had been prepared. But so were they.

When she next looked up, Cael had made his way to her. He gave her a smile that made her heart sing. There was no time for words, though, as a fresh wave of soldiers appeared. The room was so thick with ash that it was becoming difficult to see.

Erith swung her sword above her head in a circle. The ash followed the movement, gathering high. Then she lowered her blade and released magic. The windows blew out on the first floor, sucking the ash outside.

"Duck!" Cael bellowed.

Erith didn't hesitate to do as he asked. She spotted the large ball of magic that came flying over her head from behind. Erith turned as she straightened and raised her sword in time to slice another orb in two.

Eilish ignored the waves gently lapping at her boots as the five of them studied the ground. There was no barrier around the island, but there had been. Even she could feel it. That was how strong the magic had been.

"I don't like this," Shara said as she straightened.

Esther had her hands on her hips and shrugged. "None of us does."

"Where are the doorways?" Gemma asked.

Shara gathered pebbles at the water's edge and used them to mark either side of each doorway. Then she returned and pointed to each, naming its color.

"Do the colors mean anything?" Darcy asked.

Shara twisted her lips. "Sometimes, a Fae can color it themselves when they make it. Other times, it creates its own."

"In other words, no," Eilish said.

Shara briefly met her gaze. "Exactly."

"Which one do we try?" Esther asked.

Gemma shrugged a shoulder. "We have a one in eight chance of finding Aisling."

"So, eeny, meeny, miny, moe?" Eilish asked.

Once the children's counting rhyme was done and the door chosen, Eilish, Gemma, Darcy, and Esther made their way toward it.

"I don't like this. We should wait for the others," Shara cautioned.

Eilish knew she was taking a risk, but she had to do this. She was no stranger to danger. And, like Gemma had said, Aisling wouldn't hesitate to come for them if they were the ones in trouble.

"Just tell Ulrik and the others," Eilish told Shara.

"No magic," Shara warned, right as Eilish stepped through the doorway.

It was another fekking feast. Aisling stared at the table of food before turning on her heel and hurrying out. The light continued following her. After two more streets, she went into another home where the light shone and found another table of food.

She hadn't heard her name being called again. She was weak, tired, hungry, and more scared than she had ever been. Her emotions were raw, and she was on edge. Perhaps she could eat, and nothing would happen. Maybe she could do magic and leave whenever she wanted. Or…either one could kill her and give her magic to Lena, tipping the balance more in the Dark's favor.

Aisling covered her face with her hands and fought the scream of frustration bubbling up. The answers were right before her. She knew it, but she couldn't sort them out. She was too tired, her brain too locked on *what-ifs*. Too wrapped up in fear and worry.

Her stomach hurt from hunger. All that delicious food was just steps away. Her mouth watered at the aromas. She stumbled to the table and grabbed a loaf of bread, sinking her teeth into the buttery goodness. She tore off a piece and closed her eyes as she chewed. It was only after she had swallowed that she realized she was still alive. Her fear that the food would kill her had been nothing but her imagination.

Aisling's gaze darted around the table before she rushed from one place to another, grabbing food and stuffing it into her mouth.

The wall next to Cael exploded as Ulrik tossed a soldier through it. There wasn't a wall on the first floor that *wasn't* cracked, smashed, or shattered. Even the floor and stairs bore evidence of the battle. He heard a loud groan before the stairs snapped and broke in half.

Cael caught Erith's gaze. "Enough of this."

"Agreed," she said.

Together, they rapidly cut through the throng around them. The Reapers and Dragon Kings redoubled their efforts. As the last soldier turned to ash in Cael's grip, everyone stood silently, waiting for another wave. Instead, the ominous creaking of the house greeted them.

"I think we finished them," Eoghan said.

Erith turned her head to Cael. "Or Lena called them to her."

"Nay," Balladyn said. "Xaneth would take her somewhere she couldn't use magic."

"The maze," Cael and Erith said in unison.

Rordan frowned. "How do we get there?"

"We don't," Torin said. "No magic can be used, remember?"

Cael reached for Erith and looked at those before him. "There's a way in and out of the labyrinth. We'll find it."

"Xaneth may need us," Erith said. "And if Lena comes out, she'll have us to battle."

The strike snapped Xaneth's head to the side, banging it against the wall. Pain exploded in his skull, skating through his head and face. He barely had time to register that before Lena landed another punch on his cheek. The taste of blood filled his mouth. Xaneth ducked as she swung again. He rammed his shoulder into her stomach and propelled her into the wall. A grunt passed his lips as she elbowed him in the spine.

He dug his fingers into her thighs as he got ready to throw her again. The last one had cracked her skull, if the amount of blood that covered her short hair was any indication. Just as he was about to lift her, Lena raised her knee, connecting with the underside of his chin.

Spots dotted his vision. She grabbed a fistful of his hair and yanked. Hard. He felt the hairs pull from his scalp as she tried to move him away, but he wasn't going anywhere. She kneed him a second time, then a third. His fingers loosened, and she was able to slip free.

Lena put distance between them. He straightened and locked his gaze on her. He hadn't thought she would know how to fight without magic. It didn't matter, though, he had her now. It was only a matter of time before he got in the killing blow.

"So intent on your quarry," she said with a shake of her head.

Her pristine clothes were torn, wet, and stained. Her face was splattered with blood, and it dripped from the gash on the back of her head. She had removed her heels sometime during the fight—or maybe they had come off. Xaneth didn't really know or care.

"I'm not here to converse."

"That's right. You're here to kill," she stated angrily. "It's too bad you aren't thinking this hard about your lover."

At the mention of Aisling, Xaneth heard a growl. Belatedly, he realized it had come from him. "Don't speak of her."

"Why? Is it too difficult to know you'll never see her again?"

"She's alive. I'll find her."

Lena's smile was too cocky, too confident. "Nay. You never will. I've made sure of that."

He took a step toward Lena. "Tell me where Aisling is."

"Let me go."

"Never."

"Then you'll never find her."

Something broke inside of Xaneth. Something deep within him he hadn't known was there. He'd held onto hope that he would locate Aisling when this was all over, but at Lena's words, he realized he'd been clinging to a tiny, thin thread when, deep down, he knew he might never be with her again.

It was that realization which released the last vestiges of control he had on the beast. When it burst forth, Xaneth didn't stop it. Didn't hold back. He didn't only embrace who he was, he greeted the monster with open arms.

CHAPTER THIRTY-FOUR

Aisling rolled onto her back and looked up at the ceiling above her, where shadows danced from the candlelight. Had she fallen asleep? She remembered stuffing herself with food and not much after that.

She looked outside to discover it was still night. Or had she slept through another day? She yawned and contemplated closing her eyes again. Her belly was full, but she was still so tired. Any kind of movement took great effort. She had never felt so lethargic.

"Aisling."

Her eyes snapped open as awareness shot through her. Had she just heard her name? She forced herself to her feet and rushed to the open window. Aisling poked her head outside and listened.

"Aisling."

Yes. She *had* heard her name. She didn't imagine it. And it sounded like Eilish's voice. Aisling started for the door, but as she reached it, she paused and glanced back at the table with all the food. She would remember this place so she could return. She didn't ever want to be without food again.

But what if she couldn't locate the building? What if she got lost? What if she became so hungry again that she couldn't go on? Aisling bit her lip, trying to decide whether to leave the feast. Just as she was about to remain, she remembered that she had never gone hungry before. Because she had magic. All she had to do was return with her friends. And Xaneth. She smiled as she thought of him. How could she have forgotten about him? And to think she had believed herself too broken for anyone. Yet, somehow, she felt…if not whole, at least better. Because of Xaneth. He had a way of looking at her with those stunning silver eyes of his that healed her. And his smile. It was breathtaking.

Aisling forgot about the food and being hungry or tired. She was focused once more, and she knew what she had to do. She walked from the house, eager to get back to Xaneth.

"Eilish! I'm here," she called.

Aisling didn't run this time because she didn't have the energy for it—odd since she had eaten. Her body should've been replenished, but she'd worry about that later. She continued calling for Eilish. Aisling caught her name on the wind a few times, so she knew her friends were here somewhere. The city was huge. They could be anywhere. She just needed to keep looking.

Except it became harder and harder to keep going. She had to lean against the buildings to keep herself upright and catch her breath. She was only thankful for the fact that it was night, so the sun didn't bake the cobblestones and burn her feet.

When it became impossible to keep her eyes open, Aisling paused at the corner and rested her head against the structure. She gripped the stone tightly to stay upright. "Eilish?" she shouted.

Aisling frowned when she thought she heard laughter. But then she didn't have the energy to care. She cracked open an eye and spotted light from inside the building across the street. It was like a beacon. She knew she would find a place to rest and more food. She forgot about everything but getting inside. Aisling pushed off the edifice and walk-stumbled to the house. She tried to step over the threshold, but her toe caught the edge, and she fell instead.

She winced as her knees slammed into the hard stone. Aisling managed to catch herself before her face hit. It would be so easy just to lay down right here. Then she remembered the food. It took her three tries before she got her hands and knees under her. There was a smile on her face as she crawled into the house and followed the tempting aroma of food.

When she found the lighted room and another long table of food, something kept niggling at the back of her mind. She was supposed to remember something. Or was it someone? It was too difficult to recall. It was much simpler to focus on the fare before her and how good it would taste. Aisling let her mind go blank as she pulled herself to her feet. She clutched the table to steady herself and make her choices.

～

"Bloody hell," Gemma grumbled.

Eilish looked around the busy Temple Bar district of Dublin in confusion. "What the actual fuck?"

"It makes sense. Some doorways lead to places like the maze, while others to freedom," Esther said.

Darcy looked behind them, where they had walked from the doorway. "Do we go back through?"

"We have no choice but to return to the island and try a new door. But I'd rather use my finger rings than a Fae doorway," Eilish said as she held out her arm for them to grab.

Gemma nodded. "I completely agree."

As soon as they touched her, Eilish clicked her silver finger rings and teleported them to the island. Thankfully, Shara was still there.

"That was quick," the Fae said.

Esther shrugged. "It was Dublin."

"You didn't look for Aisling?" Shara asked.

Eilish shook her head and eyed the other doorways. "It was pointless. If Aisling had chosen that door, she would be with the Reapers battling Lena, and Ulrik would've alerted me."

"Ah. Good point." Shara glanced at the doors. "One in seven chances now."

Eilish looked between Gemma and Esther. "One of you want to pick this time?"

"Not really," Esther said.

Gemma walked around the stones that designated the doorways. She stopped in front of the doorway opposite the one they had taken. "This one."

"That one, it is." Eilish gave Shara a pointed look.

The Fae nodded somberly. "I know what to do. Just be careful."

"Remember," Esther said as the four of them gathered before the door. "No magic."

Eilish took a deep breath and stepped through the doorway.

"Impossible," Lena said, her voice breaking as she gawked.

Xaneth ignored her words and advanced on her. Instead of meeting him head-on as she had before, she lurched backward, her feet tangling as she kept her hands on the wall as if to hold herself up. Then, she spun and ran.

Xaneth paused, surprised she was fleeing. "You can't run from me, Lena."

He had her scent. There was nowhere she could hide on the realm that he wouldn't find her now. Xaneth followed her, though he didn't run. She was going in the opposite direction of the exit, which meant she had nowhere to go.

Xaneth followed the reek of her wickedness. He found her with her back against a wall, facing and watching him warily. He studied her in confusion. While there had been a trace of fear before, she shook with it now. Why had she run from him now and not before?

"You don't know, do you?" she asked in a shaky voice.

He quirked a brow. "What is it you don't think I know?"

"What you are."

That brought him up short. A part of Xaneth, the old part, the one that had longed for a family and revenge against

Usaeil, yearned to discover what Lena knew. But the new part of Xaneth couldn't care less.

He grinned slowly. "Your time is up. Nothing you do or say will stop what's coming."

"You'll never fit into the Fae world," she said hurriedly. "Not now."

Not now. Those words went through him like sharp needles of ice. Aisling's face filled his mind. He'd known. All along, he'd known the truth. But it was Lena's words that made it real, tangible.

He didn't know what the Dark saw, and it didn't matter. The beast wasn't within him anymore. He *was* the monster. Xaneth couldn't reverse anything now if he wanted. And he didn't want to. Lena had to be stopped. The Fae Others had to be ended, once and for all. He would do that. From the very beginning, he'd recognized that the responsibility fell to him.

Lena blinked, disbelief making her jaw go slack. "You're going to give up everything. Just to kill me?"

"I've always questioned why I wasn't killed with the rest of my family. Now, I know. For this moment."

Lena shook her head. "This isn't possible. It can't be. *You* can't be," she stated, her voice pitched higher as panic took her.

"But I am."

Heat consumed Xaneth. It was unlike anything he'd ever experienced. It didn't hurt, didn't sting. It felt *good*. Right. He'd found his quarry. And he was about to seize what he'd been sent to secure—her life.

"Nay!" Lena screamed and attempted to dash to the side.

Xaneth watched it all in slow motion. He caught her

around the neck as he had when he'd teleported them to the maze. But the fire dancing along his skin caught his attention. Lena flailed wildly to get free, but he held her easily. The flames on his arm moved toward her, seeking. She screamed and clawed at him, but he felt nothing, heard nothing.

The instant the blaze touched her skin, it engulfed her. He perceived her skin burning and the agony on her face, but he was utterly unmoved by it. She had taken countless lives for power, and the fire burned the ill-gotten magic out of her.

Finally, she stopped moving. But she wasn't dead. Xaneth still felt life within her. Her head lolled to the side, and her lids lifted so she could look at him. Her charred lips moved. He could have discerned what she said if he wanted, but he didn't care. He had done his duty.

He contemplated leaving her in the maze for a decade or two in her current condition. That would make him feel better. Yet Xaneth wouldn't. He had to finish things.

"For all your conniving and preparation, you never planned for me," he told her.

Her eyes went wide with fear right before he snapped her neck.

Xaneth didn't move until all that was left of Lena was ash. He released a sigh of relief. A glance down at his body showed that fire still danced along every part of him. It was a beautiful red-orange with occasional green and blue tips. He didn't know how it had started or if it would stop. He loved the feeling of it moving across his skin. It was like the softest caress, tinged with warmth and unimaginable power.

He looked once more at the ash that had once been Lena and turned on his heel. As he made his way through the maze to the exit, his mind locked on the one thing that mattered now —Aisling. Dread filled him. Xaneth started running. The walls passed in a blur, the red arrows mere dots that flashed as he ran. He scaled the wall to the exit with barely a thought, then busted through the door above and launched himself onto the isle.

"Easy, Xaneth."

His head snapped to the side at the male voice to find faces he recognized. It took a moment for the names to register in his mind. Cael, Erith, Eoghan, Balladyn, Rhona, and even Ulrik and three other Dragon Kings. Xaneth shifted his gaze to the eight doorways now. Lena must have added the others. And there was only one reason for that.

"Lena?" Cael asked.

Xaneth ground his teeth together. He was tired of speaking about her. He needed to find Aisling. "Dead."

"Eilish, Gemma, Darcy, and Esther went to find Aisling," Ulrik told him.

Xaneth noted the Dragon King's stony expression for the first time. He was worried about his mate. As he should be. Lena's traps were horrendous.

"That one leads to Dublin," Balladyn said, pointing to the door to Xaneth's left.

Ulrik jerked his chin to the doorway to Xaneth's right. "My mate went through there. So, that's where I'm headed."

"Nay." The word was out of Xaneth's mouth before he knew why. His gaze swung to Erith. "Leave. All of you."

"We're here to help," Death said.

"No one is going to tell me no' to go after my mate," Ulrik stated angrily.

The three Kings behind him nodded in agreement, their expressions daring him to say anything. Xaneth turned to the doorway to Dublin. Tearing down a Fae doorway made by another was notoriously difficult. Xaneth stuck his arm through and fisted his hand. Then he turned his fist upward. There was a loud crack. He yanked back his arm right before the entire door collapsed.

"Fek me," Eoghan murmured. "How is that possible?"

Xaneth glanced toward the door the Druids had used. He turned to it and put his hand on the outside of it. Xaneth felt the magic it took to create the doorway rushing beneath his palms, something that had never happened before. Then again, he was no longer a Fae. The man had become the monster.

Ulrik said something behind him, but Xaneth didn't pay attention. Hopefully, the others would keep the Kings out of his way. Xaneth closed his eyes and let the flames move from him to the doorway. There was a jolt when his fire merged with the magic of the door. It might have felt good except that Lena's lingering stench remained.

Xaneth set his jaw and stepped one foot through. He turned to the side and leaned across the threshold to peer into the other side. He instantly recognized the sound of water dripping and the dark walls of the maze. Movement caught his attention. He turned his head and saw three bodies rushing toward him.

Eilish was the first to get to him. Her smile was shaky as she greeted him. He saw the way her eyes lingered on the flames. Xaneth focused on the fire, willing it to vanish. To his surprise, it listened. Smoke wafted around him while the tips of his fingers glowed like embers.

"We're very happy to see you," Eilish said.

He pulled her back through to the isle, and Esther, Darcy, and Gemma followed. Once they were safe, Xaneth backed out and demolished the door.

Out of the corner of his eye, he saw Ulrik and Eilish embracing. Emotion caught in Xaneth's throat as he thought of Aisling. There wasn't time to think about what she would do when she saw him. He had to find her first. Xaneth made his way to the next doorway when Cael stepped in front of him.

"Move," Xaneth replied, his gaze locked on Cael's purple eyes.

Cael calmly said, "Let us help."

"If you won't allow us to go with you, then let us stay here in case you need something," Eoghan suggested.

Ulrik walked up with Eilish. "We're staying to help."

Xaneth lowered his eyes to the ground before looking at Death.

"Tell us what you need," Erith said.

Gemma hurried forward. "We found Aisling's clothes and boots."

Xaneth frowned at the news, his heart clutching painfully. There was only one reason Lena would take Aisling's clothes —to make her suffer.

CHAPTER THIRTY-FIVE

Xaneth lost hope with each entrance he went through without finding Aisling. He stepped away from the next door as it vanished. That made five destroyed in all. His heart was heavy as he turned to the remaining three. So much time had passed as he searched. He hadn't entered the previous doorways alone, and he had to admit that he was thankful for that.

Even if he hadn't wanted his friends to remain.

There was no way he could've conducted the search that quickly on his own. Still, the search was taking a toll on all of them. One of the last doorways had brought them to Big Ben in London. The other two had been more of Lena's prisons. The first, a desert with an unending sandstorm that would've blinded them to returning had it not been for those who still stood half in the doorway. Xaneth had used a rope around his waist to get back to the door after he'd searched long and hard for Aisling.

The last doorway had led them to the middle of some vast

ocean with an enormous monster with seemingly endless tentacles that tried to yank them down into the dark depths. They had fought their way free without magic, but it had cost them precious time—time that Aisling didn't have.

Xaneth shoved his wet hair from his face and glanced at his friends. They were as winded and exhausted as he was, but he wasn't going to stop until he'd located Aisling. He'd promised he would find her, and he wasn't going back on that. No matter how long it took.

What no one mentioned was what would happen if they couldn't locate her. Xaneth might have demolished the doorways, but he could rebuild them to continue his search if he had to. Just one more fact that he knew without any way of explaining it. He looked to where the doorways had stood. Aisling was smart. She wouldn't have ventured far from a door had she walked into the desert prison or the ocean. And if she had remained near the door, why hadn't she walked back through?

Those questions ran through his mind in a continual loop with only one answer: She wasn't in those places.

Xaneth clung to that thought like a lifeline. He shook the water from his face and turned to the next door. The others got into position behind him. After the argument about who would go through the doors first, no one had tried to take that position from him. He swallowed as he looked at the purple doorway.

Please, let Aisling be there.

He held onto the sides of the entrance and poked his head through to look. The sight that greeted him left him speechless. Night drenched an abandoned metropolis, the crumbling ruins stretching before him as he stood high above it. There was no moon and very few stars in the inky sky, but he didn't need light to spot the mass of wraithlike specters swirling over the city.

They were bluish white in color with a defined upper body that trailed to a billowy gown. He saw their arms and long, spindling fingers. He made out different faces and their long hair, where the ends trailed off into mist. But they moved quick as lightning. At the moment, their focus seemed to be on one location in the city as they funneled toward it, some diving before returning to the sky and doing it all over again.

One of the specters noticed him and came his way, its black eyes bright with excitement. It opened its mouth and let out a deafening scream that called others to it. Xaneth watched the being race toward him eagerly. Then he smelled them. Evil. Pure malevolence. Heat instantly suffused him as flames erupted along his body. The apparition jerked back in terror and quickly floated away. Others followed suit when they caught sight of him.

Xaneth ducked back through the doorway and turned to his friends. "I go in alone."

"What is it?" Eoghan asked.

Xaneth described what he had seen. "They're afraid of me. I have to go alone."

"After what we've experienced so far, I don't think that's wise," Erith said.

He held her gaze. "I think Aisling is there. If these things fear me, they'll stay away. I have to get to her quickly. And before you argue that you could hold your own, remember that Aisling is a Reaper. I have no way of knowing if she's injured. She's far from the doorway."

"Why did she travel so far?" Balladyn asked.

Xaneth thought of that drop. "The doorway is suspended high above the city."

"Surely, she used her magic to get down," Ulrik said.

Erith shook her head. "Not after the maze."

"I know she didn't," Xaneth said and then told them what had happened after he and Aisling had first come to the tiny isle and she wouldn't use her magic.

Cael glanced at the door. "She could be injured."

"Exactly. I have to go for her now," Xaneth stated.

Eoghan held up the rope from before. "If you won't let us come with you, we can stand at the door. Give a couple of hard tugs, and we can pull you and Aisling up."

Xaneth raked a hand through his wet hair to get it out of his eyes. "I'll be back as quickly as I can."

"You have ten minutes before we come after you," Balladyn warned.

Xaneth nodded and faced the doorway. He whispered Aisling's name in his head before stepping through. He teetered on the edge as he attempted to gauge the distance. Then he jumped. The wind whipped around him as he plummeted. He held his arms out at his sides and kept his gaze focused on the ground as it rose to meet him.

He didn't use any magic to slow his descent. Xaneth landed with both knees bent and his hands on the ground. Dust billowed around him from his impact on the cobblestones. He slowly rose and looked upward. He couldn't see the sky clearly for the number of specters above him. He did make out the door and the rope his friends had tossed through that now dangled near him.

Xaneth turned to where the spirits converged and ran toward them. Many of the apparitions dove his way, but they quickly rushed back when they saw him. He tried to grab a couple of them, but they were too far away. He ignored them and wove through the buildings, cutting across roads and racing down narrow alleys.

With every pump of his arms as he ran, came the certainty that time was running out for the woman he loved.

"Aisling!" he shouted as he ran. "Aissssling!"

She squeezed her eyes closed at the sound of Xaneth's voice. This wasn't the first time she'd heard him or the Reapers. But his voice hurt the worst because she had long discovered that no matter how quickly she answered or how fast she ran toward the sound, no one was there. No one had come for her.

Aisling covered her ears and curled into a ball on her side. Thinking about Xaneth, remembering their time together, was too painful. It was better if she forgot him—and her feelings for him. It had been wrong to think that he would be able to find her. There were eight doorways for him to choose from. And that was assuming he hadn't gotten trapped in one. She should be able to get out of this herself. She was a Reaper, after all.

Or she had been.

Had they forgotten her? Replaced her? She had left them to search for Xaneth. Her team, her family. How could she have so easily walked away from them like that? She squeezed her eyes closed tightly and tried not to think about how much it hurt that she hadn't been there to witness the Christmas season with them. She had heard all about it, and she had sworn to be there for the next holiday. She wouldn't, though. Because she was never getting out of this place.

Should she attempt magic to get to the doorway? Did she dare such a thing? Surely, enough time had passed for the battle. She inwardly winced, thinking about not being there for her family. Again. The one thing she was sure of was that Xaneth could and would defeat Lena. Aisling wished she was there to fight alongside him. She could only imagine the battle would be epic. Lena would likely try all kinds of things, but nothing would work against Xaneth. That brought a smile to her lips.

It made her think about the monster Xaneth had spoken about that was inside him. She suspected it would help him take Lena out. No doubt the Reapers were alongside him, as well, and had witnessed everything. Even though Aisling had known using herself as bait would keep her from her family, she didn't regret the decision. She might not be standing with them on the battlefield, but she had contributed in her way.

If the battle were over, perhaps they thought her dead. She felt halfway there. Hopefully, Lena *was* already dead. If so, then any magic the Dark used should have faded by now. That meant Aisling could use magic without fear of Lena stealing from her. She could teleport to the doorway and walk through it.

Though there was the hound to deal with on the isle. No,

she was better off where she was. Besides, it would take too much energy to teleport to the doorway.

Trepidation and panic rode Xaneth hard as he raced toward Aisling. He ran faster than he ever had, the buildings nothing but a blur. He kept his gaze on the specters as they congregated above a structure, taking turns diving toward it. If they were harming Aisling, he would torch every one of them.

Xaneth turned a corner and saw the building ahead on his left. He pumped his legs as fast as he could until he reached it, sliding to a halt before the broken door. Shrieks of outrage sounded as the spirits wailed at his arrival before skittering away. He ignored them and rushed into the house, his heart thudding wildly against his ribs.

He hastily looked from room to room until he found Aisling curled on the floor. Xaneth's breath left him, the air sucked from his lungs with such force that he had to grab the wall to stay on his feet. She wasn't moving.

"Nay," he whispered as if he could change the truth with a word.

When he saw an apparition come through the ceiling and sweep along Aisling with its enormous mouth open, an unspeakable rage consumed him. He released a bellow and dove for the specter. He caught it before it could get away.

The way it screamed and thrashed against his hand around its throat did little to appease him. The fire along his arm shot forward instantly. With one lick of the flames, the

spirit released one more fear-filled screech before the blaze
devoured it.

Xaneth dropped down next to Aisling. He started to reach
for her when he saw the fire on his skin. He had killed Lena
and the specters with it. He couldn't chance harming Aisling.
A glance at the apparitions showed they watched him intently.

Xaneth extinguished the flames. With smoke still wafting
from him, he tenderly moved the hair from her face that had
come free of her braid. His heart broke when he saw her
hands covering her ears.

"Aisling. Please, love, open your eyes and look at me," he
begged.

He anxiously waited for her to do something. The cold
hand of fear painfully gripped his chest when nothing
happened. Xaneth gently lowered her arm and rolled her onto
her back. Yet she still didn't open her eyes. He needed to get
her out of here. Now. But as soon as he gathered her into his
arms, the specters flew at him in a rage.

Xaneth lowered Aisling to the floor and put his hands on
either side of her head as he used his entire body as a shield.
The spirits came at him, one after another, their teeth scraping
against him and trying to reach something deep inside him.
He bellowed and let the flames on his back roar higher. The
specters screeched in fury and pain as they died painfully.

They might fear him, but they were willing to sacrifice
themselves to prevent him from taking Aisling. And they were
prepared to die to stop him.

CHAPTER THIRTY-SIX

"This is taking too long," Cael muttered.

Erith watched the rope, even though Balladyn had it in his grip.

"We should've gone with him," Eoghan said.

Ulrik shrugged. "We still can."

"Nay," Erith said. "He has to do this."

Cael's purple eyes met hers. "And if he needs help?"

"He'll let us know," Balladyn replied in a soft voice, his eyes locked on the doorway.

Eoghan grunted. "He damn well better."

Erith silently agreed. She had lost Xaneth once. She wouldn't allow that to happen a second time. Nor would she lose Aisling.

"Come on," she whispered, urging Xaneth to hurry.

Xaneth let out a bellow as he rose to his knees. Flames shot out from him in a circle and stretched to the ceiling and out the windows toward the apparitions. The blaze ate at the long table and the remnants of food.

It engulfed everything it touched.

Everything except for Aisling because he didn't allow them near her.

When the room went silent, Xaneth fell forward on his hands, spent. He looked down at Aisling. To his shock, her eyes were open. "Aisling?"

A ghost of a smile played on her lips. "I wish you were real."

"I am. I'm here," he told her.

Her eyes closed as if she hadn't heard him. She was deathly pale, her heart beating too slowly for his comfort.

Xaneth snuffed the flames once more and gave her a little shake. "Wake up, *mo grá*, my love. We're supposed to have that long talk, remember? I'm here as promised."

But there was no reply. A painful knot formed in his stomach. Xaneth knew the trip back to the doorway would be difficult, but he didn't care. He gathered Aisling in his arms and climbed to his feet.

After walking to the structure's entrance, he paused and glanced outside. Specters swirled frantically above him, screeching in anger. He wanted to teleport to the doorway. There was a chance he could, and neither he nor Aisling would be harmed. But he couldn't risk it.

Xaneth held her tightly and started running. Almost instantly, the spirits dove toward him, trying to avoid him but get to Aisling at the same time. The doorway loomed above the city like a beacon. Xaneth kept his gaze on it as he ran faster and faster, but he couldn't outrun the spirits.

He wondered how many times Aisling had looked up at the doorway. Had she fallen from it? Had she been injured? Had she used magic? He glanced at her dirty feet and clothes, and that gave him the answer about magic. He couldn't imagine what she had suffered. What had been a mere few hours for him could've been days, months, or even years to her.

He'd kept his promise, though. And he would get her home.

Xaneth didn't see the apparitions clinging to the rope until he drew close to the columns holding the doorway. They were actively trying to tear it apart. He didn't think they could, but did he really want to take that chance?

"Fek," he growled angrily. "You think you can stop me from taking her? Think again."

The spirits congregated around the doorway. As if that would thwart him from reaching it. But it did prevent him from calling to his friends. He had seen what the specters had done to Aisling, felt what they tried to do to him, and he didn't want the others falling into that.

Xaneth looked at Aisling. Her cheek was pressed against his shoulder, but her chest wasn't moving. "Nay. Not again," he murmured.

But even as he said the words, his magic built to a fevered state in an instant. It pressed against his skin from within. As it pushed to break free, flames erupted over him. He could only stare in shock as the blaze came close to Aisling but never touched her.

Xaneth heard the specters and looked up. He saw a mass of them diving for him. The magic within him tightened, intensified. He could feel himself losing control. The flames came dangerously close to Aisling. He dropped to his knees and lowered her to the ground.

The magic was so thick he couldn't breathe. It waited to burst from him. He gasped for air, struggling to pull it into his lungs, when his arms flew out to his sides, and his back arched as he flung his head back and released both the magic and the fire.

It poured out of him, annihilating everything in its path. The flames shot into the sky and stretched out like fingers, brushing against all the specters, their screams soon silenced forever. The magic was out of him, the flames doused. Xaneth hunched over Aisling, nervously waiting for her to open her eyes. She'd said he'd brought her back before. Had he done it again? As the seconds passed with nothing, his throat clogged with emotion.

"Nay," he said and gathered her into his arms.

He rocked her against him, unable to accept that she was gone. Why couldn't he have reached her sooner? Why hadn't he chosen this door first? So many *whys*.

Xaneth stilled when he felt a brush of air against his neck. He pulled back and put his finger beneath her nose, feeling her breath. His relief at finding her alive soon faded when she still wouldn't open her eyes. That was when he realized it might be the place that kept her like this.

He lifted her into his arms and teleported to the platform. As soon as he stepped through to Earth, he handed Aisling to Cael and destroyed the three remaining doorways. Only then did Xaneth turn to find that everyone had surrounded Aisling as they tried to wake her.

He stood back, apart from them—as he'd always been.

As he always would be.

Xaneth glanced at the smoke wafting up from his skin. His hands clenched. He missed Aisling already. He hadn't wanted to release her, but the overwhelming need to destroy the doorways couldn't be ignored. Because even with Lena gone, he couldn't chance anything getting through to their realm.

"She's barely hanging on," Erith said.

Balladyn caught Xaneth's attention. "What happened to her?"

"Specters were feeding off her," Xaneth told them.

Cael replied, "We need to get her out of here."

"I-I tried to bring her back," he explained.

"She needs time to heal," Eoghan told Erith.

Ulrik stepped forward. "Dreagan?"

"Nay," Erith said. "She needs my realm."

Then, they were gone. Xaneth's heart lurched in his chest, his knees threatening to buckle. He fought against the rising tide of panic to accept that the woman he loved beyond reason, the one who had faced the beast and accepted him, was out of his reach once more.

Possibly forever.

"—nth?"

He blinked and focused on Balladyn who stood before him. The Reaper had spoken, but Xaneth couldn't hear the words, could only see his lips moving. Xaneth slid his gaze to the place he'd last seen Aisling. Sound rushed back so quickly that Xaneth winced.

"I'll take you to Aisling. Come on," Balladyn urged.

But Xaneth couldn't. What was it Lena had said? That he would never fit in with the Fae? He knew he was no longer a Fae, and he wasn't a Reaper. Only Reapers were allowed on Death's Realm.

Ulrik walked up, his dark brows drawn together as he studied Xaneth. He wanted to ask the Dragon King what he saw, but Xaneth thought better of it. Whatever he was now had terrified Lena.

"You did it, brother. You found Aisling and brought her back. You should be rejoicing," Ulrik said.

"She should never have been there to begin with." The truth of those words was a punch to Xaneth's gut. "I should've gone to Lena on my own. None of you should've been involved."

Balladyn shook his head. "Don't do that. We all made the decision to fight. Especially Aisling. Don't take that from her. She's a warrior. A Reaper. She knew the risks."

"Exactly!" Xaneth shouted, his anger growing with each beat of his heart. "I did, too. I knew what Lena wanted. I knew that she would do everything she could to hurt Aisling."

Ulrik's lips twisted as he crossed his arms over his chest. "We're still standing. *Aisling* is still alive. Lena isna. Focus on that."

"Focus on the fact that..." Xaneth paused, swallowing hard as the words lodged in his throat. "That Aisling is near death? That I almost didn't reach her in time?"

Balladyn flattened his lips. "Aisling is one of the strongest people I know. She's alive because of you. She'll pull through whatever this is."

Xaneth knew Balladyn was right, but that didn't allow the anxious feelings to lessen even an iota.

"Let Balladyn take you to Aisling," Ulrik urged. "Stay with her. She's going to need you."

Balladyn nodded. "Aye."

Xaneth looked around. There was no evidence that Lena had ever been on the island. He had wiped it all away. If only he could do the same with the thoughts and memories running through his mind.

He looked from Ulrik to Balladyn. He felt heat and saw the flames dancing along his skin. "What am I?"

"We'll figure it out," Balladyn replied.

Xaneth lifted his hands. They had held Aisling, had known the sounds of her sighs, the cries of her pleasure. But that had been before he'd turned into…this. Even then, he'd known he wasn't like anyone else. Only he'd never thought he would become whatever he was. "I'm not a Fae."

"You're Fae," Ulrik said.

Xaneth dropped his arms to his sides and looked into the Dragon King's gold eyes. "I'm not. Everything is different."

"It doesn't matter. We'll sort it out. You're part of our family," Balladyn replied.

How could Xaneth remain with them if he wasn't sure what he was? What if he turned on them? What if he tried to kill them? What if he lost himself completely? He wasn't the same. That was the only certainty he had. These people were his allies. He'd had acquaintances, but this was the first time he'd felt as if he could call anyone a friend.

Then there was Aisling.

His heart hurt, longing to be with her, to hold her once

more. To pretend that he wasn't a beast. He wanted to be there when she opened her eyes.

He wanted them to have the conversation they'd spoken about.

He wanted to tell her how much he loved her. Needed her.

He wanted the future with her he hadn't dared to dream about.

He wanted it all. But he was reaching beyond his limits. He had always reached too far. First, thinking he could trick his aunt. Then trying to kill Usaeil.

And now daring to dream of a life with Aisling.

She was a Reaper. She had done too much for him already. He didn't know why Erith had allowed Aisling to find him, or why Erith hadn't called her back to the Reapers. Xaneth should never have gotten the time he had with Aisling, but he would treasure every second of it.

"I know that look. Doona be stupid," Ulrik said.

Xaneth glanced at the Dragon King. How could he explain everything that churned within him? All the emotions, questions, and uncertainty. The fear. He could hardly think about them, much less find words that would make any sense to someone else.

Balladyn grabbed his arm. Xaneth looked down at his friend's hand and saw the flames licking at his skin. When Xaneth raised his gaze, Balladyn's red eyes were piercing as they held his. "Aisling helped you accept the other side of you. She's the reason you're standing here now."

"Aye."

"Then don't walk away from that. Don't walk away from *her*."

Ulrik nodded as he dropped his arms to his sides. "Trust me, brother. I tried that with Eilish. It was excruciating."

"I need answers," Xaneth replied. "Ones neither of you can give me."

Balladyn's nostrils flared. "You're not giving us time."

Time. It was something Xaneth had railed at for many years. He had lived while his family hadn't. He had plotted so many ideas to kill Usaeil and avenge his family, but he'd never carried them out because the time hadn't been right. Then, his chances were taken from him when Usaeil captured him and locked him in his mind, where time seemed to stretch forever.

Xaneth inwardly grimaced when he recalled how he'd believed he was still locked in that nightmare and that everything with Aisling had been another trick by his aunt. Now, he knew that he'd let doubt control him and had wasted time with Aisling. He thought of the hours she'd spent in that city, clinging to life and waiting to be found, while he fought against the clock, going through other doorways in search of her.

Fae didn't worry about time. They had plenty of it. For Xaneth, he'd had too much when he didn't need it, and not enough when he required it. Like now.

He pulled his arm from Balladyn's grip. "When we first met, I knew you were honorable. You were the best king the Dark ever had."

"You wouldn't say that if you knew what kind of Dark I'd been. The fact that I was Dark at all should tell you all you need to know," Balladyn replied.

Xaneth thought about Aisling and her path as a Fae.

"Light or Dark, I saw you. We didn't get to go after Usaeil as we hoped, but you were someone I knew I could trust."

"This sounds like goodbye," Balladyn said, his brow furrowing.

"Because it is." Xaneth turned to Ulrik. "Thank you."

Ulrik bowed his head, his expression resigned. "It's what we do for friends. You're welcome on Dreagan anytime."

"Xaneth, please," Balladyn pleaded.

But Xaneth teleported away.

CHAPTER THIRTY-SEVEN

Death's Realm

Cael looked around Balladyn's shoulder to the doorway behind him. "Where's Xaneth?"

"He's not coming."

"Not coming?" Cael glanced behind him to the white tower he and Erith called home. "Fek."

Balladyn nodded solemnly. "He needs time."

"He should be here with Aisling."

"Aye, but we can't force him."

Cael wanted to do just that. "After everything he went through to find Aisling, I don't understand how he can ignore her."

"He's not." Balladyn scratched his jaw and sighed. "It bothers him that he doesn't know what he is. What's obvious is his love for Aisling."

"Will it be obvious to her, though? I know I wouldn't want to be him when she wakes and finds he's not here."

"How is she doing?"

Cael ran a hand down his face. "I don't know. Erith is beside herself with worry. She's second-guessing bringing Aisling here."

"Where else would Erith have brought her?"

"I think what's bothering Erith is that we took Aisling from Xaneth and left without talking to him."

Balladyn pressed his lips together. "He did seem lost without her."

"Bloody hell."

"You had good intentions. Xaneth knows that."

"I hope so." Cael turned to face the tower. His gaze landed on one of the upper windows to the chamber where Erith tended to Aisling. "Should we look for him?"

Balladyn clapped Cael on the shoulder. "I will."

Cael's head swung to him. "Do you think anything in your extensive library could tell us what Xaneth has become?"

"Already ahead of you on that."

After Balladyn left, Cael made his way through the flower garden to the tower. When he entered the chamber, Erith sat on the edge of the bed, holding Aisling's hand. Erith glanced at him, hope in her eyes. Cael shook his head. Her face fell as she turned back to Aisling.

"Balladyn said he needs time," Cael told her.

Erith gently released Aisling's hand and moved to the chair next to the bed. "We shouldn't have left without him."

"We weren't leaving him out."

Her lavender eyes met his. "We didn't exactly include him either, did we?"

"He knows he's welcome here."

"I'm not sure he does."

Cael walked to the side of the chair and rested his hand on her shoulder. "Balladyn is going to search his library to see if he can find anything that can tell us what Xaneth is."

"In my very long life, I've never seen anything like it."

He squeezed her shoulder. She reached up and took his hand in hers. They sat in silence for a time, each lost in their thoughts.

Erith shook her head slightly. "I feared we'd lose someone in this battle. We had injuries, but nothing serious. Because Xaneth took Lena away to fight her. Then, after all of that, he searched for Aisling."

"He wasn't alone in that."

She snorted. "He only suffered us because he knew we wouldn't leave. I don't know what happened in that place he found Aisling. The look on his face when he returned…"

"Aye," Cael said, recalling the determination and resolve in Xaneth's expression. It had made all of them take a step back.

"He should be with her. They're meant to be together."

"They will be."

Erith looked up at him, doubt lining her face. "Will they? I have a bad feeling that I made a mistake coming here without Xaneth."

"He needs time, remember?"

"Maybe I shouldn't have agreed to let Aisling be the bait for Lena."

Cael tightened his fingers on hers. "Aisling knew what she

was doing. So did you. You know her better than any of us. Her abilities caught your attention, and you watched her for years."

Erith leaned her head against the chair. "Everyone has a breaking point, my love. Even me."

"Aisling is still alive. Don't give up on her yet."

"Then why isn't she healing?"

Cael wished he had that answer.

"We all stuck our heads through the door after Xaneth. You and I are the only ones who saw the specters besides him."

Cael frowned as he squatted next to her so he could see her face. "You think he's a god?"

"What I know is that he's powerful enough to take on Lena by himself."

"You could've."

"Possibly. But her power had grown immensely. Besides," she said with a grin, "you wouldn't have let me fight her alone."

Cael cut her a look. "Nay, I wouldn't have."

"And she would've used you against me. Xaneth knew that from the beginning. It was why he kept saying that he had to do it alone. He didn't hesitate to battle her himself. There was a time I wouldn't have either. Now, however, I know the strength of having you and the Reapers at my side."

"That doesn't make you weak, sweetheart. Neither does it make Xaneth strong because he fought alone. You know the benefits of battling with your family."

"And he knew the danger that put everyone in. Which is why he separated himself from us," Erith replied. "Xaneth thinks he doesn't have anyone. And that isn't true. He has us. *All* of us."

"If he wants us."

Erith looked at Aisling. "He wants her. That will lead him back to us."

Cael hoped she was right.

If Xaneth thought Lena's death would end the Fae Others, he was wrong. He focused on hunting each of them down. Some, he gave a choice to forget the organization or die. Others drenched in evil were eradicated immediately.

He didn't stop, barely rested, and never slept. Each time he closed his eyes, he saw Aisling lying on that dirty floor, unmoving as the spirits dove at her, taking who knew what. Her soul? Her essence?

Xaneth crouched on the roof of a building in Cork as rain fell hard, coming down in sheets. He blinked the water from his lashes and searched the night for his target. He'd known the Fae Others had built up a sizable group, but he hadn't recognized the full scope of it until now. Word spread quickly that Lena was gone and the Six were no more.

Every time he thought he'd stamped out the worst of the evil, more sprang up. Any hint of power up for grabs brought the worst out of the woodwork. But he was making headway in dealing with it. Though he had to admit, he was surprised that he hadn't seen the Reapers.

His heart clenched agonizingly as his thoughts drifted to Aisling. He'd half-hoped she would come looking for him again. Then he was grateful that she hadn't. He still didn't know what he was or if he was a danger to her—or anyone. Maybe he'd spent his life alone because that was what he was meant to do—for however long he remained alive.

The only way he got through each day was by sinking into his memories of Aisling. He'd had the chance for so much more time with her. If only he hadn't kept pushing her away at the beginning. They could've had weeks. Instead, they'd only had days. But that time was more precious to him than anything else.

Xaneth turned his head to the right as the smell of evil greeted him. He caught sight of his quarry. The Dark and her three female associates sought to create another group of Six to re-form the organization. Xaneth hadn't nearly lost Aisling and become what he was now to sit back and let history repeat itself.

He straightened and trailed the group around the side of a building to the back. Xaneth dropped down in front of the lead female. She was much taller than her companions, nearly his height. Her red eyes blazed with displeasure.

"You'd do well to leave, Light," she stated with a cruel smile. "You have no idea who you're messing with."

A rush of heat flashed through Xaneth before the flames erupted over him. "Your time is up, Dark." He looked at her three friends. "All of you."

"What the fek are you?" one of them asked.

Xaneth smiled. "Vengeance."

He held the leader's gaze, waiting for them to make the first move. That was what he did now. He didn't attack first, he let them come at him, and *then* he unleashed everything he had on them. It gave him a small measure of satisfaction when he saw their fear right before they died.

The leader glanced to the right. The Dark beside her rushed Xaneth, delivering what she, no doubt, thought was a volatile attack. He knocked aside the orbs and took her life by turning one of her balls of magic on her. The leader's eyes narrowed on him. She yelled, and then she and the remaining two attacked at once.

It was over quickly. Too quickly. The rain turned the ash into nothing. Xaneth banked his flames and teleported to the roof once more. He gazed over the wet city and waited. He no longer experienced the blinding headaches, nor did he pass out. He had more strength and power than ever before.

He felt it running through him at all times, but especially when he called to the flames. That was something he could control now. Though not completely. Sometimes, when he was near any evil—even humans—the fire began on its own. But he was working on it.

The drone of the rain soothed him. Despite the torrential precipitation, people were still out and about. Most were Fae, but he spotted some humans in the mix. They were tourists, eager to see everything despite the weather.

He raked his hair away from his face and teleported to Waterford. He would search the city for any Fae Others before moving on to the next. He did it every day. Mostly, he stayed in Ireland, but the scent of evil had led him to England and even Scotland a few times. Still, he was always drawn back to Ireland.

The days ran together. He didn't know how long it had been since he'd carried Aisling through the doorway. It felt like an eternity. He had thought to call for Erith or Cael several times so they could take him to Aisling. Then he remembered who and what he was when next he tracked a Fae Other.

It wasn't that he didn't think Aisling would accept him. He knew she would. That was what kept him from going to her. Because he didn't know his limits. He didn't know yet what he was capable of. Or if he would completely lose himself to the beast within.

And if he were the cause of anything that may happen to Aisling, he'd never forgive himself.

Xaneth spent the remainder of the night moving from city to city. As dawn broke, he found himself standing on a familiar cliff, looking out over the Atlantic. He watched the orange ball of light crest the horizon and give off a dazzling start to the day as the sky turned shades of deep red, vibrant orange, and stunning yellow.

It was a sunrise to be shared. The ache in his heart doubled as he wished Aisling were with him. Unable to look any longer, Xaneth stepped off the cliff and dropped to the rock-lined shore below. He bent his legs as he landed. A wave rolled in and covered him from the knees down, but he didn't notice.

He turned and looked at the arched entrance to the cave. He stood there for several minutes before slowly making his way to it. Xaneth paused at the entry, remembering the fire, the blankets, but most of all, Aisling in his arms.

There was a reason he hadn't returned here. And he regretted doing it now. The memories were too strong. The longing too raw.

"Aisling," he murmured as he dropped to his knees.

CHAPTER THIRTY-EIGHT

Aisling opened her eyes to sunlight filtering through a sheer white curtain, billowing in the breeze from the open window. A chirp caught her attention, and she lowered her eyes to a tiny yellow bird on the sill. It tilted its head to the side and regarded her, chirping again. Suddenly, the bird ruffled its feathers, gave her one last look, and flew away.

She looked at the ceiling and noticed that she was in a comfortable bed. The more she looked around, the more familiar things seemed. Then it hit her, she was in Erith's tower. Aisling sat and stretched. Almost immediately, memories of a ruined city and merciless heat filled her, along with a ravenous hunger and exhaustion she wished she could forget.

Aisling shoved aside the covers and rose from the bed. The scent of flowers on the wind drew her to the window. She spotted Erith's lush garden among the trees, and beyond and to the side, she saw the lake and mountains. They had found her. She had no memory of it, or who had come for her. Had it been Xaneth?

She glanced down at herself and found that she was clothed in a black tank and sleep shorts. How long had she been here? It didn't matter how hard she searched her memories, she had no recollection of departing the city and coming to the tower. She felt fine. Normal, even. Which was a far cry from how she'd been at the ruins.

Her thoughts returned to Xaneth. Surely, if he had come for her, she would've remembered. She turned back to the room and spotted the chair near her bed. It hurt to find that Xaneth didn't occupy it. Then, she chastised herself for such thoughts. It was as if she were in danger here. Maybe he was exploring the tower or the realm. He was on Death's Realm. He had to be. Because to think anything else meant he either didn't want to be with her, or…

"You're awake."

Aisling jerked at the voice and swung her gaze to the door to find Erith.

Death wore a big smile as she hurried to Aisling and took her hands. "We've been so worried. How are you feeling?"

"Fine. I think."

"Cael!" Erith shouted as she glanced through the door. Then she returned her attention to Aisling. Her smile slipped a little. "What do you remember?"

Aisling swallowed, trying to find the words as Cael appeared in the doorway. He grinned at her and came to stand next to Erith. The two shared an excited look, their joy obvious. If there had been any doubts about her being a part of a family, they were dispelled immediately.

Yet it was how the two regarded her so expectantly that made Aisling want to back up a step. Only she couldn't because the window was behind her. Aisling tried to connect where she had been to where she was now—and the space between that she couldn't remember. Worse, was the longing she felt for Xaneth. The longer she went without seeing him, the more her concern grew.

Was he…dead? Had Lena…? Aisling couldn't finish the thought. She gripped the sill behind her and fought to keep her breathing even, when all she wanted to do was curl into herself and demand answers. But first, she needed to get her emotions in check.

"I need a moment," she said when she finally found her voice.

Erith eyed her for a moment, the goddess's lavender gaze missing nothing. "Of course. We'll be downstairs."

Aisling remained where she was until the couple had left, Cael closing the door behind them. Once she was alone, Aisling sat on the edge of the bed and shoved her hands into her tresses, holding her head as her hair draped on either side of her face. She cleared her mind and focused on her breathing, inhaling deeply and then slowly releasing it to keep from hyperventilating.

She stared at the thick fibers of the pale blue rug beneath her bare feet. She could still remember how her soles had blistered on the cobblestones of the city, how her stomach had cramped from the hunger. Or had it all been a dream? No. She recalled her conversation with Lena and the hound's howl. Aisling had also chosen a doorway.

It had all been very real. And she had survived it,

somehow. She wanted answers. But to get them, she had to venture downstairs and talk, when all she wanted to do was go in search of Xaneth. Because he would be here.

"If he could be," she whispered.

She sat as her gut churned with dread. Thoughts of his demise took hold of her once more. She struggled to draw air into her constricted lungs as different scenarios ran through her head, each worse than the last, until she was drowning in them.

Aisling surged to her feet and paced as she fought to get herself under control. She couldn't—wouldn't—go down like this. *If* something had happened to Xaneth, she wouldn't hold in the emotions like before. She would go somewhere private. But she wouldn't know anything if she didn't leave the room.

With that realization, she halted. She called her clothes and boots to her and shoved her hair into a messy bun at the base of her neck. One more deep breath had her shoving aside her fears and containing them for the moment. Then she walked from the room and down the stairs that spiraled along the tower's interior.

True to their word, Erith and Cael were on the main floor in the right front room they used for several purposes. Today, it was more of a salon. They weren't the only ones there, however. Eoghan and the rest of her team, along with their mates, were present. As soon as she entered the room, each of them enveloped her in a hug. Though she considered them family, hugging wasn't something they did regularly. But it felt damn good. She hadn't realized how much she needed the embraces until then.

She fought back the tears that burned her throat, nose, and

eyes. Good tears. Because she was loved and accepted completely. Regardless of her past, in spite of everything. She had called them her family, but in the back of her mind, she had always feared they didn't feel the same. She knew now that those doubts had been created by her insecurities and nothing more.

"We were so worried," Maeve said as she stepped back and released her.

Everyone started talking at once, each asking something different. Aisling looked from one to the other, trying to find a moment to answer. That was when she noticed Balladyn standing off to the side with Rhona, the Druid he had fallen in love with. Something in Balladyn's eyes caught her attention.

"Enough!" Erith shouted with a laugh. "Give Aisling time to answer. As you can see, she's hale and hearty."

Was she, though? Aisling wasn't so sure since half her heart was missing.

Xaneth.

Her eyes burned with more tears, these for the man she loved. The man she had thought to find here. Where was he?

"It's been over a month since we found you. And worry doesn't begin to describe what we went through," Bradach said.

Her stomach flipped. "A *month?*"

"A little over," Rordan confirmed with a nod.

Aisling felt another panic attack about to set in. She took in long, deep breaths to stave it off. Even though she knew Xaneth wasn't there, she still looked for him, sought him to steady her and give her answers. Hold her.

It took her a minute to realize the room had gone silent.

She looked up to find everyone staring at her with a mixture of expressions—sadness, distress, ire, and guilt. Had someone asked her a question? She shifted her feet, not liking the way they studied her as if everyone were waiting for her to break down. Truth be told, she was on the verge. She *needed* answers.

"What do you remember?"

Eoghan. Of course, he would be the one to speak now. She looked into his swirling, molten silver eyes as he studied her. She trusted him completely. He was her leader, her friend. A brother. He, like all the others, saw that she was teetering and on the verge of falling apart, but made sure she didn't.

Aisling didn't have to think too hard about his question. The memories of the city were there, waiting to assault her with every breath. She'd begun to fear it would always be like that. She swallowed. "Heat unlike anything I've ever encountered. Silence so deafening that it was unnatural. The sun was so bright I could barely see if I wasn't in the shade. And no matter how far I went, I couldn't reach the city wall."

She glanced at her feet, which were long since healed, but she'd never forget the burns she'd endured from walking on the hot stones. "Because of the maze, I was terrified to use magic. I nearly fell when I first went through the door, but I managed to grab hold of the platform for a time. Eventually, I lost my grip and dropped, but my injuries weren't severe, and I healed. After that, I did my best to stay in the shade so my feet didn't burn as I explored buildings, looking for signs of life. Then came the hunger. And after…the exhaustion. I couldn't keep my eyes open."

Aisling put a hand on her stomach because she could still feel it clawing at her. As a Fae, she had never known the likes of it. As long as a Fae had magic, they never went hungry. "I didn't want Lena to get my magic, so I couldn't chance using it. Just in case. Food suddenly appeared, but I didn't trust it. Until I had no choice but to eat. Then, all I wanted to do was sleep. I had no energy."

"Sounds horrific," Dubhan said.

She met his gaze. "It wasn't the worst thing about my stay."

"What was?" Ruarc asked.

"The voices of the people who weren't there. All of you, Eilish, my daughter." She hesitated a heartbeat, then said the name no one else had dared yet, "Xaneth."

Cathal smiled at her. "But you survived it."

Aisling didn't want to talk about this anymore. Not now. Maybe not ever. "What happened with Lena?" *Xaneth. Someone tell me about Xaneth before I go mad, please.*

"She's gone for good," Chevonne replied. "Xaneth saw to that."

Aisling had known he would do it. The knowledge didn't give her the reprieve she sought, however, because there was still the question of his absence.

"We finished off Lena's soldiers while Xaneth and Lena fought it out in the maze," Cael explained.

Somehow, that didn't surprise Aisling. Xaneth taking Lena to the maze would prevent her from using magic, and since he knew how to get out of the labyrinth, it was smart.

Eoghan caught her gaze. "He's the one who found you. Went through five of the doorways before he did, though."

Her breath caught as she hastily looked upward so the sudden rush of tears wouldn't fall. She blinked rapidly and clenched her hands into fists. He had kept his word. That didn't explain why he wasn't there now. Maybe he was on some mission Erith had sent him on. Because surely there was a reason he wasn't beside her. They had agreed to have their long talk.

"Did you see any beings in the city?" Erith asked.

Aisling had to pull her thoughts from Xaneth. She blinked twice as she tried to process what Erith had asked. "Nay. I was the only one there."

"Unfortunately, you weren't," Cael said.

Aisling frowned. "What do you mean?"

Erith glanced at Cael. "It was night when Xaneth went through the doorway. He told us about the specters."

"Specters?" Aisling asked, her confusion growing. "There was nothing there."

Eoghan's lips twisted. "I didn't see anything."

"But Cael and I did," Erith said. "As did Xaneth."

Aisling digested that bit of news. It was something else that set Xaneth apart from everyone else. She thought of the monster he'd spoken of, the beast he said was taking over. Was that what had allowed him to see the arrows in the maze and the specters?

"They were afraid of him. He went searching for you alone, but we tried to follow. The spirits steered clear of him, but they came right for us," Erith said.

Aisling felt her heart thudding against her ribs. Everyone stared at her. She wanted to scream at them to stop. Instead, she stood silently, waiting to learn more.

"They fed off you somehow," Cael added.

Aisling thought about how tired she had been, and how it

hadn't mattered how much food she ate, she never had energy to keep her eyes open, much less sit up. She thought about the voices she'd heard and how clear they had been.

She backed up a few steps until she hit a wall. She grabbed hold of it behind her, anything to keep herself standing. How could she not have known about the apparitions? Had they been the ones supplying the food to keep her alive so they could continue tormenting her to feed off her? And what exactly had they fed on?

But she knew—her soul. Just as the Dark did.

She touched her face, wondering if she had aged. She could feel no wrinkle creases, but that didn't mean the specters hadn't left some kind of damage behind. Aisling would need to take stock of her body as she hadn't done since she woke. Oh, she'd curiously glanced earlier but nothing more. Now, she had a reason to go deeper.

Erith's gaze was locked on Aisling's face. "The spirits fought Xaneth to keep you, but in the end, he destroyed them all."

Aisling was staggered by the news. Xaneth had done that? Alone? She couldn't imagine how much magic that had taken, but she wasn't shocked by it. He was unique, special. She'd always known that.

There was more. She wasn't sure she was prepared for it but waiting seemed inconceivable. No matter how difficult it would be to hear, she had to know. Aisling covered her face with her hands to mentally prepare herself for what was to come. When she opened her eyes, she was alone in the room.

"I asked them to let me talk to you alone," Balladyn said.

Her head snapped to the side, where she found him

leaning a shoulder against a wall. He pushed off it and straightened. He kept his face devoid of emotion. Somehow, that was worse. Aisling braced herself.

"Just say it. Whatever it is you have to say," she told him. "Spit it out."

Balladyn looked down as he inhaled. He didn't look at her again until he had released the breath. "Xaneth is changed."

"If you're talking about the beast he refers to, I already know."

"I'm not."

"Oh." Aisling wasn't sure she could continue standing. Her knees already trembled. She shakily made her way to a chair, grabbing the back in an iron grip before lowering herself onto it. "Go on. I want every detail."

For the next thirteen minutes and twenty-seven seconds, she listened as Balladyn explained about the flames on Xaneth's skin and that he feared what he was.

"He's trying to find answers," Balladyn finished.

Aisling alternated between shock and anger. She gripped the arms of the chair, her chest rising and falling rapidly as her gut churned. "You've not told me why he isn't here. Did Erith invite him?"

"Aye."

"He's not here out of choice, then."

Balladyn ran a hand over his jaw and took the seat across from her. "You did hear me tell you that he's trying to find out what he is, right?"

"I did," she bit out.

Balladyn rubbed his palms on his thighs. "It's clear the two of you are in love."

"Exactly. He should be here." Why did it hurt so much that he wasn't? It felt like a gaping hole in her chest that would never be filled. The broken pieces that had begun to mend were shattered all over again.

"Because he's afraid he could hurt you."

Aisling opened her mouth to argue that point, but the words died. She remembered how he'd fought that other side of himself to such a degree that it had left him with a splitting headache before falling unconscious. She put herself in his shoes and tried to imagine what it would be like to learn that she was something different but not have a name for it—or the consequences.

She swallowed past the lump in her throat. "Do you know what he is?"

"I might have discovered something."

CHAPTER THIRTY-NINE

Aisling walked from the tower long after Balladyn had dropped his news on her and departed. She had simply sat with the information, trying to decide what to do. Or if she should do anything at all. The decision she'd arrived at wouldn't be one that everyone agreed with, but it was hers to make.

She looked around the sun-soaked grounds and recalled the first time she had ventured to the realm. She had been left speechless by its beauty, astounded by the calm that'd wrapped around her the moment she passed through the doorway. It was a sanctuary, a refuge. And it quickly became home.

Was it because she was safe? It could be because all the Reapers were here. Or was it because she let herself think of it as something permanent? Whatever the reason, she never tired of looking at the splendor around her.

Her gaze slid to a distant mountain. It was so far away, she could barely make out the snow-covered peak. The Reapers had celebrated Christmas there. Aisling regretted not taking part in the festivities and the memories. She'd heard all about it from the others, wanting to share so she didn't feel excluded. But her being left out was no one's fault but hers. Because she'd been searching for Xaneth. She would never again miss something like that with her family.

Movement at her side caught her attention and pulled her thoughts to the present. She looked to find Eoghan. He said nothing, simply stood with her. She had liked him from the very first. He was a natural leader. He let each of them be who they were, using their strengths to the advantage of the entire team, as well as aiding them if they needed it. Eoghan let everyone stand on their own. He was one of the greatest warriors she had ever known, but he was also kind and generous. She wanted to know how he had become a Reaper, but if she didn't like to share, he likely wouldn't either. As much as she hated that he had been betrayed and murdered, she couldn't imagine life without knowing him.

"We ganged up on you in there," he said.

Aisling shrugged. "In a way, but it was nice to know everyone was concerned."

"Aye." He met her gaze, his liquid-silver eyes locked on her. "Do you feel any lingering effects from the specters?"

She shook her head. "Not yet. It's disconcerting to know I was unconscious for over a month."

"You needed the time to heal."

"That's a long time for a Fae. Especially a Reaper."

His lips twisted ruefully. "That's how much damage you sustained."

"You make it sound as if I were almost dead."

"You were. Xaneth brought you back again, but you didn't wake."

She shoved her hands in her back pockets.

"You took a huge risk acting as bait for Lena. Once more, your bravery astounds me."

She took a deep breath and looked back at the mountain. "I'm not sure it was being brave so much as knowing you all would defeat Lena and find me."

"You mean that Xaneth would locate you."

Just hearing his name was like a knife twisting in her heart. She couldn't quite hide her wince, and she knew Eoghan saw. He didn't miss much. "He didn't do it alone."

"You're upset with him."

It wasn't a question, and she didn't treat it as one.

Eoghan sighed softly. "I take it Balladyn told you his guess about what Xaneth is?"

"He did."

"What are you going to do?"

Aisling turned her head to him and quirked a brow. "Do?"

"I assumed you'd want to find Xaneth."

Aisling's attention was drawn to the flower garden. She spotted Death, who had stepped past a rose bush and stared at her, waiting.

"You'd best go to her. It's good to have you back among us," Eoghan said.

She glanced at him to see his retreating back as he walked away. Aisling headed toward the garden. She noticed a new stone path that now led her to the lush patch. While the realm itself was full of wildlife, Death's garden housed more in one place than any other. It was like the creatures were drawn to it, either by Erith's magic or the plethora of flowers.

The beautiful orchestra of the birdsong and the gentle breeze rustling through the trees added to the buzzing of bees as they flitted from blossom to blossom. The flutter of dragonfly wings as they zoomed around, and the beautiful glide of butterflies in their leisurely dance always mesmerized Aisling.

As she neared, she inhaled the heady fragrance of the numerous flowers. Roses, jasmine, hyacinth, lavender, lilies, wisteria, lilac, and so many more. The area was a bounty to the senses. It was no wonder Erith had put this in front of the doorway, to greet everyone as soon as they entered the realm.

"Walk with me," Erith said when Aisling reached her.

They strolled unhurriedly through the rows of flowers for several minutes. Aisling wondered if Erith was waiting on her to speak.

Death paused to smell a white peony. She gently cupped the outside of the six-inch flower and gazed down at the fluffy double petals. "Do you know one of the things I've always admired about you?"

Erith admired something about *her?* That was news, and something Aisling desperately wanted to know. "What's that?"

"The way you follow your heart."

Aisling looked away and clasped her hands behind her back. "That hasn't always led me well."

"Nothing said it would. For anyone."

Aisling swung her gaze back to Erith to find the goddess watching her. "I'm not sure if I've ever thanked you for allowing me to look for Xaneth."

"I knew we needed him. And I knew he'd only listen to you."

"It took him a while."

"But he did listen."

Aisling shifted beneath Erith's gaze, unsure of what the goddess wanted. Erith smiled softly and started walking again. Aisling fell into step beside her. Two bees caught her attention as they circled each other several times before landing side by side on a flower.

"What are you going to do?" Erith asked.

Aisling had known the question was coming, but that didn't make answering it any easier. "We've been focused on Lena and the Fae Others for too long. We have some reaping to do."

"Aye, we do. Are you sure this is what you want?" Erith's head swung to her, her gaze probing.

It was Aisling's turn to halt. She waited until Erith faced her before saying, "I chased Xaneth for weeks. I followed him and begged him to talk to me, even when he told me to leave. Then things changed between us. Something...developed."

"Love," Erith said.

"I owe him a debt for finding me in that horrible place, but he made his choice. He chose not to come here. To me. I'm done chasing him."

Erith nodded slowly. "I understand. However—"

"Nay," she spoke over the goddess. Aisling inwardly winced at her defiance, but she had to make her point. "He made his choice."

"And you think by not coming here he didn't choose you?"

"That's exactly what he did."

Erith sighed, her shoulders drooping. "That is hard to misinterpret."

"I'd appreciate it if we didn't speak of him again. I wish to get back to my duties as a Reaper. I've shirked them for far too long." Aisling stood still under Erith's piercing lavender gaze.

"So be it," the goddess replied.

Xaneth sat on the sandy beach and watched the water roll in, the rhythmic ebb and flow of the waves doing little to calm his battered soul. He'd removed his shoes and sank his toes into the cool sand. He was so deep in his thoughts, the cry of gulls overhead barely registered.

He dragged in a deep breath of sea air, letting it fill his lungs until he could practically taste the salt on his tongue. He shouldn't be here. Hadn't allowed himself to come once since... Yet here he'd been for the last hour, just sitting and contemplating. He hadn't liked where his ruminations had taken him—he never did of late.

The sound of shifting sand snapped his head to the side. He found himself looking into familiar red eyes. Balladyn said nothing as he lowered himself to the ground. Xaneth had known he'd come. That was why he'd chosen this spot near Rhona's cottage. As the leader of the Skye Druids, Rhona was alerted to any Fae who came to the island. Since it had taken Balladyn over an hour to notice him, it was confirmation that Xaneth was no longer Fae.

"I'm surprised to see you," Balladyn finally said.

Xaneth set his arms atop his knees and clasped his hands together. "Me, too."

"It took you long enough."

"I had things to do."

Balladyn's head swiveled to him briefly. "What might those be?"

"Hunting down the last of the Fae Others."

"And?"

Xaneth nodded. "I got the final member last week."

"You killed them all?"

"I gave some a choice to forget about the group. Most took the offer. Some didn't."

Balladyn grunted in response as he leaned back on his hands and stretched out his legs. "What will you do now?"

That was the question, wasn't it? He'd tried something different, and it hadn't worked. "I will continue what I've been doing."

"Hunting evil."

"True malevolence, aye."

There was a long silence. Then he said, "Why are you here?"

Xaneth swallowed, his heart racing. Could he get the words out? He hadn't come for fear of what he'd discover. Yet he had to know. His heart couldn't take it anymore. "You know why."

"Say it."

Somehow, he wasn't surprised by the demand. "I came for news of Aisling."

"It's been seven weeks since we last spoke. I called to you many times, and you ignored me."

Xaneth lowered his chin to his chest. "I know."

"She finally woke."

Xaneth's eyes closed in relief. Then they flew open as he jerked his head to Balladyn. "What do you mean *finally*?"

Red eyes full of indignation met his. "Aisling was unconscious for five weeks. Something you would've known had you cared to answer any of us. Or gone to her."

"Is she…all right? The specters didn't do any lasting damage, did they?"

A muscle in Balladyn's jaw clenched. "There's no damage that we're aware of."

"Good." Xaneth had been terrified she would never recover.

As he let all of that sink in, he realized that it had been two weeks since she'd woken. Two weeks that she hadn't come in search of him. He swallowed past the sizable lump in his throat. How could he be upset when he hadn't been there for her? It didn't matter what excuses he made to himself or anyone else, he hadn't been by her side.

All this time, the thing that Xaneth dreaded the most was Aisling dying. At least that's what he'd believed. The truth was, he'd feared she would decide that she didn't want him after she saw what he was. He knew his actions had probably led to her decision. But it proved that he couldn't be what she needed. It was why he had stayed away to begin with.

The pain, however, was still the same. The magnitude was agonizing, the weight unbearable. The significance excruciating.

Whatever was left of him from his previous life withered and died at that moment. Xaneth had what he'd come for. It was time to move on. He'd let his friends and the woman he loved down. There was no coming back from that.

"Find her," Balladyn said.

Xaneth pulled his feet from the sand and, with a thought, had his boots back on. He stood and took one more look at the water. "It's better this way."

"Explain everything to her," Balladyn said as he rose. "Lay it all out. She needs to hear it from you. Everyone makes mistakes. Ask for her forgiveness."

Xaneth looked at the former King of the Dark, now Reaper and Warden for the Skye Druids. "I wish you well, my friend."

"I can tell you what you are."

Xaneth paused and considered. Then he realized he didn't care anymore. Nothing mattered without Aisling. "Farewell, Balladyn."

CHAPTER FORTY

It felt good getting back to what she was supposed to do. Aisling had just finished her last reaping. While she waited for her next assignment, she walked along the streets of Drogheda in twilight. The industrial port town was north of Dublin, situated between Dublin and Belfast, making it just another harbor for the Fae. Not that her kind didn't enjoy smaller villages, but the hustle and bustle of the cities—as well as the tourists—were like beacons.

She had her veil firmly in place as she strolled. She didn't go anywhere without her veil in place now. The only time she lowered it was when she returned to Death's Realm, where she spent most of her free time of late. Earth no longer held the appeal it once did.

Aisling didn't search for Xaneth. Well, she didn't anymore. She hadn't been able to help herself when she first ventured back to Earth, but it hurt too much to continue. Besides, what would she say? She was afraid that she wouldn't be able to use words and would instead use her fists. And that wouldn't do any good.

As she requested, no one said Xaneth's name around her. He wasn't mentioned at all. Her family went out of their way to ensure they didn't, and it made her love them all the more. If there was one thing that'd come out of the heartache, it was that she was able to freely give her love to the Reapers and accept theirs in return.

She had bared her soul to Xaneth. That act had freed her in ways she'd seen every day since. She would never forget her daughter and the precious bond they had shared for those few months, but neither could Aisling continue carrying the weight of her baby's death. It was time to let go—for herself and her child.

A rumble of thunder made Aisling pause and look east, where dark clouds gathered. A storm brewed. By the size and darkness of the clouds, it would be a fierce one. The waves were already white-capping in the distance as the seas turned choppy, heralding the tempest.

She had always loved storms. The lightning. The thunder. The wind. Aisling considered settling in to watch the gale's approach and subsequent release. A bolt of lightning zigzagged across the sky, and she smiled at the sight of such power. Fae could do amazing things with their magic, but nothing could ever compare to the raw supremacy and domination of nature.

Her smile died when she thought about how Xaneth would enjoy the sight. Despite her resolve, he crept into her thoughts more often than not. How long would it take for her to get over him? She feared the answer was never. Thankfully, she hadn't run into him. It was one of the reasons she didn't stay long on Earth. She reaped those she was supposed to, and then Aisling returned home.

The approaching storm had swayed her to remain. Besides, she could go decades without coming face-to-face with Xaneth. No doubt he was doing his best to keep hidden from her. She snorted at that. It wasn't as if she looked for him. Not now.

"Not ever again," she murmured.

Her anger at his absence festered, gnawed at her. She needed to face that soon before it turned to bitterness. She had come too far to backtrack now and let him consume her life. He'd made his choice. And it hadn't been her.

The sting of that would last her entire life. There had been something special between them. Something rare and beautiful. He hadn't seen or felt it. That was on him, not her. She had held nothing back. While it would be easy to take the blame and say she hadn't done or said the right thing, Aisling refused to do that this time. She'd done that in the past with her ex, and that had gotten her nowhere.

Xaneth might have carried her out of that Hell, but he hadn't stuck around. That point got her every time. He'd promised to find her, which he had. But he'd never promised to stay. Balladyn believed that Xaneth would come to his senses one day after working things out, but she wasn't holding onto that. Aisling hoped Xaneth found the answers he sought. As for a second chance? She wasn't so sure she'd give him one.

A light misting of rain began. Aisling lifted her face to the Heavens, seeking the droplets. She released her hair from its gathering atop her head and let it fall down her back. It was time to braid it again. Maybe after some time in the storm.

She heard humans rushing about behind her, trying to get to their cars and inside buildings so they didn't get wet. Her hearing picked up the drum of windshield wipers as they swiped across glass.

Aisling closed her eyes and held out her arms when larger droplets began splashing against her. Thunder rumbled, long and loud, shaking the earth. Alone and veiled, she felt the sky's energy directed at the ground as lightning flashed behind her lids. She could pretend that she was the only one on the entire planet. That was how she wished to be now. Alone. With her wounded heart so she could find some way to heal.

She dropped her arms to her sides and lowered her head. Opening her eyes, she saw the dark clouds moving her way. Fast. She searched the rain clouds, waiting to see more lightning. It didn't disappoint as the blast backlit the clouds before connecting with the water. She gasped at the show, eager for more.

Aisling needed a better view. This one was good, but it wasn't great. If she stayed, she wanted to see the entire spectacle in all its glory. She knew just the place. Just as she was about to leave, something drew her attention. She turned and stilled when her gaze landed on none other than Xaneth.

He stood a few feet behind her, his only movements those of the rise and fall of his chest and his eyes blinking the rain from his lashes. Aisling had dreaded the moment. She had hoped it wouldn't happen, while secretly praying it did. She had seen this scenario play out a thousand different ways.

Now that he stood before her, all she wanted to do was get

away before she unleashed her wrath. She didn't want him to know how gravely he'd wounded her or how he'd shattered her pieced-together heart once and for all. How he had trampled on her dreams without a care.

His silver eyes searched hers. She kept her expression carefully blank. He would never know the tears she had shed for him and the future that could've been theirs. He would never know how she had taken herself far from everyone and screamed her anguish and grief until she curled into a ball when there was nothing left but the dull, throbbing misery of heartache.

"Aisling," he whispered.

She heard the pleading in his voice, but she refused to break. It took everything she had to turn away. She teleported away before she did something stupid like answer him. Aisling found herself on a small inlet, the cove giving her a grand view of the thunderstorm barreling down on her—a tempest that matched her feelings. The rain hid the tears she was unable to hold back.

Her heart raced, and her lungs seized. Why did it have to hurt so much? Why did he have to run from her? What was wrong with her that made her unlovable? Why had she given her heart to someone who couldn't return her affections?

She gasped for air, her throat closing from the thick emotions that robbed her of breath. So many things that she wished she would've said to him raced through her mind, but she knew it was better that she hadn't. Her pain was too raw, too fresh.

Aisling squeezed her eyes closed. The storm had been ruined for her. Retreating to Death's Realm was her best option. So much for the bravery Eoghan spoke of. She was anything *but* brave.

"Aisling."

She jerked at the sound of Xaneth's voice behind her.

"Please, don't leave," he hurried to say. "Just…hear me out."

She tried to teleport, but he grabbed her wrist and prevented her. She gaped at his hand holding her. She jerked her arm out of his grip and spun to face him. "That was a mistake."

"I don't deserve it, but I'm asking for a little of your time," he said, holding up his hands in front of him. "Please."

"No."

Damn if he didn't stop her from teleporting again. This time, Aisling didn't pull away. Instead, she lashed out with all her anger.

Bloody hell, she was the most magnificent creature Xaneth had ever beheld. Especially when she was furious. He had been looking for her since he'd left Skye. He hadn't actually thought to find her, but when he had, he had drunk in the sight of her, realizing for the first time how much he'd missed her.

He blocked and dodged a few of her attacks, but not once did he strike back. She had every right to her anger. And he would take every hit she threw at him.

"Fight!" she bellowed.

The rain pelted them, the wet sand moving easily beneath

their feet, gripping and sticking to their shoes. Lightning struck, and thunder rumbled almost in unison, growing louder and louder as the storm raced toward them.

Aisling's long, black and silver hair fanned around her as she spun, her crimson eyes glittering with rage. She could've delivered orbs of magic meant to do him considerable damage. Instead, she struck him with her hands and feet, pelting him with blow after blow.

She lifted her leg as she spun, her foot connecting with the side of his head. The impact knocked him off balance. Xaneth struggled to stay on his feet. He shook his head to clear it from the hit. He would let her hit him all she wanted, but first, he needed to tell her everything.

Xaneth grabbed her wrists and held them above her head. She hollered in rage and tried to get free. He spun her, pinning her back against his chest.

"I'm sorry!" he shouted over the rain. "I should've been there!"

In answer, she threw back her head, connecting with his nose. The crunch of cartilage told him it was broken.

How dare he? Aisling stomped on his foot and twisted to get away from him. Being this close was too much. Hearing his voice, feeling his body. It was a kind of torture she couldn't endure.

Aisling managed to free a wrist and elbowed him in the stomach. She took a step away, but to her shock, he managed to grab her again. This time, he held her so she faced him. She smiled at the blood running down his face from his broken nose that had already healed.

"I'll take whatever you dole out to me."

She snorted and lifted her knee that she directed to his groin. "Fek off."

He managed to turn to the side at the last second, her knee glancing off his hip instead.

"Aisling, I let you down. Let me try to make it right."

She glared at him, her chest heaving. "You want to make it right?"

Xaneth hesitated at her calm voice. "Aye."

"Then go away. I never want to see you again."

He'd known he would have to work for it, but hearing those words was agony. "Let me ex—"

"Explain?" she said over him. "I already know what you'll say. Balladyn told me."

Xaneth shook his head. "Not everything."

"I don't want to hear anything you have to say. You had your chance."

She shouldn't notice the hurt in his eyes. Or be bothered by it. Not after what Xaneth had done to her. But damn if she didn't want to take her words back. She had stopped trying to pull out of his hold. The rain came down in buckets now, drenching everything. Lightning lit the sky like camera flashes, but she didn't pay any attention to the magnificent display.

"Aisling," he whispered huskily.

Suddenly, his face tightened. He lifted his gaze over her shoulder and released her. She watched as flames erupted across his body and head. Aisling glanced behind her to see a group of seven Dark.

"Go," Xaneth told her.

Aisling rolled her eyes as she faced the group and dropped her veil. "And let you have all the fun? I don't think so."

There were no more words as the first orb came at Aisling. She sidestepped it while hurling her own. It fell wide, but it had been a distraction as she rolled and came up with spheres of magic in both hands. Her battle was over in seconds.

Aisling stared down at the pile of wet ash mixing with the sand, sad that she'd had to take a life. She then turned to her next target only to find that Xaneth had already taken out two and was fighting the last four.

He moved so fast that it was hard for even her to keep up with him. First one, then a second of the remaining four teleported away. Xaneth faced the last two, waiting for them to make a move. Meanwhile, the two who had jumped returned behind Xaneth. Aisling intercepted them, making quick work of them.

When she turned back to Xaneth, he stood watching her, the rain making the flames hiss. She looked into his eyes to see they had turned inky black. She reached out a hand to touch him, but Xaneth jerked back, his brow furrowing.

"Nay," he said with a shake of his head.

Aisling squared her shoulders and tried again. This time,

she anticipated his move and was able to grab hold. The panic on his face made her heart catch. Aisling looked down at where she held him to see the flames encompassing her hand.

"Does it hurt?" he asked so low she thought she imagined the words. Then his gaze lifted to hers, searching, seeking.

Aisling couldn't find her voice, so she shook her head instead.

The relief that swept over his face told her more than his words ever could. His black eyes faded, gradually returning to silver, and the flames died. The desire she saw reflected at her made her stomach flutter. A bolt of lightning hit the ground mere feet from them. She felt the force of it, the energy that sizzled in the air, followed by the deafening boom of thunder. But all she saw was Xaneth.

They reached for each other at the same time, their mouths fusing as passion seized them. He cupped her face, his mouth hungry as his tongue swept into her mouth to mate with hers. The wind whipped violently around them, but they were too lost in each other to notice. She clung to him, wanting to get closer. He lowered his arms to wrap them around her, then bent, his hands cupping her arse before hauling her up to press his thick arousal into her stomach.

"I'm sorry," he said between kisses down her neck. "I'm so damn sorry."

Aisling dropped her head back as her center throbbed, needing him inside her. His fullness, his length. She moaned when he tore her shirt and bra away and closed his lips over her nipple, suckling. It felt so good. Each pull of his lips sent need straight to her sex, making it throb.

Then she was on her back, the gritty, wet sand meeting her

flesh. Xaneth hovered over her, his hands on either side of her head as he watched her. Aisling reached between them and grasped his cock, moving her hand over its velvety thickness. Unable to wait a moment longer, she brought him to her entrance.

His eyes flared when he felt how wet she was. With one thrust, he was inside her. His moan, visceral and primal, made her breath catch. She brought his head down for another kiss as he began moving. Their hunger and yearning for the pleasure that awaited drove them. He plunged into her, hard and deep. The walls of her sex clutched at him, savoring each glide of his length in and out of her, bringing her ever closer to climax.

She locked her ankles around his waist as he tilted her hips toward him. On his next thrust, he rubbed against her sensitive clit. She moaned at the incredible feel of him, of *them*, together. She felt the ground tremble. Xaneth lifted his head from hers. Their eyes met as light flashed around them in a steady stream. Desire tightened low. She could feel the orgasm building rapidly. Xaneth's eyes glittered as if he knew.

He smiled right before she stiffened, her body clutching his rod while waves of pleasure rippled through her. He buried himself deep and let out a bellow as his cock pulsed inside her. She felt his length throbbing. She squeezed her legs around him as her body continued quivering from the remnants of her climax.

When she opened her eyes, Xaneth leaned over her, protecting her from the worst of the rain. He pulled out of her a little before thrusting his hips. She moaned as her body shuddered with one last tremor that was a mini-orgasm in and of itself.

"I love you."

Aisling's heart skipped a beat. She stared at him, unsure if he had really said the words.

Xaneth swallowed hard. "I love you more than I thought it possible to love anything. I stayed away because I feared my flames would cause you harm. You have no idea how challenging it was to do that. It's an excuse, I know. I'll—"

She put a finger to his lips to quiet him. All her hurt and pain had been erased with three little words and the truth of them shining in Xaneth's eyes. "Say it again."

He searched her face for a moment. Then, a grin turning up his lips, he said, "I love you."

Tears overflowed her lids, falling onto her cheeks to roll to her temples. "I love you."

Xaneth gathered her in his arms and held her tight. "I'm never letting you go again. *Never*."

It felt so good to be in his arms. Aisling never wanted to leave them. And she wouldn't. They were a team. Together.

He leaned back to look at her, and she saw his tears, even through the rain.

"You're not alone anymore," she told him.

Xaneth kissed her softly, lingering. "I haven't been alone for some time. I may not have said it, but I knew it. You're all I've thought about for months, even before my aunt captured me. But especially these last seven weeks."

"The past is the past. We have the present and a future."

A bit of the happiness dimmed from his eyes. "About that. I need to find out what I am."

"Would you like for me to tell you?"

Xaneth stilled. He was desperate to know now. But there was also the fear that he wouldn't like what he heard. Either way, he had to know. For them. For him. He couldn't continue ignoring it. He nodded once.

"A Hellhound."

His brows snapped together. "That's…not possible."

"Actually, it is. Balladyn found reference to one of the first Kings of the Light, which is your ancestor. It seems a Dark tortured his brother to the point of death. Everyone thought the Light was dead, but he merely transformed."

"Into a Hellhound?" Xaneth asked in a shocked whisper.

Aisling grinned, her eyes sparkling with flashes of lightning. "From what the king and the scientists could decipher, it had something to do with a unique combination of his blood, the magic he possessed, and the torture. The drawing Balladyn found was of a Light with flames on his skin and black eyes. Just like you."

He digested that, trying to imagine how his life would be going forward. "What happened to him? This Hellhound."

"Have you ever seen Balladyn's library?"

Xaneth nodded. "Once, when he was King of the Dark, he brought me to his chambers. He knew I used glamour to disguise that I was a Light in his court, but Balladyn didn't care because we had a common enemy in Usaeil."

"So you've seen his impressive collection." She nodded. "I hadn't until recently." She smoothed his hair from his face.

"On the shelves of books was a journal from the King of the Light, who spoke of his brother, the Hellhound. The king wrote about his brother's exploits and how no one was more powerful than him."

Xaneth raised a brow when she paused. "And?"

"Light and Dark Fae alike feared the brother. The Hellhound wasn't welcome anywhere. One day, the king said his sibling was just gone. Disappeared from the Fae Realm."

Xaneth recalled Lena's words about how he would never fit in with the Fae. That shouldn't bother him because he'd never really fit in anywhere. But it did unsettle him.

"That won't be you."

He focused on Aisling's crimson eyes. "Why?"

"Because your home, if you want it, is with me. Here, on Death's Realm, or wherever you want to live. I'll be with you. You have a family with the Reapers. You always have."

Xaneth pressed his forehead to hers. She offered everything he'd longed for. He could hardly fathom that it was all within his grasp.

"Also, it seems the former Hellhound had the same penchant for smelling evil and eradicating it as you do," Aisling told him.

"Did he? What does that mean for us?"

She brought his head down to her as she smiled up at him. "It means, my love, that we work well together. Reaper and Hellhound."

That's all he needed to hear. They shared a smile before he claimed her lips in another searing kiss.

EPILOGUE

Two weeks later…

Aisling closed the journal and set the book aside. She looked at the other end of the sofa where Xaneth sat, rubbing her feet as he stared into the distance. She stared at his profile, basking in the quiet time they'd had since arriving on Death's Realm.

She clasped her hands in her lap as she reclined against the pillows stacked against the arm of the couch. No one had intruded upon their time, thankfully. A day after their arrival on the realm, Aisling had found the journal on her doorstep. She knew Balladyn had brought it for Xaneth.

At first, he hadn't wanted to read it. But over the past few days, he had devoured the pages of the book, learning more about the first Hellhound. Then he gave her the journal to read.

His long fingers rubbed the arch of her foot as he glanced at her. Silver eyes probed hers. "Well? What do you think?"

"I think the Hellhound was lucky to have had such a relationship with his brother. Otherwise, we wouldn't know any of this." She shrugged. "The entire journal was dedicated to writing down everything about the Hellhound."

Xaneth chuckled. "And Balladyn stole it from the Light Castle."

"I know," she said with eyes wide, laughing. Then she sobered. "Just because things are written in that book doesn't mean they will happen to you."

He nodded solemnly. "It's a starting place, but it's made me think. I'd like to have my own journals."

"I think that's a good idea."

"It's too bad we don't know where the first Hellhound is. It'd be nice to compare how we were transformed to see if there are any similarities. Don't you think it strange that he just disappeared?"

She raised her brows and nodded. "Very much so. Then again, I've seen some of your abilities. They're impressive. Who knows what you could do if you put your mind to it."

"Which is something else I plan to find out. I want to know my limits."

"If there are any."

He twisted his lips. "Everyone has limits."

"Not you, my love." She sat and shifted to straddle his lap. "Your power is limitless."

His hands rested on her waist before he caressed upward to tangle them in her hair. "My love for you is limitless. As is my need to be inside you."

"Oh?" she murmured.

"Shall I prove it?"

"Do you even need to ask?" she retorted.

They laughed before he pulled her forward and took her lips. The kiss turned heated as she felt his arousal.

"I love you, *mo grá*. You are my heart."

She looked into his silver eyes and smoothed her hand down his face. "And you're my soul. Now and always."

Erith stood in the open window of the tower and watched the setting sun. She heard Cael come up behind her, and it made her smile. She held out her hand for his. He intertwined his fingers with hers.

"You did it," he said.

She leaned her head to the side as he moved her hair out of the way to kiss her neck. "Did what?"

"You got everyone here. Our family."

She turned to face him. "*We* did it."

"I might have done a little to help," he said with a wink.

Erith rose on her tiptoes to kiss him. "We both know you did more than a little."

"What matters is how things ended."

"True. Though can we really say this is the end? We're just learning about Hellhounds."

"Let's not forget Zora."

She wrinkled her nose. "Ah. Zora. I think it might be time to pay that realm a visit since things are under control for the moment. I'd like to see how Con, Rhi, and the twins are doing."

"It might be better if we don't. Maybe things are going well enough that we're not needed."

Erith shrugged as she linked her hands behind Cael. "If you want some private time with me, that's all you have to say."

"I want some bloody private time with you," he said as he swung her up in his arms.

Erith laughed as he took the stairs two at a time before striding into their chamber. She would always worry about the Reapers and their mates. No doubt there would be more children soon. And now there was a Hellhound in their midst. Nobody knew what that meant for them, but she was eager to find out. The balance of good and evil had been restored. The celebrations were over, and now it was time for peace, because there was no telling how long it would last.

She rose on her elbows and watched with a smile as Cael stripped out of his clothes. With a snap of his fingers, she was naked. Erith reached for him, sighing at the delicious feel of his weight atop her.

Then he kissed her, and she gave in to the passion that awaited.

～

Isle of Skye

Rhona walked out onto the porch where Balladyn stood, looking at the water. Clouds hung low in the sky, dappled by morning sunlight, the mist clinging to the trees and mountaintops like a sleepy lover.

"It's quiet," he said.

She came up beside him and handed him a cup of tea. "That's good."

"Nay, sweetheart. It's too quiet."

She didn't need to ask what he meant. The Druid murders and the killing mist had left everyone on Skye shaken. They had no answers, no motives. They did, however, have a suspect —pointed out by someone else. But it was a place to start.

"Things are just getting started here," Balladyn said as he sipped his tea.

Rhona linked her arm with his. "Maybe."

"You're not worried?" he asked as he looked at her.

She grinned and shook her head. "Look at this beautiful day. We spend enough time bogged down with untangling our enemies' motives and working out how to protect ourselves and others. We deserve a day to ourselves. Free from all of that."

"Hmm. You may have a point. All right. What would you like to do today?"

"Anything?"

"Anything."

"Does that include binge-watching something?"

He grinned and pulled her against him. "Even if it is our twentieth time of watching *Bridgerton*."

"Damn," she murmured and eyed him. "I think I did good when I roped you into loving me. I don't know any other man who would be so amazing."

Balladyn chuckled as he bent to kiss her. "I'm the one who got lucky."

"You certainly did. And just for that, let's do the Cuillin Ridge hike."

His red eyes lit with excitement. "Don't tease."

"No teasing. I've already got everything packed."

"Then let's go," he said as he took her hand and dragged her into the house. "Adventure awaits."

Thank you for reading **DARK ALPHA'S FURY**! I hope you loved Xaneth and Aisling's story as much as I loved writing it. Next up in the Dark Universe is the second in the Skye Druids series, SHOULDER THE SKYE.

Passion will test the boundaries of life and death.

Buy SHOULDER THE SKYE now at www.DonnaGrant.com

To find out when new books release
SIGN UP FOR MY NEWSLETTER today at
http://www.tinyurl.com/DonnaGrantNews.

Join my Facebook group, Donna Grant Groupies, for exclusive giveaways and sneak peeks of future books.

Keep reading for an excerpt from SHOULDER THE SKYE…

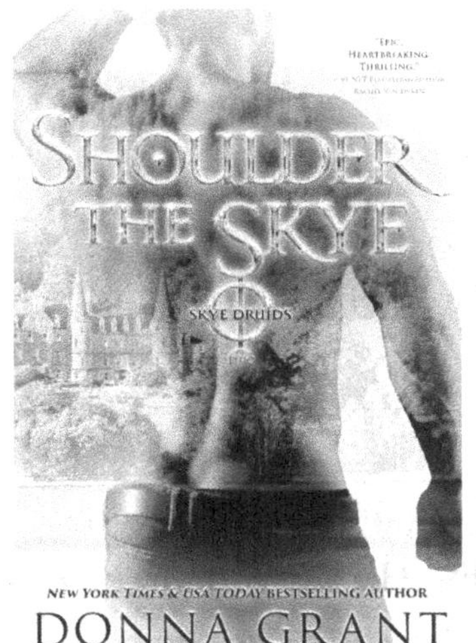

In her sexiest Skye Druid novel yet, *New York Times* and *USA Today* bestselling author Donna Grant weaves an intricate tapestry of magic, secrecy, and ultimate desire.

Bronwyn Stewart knows heartache. Death and danger have haunted her every step, but she's prepared for what's hunting her. Or as prepared as she can be. There's only one outcome —and she's ready for it. But a wickedly handsome Druid from her past returns and refuses to let her face the oncoming battle alone. He stirs something long buried within her. For the first time in years, a spark ignites within her that soon turns into a blaze that can't be extinguished.

Forced to leave his beloved isle years ago to protect his family, Elias MacLean fears he'll never see his home again. But Fate has other ideas. When a mission leads him back to Skye to investigate a rash of Druid murders, he finds another mystery to unravel—that of a gorgeous, reclusive *drough*. With foes lurking around every corner and an undeniable hunger that grows with every kiss, Elias risks it all for the woman he's fallen for. Together they unleash an all-consuming passion that won't be denied.

Chapter One

Isle of Skye

It was a joke.

Or a nightmare.

That was the only conclusion Elias could come up with as he stared at the two couples before him. His sister's light blue eyes held a note of misery. Beside Elodie was Scott, the man who had helped her when he hadn't been there. Scott's face was as impassive as his assessment was cool, his arms crossed over his chest as he met Elias's gaze.

Next to Scott was Rhona, the leader of the Skye Druids. Concern lined her face, but her green eyes held a fierceness that only someone of her position could have. On Rhona's other side was the imposing figure of Balladyn. He wasn't just Rhona's lover and Warden of the isle, he had also once been a legendary Light Fae turned Dark before becoming *King* of the Dark. Now, he was a Reaper.

"Tell me it isn't true," Elodie begged Elias. "Tell me George is wrong about you being a murderer."

Georgina Miller, also known as *George*. Just hearing the name made Elias want to punch something. Hard. He fisted his hands in an effort to control the surge of anger that bubbled up within him. Balladyn's red eyes lowered to Elias's hands before the Reaper quirked a black brow.

The fury that clogged Elias's throat was so thick that it took him two tries before he could answer. "Of course, George is wrong. How could you even think that I was the one killing Druids?"

"George said—" Scott began.

"I doona give a flying fuck what she says!" Elias shouted. He closed his eyes and sucked in a breath, hating that he'd lost control. The outburst brought back memories of his youth and the father he wished he could forget. Elias didn't open his eyes until he had his anger tightly leashed once more. Then he looked at each of the four before him. "George is wrong."

Elodie smiled, though it looked forced. "I knew it wasn't you."

"I'm no' saying George is never wrong, but she's a seer," Scott said.

Rhona held up a hand to quiet everyone. "I've yet to talk to George myself. I'll listen to what she has to say, but I'll also do my own investigating. Seers are a rarity in the Druid community, but that doesn't mean they aren't infallible or see the entire picture."

While it wasn't an acquittal, it was all Elias would get for the moment. He felt Balladyn's penetrating gaze and looked into his red eyes. The Reaper could use glamour to hide the eye and hair coloring that signaled him as a Dark Fae, but he didn't. And Elias respected him for that. He'd had few run-ins with the Light and even fewer with the Dark. He tended to steer clear of the Fae as a whole, which was harder than it sounded since they could blend in and walk among humans so easily.

"It's going to be okay."

Elias looked down at his sister, who had moved closer to him. She squeezed his arm as their gazes met. He'd returned to Skye for her, but in the end, she hadn't needed him. Their family was so fucked up that he didn't like to think about it, but it seemed that things were finally beginning to turn around for them.

Elodie had her magic once more, and she knew the truth of how she had saved their mother, sister, and both of them from their father. Her actions—and the resulting panic attack— however, had ended in their mum erasing Elodie's memories and binding her magic while also taking the blame for Edward MacLean's death. Elias had left Skye soon after so he wouldn't inadvertently say something that reversed his mother's magic and brought all the heartache back to Elodie.

But that meant leaving his sisters and his home behind for fifteen years—long years he had spent trying to outrun the past.

Now, Elias was back on Skye, Elodie's memories had

returned, and their mother, Emily, was set to be released from prison soon. The only one blessedly ignorant of everything was Edie. She was the only MacLean who had a normal life, and he was grateful for that. She had remained on Skye, gotten married, and now had two beautiful children. If anything proved that he and his mum had done the right thing the day his father died, it was seeing Edie and her family flourish.

Scott came up behind Elodie and nodded at Elias. "You're right. George hasna given us any proof of you being a killer. I shouldna have accused you. I'm sorry."

"Doona worry about it. You trust her. I would've done the same in your shoes." It was a lie. Elias had learned long ago not to accept someone's word—no matter how much he trusted them. He always verified things for himself.

"Then I guess we'll see you at home later?" Elodie asked, her gaze searching his.

Elias glanced at Rhona and Balladyn. The couple had more to say to him, which was fine since he wanted to get it out of the way. He nodded at his sister, and she shot him a wide smile before she and Scott filed out of Rhona's cottage.

When the door shut behind them, Elias turned his head to Rhona. For as long as anyone could remember, Corann had led the Skye Druids. There were no pictures of him, but if you asked the eldest of the community, they would say that he'd looked ancient, even when they were young. But his actual age was anyone's guess.

Corann had died defeating the Others—a group of Light and Dark Fae and *mie* and *drough* Druids from this realm and another—and had chosen Rhona as his replacement. Even in his time away, Elias had kept tabs on the happenings on Skye. He knew the respect Rhona had earned before stepping into Corann's role. But her actions with the Reapers and her connection to the magic through Balladyn set her apart from anyone on Skye—or on the planet.

Rhona might still be finding her way, but she had the wisdom of someone much older than her young years. Obviously, Corann had seen that, as well. She was a good choice as leader—especially in such turbulent times.

Because not only Druids were being murdered. There was a malevolent force on Skye. Someone was controlling the mist that had attacked Elias, though whether it was the same person killing the Druids had yet to be revealed. Then there were the Druid Others, based on the original group who had tried to take over their world.

Elias blinked and found Balladyn standing before him. The Reaper quirked a black brow again and held something out to him. Elias looked down to find a tumbler filled with amber liquid.

"Thought you could use this," the Reaper said in his Irish accent.

"Thanks." Elias lifted the glass and inhaled the scent of whisky. He brought it to his lips and savored the flavor as it touched his tongue and slid smoothly down his throat. Dreagan whisky, made by the Dragon Kings, an immortal group of ancient beings who could shapeshift into humans. He'd met one recently, and it had been as awe-inspiring as he'd thought it would be.

Rhona turned and walked to the sofa. Sitting, she motioned Elias to the chair. "Have a seat."

Elias knew it wasn't exactly an order. He could leave. He hadn't lived on Skye in years but he *was* from the isle. That meant he would always be considered a Skye Druid. He made his way to the chair and lowered himself into it. Balladyn moved to the opposite side of the room, crossing his arms over his chest and leaning a shoulder against the wall, the Reaper's red gaze never leaving him. Elias listened to the rain pinging against the windows as he anticipated the inevitable questions. He didn't have to wait long.

"Why would George accuse you of the murders?" Rhona asked as she tucked a strand of red hair behind her ear.

Elias shrugged and finished the whisky. "I doona have a clue."

"Have you ever met her?" Balladyn queried.

Elias shook his head, suddenly feeling weary to his bones. "Never. But I know of her."

That got Rhona's attention. "How?"

"You can discover a lot by asking the right people."

There was a hint of a smile on Balladyn's lips. "And that's what you did?"

"Aye. It isna some great gift. It's just taking the time to study an area and the people within it. It doesna take long before you begin finding those who like to talk." Elias turned the empty tumbler around in his fingers. "There are always those who say more than they should."

Rhona nodded. "True. What did you find out about George?"

Elias thought about that for a moment. He didn't know Rhona or Balladyn. He didn't know George either. Most people in his position would attempt to make George out to be corrupt or guilty in an effort to get others on their side. It might work for a short while, but it rarely lasted in the long run.

Despite his anger at George for her accusation, Elias decided to be candid. "She works hard to find Druids in Edinburgh and bring them into her organization. She's well-liked."

"Not by you, though," Rhona pointed out.

Balladyn grunted. "And given the anger in your voice, it goes much further than her recent accusation."

Elias ran a hand down his face. He sat the tumbler on the table beside him and leaned forward to rest his forearms on his thighs. "Nay, I doona like her."

"Why?" Rhona pressed.

Elias looked at the floor for a heartbeat before meeting Rhona's gaze. "Call it a hunch."

"I'm going to need more than that."

"I've traveled all over the world, met a lot of people, and I've seen many just like her." Elias paused, trying to put his thoughts into words. "I doona have specifics, exactly."

Balladyn pushed away from the wall and dropped his arms to his sides. "Something's bothering you. What is it?"

"She's never wrong. In everything she's seen through her visions, she's never wrong."

Rhona's brows drew together in a frown. "That's not normal. I don't care how powerful a seer is, no one gets everything right."

"Precisely. She's wrong about me," Elias stated. This time, he let his fury come through. "I willna say I've no' killed, but it was always in self-defense."

Balladyn stalked closer with his eyes narrowed. "Oh?"

Fuck. Elias had said too much. He shouldn't have let his anger get the best of him. But to be called a murderer? To be blamed for the killings he was actively trying to solve? It was too much.

"Elias," Rhona pressed.

He looked from her to Balladyn. There was no way he would get out of here without telling them something. Besides, they'd find out soon enough anyway. Probably from him. "I've been tracking the murders."

"What? How?" Rhona asked as she scooted to the edge of the couch cushion, curiosity and interest propelling her. "There are murders everywhere, every day. How do you know someone is a Druid?"

Elias slowly sat back. "It's the *type* of killings."

"The mist that attacked here," Balladyn said. "Is that happening in other places?"

Elias shook his head. "No' exactly. But there *are* things like that. Things out of place. Unexplained murders and such. No' to mention the notes that say *bàs ort*, death to you."

"Where?" Rhona asked in a soft voice.

Elias released a breath. "Everywhere we look."

"We?" Balladyn asked.

Elias shrugged, hoping to deflect. "A slip of the tongue."

"I doubt that." Rhona's green gaze held his, daring him to lie. "An operation this big would take others."

Well, fuck. Elias wished he could take back the words, but he couldn't. He flattened his lips and nodded.

"How many of you are there?" Rhona pressed.

Elias shoved to his feet. "I've said more than I should've already."

"It looks suspicious when a group wants to remain a secret," Balladyn stated.

Elias slid his gaze to him. "The Reapers remained secret for how long?"

"That isn't the same."

"Is it no'?" Elias argued.

Rhona rose and stepped between them, her eyes on Elias. "You've made your point. We may not know each other well, but my goal is to protect the Druids on Skye."

"And mine is to protect *all* Druids. I respect your position, and I ask that you give me the same courtesy," Elias replied.

Tension radiated from Balladyn. "She's not been accused of murder."

"Stop," Rhona told Balladyn. Her long, red hair swung behind her as she turned back to Elias. "One way or another, we're getting to the bottom of this. Work with me. And just so you know, I'm going to ask the same of George."

Elias wasn't surprised. It was the same move Corann would've made. No doubt the old Druid would've been proud of Rhona. It was a smart decision. Unfortunately, it wasn't one he agreed with. "I can no' work with George."

"Rhona's not asking that of you. She is asking you to work with *her*," Balladyn corrected.

Elias studied the Druid leader for a long minute. "In the short time I've been back home, I've seen the lengths you'll go to in order to protect the Druid community. Corann made a good choice with you."

"Wait, Elias," Rhona called.

But he ignored her as he strode from the house. Elias half-expected Balladyn to teleport him back inside, but no one stopped him as he walked through the rain and got into the rental car. He waited until he was a few miles from the cottage before pulling over and putting the vehicle in park.

"Fucking hell!" he yelled as he slammed his hands against the steering wheel.

Elias gripped the leather so tightly that his knuckles turned white. There was a reason George had pointed the finger at him. And he was going to find out what that was.

Buy SHOULDER THE SKYE now at
www.DonnaGrant.com

ABOUT THE AUTHOR

New York Times and *USA Today* bestselling author Donna Grant® has been praised for her "totally addictive" and "unique and sensual" stories.

She's written more than one hundred novels spanning multiple genres of romance including the bestselling Dragon Kings® series that features a thrilling combination of Druids, Fae, and immortal Highlanders who are dark, dangerous, and irresistible. She lives in Texas with her dog and a cat.

www.DonnaGrant.com
www.MotherofDragonsBooks.com

facebook.com/AuthorDonnaGrant

instagram.com/dgauthor

bookbub.com/authors/donna-grant

amazon.com/Donna-Grant/e/B00279DJGE

pinterest.com/donnagrant1

www.ingramcontent.com/pod-product-compliance
Lightning Source LLC
Chambersburg PA
CBHW010142200726
48285CB00011BB/2794